The California Experience

The California Experience:

A Literary Odyssey

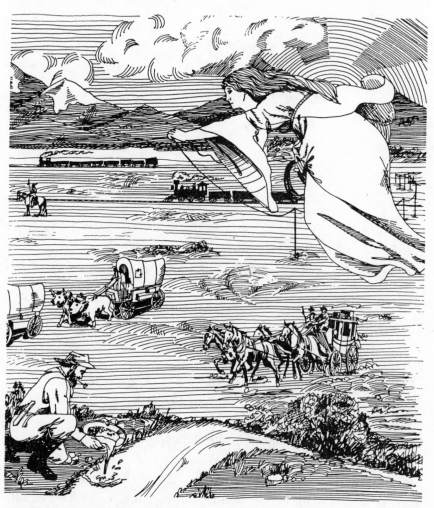

Warren A. Beck

Peregrine Smith, Inc.

SANTA BARBARA AND SALT LAKE CITY

1976

Library of Congress Cataloging in Publication Data

Main entry under title:

The California experience.

    1.   American fiction. 2.   California—History—
Fiction. I. Beck, Warren A.
PZ1.C127   [PS648.C3]   813'.081   76-10296
ISBN 0-87905-035-7

Manufactured in the United States of America

Contents

Preface

The goal of this work is to make available selected excerpts from historical fiction. Special emphasis has been placed upon how people reacted to the momentous events of yesteryear and the setting in which they lived. The organization into chapters is intended to make the selections more comprehensible. It is the hope of the author that this book will be read along with a general history of California; however, the chapter introductions and the headings make it possible for the book to be read by itself.

The author has benefited from the assistance of many people in the preparation of this work. The Los Angeles Public Library has been most generous in providing the author with the loan of many obscure and even rare novels which could not have been found elsewhere. Special thanks are due two good friends who read the manuscript and made many helpful suggestions: Jackson K. Putnam and Edward H. Parker. A former student and friend, Myles L. Clowers of San Diego City College, has assisted in many ways. My son Kent, a busy graduate student, has helped the project by suggesting several selections and even the title. A final word of thanks is due my wife, Phyllis, who performed the arduous tasks of xeroxing and typing.

Introduction

The objective of the historian is faithfully to re-create the past so that it becomes comprehensible to the present. The historical novelist has the same objective and often uses the same historical sources in much the same manner as does the historian. The distinction between the two lies in the way each presents his recreation of the past to the reader. Novelist Upton Sinclair claimed of one of his works: "The picture is the truth, and the great mass of detail actually exists. But the cards have been shuffled; names, places, dates, details of character, episodes—everything has been dealt over again." Other novelists often make simliar claims: "there are no real persons in this story (except for actual historical individuals); there are little bits of hundreds of real persons, which creative imagination has endeavored to fuse into something more real than reality."

This then is the fundamental difference between the historian and the historical novelist: the former, in theory at least, is a dispassionate recorder of events, while the latter uses creative imagination to make things "more real than reality." In other words, the novelist as creative artist finds meaning in historical events and personages and filters them through his own emotions before presenting them to his readers. In this process, he sometimes exaggerates to provide a better setting or to make his characters more alive and believable. The novelist may even inject his own values into the circumstances he is writing about. A poor historical novelist may become so concerned with telling his story that he violates historical truth either in the description of events or in the creation of historical personalities. While no less concerned with telling his story, a good historical novelist will only embellish or embroider historical truth without violating it. In doing such, he may legitimately create fictional characters or render possible explanations to fill the many voids contained in the verified data of any past set of circumstances.

In exploring the question of what impact the natural environment has had upon man and historical events, the historian might raise questions like the following: What has been the effect of California's isolation both from the outside world and from various points within the state? What are the political results of great size? How did the lack of navigable rivers or the presence of the Sierra Nevada retard settlement? The historical novelist, on the other hand, would explore the same questions by showing how the forces of nature have altered the lives of individuals. How has an historical character reacted to issues created by the environment? What is the effect of desert living on an individual, or of being all alone in an isolated mountain valley? Events are personalized and dramatized for maximum effect, sometimes to the point of exaggeration.

Thus, while the historian provides statistics as to the numbers of those seeking the benefits of California's climate and the economic impact of the money such migrants bring into the state, Stewart Edward White's main character in *Rose Dawn* stresses how the natural beauties of the Golden State provoke him to rapture. California's periodic and devastating rain storms and destructive fires can be the subject of scholarly monographs, but George R. Stewart's *Storm* and *Fire* tell how these events of nature relate to the lives of people. Earthquakes and landslides are fit subjects for scientific inquiry, but Gavin Lambert in *The Slide Area* and Myron Brinig in *The Flutter of an Eyelid* show how such natural calamities affect man. Brinig's cataclysmic theme was predicted by the poet Robinson Jeffers—"someday this coast will dip and be clean."

Some historians claim that their discipline is a science and that after examining the documents or assessing other historical evidence, they are prepared to render an objective judgment. Nevertheless, the historical works produced about Hispanic California, for example, tend to refute such a claim of historical objectivity. Many works depict this period as a Spanish Arcadia in which everyone was happy and problems did not exist. The Indians are seen as well-adjusted wards of the mission Fathers and life on the ranchos as little more than a continuous round of fiestas. Other works, claiming to be just as scholarly, disparage the Hispanic era and stress the shortcomings of the primitive way of life of the rancheros. In other words, qualified historians are reaching different conclusions after examining the same or similar evidence. Thus, admittedly unobjective historical novels may not be so much different from "objective" works of history after all.

The novelist as creative artist can deepen our understanding of the state's past by providing insights into historical events. In the excerpt from *The Road to Glory* Darwin Teilhet does not resolve the question as to whether mission life was good or bad for the Indian; he does, however, present the aims and fears of the clergy for their charges. Jonreed Lauritzen in *The Cross and the Sword* relates the basis of the conflict between church and state. *Angelo's Wife* by Virginia Myers argues the case of the rancheros versus the missionaries. Anne B. Fisher in *Cathedral in the Sun* portrays a possible reaction of the Indians to Hispanic life and especially to their treatment at the missions. These excerpts may be fiction, but they correspond to actual historical treatment, and in reviewing the differences in viewpoint the reader will be in a better position to make his own judgment. For example, Stewart Edward White in his meticulously researched and historically accurate picture of ranch life in *Folded Hills* presents a contrast to the way Gertrude Atherton romanticizes the activities of rancheros in *The Splendid Idle Forties*.

Of all the events in California's history, there is none more controversial than the American take-over. Traditionally, historians have stressed the theme of brave Yankee frontiersmen who carried the flag to the Pacific shores by sea for purposes of trade, and, cooperating with the pioneers who breached the lofty mountains and hostile deserts, added this outpost of Mexican rule to the Union almost as if it were ordained by Divine Providence. In the past two generations, scholars have taken a more hostile view of the manner in which the United States acquired such a large expanse of Mexican territory.

The historical novelists of the era have relied upon memoirs and, much in the manner of earlier historians, have tended to exaggerate the high adventure qualities of the historical characters depicted. In both *Follow the Free Wind* by Leigh Brackett and *The Mothers* by Vardis Fisher, historical memoirs are used to provide the basis for the story. However, such documents have their weaknesses, as man tends to inflate the story he leaves behind for posterity. Brackett accepts most of the wild claims of Jim Beckwourth, and Fisher makes the sordid Donner tragedy into high adventure. The excerpt from *Folded Hills* by Stewart Edward White, on the other hand, is as accurate as most historical accounts and gives an insight into the confused reactions of Americans living in California who couldn't understand Frémont's motives at Hawk's Peak. War has always been a personal affair, and the antagonisms which developed between the rude and overbearing Anglos and the native Californios is vividly portrayed in *The Dons of the Old Pueblo* by Percival J. Cooney. The most heroic episode on the Anglo side was the ride of John Brown to San Francisco to bring aid to the beseiged garrison at Los Angeles, while the most heroic episode on the Californio side was their victory at San Pasqual. In her account of the latter event, Gertrude Atherton in *The Splendid Idle Forties* considerably embellished the human side for greater fictional impact.

The Gold Rush was the most exciting and glamorous epoch in the history of California. More books, both fiction and non-fiction, have been written about this brief period than any other. The historian can summarize the documents, memoirs, letters, and newspaper accounts, but the human drama has been better presented by the novelist. The disruptive impact of gold fever upon one Ohio family and how this malady influences the lives of men, women, and children is portrayed in Todhunter Ballard's *Gold in California*. The scene presented can serve as an example of what took place in thousands of homes across the country. Throughout history man has sought to escape the tedium of everyday life by going on a crusade of one sort or another. This spirit is recaptured in Ruth Eleanor McKee's *Christopher Strange* where the main character looks to California's gold fields as a solution to all of his problems. Discovery of gold is a common fantasy of most people at some time in their lives. Robert Lewis Taylor imparts a "feel" for the excitement which such a moment brings in *The Travels of Jamie McPheeters*. The more prosaic tasks of outfitting miners through the port of San Francisco, the emerging entrepôt, and the supplying of the mines is the subject of *The Golden Days of '49* by Kirk Munroe and *The Pardners* by John Weld.

In treating the Indian the historian is frequently at a loss because the documentation he relies upon is not available. Making matters worse is the fact that the few descriptions of the "first" Californians which do exist are unflattering and sometimes unfair. Even among the anthropologists who study pre-literate peoples there is wide disagreement concerning the natives. What life was like for the Indians before the white man came in 1769 is a legitimate question. George R. Stewart, using his creative powers, imagines what the world might have been like in *Sheep Rock*. Authorities seldom agree as to why the Indians fled the missions, but there is no question that they were maltreated by Spanish and Mexican soldiers. In *Ranchero*, Stewart Edward White recreates an incident wherein an Anglo ranchero rescues natives being attacked. White's scene was historically accurate and he was usually a sympathetic commentator on the Hispanic world. However, neither historian nor novelist can effectively go back more than a century in time and be certain that he is recapturing the true emotions of people removed by such a time span. Anne Fisher in *Cathedral in the Sun* relates the manner in which an Indian woman has her land taken from her after the secularization of the missions. The author becomes emotionally involved with the plight of her character and moralizes on the injustices which occured. *Ramona* by Helen Hunt Jackson has been the most popular novel ever written on the sad state of the "first" Californians. Here too, the author identifies with her fictional characters and exaggerates to the extent that the reader is horrified by the events depicted. Virginia Myers in *This Land I Hold* relates the shock experienced by the Indians who came to Los Angeles. The squalid scene described is found in many memoirs and is historically accurate. The novelist often takes a true incident and, by filtering the facts through his own emotions, makes the episode and his characters as true as life itself.

The novelist can take known historical personages and make them come to life in fiction. It is of small concern that the actual words attributed to them cannot be verified so long as such conversation rests within the recognized historical roles that they played. The years after the American conquest of California were rich in strong personalities. In *Eagles Fly West*, Ed Ainsworth combines fictional characters with historical personalities who debate the issues at the Constitutional Convention. Two dominant personages in the early period of statehood were Senators William Gwin and David Broderick. Richard Summers' *Vigilante* relates the details of a political understanding between them. There is no authentic historical account of this meeting, but it may well have occurred the way Summers envisioned it.

Many novelists have been challenged by the decline of the Californios after American occupation. They have attempted to explain why the once dominant rancheros lost their land and positions of power. Virginia Myers in *This Land I Hold* contends that the relaxed and friendly dons could not understand the legal and business-like environment developed by the Anglos. Muriel Elwood in *Against the Tide* (as the title suggests) blames the desire of the Californios to cling to the habits and customs of their ancestors for their eventual displacement. Some authorities believe that the confusion over land titles made the collapse of the Hispanic element in California inevitable. In *Stampede* Stewart Edward White personalizes the often confused legal tangle occasioned by disputed land claims by depicting its effect on one family. Gertrude Atherton, whose work has been so influential in romanticizing life in Spanish California, takes a different stance in *The Californians*. There she lauds the strong Californios who made it in the Anglo world and has little sympathy for those who failed.

The historian, using statistics, tax figures and the like, can show the process by which California's economy was transformed from predominantly a ranching base to one encompassing mining, agriculture, and trade. On the other hand, the historical novelist can better show what these economic changes meant in the lives of people; for earning a living has always been one of man's foremost pursuits. Once the excitement of the Gold Rush period faded, mining continued to be important, but fictional writers tended to neglect what had become a prosaic activity. Yet, Clements Ripley in *Gold Is Where You Find It* makes the story of the struggle between farmers and the hydraulic miners who ruined their lands one of high drama by having two brothers as the main antagonists. The economy of the young state had its ups and downs, and hard times came in the 1870s. In this decade the working men of San Francisco followed Denis Kearney—who burst on the bay city like a meteor and just as quickly faded into obscurity. Kearney blamed the plight of the city's workers on the Chinese, and Mrs. Fremont Older in *The Socialist and The Prince* relates the fear that this reformer provoked among the city's elite.

The boom of the eighties in Southern California enticed large numbers of people to that part of the state. However, it brought out the worst among the land sharks. Theodore Strong Van Dyke, a Princetonian who was a health-seeker, saw the boom as "the greatest piece of folly that any country has ever seen." His *Millionaires of a Day* is a genial satire peopled with weird characters such as General Tiddlebug, Captain Popsure, and Major Bluebottle. This novel is like many on California in that its weakness as literature is offset by its qualities as a memoir.

Frank Norris, who studied in Paris and at Harvard, was one of the state's most widely acclaimed authors. A naturalist, he became enthused with man's struggle with the elements to produce wheat, the staff of life. In *The Octopus* he pictures a poet eager to write a work which would embrace a whole epoch and express the voice of all of the people. Woven through his masterful portrayal of man producing wheat is symbolism illustrating how the railroad (the octopus) was raping the countryside.

The dawn of the new century found Californians concerned with new issues. The San Francisco earthquake and fire remains the most celebrated disaster in the state's history, and a vast number of novels have been written about this catastrophe, some of them moralizing about its causes. Royce Briar in *Reach for the Moon* uses a literary staple by casting his lead character in the midst of the turmoil of the earthquake. Conflict between capital and labor dominated the first years of the century, and Wallace Stegner uses this as the basis for his novel *Joe Hill*. Stegner, an English professor who writes both fiction and history successfully, built his work around the life story of the Swedish immigrant whose songs had great impact in organizing and inspiring the working men and women of America and whose execution helped make him a martyr.

Upton Sinclair, author of seventy-nine novels, was perhaps the most widely read of all California writers. More famed as a social critic than a literary giant, he wrote the novel *Oil* because his wife had inherited some lots on which petroleum was found. Sinclair described the contest over the division of royalties as "human nature in the raw, and this was the first time I had seen it completely naked." Although an enemy of the oil industry (the author liked to repeat a parody of the doxology: "Praise God from whom oil blessings flow, Praise Him, oil creatures here below,") this novel was really a picture of Southern California civilization with an excellent insight into the rapidly expanding oil industry. It contains little social protest as such and only makes a tenuous effort to connect the Dohenys of California with the oil scandal in Washington.

In the twentieth century, agriculture became and remains California's leading industry, and *Jacob Peek* is possibly the first novel about the raising of oranges. Written by an Englishman residing in Riverside, the book stresses how man's ingenuity ultimately wins out over nature, one example being the use of smudge pots to save the fruit from frost. This novelist, Sidney Herbert Burchell, also satirizes the exorbitant claims of Southern California's realtors. *The Winning of Barbara Worth* by Harold Bell Wright is one of the earlier attempts fictionally to relate man's efforts to irrigate the Imperial Valley. Tremendously popular, this novel was mawkish in the extreme with the author's clerical status evident in the extensive moralizing. Wright saw Western America as superior to the East and believed the desert represented an opportunity for man to build a simple and happy society. A later water episode is placed in the Owens Valley and concerns itself with the reaction of individuals to Los Angeles' efforts to turn that verdant land into a desert by taking all of the water. In *Golden Valley*, an engineer representing the city's water-seekers falls in love with the daughter of a rancher and thus quickly sees the error of his ways. The technical aspects of the water problem are especially well handled in this narrative.

The social historians of California note that the state has a disproportionately large number of cultists and faddists. The scholars explain their presence as a natural result of the rootless and mobile society but, somehow, the cause and effect relationship of historians does not tell the full story. Religion is another area of man's activity in which a novelist can probe the psyche and arrive at answers more satisfying than those of the scholars. E. M. Nathanson's bizarre treatment in *The Latecomers* of the young man who had himself nailed to a cross to expose evil may express the latent impulses of many Christians toward crucifixion or the subconscious death wish of cultists. Nathanael West in *The Day of the Locust* claims that the boredom of their everyday lives and their lack of the intellectual capacity to enjoy leisure drives Californians to follow cultist leaders. West's people are ravaged by the locusts of their own fantasies so that they are destroyed in one mad apocalyptic riot. Upton Sinclair who, as previously noted, wrote an epic novel *Oil!* about Southern California life, has as his main character a leading revivalist who has discovered the new instrument of radio as a means to win converts. To Sinclair also it is the lack of meaning in their lives which drives people to identify with the strong religious personality. The extent to which religious cultism is a medical phenomenon instead of a spiritual one is the subject of Garet Rogers' *Prisoner in Paradise,* a skillful satire on health faddists and the ruthless villains who prey upon them. Jane Levington Comfort's *From These Beginnings* is, in the main, a sympathetic account of cult addicts who follow the teachings of theosophy. On the other hand, Myron Brinig in *The Flutter of an Eyelid* treats the subject with a literary meat-axe. In fact, his exposé of California religious cultism was so severe that one person who felt he was maliciously treated forced the publisher to withdraw and revise the book under threat of a libel suit. All the crackpot nature of Southern California life is laid bare, with the conclusion of the novel stressing that mankind would be best served if California slid into the Pacific Ocean.

The brief span of two decades between the wars saw the enthusiasm of the 1920s give way to despair among writers of the California scene during the depression years of the 1930s. In *The Boosters* Mark Lee Luther pleasantly satirizes the boomer mentality of the 1920s. The main character is an architect who is at first repulsed by the zaniness of Los Angeles in that period but ends up by becoming a booster himself. Robert Carson in *The Outsiders* records the history of Los Angeles from the 1880s to the 1960s in the saga of a single family. The author is able to recount the exhilarating growth of the city and to predict its ability to solve the problems of the 1920s without falling into the pitfalls of boosterism.

Perhaps one reason the civilization of Southern California came in for so much criticism arose from the presence of Hollywood, the motion picture capital of the world. The image projected by the movies was not a flattering one. Aldous Huxley turned his talents from satirizing English society to giving Hollywood and Los Angeles the poison pen treatment in *After Many a Summer Dies the Swan.* This Englishman gives a description of Los Angeles which is the most caustic ever penned, with the possible exception of Evelyn Waugh's *The Loved One.* Nathanael West in *The Day of the Locust* creates a main character who is a painter for the movie studios. The painter, like the novelist, looks into people's souls and often sees the baseness. West also was fascinated by the architectural melange in Hollywood, viewing it as a reflection of the people who lived in the weird houses he described.

California had firmly established herself as the promised land and when the homeless and jobless streamed in during the depression, lured by the promises of the past, the state faced many problems. Upton Sinclair in *Co-op* sought to popularize the cooperatives as one means of handling the depression's problems. In his novel he drew upon impressions of such activities all over California. Thus, Pipe City could have been anywhere in the state, as the scene described was a common one with men struggling to protect themselves as best they could. John Steinbeck took a biblical approach to show his sympathy for the unfortunate migrants who entered the state during the depression in *The Grapes of Wrath*. Often described as a primitivist, Steinbeck tended to glorify the exploits of the humble. An epic story-teller, Steinbeck made his characters so gripping that this novel was the most popular protest work of the decade. Labor turmoil in San Francisco is the subject of *Flint* by Charles Norris. This novel covers many subjects and includes composite characterizations of many men prominent on the state scene in the 1930s. This younger brother of Frank Norris wrote several widely acclaimed novels.

The outbreak of World War II ended the depression in California as it did in the rest of the nation. The war also brought a large outpouring of personal testaments about participation in some phase of the conflict. Such novels are, in reality, memoirs thinly disguised as fiction and should be recognized as valid historical sources despite their shortcomings as literature. For the truth is that most people looked upon their war experience, even if it was only on the home front, as unique; and it has gained an added importance in their minds as the years have passed by. Thus, there are excellent examples of novels to illustrate how people's lives were changed in the state during the war.

Seymour Kern writes in *Samson Duke* how an eastern real estate investor was able to predict rising property values and thus profit from his insight. Above all, he was able to use an investment to ensure a deferment from army service. *Harvest of Hate* by Georgia Day Robertson is the work of a person associated with the Japanese who understood the anguish which accompanied their internment. Working in industry was a novel experience for many young women. This opportunity to escape the routine of the housewife, earn good money, and feel that they were contributing to the war effort was a great event in many lives. Richard Stern in *Brood of Eagles* has written of a California aircraft family in epic and authentic fashion. The movement of Arkies from their homes to the Bay area shipyards is the subject of *Skip To My Lou* by William Martin Camp. The manner in which people were lured from their native surroundings to the discomfort of war swollen cities is skillfully told through believable characters. In addition, this is a personal testament that finds much humor in the travail of simple people.

There was no joy in the efforts of blacks to find employment in the shipyards that were enticing white workers from two thousand miles away. This problem is explored in Alexander Saxton's *Bright Web in the Darkness*. The difficulties confronted by Mexican-Americans in achieving equality in Los Angeles during the war years are treated in *Teach the Angry Spirit* by Cornelia Jessey. The fear felt by barrio youths as they were subjected to brutal attacks is the main theme of this work.

A character in the novel *Mayo Sergeant* laments that he returned to

California "very much the same as I was when I enlisted to avoid the draft. Upon my return I found the state, itself, had changed while my back was turned." The mass influx of people and the growth of industry especially transformed Southern California and the sprawling Bay area. The new age of technology which emerged prompted many novelists to be highly critical. Some, like Maxwell Griffith in *The Gadget Maker*, simply trace the transition from mass production of wartime aircraft to the limited work for a peacetime market and finally to the making of missiles in the 1960s. The many novels written about California's aerospace industry depend for their interest upon a wealth of technical detail presented so that it can be understood by the layman, with the plots stressing near mishaps in launching and pride in the final triumph as the missiles disappear amid the stars.

Much of the change in post-war California resulted from the mushroom growth of subdivisions, high-rise office buildings, and apartments. *Mayo Sergeant* by James B. Hall is about an unscrupulous real estate promoter prepared to use every method to succeed, but who comes to grief in the end. The novel's locale is the Newport Beach area of Orange County, and its handling of the sale of housing to the retired is made more acceptable by the injection of humor.

Strikes among the predominantly Mexican-American agricultural workers and how they change the lives of the participants is the subject of *Macho* by Edmund Villaseñor. Another type of social unrest was reflected in the emergence of secret right-wing societies. What one such group does to innocent individuals is detailed in *The Lost and The Found* by Ann Chidester. Political novels have been especially popular since World War II and one of the best of these is *The Ninth Wave* by Eugene Burdick. Although its primary theme is how fear-mongers generate hate to ensure election, it also provides an insight into the new Californian. The leading character is one who always waited for the biggest wave when surfing, the ninth wave. By implication then, the Californian who makes it waits and recognizes the big chance and seizes it.

The era since World War II has been marked by the struggles of ethnic minorities to attain political, social, and economic equality. The early fiction on this subject was usually written by whites attracted by the uniqueness of an alien culture or by injustices perpetrated against a helpless people. Grant Carpenter in *Night Tide* displays an acute understanding of and sympathy for the Chinese as they struggled to make a living in the hostile environment of California. On the other hand, Gertrude Atherton in *Ancestors* shows little sympathy for the Japanese but understands that the attacks upon them originated in the economic fears of whites. Chester Himes in *The Lonely Crusade* writes a personal testament of a black struggling to better his position in the Golden State. Of the large number of Mexican-American authors who have sought to define their position in the Anglo World, none has succeeded better than Raymond Barrio in *The Plum Plum Pickers*. *The Rabbit Boss* by Thomas Sanchez, himself an American Indian, seeks to understand the contemporary native Californian by exploring the lives of four generations of Washo, a tribe on the California-Nevada border. The novel is often confusing as its uses mysticism and Indian lore to convey its message. However, there is no question as to the message Joseph Wambaugh is trying to send the reader in *The New Centurions.* There is no subtlety in the fact that police power is an effective means of checking a race riot. Wambaugh was a policeman who helped subdue the disorder in Watts in 1965, and much of his writing is probably personal experience.

In the years since World War II a new society has emerged in California. Some have seen it as the full realization of the American dream, while others have seen it as a precursor of a national nightmare. When the tremendous population and economic growth slowed in the middle 1960s, many began to question whether the millenium had really been attained in the state. This wave of skepticism was heightened as a result of the youth revolt. Sociologists and journalists have readily interpreted these changes, but the creative instinct of the novelist probably has better understood the full meaning of the events of these tumultuous years.

While most people were lavishing nothing but praise upon the Golden State in 1962 when it passed New York as the nation's most populous, Richard Armour found many things to question. In his poem, "I Loved You, California," the state's leading humorist couches some biting questions about the new society in a jesting framework. Even in the midst of economic plenty, large numbers of Californians seem to be lonely, restless, and without personal peace. Vilhelm Moberg in *A Time on Earth* explains this as a result of the fact that the state is populated by people from other places who never really feel they belong in their adopted state. Carol Evan in *Glad and Sorry Season* constructed her novel in the form of letters and telegrams sent to New York City friends as reports on her Los Angeles activities. She is especially concerned with a radio talk show, a form of therapy for those who feel abandoned and lost in modern California.

In the 1950s the "beat" generation was spawned in the Haight-Ashbury district of San Francisco. A leading spokesman for this youth counter-culture was Jack Kerouac. He wrote numerous poems and novels to explain its genesis, one of which was *The Dharma Bums.* Wallace Stegner performed a similar chore for the hippies of the 1960s. In *Angle of Repose* (the title comes from the maximum angle of slope at which sand will remain in place on a hillside), Stegner seeks to explain the chaotic present generation by examining a more placid past. His work is based on the life of Mary Hallock Foote, and the moralizing of the author is performed by a fictional narrator who is himself so believable that the reader may easily come to accept whatever conventions he dictates. Ross MacDonald, a Santa Barbara resident and writer of mystery tales, was angered over the oil spill that damaged the beaches of that city in 1969. He therefore used it as the main theme in *Sleeping Beauty,* stressing that the oil did as much injury to people's lives as it did to the beaches. In *The*

Outsiders Robert Carson uses his characters as a vehicle to express his fears for the future of the California he loves.

Thus, as these selections show, the creative art of the historical novelist can enrich man's understanding of the dramatic past of California. The historian, with his emphasis upon facts, may be indispensable to a study of the Golden State; but the artist as literary man, with his glimpses of beauty and poetry, can bring that past to life for the present generation. In the final analysis, the historian and the historical novelist need each other, and by utilizing the best of both worlds, the reader can broaden his knowledge of California's yesterday.

The California Experience

Chapter 1

The Land

The Land

One of man's oldest fantasies is the belief that there exists somewhere a perfect place. In this terrestrial paradise want is unknown, the land itself is beautiful, food falls from the trees, the sun is always shining, and the weather is a delight. References to the Garden of Eden can be found in the books of Genesis and Daniel. Columbus and other explorers were sure they had found this terrestrial paradise in America. The search by Ponce de Leon for the fountain of youth in Florida and Francisco Coronado's quest for the gold-laden seven cities of Cibola in the Southwest symbolize the continuing belief that such a land did indeed exist. The Spaniards who found the gold of the New World were certain they had found this mythical paradise. Although at first repelled by the harsh and forbidding climate, the English also came to believe that this bountiful land of America was truly a paradise.

One of the basic tenets of American frontiersmen was that somewhere there was a promised land where the soil was richer, the grass greener, and the air purer. Wallace Stegner, in *The Big Rock Candy Mountain*, expressed this never-ending quest in these words: "There was somewhere, if you knew where to find it, some place where money could be made like drawing water from a well, some Big Rocky Candy Mountain where life was effortless and rich and unrestricted and full of adventure and action, where something could be had for nothing." To many, "born with itch in their bones," California was the terrestrial paradise. The Golden State became a symbol to those seeking a better life. Here gold could be found for the taking, rich lands for ranching or farming could be had by all, high paying jobs in factories were waiting to be filled and, to some, California was the place where chronic bodily complaints would disappear. From frontier days to the last quarter of the twentieth century, in boom times and in depression, California was the promised land to millions who yearned for the better life.

Countless writers have stressed this promise of California. This was what spurred on the Okies that John Steinbeck depicted so movingly in *The Grapes of Wrath*. In Stewart Edward White's *The Rose Dawn*, one character says, "I tell you, Puss . . . where would they find another place in the world with a sun and sky like this! Think of it back East where they came from! Snow, ice, wind!" In Lewis Browne's, *Oh Say Can You See!* a new arrival simply cannot believe what his eyes behold: "The name was there on the station-wall: he could see it—SANTA LUCIA—bold and black in the floodlit glare. But though his lips read it off half-audibly, he was still incredulous. For months and months already he had been dreaming of this place, and for weeks he had been traversing land and sea to reach it. Yet now that he was here, he had a feeling he was still dreaming. There was something unreal about the scene: about that illumined doll's-house of a station, with its stucco arches and clambering vines; and about the tousled palms standing like sentries against the star-lit sky. It was all too neat and clean, too pretty, too much like a picture." In fact, through much of the fiction with a California setting there runs a touch of fantasy, as if the authors themselves were unsure of their descriptions of this fabulous land. Perhaps they suffer from the dilemma suggested by Carey McWilliams in *California: The Great Exception* "The analyst of California is like a navigator who is trying to chart a course in a storm: the instruments will not work; the landmarks are lost; and the maps make little sense." But even with their stress upon the promise of the land, through the years, writers have had to face a growing realization that California also has its shortcomings, and that man has to contest with nature for control of this Garden of Eden.

1   The Naming of California

The belief that the Golden State was the long dreamed of terrestrial paradise originated, along with the state's name, in an early sixteenth-century Spanish romantic novel. This work, *Las sergas de Esplandian* (*The Deeds of Esplandian*), was read widely by the Spaniards at the time of the Mexican conquest. The place name of the novel's mythical island was applied to California as early as the decade of the 1530s. The image of California as an island was not corrected until the beginning of the eighteenth century as a result of the explorations of Father Eusebio Kino.

Now you are to hear the most extraordinary thing that was ever heard of in the writings or in the memory of man . . . . Know that on the right hand of the Indies, there is an island called California, very close to the Terrestrial Paradise. This island is inhabited by black women who have no men among them and who live as Amazons. These women are large, of great physical strength, and are very courageous. Their island was the strongest and most rugged in the world with its steep cliffs and rocky shores. Their weapons were all of gold, as was the harness of the wild beasts which they tamed and rode. In all the island there was no other metal.

They lived in caves which had been carved out of the rock with great difficulty. They had many ships with which they sailed out to other places to obtain plunder. They carry the men they capture back to California. With some they have carnal relations and as a result many of them become pregnant. If they give birth to a female they keep her, but if the child is male

Translated from *Las sergas de Esplandian* by Garci Rodriguez Ordóñez de Montalvo. Published ca. 1510.

they kill him. They do this because they are firmly resolved to keep the males so small in number that they can control them; they only allow those to live which are thought necessary for the perpetuation of the race.

In this island called California, with its rough terrain, there are a great number of wild animals, among which are griffins, not found in any other part of the world. When the griffins give birth to their young, these women go out and trap their young whom they take to their caves and raise them. Being very strong they are able to control these griffins and feed them the men whom they took prisoners, and the boys to whom they gave birth. The griffins are so domesticated that they would do the women no harm but would kill and eat any male who came to the island.

Over the island of California reigned a mighty queen, Calafia. She was a very large person and more beautiful than all of the other women. She was in the flower of womanhood, very brave and was eager to perform valorous deeds; she was ambitious to surpass all of those who had ruled before her.

2   Everyman's Eden

California has truly been for many the land of promise, where man could find gold, fame, health, and adventure. Since Diego de Borica, who became Spanish governor in 1794, wrote to friends that if they wanted to "live much and without care, come to Monterey," to the last quarter of the twentieth century, man has tried to realize the American dream in California. In this selection, written about the 1880s when health seekers, real estate speculators, and tourists were flooding the state, emphasis is upon the unique beauty of the land itself as the greatest lure.

The trails started in the cañons with their shady oaks and sycamores, their parks of grass and flowers, their leaping sparkling streams with boulders and pools, waterfalls and fern banks; they climbed by lacets to a "hogsback"—or tributary ridge—through overarching cascara and mountain lilac; and so proceeded to upper regions. The sun against the shade and the chaparral warmed to life many odours. White of cascara, blue of lilac powdered whole mountain sides with bloom; the leaves of the mountain cherries glittered in the sun, and the satin red bark of manzanita glowed. The air was like crystal under the blue sky, and the single notes of the mountain quail rang clear as though the crystal had been struck. Cañon slopes fell away grandly. Great mathematical shadows defined the sharp ridge—and the abrupt foldings of the hills. The sky was a steady, calm watchful blue. No wonder old boys—old, but always boys—turned light hearted and played pranks that would have made their children or grandchildren ashamed—if they had known! Especially as George Scott, the amused cynic, never went riding. He spent his mornings at the beach,

From *The Rose Dawn* by Stewart Edward White. Published 1920.

watching the bathers, snubbing the forward, and uttering caustic comment.

But it was when they stopped on some outlying spur and looked abroad on the scenery that the real charm of the country gripped them.

For over the panorama below them lay a misty peace, a suspended stillness as though a great Spirit had sighed in his sleep and had for a contented moment held his breath, and the moment was as the Biblical thousand years. From above, the folds of the lesser hills were soft and rounded, and on them showed the dark spots of the trees. The sea rose up from the depths below them until it met the horizon at the level of the eye. This gave it the curious effect of being the opposite wall of a cañon on the bottom of which lay Arguello and the farms and the *ranchos* and the shore. A yellow haze mellowed it. From incredible distances and with incredible clarity, rose single sounds—the stroke of a bell, the lowing of cattle. The pungent aroma of sage brush—Old Man—hung in the air.

The old boys used to stop and look on all this with great inner appreciation, but with outward indifference. At length Boyd himself broke out:

"Where on the globe," he cried, "will you find anything even approaching this? The climate is perfect; the people—look at the way that country lies! There's not another place in the world where you can ride a horse in high mountains and come home on a beach two hundred feet wide, and do it all in one afternoon! There's not another place like it in California! Why look at the size of that valley, and consider how many people, wealthy people, will flock in here when a few of them get to know it as we know it! There won't be room for them! Why, the fellow who owns real estate—"

They crowded their horses around him whooping with amusement, slapping him on the back, while even the staid old horse fidgeted.

"He's got it!" they cried. "It's bit him!" "The old cuss has a bad case; he'll come back!"

Boyd stood their banter with a grin that was at first a little shamefaced, but soon became triumphant. His was not a nature to take it lying down.

"Yes, I've got it, you poor nincompoops; and I'm bit. But I'm not coming back. Why? Because I won't have to. I'm going to stay. Just soak that up, will you? You got to go back and attend to your business. I don't have to unless I want to; and I don't want to. While you are sweating away in those pleasant eastern summers, or thawing the icicles out of the whiskers of hope before you can get away next winter, you just think of me right up here, or right down there picking oranges and flowers and filling my system up with this good air!"

"You don't mean that, do you, Boyd?" inquired Saxon, the shoe man.

"Of course I mean it."

"How about your business?"

"To hell with my business! It don't need me any more: and I don't need it."

"I don't know," rejoined Saxon doubtfully. He with the rest was sobered down from vacation irresponsibility by Boyd's decision to do what each had secretly played with as a fascinating but impractical possibility. "How about yourself? You'll get sick of this sort of a thing as a steady diet."

"I'll get me a place," said Boyd, stoutly. "I'll buy me a ranch over the mountains. There's a big future in this place. It's asleep now; sure thing. But it can be waked up. It ought to be waked up. Judging from what I've seen, that would keep a man busy for a while. Oh, I won't take root, if that's what you mean. You fellows are as blind as bats. All you see is a sleepy little backwater town that you have a good time in. It's got a great future."

"So confounded future that you won't live to see it—except of course that more and more tourists will come. You aren't going into the resort business, are you, Boyd?" observed someone else.

"I may. Do'no yet. But you can stick a railroad up the coast, and bore a tunnel in through these mountains here for water so you can irrigate the way they've begun to do at San Bernardino, and cut up these big ranches into farms with water on them, and—"

But his companions burst out laughing.

"You're in the traction business," Saxon suggested. "How about it? After you get all these mountains knocked down and kicked out of the way for your railroad, how about a new mule for the street car system?"

"I may take hold of that, too," rejoined Boyd, after the renewal of laughter.

He had not before seriously considered abandoning the East, but suddenly he could see no reason against it. Since his last merger he had practically retired from active management of the concerns that brought him his enormous income. He had no other family ties than those that bound him to his son, Kenneth. To a man of his temperament new friends quickly replaced the old. The vision, genuine though narrowly commercial, that had made him what he was, pierced the veils of apathy behind which Arguello slumbered to a sense of the rose dawn of a modern day. Now, suddenly, there on top of the mountain he came to a decision.

3   The Slide Area

The impermanence of the earth's surface has frightened settlers away from areas which experience this problem. During the winter rainy season headlines like the following are all too common in some sections of California: "Mudslides Bury Row of Houses" or "Soggy Hillside Gives Way, Roars Down on Eight Homes." The condition has been worsened by the use of huge earthmoving equipment which has enabled man to carve out building lots on hillsides. As a result, houses are crushed by mudslides or go cascading over cliffs into the ocean. The following selection illustrates how new arrivals are constantly mystified by the nonchalance Californians display when the land collapses around them.

The ocean appears suddenly. You turn another hairpin bend and the land falls away and there is a long high view down Santa Monica Canyon to the pale Pacific waters. A clear day is not often. Sky and air are hazed now, diffusing the sun and dredging the ocean of its rightful blue. The Pacific is a sad blue-grey, and nearly always looks cold.

Each time I drive down here it feels like the end of the world. The geographical end. Shabby and uncared for, buildings lie around like nomads' tents in the desert. There is nowhere further to go, those pale waters stretch away to the blurred horizon and stretch away beyond it. There is no more land ever.

High lurching cliffs confront the ocean, and are just beginning to fall apart. Signs have been posted along the highway, DRIVE CAREFULLY and SLIDE AREA. Lumps of earth and stone fall down. The land is restless here, restless and sliding. Driving inland towards the mountains, it is the same: BEWARE OF ROCKS. The land is falling. Rocks fall down all over and the cliffs called Pacific Palisades are crumbling slowly down to the ocean. Who called them Palisades, I wonder? They cannot keep out the Pacific. There are mad eccentric houses above the Palisades, with turrets and castellations and tall Gothic windows, but no one wants to live in them any more in case the ground slides away.

It has slid again this afternoon. On one section of the highway a crowd has gathered. An ambulance stands by, winking red lights. A sheriff directs operations. From a great pile of mud and stones and sandy earth, the legs of old ladies are sticking out. Men with shovels are working to free the rest of their bodies. Objects are rescued first, a soiled tablecloth and a thermos flask and what looks like a jumbo sandwich, long as a baby eel. Then an air cushion and more long sandwiches, and a picnic basket, and at last the three old ladies themselves. They are all right. They look shaken and angry, which is to be expected. A few minutes ago they had been sitting on the Palisades, in a pleasant little hollow free from the wind. The cloth was spread for a picnic. Miss Natalie O'Gorman laid out sandwiches on a plastic dish, her sister Clara unscrewed the thermos flask to pour out coffee, and their friend Willa North decided to blow up her air cushion.

Absolutely silent at first, the ground beneath them disappeared. The slide meant for a moment that there was no ground at all, it ceased to exist, and then as it gained momentum and scudded away like clouds breaking up in a gale, there was a light rumbling sound. The three ladies, Natalie O'Gorman with a sandwich in her hand, her sister with the flask and Willa North with her mouth pressed to the air cushion, went with the land and were practically submerged by it at the side of the highway below.

Now they are brushing their dresses with distracted motions and shaking little stones out of their bosoms and little clods out of their hair. Everyone is saying it is a miracle. Natalie O'Gorman would like to find her hat. Bones are felt and nothing is broken; they are scratched and bruised,

that is all. 'We are all right,' they tell the crowd. 'Yes, we are quite all right.'
Willa North says: 'I was taken completely by surprise!'

I drive on, past another SLIDE AREA sign. The beaches are still quite
full. A group of tanned young men are wrestling and playing ball. Two
girls watch them, eating hot dogs. An old Negro in a tattered blue suit
walks by the edge of the ocean, a mongrel dog following him. Out to sea,
someone is surfing. Stretching his arms, the muscular young lifeguard
watches from his tower.

. . .

I find myself remembering how the summer began. The cliffs weakened
under heavy spring rains, rocks and stones rolled away, then whole sections
crumbled and fell. Houses skidded down with them. There were some
deaths. For several miles the coast highway was closed. The newspapers
rumoured that a long geological survey would be undertaken. Had the
highway been cut too deep into the cliffs? Would the land go on falling?
Perhaps the area would have to be abandoned and a causeway built out over
the ocean. Meanwhile, the ruins were shovelled away, FOR RENT signs
went up on beach houses, a few bars and restaurants closed. After three
months, the highway was opened again without explanation. Driving
along, you saw jagged hollows and craters scarring the cliffs. They looked
almost volcanic. WATCH FOR ROCKS. The sun grew stronger. Cars
massed along the highway, the long pale stretch of pleasure beaches
became filled with people. And the slides were forgotten, nobody talked
about them any more.

'Well, there's no point in scaring people. Remember those old ladies
who went over the edge? I told them then it wouldn't be the end of it, but I
told them not to scare anybody.' The engineer who said this was stocky and
unruffled. He had thickly-rimmed spectacles and a briar pipe. The city
authorities had consulted him after the houses fell down. 'We'll handle the
whole thing quietly, in our own way. That's what I told them.'

'Then how serious are the slides?' I asked.

'I guess you could call the last one a little serious.' He puffed at his
pipe. 'Quite a bit of land fell away that time. Took quite a few houses with
it.'

'People, too.'

'Sure. People, too.'

'Shouldn't something be done?'

'We need more information.' The engineer's pipe was drawing badly.
He lit another match. 'We want to see what happens after the rains next
year.'

'You mean, wait for the same thing to happen again?'

'So what else can you do?' The engineer shrugged. 'Make a big project
out of it and spend a lot of money? Scare a lot of people and take their
business away? It's not worth it. Time's on our side.' He gave a reassuring
nod. 'Maybe the foundations *are* shaky, maybe we'll have another slide

after the rains next year, but it's a slow, easy process. It'll take years and years before you notice a real difference.'

'A few houses more or less don't really matter,' I said.

'Well, that's not exactly the way I'd put it.' He shrugged again. 'You know what I think? People should be a little careful and not live too near the edge, that's all.'

4 Earthquake Country

One of the most enduring themes in California fiction concerns earthquakes. Scores of novels have been written about the great San Francisco quake and many more on quakes in general. These novels usually reach their climax at the moment the dishes begin to rattle and the chandelier begins to sway. A favorite treatment depicts California breaking off at the San Andreas fault and sliding into the Pacific Ocean.

The following is from the pen of an east coast author who disapproves of the California life style and suggests that it would not be a great loss if the state did fall into the ocean. After satirizing virtually all that he has seen in the Golden State, Myron Brinig closes a courtroom scene with an apocalyptic vision of just such a disastrous end.

The case of the State of California versus Mrs. Forgate had dragged on for a number of days before the prosecutor made his final speech to the jury, on October the Thirtieth. Where, in other parts of America, the coolness of autumn was in the air, California was still warm with clear, blue skies, cloudless and lit by great golden globes of sun. The court was a hive of humanity, but unlike the useful insects, these were parasites on the body of a vast, perspiring scandal. They were less insects than voracious vermin that one might find after lifting a corpse that had been dead for a long period of time. In this court room, then, were bodies, intestines, prejudices: the common fools; and the only figure of distinction among them was the defendant, who had become so resigned to her fate that she had recaptured her old air of cold, malevolent disdain.

In the last few weeks of her imprisonment, she had returned to Proust, and had, just prior to entering the court room, finished reading the last volume of LE TEMPS RETROUVÉ. Now why should she not die? Death is a magnificent culmination for one who has lived as completely and colorfully as Mrs. Forgate. She seemed to have passed through all stages of existence. She had been an innocent virgin and had lost her virginity. She had known calm landscapes, grasses at dawn and a clear, silver moon at night. She could place a pastoral scene by the side of one decadent; a civilized mind so depleted by mental excesses that only a violence of insanity remains. She had loved and hated, given and withheld herself. She

From *The Flutter of an Eyelid* by Myron Brinig. Published in 1933.

had traveled in nearly all countries of the world, had watched the slumbrous indigoes, nephrites and almandines of the South Seas as well as the silver and steel snowscapes and raw steppes of Russia. She had known possession and jealousy and won and lost. She had read Flaubert, Proust, Poe, Baudelaire, Strindberg. She had heard Wagner and Debussy, Beethoven and Brahms. And she had killed. Her life was therefore complete as any life can be, masterful and masterly. Now who were these fools that they should judge her?

She looked forward to a painful death. Millions and millions of men and women had died, to be sure, but in comparison to these millions, but an insignificant number had been hanged. That was a distinction considering that the mass of humans are such boors, cattle and fleas; surely, it was an honor to be put to death by such oafs, morons and cowards. If Mrs. Forgate's jury had been made up of Arthur Machen, Proust, George Sand, Huneker, Duse, Huysmans, Keats, Lincoln, Whitman, Poe, Pater and Wilde . . . ah, then, what an interesting trial! Acquittal or conviction, what a drama, what a sublime spectacle this would have been! But these blowsy housewives, merchants, mechanics—what could one expect from them? Lacking innocence and humility on the one side and aristocracy and intellect on the other, who were they to pronounce guilt or freedom? What importance had they in the cosmos? Mrs. Forgate was intensely happy. She thought that her intellect had grown in stature since her imprisonment. These circumstances were what she had required in order to round out a perfect life—all experience in one body and mind. Who among the jury, the lawyers or spectators could boast of one-fiftieth of such distinction? Let them preserve Society, since, in our time, it is, at best, the drool of a complacent, jelly-fleshed nit-wit. . . .

The sun moved toward the center of the heavens, unconcerned with life on earth. It was a still, hot day. The glass of the huge court room windows was stricken with a staring pain of light. The entire coast-line was thin and desperate with silence. Trees were quiet, and there was scarcely a murmur of the sea, flat and brilliant as the surface of a polished table.

The prosecutor, a soiled, debilitated looking man, arose from his place to address the jury. He suffered from diabetes and doctors had told him that he had not long to live. He was sullen and bitter since it seemed to him that life had never been very colorful or exciting. In his youth, because of his family's poverty, he had been compelled to go to work in a coal mine. Later, in Chicago, he had studied law in a night school while working days in a shoe factory. All his life had been passed in bitter work and slavery to the end that one day, he might hold in the palm of his hand, the fate of those members of the privileged classes who had scorned him in his youth. As a defense attorney, his successes had not been particularly notable. But as a prosecutor, he was famous for his brilliant savagery, and murderers that he denounced were fascinated by the killer's instinct in him that they knew was in themselves.

Mrs. Forgate's case had attracted attention all over the world, and the prosecutor, at the opening of the trial, had the feeling that his greatest moments were before him. He decided that he would torture and crucify the accused unmercifully, and had not the slightest doubt that she would be hanged. But after a few days, his glowing exaltation had subsided into his old bitterness again, since it was obvious that Mrs. Forgate was not upset by what he said, and sat disdainfully, answering the pointed questions he addressed to her. She looked on him as an aid to her extinction; and, becoming aware of her partisanship, the prosecutor was strangely defeated and humbled for the last time in his career. He might be a killer, but Mrs. Forgate possessed a finer subtlety, far more poise and distinction in the same line. And so, as the trial progressed, he came to regard her as a great woman, and a secret understanding was formed between them. Mrs. Forgate was sorry for him; and he, on his own part, was resigned to her superiority.

Up in San Francisco, the waters about the Golden Gate were dark and sinister. In the Sierras, the Redwoods stood like rows of prisoners awaiting the guillotine. The streets of Santa Barbara were sodden and soaked with the yellow heat. San Diego was numb, paralyzed on its rack of barbed, excruciating fire. Near Palm Springs, the desert lay bereft of the varied, contrasting colors of its flowers that had bloomed after the winter rains. The desert was toneless, denuded, a dry, airless plain between Heaven and Hell.

The prosecutor commenced his summing-up with a formless ferocity of words, expected and trite. He called the jury's attention to Mrs. Forgate's indifference and exhorted them to study her soulless expression. She was a born criminal, he said, a callous, cruel killer . . . and had it not been proved that she had poisoned others when she had lived in Italy? Italy, where she had lived a life of rotten and rank decadence, went on the prosecutor, thinking how unfortunate it was that he had never been there. But somehow, there had not been time, and when there had been time, no money. Italy! How the prosecutor longed for other shores and climes than he had known! How he wished that he had owned the courage to kill with poisons and weapons rather than with words! He might have killed his wife, for instance. How sick he was of her, a dowdy, misshapen woman, a member of numberless clubs, clubs for the betterment of this and that, political clubs, temperance clubs, bridge clubs, charity clubs. Everything she did and said was with an audience of women in mind, and she could not even read a book without the thought, I'll tell the club about it. And his children, gin-drinking, partying, motor-car speedsters and nonentities, how he would have loved poisoning off the lot of them! Instead, he was poisoned with diabetes . . . sugar in the blood . . . and now he would never find time to go to Italy, to look in at the art galleries, to stroll through the streets of Florence.

"I demand the extreme penalty!" he shouted. "For if such a woman is permitted to roam free, her hands dripping blood and poison, our glorious state of California might as well destroy itself or be destroyed. . . ."

The prosecutor's index finger, a gleaming point in the sunlight, was uplifted. Sylvia's eyelids fluttered in surprise and she moved closer to her husband. And Mrs. Forgate sat like a figure of stone in her chair. The walls of the court room trembled, at first imperceptibly, then sharply. The floor slanted downward and there was a shattering of windowglass. The chandeliers swung back and forth like trapezes in a circus tent. And all of California, from the Siskiyous to Mexico, from the eastern border to the coast, started sliding swiftly, relentlessly, into the Pacific Ocean.

.   .   .

The rugged cliffs that stand over San Francisco Bay crumbled as though blown up by dynamite, and buildings of the city collapsed, cracking in half like tall soldiers whose stomachs are penetrated by machine-gun bullets as they advance toward the enemy. At Carmel, startled flocks of gulls wheeled and screamed above a slanting destruction of rock and sand. The waters rose, the shore sank, and in a few minutes, only a few rocks could be seen protruding above the desolation of sea. Seals dived deep to escape the falling and ponderous landslides, and schools of fish were disorganized and scattered to unknown blind deep-sea tunnels and temples of rock. Los Angeles tobogganed with almost one continuous movement into the water, the shore cities going first, followed by the inland communities; the business streets, the buildings, the motion picture studios in Hollywood where actors became stark and pallid under their mustard-colored makeups. From the sea, this furore of finality was a mammoth spectacle, as if the land were on wheels rolling into the depths of an invisible grave. And as the land stood on end, like a sinking ship, the waves rose high with a hungry, mad roar, solid walls of water iridescent and exquisitely green in the sharp sunlight. There was a breathless embrace of land and ocean, and of this conception death was born. Horrified cries and screams pierced the atmosphere, a continuously moving wheel, a spectrum of sound.

Only winged creatures could escape; and all the singing birds released themselves from firmness into a sparkling freedom of swift air, until the blue of the sky could not be seen for birds flying away, to the sun and the seas and shores of Mexico and South America: The small pink and white, blue and orange stucco houses of the shore were blown like colored sands into the tempest; stone had no invulnerability, and wood was soon soaked and rotted. Trees were uprooted, and like captive women, dragged by their green hair into the mad, tumultuous arena of death. Huge boulders were ripped from their smugness and fell like great meteors, many of them crushing men and women and children in their descent. Presently, the birds in the sky were fewer; the sky was clear, the sun bright and harsh, moving like a golden chariot of triumph over a field of carnage.

For a few minutes, perhaps three or four, the interior of the court in which Mrs. Forgate's case was being tried, retained something of its rectangular shape and formality. But that destruction was imminent, death and cold, no one in the room could doubt. There were moans and whimperings, sad and insane, Protestants huddling together with Catholics, but Jews sought out other Jews. The Judge held on grimly to his gavel, as though by pounding on his desk, the flood would grow timid and subside, the land become firm and stationary once more. But not all his poundings could halt the trend to the sea. "Case . . . is . . . dismissed . . ." mumbled the Judge, and continued to hold tightly to his gavel; but now it was a pathetic symbol of an authority that could be no more.

Mrs. Forgate continued to grip the arms of her chair, and as she moved down into the sea, she saw the arms of the prosecutor reaching out for her. His features were set in an expression of demoniac delight. "You thought you'd be hanged, eh?" he gurgled, striving to retain life for a few seconds more. "Well, for once, you've been cheated. . . ."

And the extraordinary Mrs. Forgate sailed downward into the deep gold and green of the under-seas, immovable and cold as a statue, making no slight movement either in her face or frame. "But this is . . . a splendid, spendid end," she called as a shark moved forward like a curling dagger to snatch out her eyes. He was too late to give her pain. . . .

For days and weeks, flotsam and jetsam of wreckage floated over the sea, pieces of fragments and odds and ends of color that had once been California. But after a year, no one could know that California had once existed in this place, though the sky was ever blue and the sun was ever brilliant, going his grandiose way from East to West.

5   The Santa Anas

California's climate remains one of its greatest attractions. Yet, it also has its drawbacks. Some writers have complained of the enervating influence of too much sunshine and too little change in the weather. The Santa Ana winds (devil winds) which become extremely dry in their flow from the Great Basin towards the sea, are thought by some to influence man's behavior. Raymond Chandler described it thus in *Red Wind*: "There was a desert wind blowing that night. It was one of those hot dry Santa Anas that come down through the mountain passes and curl your hair and make your nerves jump and your skin itch. On nights like that every booze party ends in a fight. Meek little wives feel the edge of the carving knife and study their husband's necks. Anything can happen." The succeeding passage suggests a similar influence.

Shrieking and moaning, the wind swept in from the desert. . . . It was one of those summer days rare to the Pacific coast, but poignant, when through the yellow sunlight there sift vague phantom shapes of impalpable dust

From *On The Lot and Off* by George Randolph Chester and Lillian Chester. Published in 1924.

which bite the skin and smart the eyes, and are the prickling forerunners of a three-day withering heat from out the very heart of the vast shadeless inferno up yonder in the waste places. It was such a day as lowers the vitality and depresses the spirits and sets the nerves on edge, and when vitality ebbs and depression reigns and nerves are aquiver both men and women do things which they might not otherwise have done; so no one knows what tremendous extent of folly and of tragedy may be chargeable to this same shrill shrieking, moaning, sobbing wind from the deadly desert.

6 The Spitcat

California's natural environment, hospitable to man in so many respects, is disaster prone. Thus, the state has suffered many natural catastrophes such as floods, droughts and earthquakes. But none is more feared than fire. The virtual absence of rainfall for much of the year and the hot, drying Santa Anas, make brush and grasslands tinder dry. Man is responsible for many of the fires but natural causes are also present. The following excerpt concerns a fire started by lightning. The author spent two summers with the United States Forest Service gathering material for this fictional, but very realistic novel about fire. Note the comparison of the life of a fire with the life span of a man.

As the quiet of evening fell on the steep slope above Onion Creek, the pine tree was little changed. Its tip had lopped over, like a wilting plant. A faint tar-like odor hung in the still air. There was also a slight charred smell; but, intense as the heat had been, the plentiful sap had oozed in quickly and kept the wood from burning.

Nevertheless, at the base of the tree where the discharge had run along a buttress-root at the surface of the ground, the lightning-stroke had heated a few dry needles to kindling-point.

Lying on the surface they had a good supply of air, and had continued to smoulder. Now, as the evening down-canyon wind began to move gently along the slope, a tiny column of smoke, as from a dying cigarette, curled faintly into the air.

. . .

On the ridge above Onion Creek, like a sickly new-born infant gasping in the cradle, the fire had barely lived through the night. In the chill that descended upon the mountains in the early morning it had cooled gradually until only a few glowing spots still maintained life. With the cold, the humidity of the air rose until it approached dewpoint, and the condensation of even the slightest film of dew would certainly have quenched the last coals.

As the chill deepened, however, the air along the ridge-top grew colder more rapidly than the lower air, and thus also becoming heavier, it began to slide gently down the steep slope. This draft came as a saving stimulant to the dying sparks. Moreover, this air was drier, so that a dew formed only on the lower slopes of the ridge where spray from the little brawling creek saturated the air. The fire thus continued to glow faintly.

At last, in the dawn, the glow seemed to fade out, but actually the fire was stronger, and inevitably after sunrise it grew stronger still. In the warmer, drier air it no longer had to expend its own heat in driving off the moisture from every pine-needle. During the night the fire had been like a shivering infant forced to expend the energy of its own food in merely keeping itself alive. Now it was like a well-blanketed infant, ready to stretch out arms and grow.

.   .   .

On the steep canyon-side the little fire that had sprung from the lightning-stroke still ate slowly ahead in the duff of pine-needles. . . .

When a baby, weak but tenacious of life, lies in his cradle in village or city, no fairy-godmother is needed to make some predictions for the future. Any sensible person can foretell that, barring great cataclysms, the child's early life will be shaped almost entirely by the immediate environment, though in later years he will grow to the strength and dominance of manhood, and may then in some measure determine his own career and even the history of his nation.

During its four days of life the fire had been infant-like, wholly at the mercy of its surroundings, but growing a little larger and stronger. It tended always to advance up-slope, but also to follow the path of the afternoon wind, which blew up-canyon, at right angles to the slope. As a result, the fire split the difference between the two forces, and went sliding upwards.

.   .   .

And now, after midnight on the fourth day of the dry wind, the Spitcat Fire still crackled and blazed in the bushes, and roared up in the clumps of young trees, and now and then (even in the coolness of the night) sent a tall tree towering still taller in a searing blast of hissing white-yellow flames. Its threat was worse than ever. If its outreaching arms stretched to the south and united, they would doom all the rich forest that covered the rolling country between Swayback Ridge and Cerro Gordo. But with an east wind the fire might sweep across the low divide into the drainage of Potter Creek. An unexpected shift of the wind to south or west could be even worse, for along the many miles of lightly held line the blowing of a single spark might send the fire off in a wholly new direction.

Because of the accumulation of heat and the ever-increasing length of line and the heightened possibility of accident, danger had grown even out of proportion to size until now it assumed a nightmarish vastness. The fire, instead of growing weary and middle-aged, sprang upon each new clump of bushes with youthful vigor and enthusiasm, like a wild beast seizing its prey and growing stronger by what it feeds on.

.   .   .

It was as if some running conflagration had swept from Spuyten Duyvil to the Battery, leaving two-thirds of Manhattan Island in a blackened swath behind it. Yet the Spitcat Fire would not be very memorable even in the annals of Region 5. Any old-timer could recall a score of greater ones, and would only expect that the years to come would bring many more. In comparison with the Tillamook, which in eleven flaming days had wiped out 311,000 acres of the best forest in Oregon, the Spitcat was a mere waste-basket blaze.

Even so, the costs of suppression alone would run well over a hundred thousand dollars. Two men had been killed, and a score of others had suffered injury. The value of the burned trees would pass a million dollars, figured at current prices and with no allowance for timber famines of the future.

Yet the damage could not with justice be calculated merely in terms of the present. Already the turbid streams showed that even the light rain was washing away the earth. Where previously pines had just been able to find root on the thin-soiled ridges, now half-bare rocks might be left, where only gnarled junipers would cling.

Though the Spitcat had burned for only a few days, yet its effects could be reckoned ahead in centuries. Looking across the country from a peak, an unskilled observer would have seen many tall trees still standing green, and might have thought that surprisingly little damage had been suffered. But many of those trees had been fatally scorched around the bases, and many others were so damaged that they would soon fall prey to boring insects.

And everywhere the small trees had been wiped out, as if a plague had swept through a nation, sparing some adults but killing all the babies and children. In the next few years the still-standing older trees might reseed the ground beneath them, but once they had been logged off or fallen from disease or mere old age, only tiny saplings would remain—not vigorous young trees reaching up fifty or a hundred feet already.

But that would be the best that could be expected. Where the crown-fires had raged, no trees were left to spread seed, and brush would spring up faster than forest. Once established, it would remain for many years, perhaps for centuries, yielding only foot by foot as the forest pressed in around the edges. Indeed, some said pessimistically that the forests of California had established themselves in some wetter cycle of centuries and that the brush, once rooted, would remain until some wetter cycle returned.

The flaming disaster of those few days would not be undone in a hundred years. Even after five hundred, a skilled forester might still be able to trace the scar of that old burn.

More also had vanished than any man could assay in dollars. There had been a green and gracious forest, full of the rustle and movement of life, beneficient to men. Now there was only blackness and ugliness and desolation, and over it all a heavy and terrible silence.

7 The Storm

Unlike most of the United States which has four seasons of the year, California has only two: wet and dry. During the winter months the westerly winds blow in from the ocean, bringing precipitation. Rain falls from September to April but most of it occurs in December, January and February. Rain during the summer is virtually unknown. There are only a few rainstorms, and their arrival is a highly significant event in the lives of Californians as is seen in this selection.

Early in November, had come "Election-Day rains." Chilling after the warmth of October, low-lying clouds blew in from the southwest, thick with moisture from the Pacific. The golden-brown hills of the Coast Ranges grew darker beneath the downpour. In the Great Valley summer-dry creeks again ran water. Upon the Sierra the snow fell steadily. The six-month dry season was over.

Between drenching showers the sun shone brightly, warming the earth. Thousands of hillsides were suddenly green with the sprouted grass. In the valleys, overnight, the square miles of summer fallow became fields of new wheat and barley. Stockmen talked jovially to one another—a good year! Farmers in irrigated districts thought comfortably of rising water-tables and filling reservoirs. In the towns the merchants gave larger orders to wholesale houses.

November ended with two weeks of good growing-weather. The grass and the grain sucked moisture from the soil, and spread lush blades in the sunshine.

December came in—days still warm and sunny, nights clear, with a touch of frost in the valleys and on the higher hills. Farmers began to look more often to the south—but there were no clouds. Stockmen no longer went about slapping one another on the back; instead, they went secretly and inquired the price of cotton-seed meal at the Fresno mills. As the weeks passed, storekeepers grew chary about granting credit.

By Christmas, the green of the pasture-lands and the wide grain fields showed a faint cast of yellow. In favored spots the grass was six inches tall;

but the blades were curled a little, and at the edges were brownish red. Where cattle had grazed, the ragged ends still showed.

The city-folk went about congratulating themselves on the fine weather. The tourist trade was flourishing. On New Year's Day the sports experts broadcasting the football games talked almost as much about the fine weather as about the passes.

But just after the first of the year pessimistic crop-reports from California helped send the price of barley up a half cent on the Chicago exchange. That same day, six great trucks with trailers, heavy-laden with cottonseed meal, plugged up the highway from Fresno; the richer stockmen had started to buy feed.

So, in the first weeks of the new year a winter drought lay tense upon the land.

                                        .   .   .

The Chief studied the map. As had happened often before, he wished for the moment that he were engaged in some simple line of work such as being a G-man or teaching literature. All very well for the others to predict rain— the one had his inner light, and the other his textbooks. And neither of them was responsible. But the Chief knew what would happen if he went to the typewriter and tapped off RAIN on the forecast blank.

That single word would be about as big a news-story as could break in California. Thousands of people would change their plans; hundreds of industries, big and little, would make adjustments. Money would be spent, wisely and foolishly. The very process of adjustment to that single word would mean damaged property and jeopardized lives. Then, if the rain did not come, everything would be ridiculous anti-climax, with people blaming the weather-man.

Say that he wrote FAIR or even UNSETTLED, and the rain came. Then people would go on with their fair-weather plans, and would be caught wide open. His error might mean millions of dollars loss of property and the snuffing out of more lives than a man liked to think about. . . .

So today he doubly checked all the possibilities. He quickly studied the chart of upper-air winds and temperatures, and the maps showing rise and fall of pressure and temperature. Then he returned to his own map.

The telephone rang. "It's the *Register* for the forecast," said Mr. Ragan.

"Hn-n? Tell 'em to wait ten minutes."

The Chief sighed, and thought of the Old Master's favorite quotation: "The duties of this office permit little rest and less hesitation." Well, ten minutes was enough.

From his point of view on the California coast, the Chief saw himself on neutral ground at the center of four great forces. What happened would depend upon their relative strength and the resulting way in which they shoved one another around. Just to his south, the Pacific High still stood; it was probably the weakest of the four and was retreating, but it still possessed much capacity for passive resistance. Far to the north the great mass of polar air was rushing southeasterly across the prairies. Its most southerly isobar, however, bent around Seattle, and formed a disturbing southwesterly point. If it spread farther, this bulge might block the storm away from the coast. The third force was the storm over Winnipeg; its indications were definitely favorable. The fourth force was the storm which was approaching the coast; it too seemed to have plenty of energy and to be moving in the right direction.

With the slight exception, all the immediate forces thus seemed to be working for rain. But the Chief knew that more distant forces could have their influence—the new storm on the Texas coast, for instance. It too happened to be a favorable indication. There must be many forces even beyond the range of his map. Something happening anywhere in the temperate zone, in the northern hemisphere, or for that matter anywhere in the world, might falsify his forecast. But that was only a possibility, and a man must forecast probable, not possible, weather.

He made his decisions, and his actions suddenly came to have a continental, almost a god-like sweep.

"Hey, Whitey," he called, "get on the telephone and order up storm-warnings on the coast—Point Arena to North Head." He turned to his typewriter.

But the nearest telephone rang before Whitey could get to it. "It's the *Register* again," he said. The Chief committed himself to the inevitable.

"Complete forecast in five minutes. But tell 'em to set the headlines and get ready—it's RAIN."

(From the *Register*. Page one.)

RAIN PREDICTED. *Large Storm Nears Coast*. The U. S. Weather Bureau this morning forecast that rain would fall generally throughout the central and northern parts of the state beginning late Sunday afternoon. A storm of large proportions is now centered a thousand miles west of Cape Mendocino and is advancing rapidly. Officials of the Weather Bureau declined to state what would be the duration of the storm and the amount of precipitation, other than to say that it would be considerable.

Valley farmers in those regions which have been suffering heavily from drought are jubilant. Snow-sports enthusiasts were today preparing to return to their favorite haunts.

In the meantime, while California enjoyed its accustomed sun, reports from Montana indicated widespread suffering in the wake of a cold wave. Thermometers were tumbling, with lowest temperature in the United States reported from Havre at twenty-nine below zero. Three people were lost and feared dead in a blizzard near Wolf Point, Montana. (For details, see Page A-4, Col. 3).

EXTRY! EXTRY! EXTRY! ! ! Well, folks, this is Ye Old-Time Newsy calling you the headlines over KTEY.

And the first big news this morning for all you folks in California is that there's goin' to be rain. Yessir, rain. I'll spell it—R-A-I-N. Those little drops of water coming down—"little" maybe, but plenty of 'em. That's what the old Weatherman says. So get out the umbrella and the old gum shoes. But you people in the South, don't get too excited—just showers down your way. Now, of course, Your Old Time Newsy doesn't guarantee this rain; he's just bringing you the report. But what I say is any re*port* in a *storm!* Ha, ha, folks! Don't mind me; it's just a way I have.

"O.K., oil's O.K. Say, how about lettin' me make you a deal on some new front tires; those old ones are pretty smooth. There's a rain comin'."
"Sure, so is Fourth of July."
"Naw, I mean it. Just got the news on the radio."
"Say, is that right? Well, in that case I better be movin'. Got a roofin' job on my hands. Thanks."

"Gimme a beer. Say, what's this about it goin' to rain?"

"No Billy, you can*not* plan to go with Bob tomorrow. They say it's going to rain."

"It's going to rain."

"Going to rain."

"RAIN!"

.   .   .

The manager of the Palace Department Store read the forecast in the morning paper and immediately went into action. For the coming week he had planned an emphasis upon hats, baby-carriages, and bed-sheeting. He shifted it to ski-clothing, rain-equipment, and blankets.

The Director of the Observatory gave up his plans for some lunar photography.

The proprietor of the Gaiety Amusement Park shrugged his shoulders. He had gambled his last dollar on a fair week-end. Rain would break him. He called up his lawyer, and said he would probably have to make an assignment on Monday.

In the Eagle Lumber Yard the owner kept his men working over-time on Saturday afternoon, and picked up two extra helpers. He had a lot of finished lumber in the yard, and to save it from getting wet and warping was hundreds of dollars in his pocket.

When the advertising manager of the *Register* checked up the results he decided that the paper had broken about even as far as the rain was concerned. The real-estate companies had called off most of the advertising because they knew how cold and gloomy empty houses seemed in the rain, even if you could get people out to look at them. But he had five new ads from resorts in the snow-country, and a tire company had broken out with a half-page announcing a new non-skid tread.

The effects of the forecast tended to spread out link by link until they formed long chains. The shrewd proprietors of several restaurants called up the factory, and reduced their orders for ice-cream. The manager of the factory found his needs for milk and cream lessened, and passed on his word to the dairy. Since the cows could not be forced to co-operate, the dairy company diverted the surplus to its subsidiary corporation which manufactured butter and cheese. The manager then hired two extra men, whose wives on the strength of the prospective jobs spent more freely than usual at one of the smaller retail stores. The retailer optimistically imagined an up-swing of business, and said he would take the new car over which he had been hesitating. At this point, however, the chain of effects turned back upon itself and ended. For the store-keeper, later in the day, read the forecast, and believing that his retail business always suffered in rainy weather, he called up the automobile salesman and cancelled the order.

Chapter 2

The Hispanic Era

The Hispanic Era

Spain established colonies in California mainly to keep other countries out and prevent the area from being used as a base for an attack upon Mexico. The Franciscan Fathers assisted the crown, and for a time their missions to convert the Indians to Christianity were the dominant social institutions. Early Spanish colonists found little evidence that California was to become a terrestrial paradise as they were threatened with starvation during the first decade of settlement. The long dangerous sea voyage from Mexico discouraged prospective colonists from using that route, and when the Yuma crossing was closed by hostile Indian action in 1781, few additional Spaniards made their way to California. By 1820, as the rule of Spain was drawing to a close, there were only some 3,270 non-Indian residents of the province.

There were twenty-one missions scattered along the coast from San Diego in the south to San Francisco Solano in the north. Only four forts or presidios (San Diego, Monterey, San Francisco, and Santa Barbara) protected the area from foreign invasion. Towns or pueblos were founded at San Jose, Los Angeles, and Branciforte. Private ranchos were the last of the institutions, but only twenty-five were created under Spain.

Spanish control of California ended as a result of the revolution in Mexico. Then from 1821 to 1846 California was ruled from Mexico City. During this period there was a continuation of Spanish institutions, but there were also extensive changes. Trade with foreign nations was allowed, and the hide and tallow trade flourished. Perhaps the most significant event was the secularization of the missions. Political turmoil was a problem during the Mexican period. In addition, the era saw an intrusion of foreigners into the province coming from both land and sea.

Although California's Hispanic period lasted but three generations, there is a veritable cascade of fictional works about the period. Anglos, weary of the kind of world spawned by the Industrial Revolution in late nineteenth-century America, sought a society different from their own. In Spanish California they believed an ideal civilization had existed where simple people lived for the pleasures of everyday life with but little thought for the future. In the late nineteenth and early twentieth centuries, a school of writers emerged which sang the praises of the arcadian life before the Anglo arrived to corrupt it. Novels set in the Spanish ranching era were particularly popular. Some pointed up the difference in social values between the two cultures, often using inter-marriage as the vehicle with which to illustrate their point. It might be noted that many writers who were liberals in American politics found everything to praise and nothing to criticize in a feudal society wherein perhaps 100 families dominated the political, social, and economic life of Hispanic California. The mission fathers were eulogized by Protestant authors for having civilized the

Indians. Unfortunately, few writers were astute enough to understand that the mission system disrupted the native way of life without adequately preparing the Indian for his role in the dominant Hispanic society.

8 The Road to Glory

The initial settlement of California was, in the main, an accomplishment of the Franciscan missionaries. Financed by the Pious Fund, the enterprise was intended to save Indian souls and, only incidentally, to advance the Spanish frontier. Most famed of the California Franciscans was Father Junipero Serra. A native of Palma, Mallorca, Spain, he exhausted himself in his tasks of establishing new missions and supervising the work. Despite his numerous illnesses, young men were pressed to keep up with this remarkable friar. The following glimpse of mission work is written from the point of view of the clergy.

Father Serra spoke to one of the Indians who unloaded two more leather sacks among those piled on the donkey's saddle frame. One sack must have contained at least fifty paired leather sandals, which Father Serra explained had been made at the Mission San Buenaventura. The other sack held a dozen newly woven monks' robes of wool clipped and carded from the flock of sheep at the Mission San Luis Obispo. In less than ten minutes Hugo had sandals on his feet and was wearing a warm monk's robe which still had a faint sheep smell in its heavy coarse fibers.

It was when two of the Indians helped Father Serra to his feet that for the first time Hugo saw how old he really was. It appeared a painful effort for Father Serra to rise, even when helped. For a moment the weathered face went gray. Then Hugo saw Father Serra give himself a sudden shake, put his weight on both feet, and the good brownness of wind and sun and rain was again in his face; the appearance of firmness once more fell around him like a mantle; he was an old warrior ready to go forward again. Hugo felt an involuntary tug of admiration.

The cuadrilla of Indians, Father Serra, and Hugo, set off on the road which Hugo found led more and more to the northeast and away from the ocean. Within half an hour the road was climbing upward into a range of mountains and along mountain valleys. Now and then, far below him, he caught sight of a blue thread of water that disappeared and reappeared as if the mission road followed above the line of river.

Sometimes Hugo glanced behind him, seeing the four Indians following with the donkey. In Mexico City it was assumed that the California savages went around naked; he could remember hearing captains on visits to the Admiralty say the savages kept themselves warm in cold weather by covering themselves with thick coats of mud; that the women tattooed themselves with rows of dots, while the men painted their faces and legs to frighten invisible demons. Either the sea captains had lied, Hugo decided, or the Indians in the cuadrilla had become civilized enough to throw off those old habits.

These Indians all had reed hats tied to their heads. One wore an ordinary woolen poncho. Two wore coats of woven grass and feathers, but underneath their coats were ordinary trade shirts and cotton pantaloons. Two of the Indians had long beards, braided like Marica's pigtails. While on their shoulders they carried bows and bark quivers filled with arrows, only the giant Indian had a musket which looked like an ancient firelock. Hugo guessed it was probably more lethal to the one who pulled the trigger than to any wild beasts yawning in front of the bell muzzle.

He finally asked, "These Indians in your cuadrilla, Father Serra, are they your own servants or do they belong to the Mission San Antonio?"

Without slowing his pace, Father Serra gave him a quick glance. "*Belong* to San Antonio? My son, are you thinking of our missions as *encomiendas?* We missionaries have established no system of encomiendas where Indians are attached as chattel slaves to land granted by the Crown to persons of Spanish blood."

They came down into a glade, to ascend again. As the road lifted above the trees, once more Hugo had the immense view of the encircling mountains.

"Brother Yuobo is a lay brother," Father Serra was explaining, "accompanying me from the San Carlos Mission at Monterey. He is of Spanish and Yuman Indian blood and serves me out of love of God. The other three are Christian Indians from the San Luis Mission, yes. But not my servants. They do me the honor of accompanying me on this stage of my journey. Nor do they belong to the Mission San Luis. Rather, San Luis belongs to them and the people of their tribes. We missionaries are their stewards and servants."

That was a strange way to put it, thought Hugo. Stewards and servants of these California Indians? To say that the Mexican Indians were made slaves by the encomienda system was almost treasonable. How were the big haciendas of Mexico to continue if the Indians were freed from the land? Hugo knew that the Mexican Indians were taken care of by the great hacienda owners. They were given food and shelter and sometimes even money for the fiestas. They weren't slaves. They were—peons; that is what they were called. Until now this old lame sturdy priest had appeared as reasonable and matter-of-fact as the parish priest of the Rio Verde whom Hugo remembered so warmly. He felt distressed to discover that Father

Serra was obsessed, after all. His expression must have revealed something of his distress, too, for Father Serra gave him another searching glance.

"My son, are you at all familiar with the works of Friar Bartolome de las Casas?"

At first Hugo failed to connect that question with the previous conversation. It only evoked a picture in his mind of a worn stone statue, the statue at the north of the great plaza in Mexico City which he had passed every morning and evening going to and coming from the palacio. He recalled that statue had been erected to commemorate a friar of that name. The green encrusted plaque at the base said, "*Stranger, stop and venerate, for this is Friar Bartolome de las Casas, Father of the Indians,*" or words to that effect. He said he remembered the statue, but that was all.

"No one has told you that over two hundred years ago Father Bartolome even denied the sacrament to his countrymen who murdered and enslaved the Indians?"

"I'm afraid I'm not as familiar as I should be with Friar Bartolome's work."

"Too few are. Through Friar Bartolome and others like him in the Church, the *Code for the Indians* became a part of the laws of the realm in the year of our Lord fifteen forty-eight. 'No person in war or peace may take, apprehend, use, sell or exchange as a slave, any Indian—'

"I quote you from the famous article twenty-six of the Indian Code. Make no mistake, my son. If I denounce any system forcing Indians into slavery, I speak as a devoted and loyal subject of the Crown, for those old laws still stand unrevoked. If the Viceroys and officers of their Majesties have failed to enforce the laws, at least in this province we observe them faithfully in our missions. Under the laws of the Crown, the Indians own the missions. We missionaries are only their guardians until the time soon comes, by God's compassion, when our Indians will be wise enough in the ways of living as Christians to relieve us of our responsibilities."

After following a turn of the road, Hugo let himself comment, "In Mexico I've heard no settlers are allowed to use any land cleared by the Indians."

"In God's holy sacred name, if you cleared your land and built your house, would you wish a stranger to take it from you?"

Hugo said, "No, Father," and thought that it wasn't the same thing, though. He wished he had never brought up the subject of Indians. So he said nothing more. He needed all the breath in his lungs to climb the long grade.

It was a steep climb, this time. At the top he looked across a wooded valley toward another ridge, a quarter or half league away. There was no halting up here for a short rest. Father Serra was going on down into the valley. Hugo stayed with him, glancing over his shoulder once or twice to see the cuadrilla and donkey following. . . .

He was tiring again, but Father Serra didn't appear to notice. Father Serra had settled into a marching gait, now scarcely even limping. He said he hoped to make two more leagues before sunset. Then, because his mind must have been upon the ship or upon a commendable young girl aboard, he said he was sorry he had missed the supply ship at San Diego. But he had not been able to delay his stay at San Diego longer. He had had to leave early in the month to complete his annual confirmation tour of all the missions along the coast.

"Father," Hugo asked, thinking again of Marica's protest, "must you go every year this great distance from San Diego north to San Francisco to visit all the missions?"

It was necessary, Father Serra said, as matter-of-fact about it as a priest speaking of the need to visit a church a league away from him. "Each year, hundreds of Indians at each mission are ready to be confirmed as members of the Holy Church. While the pair of missionary friars at each of the nine established missions has the authority, as priests of the Church, to baptize the Indians as neophytes and labor over the catechism with them, only the Father-superior of the missions is invested with the authority to administer final rites of confirmation."

Hugo knew that ordinarily only a bishop could pronounce the rites of confirmation. He had always assumed, however, that any priest could be invested with the authority when a bishop was unavailable.

Yes, that was true, Father Serra patiently explained, as they went over a great knee of mountain where the air was so crisp Hugo's lungs ached. But through Papal grants, the Spanish Crown was head of the Church in all the realms under the Crown except in matters of spiritual doctrine.

"It is a great distance to Spain," Father Serra continued gently. "Even the simple request to grant a California friar the faculty of confirmation has to receive the King's royal approval."

Hugo listened with increasing attention. That afternoon of their first day on the road Father Serra told him that the faculty of confirmation had been granted by the Royal hand nine years ago. It was limited solely to Father Serra for a period of ten years. Because of delays and the great distance from here to the mother country, Father Serra had not received the confirmation papers until two years after the grant was given him. But one year remained now, and perhaps the King would refuse to renew it. Father Serra could not say.

"It is as God wills for His Majesty to decide," he said. "Meanwhile, as long as God gives me strength, I will go up and down this new land when there are so many baptized Indians waiting to enter into the Holy Church."

No wonder Father Serra was always in a hurry, not wanting to spare himself! Two years to get a grant from the King? It reminded Hugo all over again of how remote this province—closed off by sea and mountains and deserts at the south—was from the rest of the Spanish realms. . . .

He noticed that the donkey was tiring. The Indians were lagging further behind, prodding and pushing at the balky beast. If anything, it seemed to him, Father Serra was going along even faster, like an old horse warmed up and feeling young again. Suppose along the trail they should walk into even one of those brown bears coming in this direction, one about as big as the donkey and twice as heavy, and maybe feeling hungry? He looked back at the cuadrilla again; they were much too far behind. And what good would a bow and arrow or even an old firelock musket do against a bear charging down with gaping jaws? Hugo thought that Father Serra ought to have been escorted by a company of soldiers. After all, he was Father-superior of the missions, at present holding greater temporal authority than even the Governor over the thousands of savages in this wilderness. Yet he went trotting off, league after league, with only three converted savages and a mixed-blood lay brother for guard!

After once more forcing his legs to bring him abreast of Father Serra, Hugo recovered enough breath to ask, "Were there no soldiers available at Mission San Luis to give you a suitable guard?"

"By Governor Fages' orders, no soldiers garrisoned at any of our missions are permitted to be absent overnight."

"Not even to accompany Your Reverence as a guard on these long marches between missions? You should demand a guard of soldiers."

"Now, why should I demand soldiers?" asked Father Serra. "Am I not under God's care, as we all are, with His Son watching over us as the shepherd watches his flock?"

9   Church and State

Although the mission was the dominant institution in Hispanic California, there was also a secular life, and the latter was often in conflict with the clergy who wanted to retain the province as their preserve. The Franciscans tolerated soldiers as a necessary evil but bitterly objected when Governor Felipe de Neve planned to establish pueblos (towns). This effort, which was intended to reduce the expense of defending the frontier land, was resented by Father Serra who expressed the fear that his Indian charges would suffer from such action.

With a procession of laden mules, soldiers, workmen, neophyte Indians, Serra, with Fathers Lasuen and Amurrio, followed the trail over the hills and along the shore the seventy miles to the site at the joining of San Juan Creek and the Trabucco. Here on the first of November, 1776, they dug up the bells that had been hastily buried when word had come of the uprising at San Diego the year before. With the bells hung on crossbars and ringing their message over the quiet countryside, and with a new altar built in a temporary ramada, Serra celebrated the first Mass at Capistrano.

If there was to be a star in this crown of missions, San Juan Capistrano was the likely place for it. It had not only the restful beauty of its setting. It was midway between San Diego and San Gabriel. It was, above all, virginal and free of the taint of anger and hatred that surrounded the two older missions. It would draw strength from both, it would give them a rebirth by showing the Indians what the church could mean to them when it functioned alone, without soldiers.

Serra stayed for many weeks, helping the little his strength allowed him in building, seeing to it that supplies were on hand from San Diego, calling for more neophytes from San Diego and San Gabriel to help with the molding and laying up of adobes. When the first chapel was finished he held services and preached to the converts. He prepared the registry books, inscribed the title pages.

Pleased with this beginning and the resurgence of energy it promised toward filling-in the gaps in his mission chain, he left for Monterey. All along the way he found the missions prospering. At San Gabriel there were good harvests of wheat, corn, and squash. The cattle and sheep herds had increased until there was mutton to feed friars, laborers, soldiers, and converts. In the luxuriant valley of San Luis Obispo under the green mountains of the bears, there was even greater abundance. At San Antonio, too, the mission had prospered, and more pagans were coming every day to eat at the Lord's table.

Weary, but for once in his life almost content, he arrived at Carmel. Here he heard the good news that Mission Santa Clara de Asis had been founded in the rich valley south of San Francisco Bay, and here Father Tomas de la Peña had celebrated the first Mass on January 12, 1777.

There was other news, less pleasing to him. Governor Neve, now with official headquarters at Monterey, had been busy—as a conscientious and intelligent governor should be—thinking out ways to make the administration of California more effective and less expensive to the crown. He had made his people a present on Christmas Day of a reglamento—a set of laws which were to govern the administration of presidios, towns (pueblos), and, to some degree, the missions.

A copy of the twenty-seven page reglamento had been sent to Carmel for Serra to study. He read it carefully, approved portions of it, but when he had finished he sat thinking in cold despair. The reglamento was, whether or not it was so intended, a pattern for the methodical destruction of the mission system.

"God grant me humility and patience—above all, patience. But let me not yield one breath to the power of Satan."

His eyes burning after a night of sleeplessness and prayer, he limped with the speed and determination of a militant angel bound to defend his vision of paradise, to Monterey.

Governor Neve received him with cordial reverence, but when he saw the intensity in Serra's visage, his own large brown Spanish-Arabic eyes burned with defensive arrogance, his fat jowls firmed, his long lips became set.

Serra wasted no time with amenities. "I have read your *reglamento*. I have studied it carefully, in the hope that it might show an indication of your good intent. Some portions of the paper I can accept. But on the whole your plan disturbs me profoundly."

"I am disappointed, your reverence. Of course I could not anticipate that you would agree with me on every point. We look at things from different sides of the wall. But—"

"In the eyes of God there are not two sides to anything—unless we grant that there is the side of truth and the side of evil."

"Are you implying that I am on the side of evil, your reverence?"

"Not by intent, Governor Neve. I believe you have a sincere wish to administer California justly and well. But your *reglamento* indicates that you have not made a thorough study of conditions here, nor of the needs of the people and the missions. If your laws were put into effect they might do irreparable harm to both."

Neve straightened in his chair and looked over Serra's head with the aloofness of a proud parent inviting criticism of his brain child. "I am willing to acknowledge any errors in the *reglamento*, Father. But you must understand that I was not sent here by the Viceroy because of my lack of experience in administrative affairs or ignorance of what is best for the people. Would you be kind enough to explain your objections?"

"To begin with, you intend to locate pueblos close to the missions. This would mean that colonists would most certainly take the most desirable land around the missions for their farms and pastures, and in the end deprive the missions of their means to employ the Indians and to feed them and properly instruct them in the ways of Christian living."

Neve indulged in a slight smile. "My dear Father Serra, what better way to teach the barbarians good Christian living than to show them an example, by putting before them families who are already Christians?"

"And depriving the missions of their power to help the neophytes?"

"The subjects of the King, the Spaniards who are already baptized, come first."

"If you will read again the instructions of the Viceroy you will see that he insists that the work of the missions comes first."

"That is a matter for interpretation. I see no reason why the presence of colonists near the missions will impede your work with the Gentiles."

"I have already said that the colonists will take the best land and pastures. I will go further and say that in my experience the kind of colonists who are sent to the frontier do not always set a good moral example to the pagans. They are often, God forgive them, lecherous, given to drink and careless habits, and they neglect their obligations to the Church, they go seldom to Mass and to confession. Often they abuse the Indians. They are interested in their own welfare, not the Indians', and if an Indian gets in the way he is dealt with cruelly."

"I could suspect, Father, that you hope to keep colonists out of California and hold it as a preserve for Indians and priests."

"You are intelligent enough to know that is not true. I have stated to the Viceroy that California could never be a strong province of the empire until colonists with families made it their home. What I say to you is this, there is enough land in these valleys for thousands of colonists. It is not necessary for them to crowd in about the missions."

"It is a matter of good administration, Father. How can we protect the colonists, and the missions, if families are scattered in remote valleys away from the presidios?"

"May I speak frankly, Governor? I am sure that the Indians of California are so unwarlike, so gentle and hospitable that they would never make trouble were it not for some soldiers and colonists who mistreat them and stir resentments."

Neve chuckled, a little amazed and quite uncomfortable. "Then why do you require a soldier guard at the missions, and soldier protection when you travel in California? If the Indians are so harmless and amiable we may as well give up the presidios and withdraw our troops. It would save the King a good deal of expense."

"The King's law requires that we have presidios and guards."

"Quite. And since we must maintain presidios and guards, and since Spain is at war with England, we must find other means of stopping drains on the King's treasury. That is why I have provided in the *reglamento* that the Indians govern themselves by appointing an *alcalde* for each tribe, under the authority of the King, to keep the peace and govern his people. This will save administrative expense. It will make it possible to cut down the number of guards, also the number of missionaries."

Serra could see no way of changing Neve's mind. If he was not aware of the Indians own loose way of governing themselves and their inability to understand the Spaniard's ideas of morals and justice, no argument would have any effect. But the matter of limiting the missionaries to one at each mission was a subject that had been argued back and forth from California to Mexico City, even before Neve came. The missionaries had strongly objected and the College of San Fernando had upheld them. In this lonely country, to deprive a missionary of any companionship but that of aborigines and ignorant soldiers would have been to deprive him of his sanity. And to limit the one missionary to ecclesiastical duties, with no one to assist in educating the Indians, to train them to farm and care for the livestock, to make clothing and leather goods, to grind flour and do the numerous other chores around the mission, would be to eliminate the one means the Fathers had of reaching the pagans and disciplining them. Serra said, "Your scheme to provide for only one friar at each mission is also an economy measure, Governor?"

"As I have said, we are bound to stop the drain on the King's treasury while we are at war."

"We are not at war with God. Why then are you so intent on depriving us of the chief means of saving souls for His kingdom?"

"We are in the service of the King, who rules by divine right, your reverence. It is our duty to do our best for both God and King. We have to perform that duty as we see it."

"That is what *I* intend to do, Governor."

For once, Serra had the advantage. Neve could not change the administration of the missions without a special order from the Viceroy, which could not be had for months, even if Bucareli should favor it—which he probably would not. Meantime Neve must come to the president for supplies for his troops, flour, vegetables, fruits, beef, and mutton. He could not change the guard or the major-domo at a mission without the consent of the missionaries. He could put none of his plans into action without the support of the missionaries.

Nevertheless, he went ahead with his efforts to put the *reglamento* into effect. He had Moraga bring a number of Anza colonists from San Francisco Bay to settle near Alviso, south of the bay and not far from the Mission Santa Clara. He expected other colonists, recruited in Sinaloa and led by Rivera, to arrive in California and provide him with families for his system of pueblos. But Rivera and his colonists had another rendezvous. . . .

10   Indians and the Mission

The original purposes of the missions were to Christianize the Indians and bestow upon them the blessings of Hispanic civilization so they could become good tax-paying subjects of the Spanish crown. The first objective was partially realized, but the latter one was not. The following selection tells how an Indian viewed life at one of California's twenty-one missions. Juan's reaction was typical, as runaways from the missions were common. The events referred to were raids perpetrated along the California coast in 1818 by Hippolyte de Bouchard, a Frenchman in the service of the Argentine, then in rebellion against Spain.

Juan O-nes-e-mo wriggled his half-naked body lower into the dried yellow grass so that he would be better hidden. The warm California sun was comforting on his back, and helped to ease his conscience a bit. Somehow, as he lay there in the luxurious freedom of the golden November hillside, and watched the Padres of San Carlos de Borromeo move among the Indians who were grinding corn for the Mission, Juan wondered if the meals and the saints and the chants were worth the never-ending work of being a Christian Indian.

Te-mo, a savage Indian from the *rancheria* a mile or two up the Carmelo, slid down beside Juan. They had promised to meet and fish for trout under the sycamores along the river, on the first day the fog lifted. Te-mo grunted and picked at the brown cotton pantaloons that the Padres made Juan wear.

"You scare fish with these," he said in Room-se-en. His own language sounded good to Juan's ears after Mission Spanish.

Juan slipped out of the Christian lowers, and felt even more freedom. Together they crawled through the tall yellow grass to the river. Te-mo didn't like sliding on his belly like a lizard to keep from being seen, and he told Juan so.

"All this because you like saints," he chided, "and can't go for fish, because the Spanish soldiers will find out you are away and beat you for missing the work."

"Something more at the Mission besides saints," Juan told him. "They give presents to Room-se-ens there, and food thrée times between sunup and dark."

They had reached the tules in the river bottom, and going was faster, for they could move forward on their feet now without danger of being seen by soldiers.

"They give you food that is hot and burns the stomach," Te-mo grunted. "You work too much. See how you carried rocks to build the Mission, on your back in thongs, from a place a whole day away. You sweated and pulled at your bowels along with seven other young saint-loving Room-se-ens, to bring the cypress beam all the way from Point Lobos. A beam to hold up adobe and make a Mission door to open for Spaniards! All Indians get is food and songs for work!" Te-mo sniffed, and his fingers were soon busy weaving a net from willow branches. "I don't like saints. The carrying thongs cut on the backs of Indians and make blood come."

Te-mo was like the Satan Padre Amores talked about. Te-mo was trying to make things seem better away from the Mission. It *was* true about the work. Padres made Indians work very hard building the Mission of San Carlos. Many a time Juan's bones ached with weariness, and great swellings came where raw-hide thongs pressed deep into the flesh of his back. But not even Te-mo or Satan himself could take from an old man the memory of his youth, of building a church. He remembered the beginning of San Carlos as if it had been only a full moon back.

First Padre Junipero Serra had blessed the bare yellow earth. He made Indians keep eyes looking down while he talked to God and the saints. Another brown-robed Padre passed among Indians, and gently pressed his hand on the head of Juan, who looked up to watch a gull flying high against the wind. After the head bowing, Indians had smoothed and flattened the earth with sticks, and then a Padre went with them to bring rocks from the hill across the river.

Many moons they worked, through rain and sun, from sunup to dark, until at last Mission walls were up and a beautiful tower, that was taller than any tree, stood against the blue sky. Te-mo could never know the happy feeling inside that O-nes-e-mo knew, when he climbed up and put the cross on top of the tower, while Padres and Indians sang the chant! Backaches, beatings, nothing could take that happiness away from an old man.

Junipero Serra and the other Padres had given their humble Indians their cathedral in the sun.

"The church bells are beautiful when they ring, and corn is better than acorns for meal," Juan managed at last.

"I can lie on my back in the sun all day," Te-mo said, "and snare rabbits with grass, or catch lizards for supper, or fish in the Carmelo for trout." He let down the coarse net made of laced twigs. "My woman grinds acorns for flour, and I get no saints or bells, and no whipping posts with Spanish soldiers to lay on the whip."

Juan knew better than to make a fish trap of his own, for trapping was Te-mo's pride. Instead he broke up bits of dry willow and soon had a tiny smokeless fire started. He was very careful not to put on too many sticks at once, for if the soldiers saw smoke they were sure to come.

"Padre Amores tries to keep soldiers from beating," Juan said after a while. "The Padres are good."

Te-mo lifted up his net and removed five big speckled trout by their gills to the grass. "You have no more chance to miss a flogging than these have to miss being eaten, when the soldiers at the Mission *rancheria* cry out 'Indian hunt' and start running. I know. I watch."

Juan slipped a fish on a willow stick and started toasting it over the fire he had made. It was good to have food away from the Mission. In many ways this Satan Te-mo was right. Once, long ago, Juan too had spent the days naked, snaring lizards, and toasting them, and had been able to lie in the sun and be waited on, and given herb tea each time his woman was to drop a baby. He took a long breath. But that was long ago, before the earthshake sent down earth and fastened his woman and children up in a cave until they were dead.

As if to reassure himself about the saints, and the chants that Padre Junipero Serra sang in the tule shelter long ago, Juan spoke his thoughts.

"The Mission *rancheria* of San Carlos de Borromeo gave me my fourth woman, and she is dropping a son for me before next moon. Pretty good for a man beginning to shrivel in the arms and behind, Te-mo."

"You could do *that* without the saints and hard work; maybe do even better. I have a child for each toe and finger, and no bells ringing for me to sing before the sun-up. And I keep to Room-se-en talk and Room-se-en name too. Mission Indians lose even their names. The Padres turn everybody into Juan or Thomas, or Pablo." Te-mo boned his fish and ate it in three bites, then shoved another on the toasting stick.

Suddenly the air was filled with shouts. The bell began to ring and it was not time for Mass.

"Pirates coming over the hill to rob us!" Padre Amores shouted. "Quick, gather up altar ornaments, the hides, the corn, and run!"

Juan crawled up the river bank to look. Padres, Indians, Spanish soldiers were running into the church and the storehouse.

"Monterey is burning," someone cried. "Come quick, before the pirates get our tallow."

"Soldiers have missed you," Te-mo said as he came up alongside of Juan. "I will kill you. That is better for a Room-se-en than the thong cuts from the soldiers, and to be tied to a post in the sun to feed the flies with your blood." He was breathing fast as he lay on the grass.

"No," Juan said. "They don't want me. If you had heard the Spanish, Te-mo, you would know. Monterey is burning and thieves are on their way over to rob the Mission of the Carmelo. The Padres are leaving. Monterey is burning up. They tell everybody to run."

Te-mo put his hand on Juan's brown arm. "You will not be flogged then. You can come home to the *rancheria* with me and turn back into just O-nes-e-mo. The Padres are running away. They will never miss you now. Up the Carmelo are mice, little tender ones, to eat instead of hot burning food. Buckeye meal well washed in running water is better for Room-se-en's stomach than Padre corn, and no work, or whipping, or saints to bother you."

Juan realized that now was his chance. "But the son? The boy that is to be dropped? My woman is there with the Padres," he murmured, still watching the furious activity at the Mission compound. Even Ramerez, and the Cornellos, and other Spanish folks were working madly; just as hard as Indians! Usually only Indians did hard work at the Mission.

"Your woman drops the baby alone. The Padres will take care of the boy, never fear. They want him to work. When he is grown large enough, we will make a forage and take him back to the hills," Te-mo said. "Come! Go while they are busy saving the saints and other things except bad Juan O-nes-e-mo."

Freedom to roam. No more dawn to dark at skinning animals and rendering grease for altar candles. No more sitting still in the compound to make shoes for the Spanish Señoritas in Monterey. Shoes that the Padres sold. And no more whippings if he went away to lie in the sun for a day, after a long stretch of foggy weather. Juan lay back for a time, listening to the bustle and excitement at the Mission, and thinking of the new freedom he had, like Te-mo.

11 The Day of the Ranchero

When Governor Felipe de Neve left California in 1782, the struggle of the infant colony to survive was over. As cattle multiplied and the missions and pueblos produced crops, there was no food shortage. Emerging as the dominant class were the holders of large land grants. The following selections describe the life of a Yankee who had obtained land. Note especially the operation of the rancho, how boundaries were marked, and the trade pattern which developed. Stewart Edward White is the author of many splendid fictional works detailing the history of the Golden State.

All these things were a matter of great interest. Travelers went out of their way to stop at Folded Hills, where they were welcome and abundantly entertained. They praised and enjoyed; but it is curious and significant that they did not imitate. Nevertheless Andy was considered of remarkable energy and enterprise and ingenuity, and a valuable citizen of the commonwealth. It was he, and a number of others like him, who established a favorable reputation for Americans that persisted even after the first immigrations, and into the very gold-rush days. Though the Boone rifle hung on the wall, and though to himself Andy seemed to have settled down to peaceful content, nevertheless his destiny bore him on.

The frame of his routine seemed established. It was a frame capacious to contain many varieties.

He was a true *ranchero* and followed the customs of his kind. Each morning he was awakened at dawn. He drank chocolate in bed, at the same time naming, to the servant who attended, the horse he would ride. Attended by Panchito he rode the range until about nine o'clock when he returned to the *casa* for breakfast. After four hours of riding this was justified as a hearty meal. When he had finished this, and had dawdled a little with the fascinating Djo, he mounted another horse until near one o'clock. An hour and a half later, after a light meal and a short siesta, yet a third horse was brought, on the back of which he remained until dusk. All his business, practically, was conducted from horseback. The saddle was his movable throne, or council seat, as it were. He went to bed early.

That was the ordinary pattern of his days. It was simple, almost monotonous when viewed from a far perspective. Leaving aside the spiritual content of love of wife and child, of social contact with visitor and resident, the merely material problems and exactions were sufficient to keep the frontiersman's active interest fully occupied; at least for the present. When Andy rode on the *palomino*, Ramón's gift, or one of the other "mannered" horses—the *generosos*—of his favoring, he did more than take horse exercise. The handling, to the best advantage, of fifteen thousand or more head of cattle is a highly technical matter. Panchito and the *vaqueros* knew their business, none better. Andy was a frontiersman trained through years of dangerous necessity to keen observation. But in this one matter of cattle—and horses—he never quite equaled his men. They seemed not only to know the individual animals by sight, but to be able to recognize them almost as far as they could see them. This ability was a continual astonishment to Andy. Panchito would rein his horse, and stand in his stirrups, puckering his dark eyes in focus upon a distant hillside.

"It is as I thought, *señor*," he would say presently. "Last week those ones were at Boca Estrecha. Juan, ride you to Boca Estrecha and find out why those ones have come away."

And Juan would ride, and later would report his findings—the water was low; there had been a fire; a plague of locusts had swept clean the grass; a grizzly had come down from the hills; or possibly it was merely a case of drift, a sudden aimless seizure of the wandering foot. One must know these things and be guided by them, must carry in one's mind a bird's-eye picture of the entire *rancho* and its shifting distributions and conditions. And of course there were the small daily jobs that were never ending; a creature caught in a bog hole to be extricated; the injured or sick to be roped and thrown and treated; the increase to be noted, sometimes to be branded and marked in the field. At least once a fortnight there must be a rough and informal *rodeo*, with every man asaddle driving the cattle to established rendezvous, where they were held for an hour and then permitted to disperse. This maneuver was essential and could not be omitted or postponed. Its object was to accustom the animals to handling. Otherwise they would soon scatter in the brushlands and become true wild beasts, elusive as the deer themselves. In spite of all vigilance a certain number did thus revert. They inhabited the chaparral and were a total loss, except for the few that could be hunted down and roped and brought in by means of the especially tamed cattle, the *cabestros*, to which they were lashed by the horn.

In the spring of the year was held the great *rodeo* when the calves were branded, the excess of bulls castrated, and the cattle that had drifted in from contiguous *ranchos* separated out and driven home. This was also a festival; or rather a sequence of festivals, for each *rancho* in turn had its *rodeo*. These were great gatherings. Every owner of stock was supposed to attend, bringing all his grown sons and all his male servants and dependents. The obligation was rigorous. The only permitted exceptions were the "unmounted"—that is, the mechanical workers—the sick, and those above sixty years of age, and the "non-owners." A non-owner was defined as one who had less than a hundred and fifty cattle. Each brought not only his *remuda* of horses—from six to ten per man—but his own little herd of *cabestros* by means of which to hold and handle such of his cattle as might be found. One of the older men of position and influence was appointed *juez-de-campo* to settle disputes, should any arise.

The gathering was notable. Ordinarily the women of the *ranchos* and *haciendas* came along for the fun of the thing. Though not a formal fiesta, there were feasting and music and dancing and love-making. The dances had not the stately formality of the *baile*. They were made up impromptu by those nearest at hand; *valecitos casaros* they were called. They ended early. The women were indefatigable and would have continued all night. They poked fun at their escorts for not holding out better. But the latter were tired business men after their hard day's riding, which had begun at dawn.

When the round of *rodeos* had been finished came the *matanza*, when the selected cattle were slaughtered, their hides prepared, and the tallow tried out and packed in skin containers, ready for transportation to the seacoast to be sold or traded to the Boston ships. Only a small proportion of the meat could be utilized. Andy was always troubled at this waste, but he could not see any way out of it, though he saved more than did his neighbors, drying quantities of jerky, which he found to be moderately acceptable to some of the poorer people near the sea. Panchito shrugged his shoulder.

"There is no waste, *señor*," he expostulated. "This is the fat season for some. And are they not also the creatures of God who must be fed?"

And indeed the California of that day was aswarm with vultures and coyotes bred to this abundance. The night hills were vocal with the diabolic ululations of the little wolves. The sky was never vacant of the slow-circling birds. With the passing of the great cattle ranches the vultures disappeared, where or why no man knows. Certainly not through the efforts of man, as in the case of the coyote. Nature withdrew them, their need fulfilled.

Andy was not entirely convinced.

"And how about the rest of the year, when there is no *matanza?*" he inquired. "How then are they fed?"

"That," said Panchito, "is the affair of God."

At the time the *rodeo* was held at Folded Hills, appeared a dignified and courtly gentleman, who traveled in some state. He introduced himself as named Castañares, adding that he was *alcalde* of the *pueblo* of Monterey. He apologized further for what he called his "slight delay." Andy had difficulty in making out what it was all about. When finally he understood, he was dismayed. He had thought the governor's grant had given him legal ownership of his land. It seemed not. The title amounted to nothing until the land's boundaries had been properly measured and marked by the proper official, who was Judge Castañares. All the labor and improvements meant nothing, less than nothing, if a governor should change his mind, or someone of influence should come along covetous of the land. He had been nothing better than a squatter. He shivered a little at the thought; but no one else seemed disturbed. The day following the *alcalde's* arrival he, two mounted assistants, Ramón and Estevan Rivera as witnesses, together with Andy himself, rode to the southwest corner of the grant. This corner was supposed to start upon El Rancho Soledad, but the monuments of the latter holding had disappeared, or could not be found, at least without a more diligent search than the *alcalde* was inclined to undertake. He perused his copy of the Soledad grant, and peered about him, and finally gave it up.

"It is undoubtedly somewhere in this valley, *señor*," said he to Andy, "and I do not imagine you and Señor Linares will quarrel over a few tufts of sagebrush.

So he caused to be piled a heap of rounded stones from the wash, and on it planted a wooden cross. This was the official starting point and was called the *mojonera*. Its existence was solemnly witnessed by Ramón and Esteban. The *alcalde* then began the business of marking the boundaries of the seven leagues comprised in the grant. This was a leisurely process and must consume several days. Andy's business at the *rodeo* did not permit him to assist; though he rode with the party for an hour or so. The process was very simple and not at all laborious. Señor Castañares rode ahead, following the proposed boundary line, sometimes in consultation with a small pocket compass, sometimes with an eye on the sun, but frequently following merely his sense of fitness as to where a proper *rancho* should end. He was followed by a man on horseback dragging a fifty-foot *reata*. This was the measure of length. The horseman noted in a lazy sort of fashion how often he thought this fifty feet spanned the course of the party; and announced each five units in a somnolent voice; whereupon the clerk, who rode another horse, made a mark in his little book. As long as Señor Castañares held his mount to a foot pace this rough measurement was not as inaccurate as it sounds; but when, as occasionally, he indulged himself in a canter, the measurement entered the realms of fantasy. Nevertheless the *reata* man continued to announce results in all confidence.

The *alcalde* said nothing, save when the little procession came directly against some natural object in the line of its course. Then he would fling over his shoulder to his clerk, "A large live-oak tree," "A white oak riven by the wind," "A curious rock," or the like.

After the latest of the little tallies in his book the clerk would note down the observation, which constituted it duly an official landmark. Later, when Andy received the parchment that represented his grant, all these things were imposingly set forth. It read well: south three hundred and fifty *estradas* to a large live-oak tree, thence a hundred and twenty-five *estradas* to a white oak tree, riven by the wind; thence two hundred and ten *estradas* to a curious rock; and so on. The document had a beautiful seal, and ribbons. Andy was quite satisfied with it. A degree or so of compass bearing; the perishability or surprising similarity of trees, or the abundance of rocks that might be called curious was not to be called to his attention for many years to come, and certainly not by his present neighbors.

After the cattle had been separated and the unmarked animals branded, there remained only the business of the *matanza:* the gathering of the annual crop. It was customary, Ramón explained, for a well conducted *rancho* to slaughter about four fifths of its increase each year. They were driven from the rodeo to the *matanza* ground near the stream. Here each *vaquero,* riding at full speed after his victim, struck it skillfully with his knife in the back of the neck. Rarely did he miss his first stroke, and rode immediately on after another. The *vaqueros* were closely followed by three of the Indians on foot, the *peladores,* who quickly stripped the hides from the carcasses. Though afoot, they were protected by the herdsmen who held together the main band. After them came, in turn, the remaining Indians, the *tasajeros,* who cut up such of the animal as it was desirable to save. A very limited amount of the choicest of the meat was taken from each creature, perhaps fifty or a hundred pounds, to be dried for emergency rations; but the tallow was worth something. That nearest the hide, the *manteca,* was especially prized and was dissected carefully away from the coarser interior fat, the *sebo.* The *manteca* was of fine quality; it could be used as cooking fat and made superior candles. Any surplus was readily disposable to the Russians, there to the north, who appreciated its superiorities. The *sebo* went to the Boston ships, in trade. One could get as high as a dollar and a half for each *arroba** of it.

Behind the *tasajeros,* again, came the Indian women with leather baskets to gather up the tallow and to load it on the waiting *carreta.* On returning to the *rancho* theirs the task of trying it out in great iron pots, procured from the whalers, and running it into hide bags each of which would weigh, when filled, some hundreds of pounds. The *sebo* tried out easily; but the *manteca* was more delicate, required closer attention to prevent its burning. Vicenta herself kept a distant eye on the *manteca* kettle, and woe to its custodian if she relaxed her vigilance for a moment's gossip!

As many cattle as could be thus cared for were killed each day. The remainder were corralled for the night. They had drunk at the stream, but had been given no opportunity to graze.

"It does not matter," Ramón answered Andy's expostulation. "They are soon to die anyway." It was that puzzling blind spot again.

The *matanza* lasted for three days. Then the hides were stretched for drying, the tallow tried out and run into the skin bags, the meat cut along the grain into strips to be hung out for jerky. The crop for the year was gathered. The *rancho* itself would need many of the hides—strips of reatas, for building corrals, for binding wagons, for a dozen purposes; it would use the best of the tallow for candles, for soap, for cooking fat; it would save a little of the jerked meat in case of expeditions beyond the cattle country. All the rest was to be transported in the *carretas* to the *hacienda,* there to be stored until the arrival of the Boston ship for trade. And there, in miniature, Andy had seen practically all the gainful business of the country. There were, to be sure, a few productive avocations, but for strictly home benefit. The missions and some of the more progressive *hacendados* raised fruits, grain, a sufficiency for themselves and everybody else, including the Russians to the north, when they wanted to come and get it. But the majority did not bother. Why should they? There was already plenty, to be had for the mere sending. The Californians were, on the whole, rather fond

---

* About 25 lbs.

of agriculture; but what to do with more? There was no market. And Mexico, through its governors, tried by every means to discourage foreign trade. They clapped prohibition duties on all imports; they imposed the most harassing regulations as to harbors and inspections. If Mexico had its way, apparently, the Californians were to be deprived of every luxury, every necessity, even, that could not be produced at home, on the spot—or supplied at scandalous prices and in inadequate quantity and quality from Mexico. That was the nub of the situation. That was the underlying basis of the hostility, the resentment of the Californian against the Mexican. Were it not for a few informal local modifications, conditions would be impossible.

Andy learned these things from Ramón as they rode together. Ramón's foreign education had given him the advantage of a perspective, an outside point of view. He was able, when he chose, to discuss such matters intelligently. But he refused to take them seriously as, he explained, did some of his countrymen.

"They get very mad," said he. "They say he's an outrage, that Mexico keep the California by the throat and choke out of her the life." He shrugged his shoulders and laughed. "That is true—when you talk about it. But the señorita, she have her silk and her lace and her *camisa* and her stocking and her comb and her jewel and all those things; and the señor he have all the thing he like; and in the *casa* is mirror and table and bed and wine of France and Spain and all the thing people want just the same. Me, I think he's a joke to talk that way. He's fix all right and comfortable for everybody."

He went on to explain. Andy discovered, as other Americans have been discovering ever since, that laws mean little if they run counter to a people's feeling of justice. It was a fact that under these laws the luxuries of living were impossible. Nevertheless, there they were. Their presence was strictly illegal, of course, but it was brought about very simply. A certain amount of plain smuggling accomplished something: so smuggling had become an esteemed occupation. But that was risky, and resorted to only by the more adventurous, rather through love of excitement than from necessity. Certain tacitly accepted customs were simpler. The shipmasters carried only a portion of their cargoes readily accessible for inspection, the rest being concealed in "secret" places in the vessels. Or a portion of the cargo was transferred, at one of the outlying islands, to ships that had already made their entries and received their papers. Fictitious invoices were a matter of course, and as no oath was demanded, even the most puritanical Boston skipper did not hesitate to offer them.

Naturally these expedients were in reality very flimsy. They would never have stood against real determinaton. The "secret" hiding places on the vessels were actually merely a removal of the goods from plain sight. Every Californian, even on the remoter *ranchos* of the interior, was correctly informed when a smuggler was to land on the beach at Refugio and was on hand with his hides and tallow to purchase his fancy. As for the checking of invoices, that was a farce, conducted at a cabin table over a glass of wine.

Sometimes, a great many times, this complaisance was venial, arranged on a percentage basis. More rarely it was a result of common sense, when the Mexican official in charge realized perfectly the impossibility of enforcing orders delivered ignorantly from a perspective of thousands of miles. They made an impressive show, as when one governor commanded that in no seaport must any building be erected nearer to the beach than two hundred *varas*, but no real effort toward enforcement. The regulation named was supposed to discourage the illegitimate landing of goods. Of course, it did nothing of the sort; but it looked well in official reports to Mexico City.

But occasionally some simple-minded unimaginative martinet—like Victoria—came along, who took things literally. Then there was trouble. Otherwise Ramón could not see why there was the slightest occasion for trouble. Things went along all right. Naturally the government had to have some money to meet its expenses. Naturally the officials wanted to make something for themselves out of their offices. There were no taxes whatever, and nothing from Mexico. The missions were there to contribute, surely; but even the fattest cow gives only so much milk.

Andy was no great stickler for legality; but he had breathed in with his boyhood the Anglo-Saxon passion for regulated form. He was a little doubtful and even a trifle shocked at all this.

"You should talk to my cousin, Guadalupe," said Ramón carelessly. "He reads books, and he get very excite over what he call the rights of man. Why make the fuss?"

Andy did not really know. He was not even coherent enough to be able to tell Ramón the real reason for their difference; that he was of the race that makes a fuss about intangibles, and Ramón was not.

12   The Splendid Idle Forties

Some students of early California have extolled life in the era of the ranchero, even describing it as a Spanish Arcadia. Foremost of the exponents of this view was Gertrude Atherton. She lived to be ninety-one and in some fifty-six volumes created a fantasy about life in California that is still accepted by those more interested in mythology than truth. The following is indicative of her kind of writing, in which she generally ignored the fact that there were but a handful of wealthy landholders and life for most of the people was not "the gayest, the happiest, the most careless life in the world."

Within memory of the most gnarled and coffee-coloured Montereño never

From *The Splendid Idle Forties* by Gertrude Atherton. Published 1902.

had there been so exciting a race day. All essential conditions seemed to
have held counsel and agreed to combine. Not a wreath of fog floated across
the bay to dim the sparkling air. Every horse, every vaquero, was alert and
physically perfect. The rains were over; the dust was not gathered. Pio Pico,
Governor of the Californias, was in Monterey on one of his brief infrequent
visits. Clad in black velvet, covered with jewels and ropes of gold, he sat on
his big chestnut horse at the upper end of the field, with General Castro,
Doña Modeste Castro, and other prominent Montereños, his interest so
keen that more than once the official dignity relaxed, and he shouted
"Brava!" with the rest.

And what a brilliant sight it was! The flowers had faded on the hills, for
June was upon them; but gayer than the hills had been was the race-field of
Monterey. Caballeros, with silver on their wide gray hats and on their
saddles of embossed leather, gold and silver embroidery on their velvet
serapes, crimson sashes about their slender waists, silver spurs and
buckskin botas, stood tensely in their stirrups as the racers flew by, or,
during the short intervals, pressed each other with eager wagers. There was
little money in that time. The golden skeleton within the sleeping body of
California had not yet been laid bare. But ranchos were lost and won;
thousands of cattle would pass to other hands at the next rodeo; many a
superbly caparisoned steed would rear and plunge between the spurs of a
new master.

And caballeros were not the only living pictures of that memorable day
of a time for ever gone. Beautiful women in silken fluttering gowns, bright
flowers holding the mantilla from flushed awakened faces, sat their
impatient horses as easily as a gull rides a wave. The sun beat down,
making dark cheeks pink and white cheeks darker, but those great eyes,
strong with their own fires, never faltered. The old women in attendance
grumbled vague remonstrances at all things, from the heat to intercepted
coquetries. But their charges gave the good dueñas little heed. They
shouted until their little throats were hoarse, smashed their fans, beat the
side of their mounts with their tender hands, in imitation of the vaqueros.

"It is the gayest, the happiest, the most careless life in the world,"
thought Pio Pico, shutting his teeth, as he looked about him. "But how
long will it last? Curse the Americans! They are coming."

13   The End of the Missions

Conflict between church and state over the status of the missions was
common to all of Spanish America and was not confined to California. No
plans existed for secularization and the clergy argued that the Indians
would have to be their wards indefinitely. In the following, a distraught
Franciscan voices his objections to secularization and his fear of what
would happen to the Indians if they were freed. Unfortunately, his dire
predictions were realized. The lands and livestock of the missions were

coveted by the laity, as were also Indians to work their fields and do their chores.

When the Dos Rios party rode again into their patio they saw a horse with strange trappings tethered to the post. Their pleased surprise was slightly dampened when a servant told Francisco that it was Father Gabriel from the mission, instead of the well-loved Father Patricio. However, they allowed nothing but unalloyed delight to show on their faces when they greeted him.

"Father Gabriel," Francisco said going into the *sala*, "this is indeed most pleasant. I can't think of a time when you have honored my house with a visit before. I am deeply gratified, sir."

Father Gabriel refused, almost brusquely for a Spaniard, the refreshment Petra had started to call for. "I am fasting," he said coldly and turned immediately to Francisco, requesting a private interview. The Estradas covered their surprise smoothly, and Francisco led the way to his office.

The priest seemed to have shrunk. He was thinner, drier, less alive than he had been before. He had ridden to Dos Rios on a fast day and refused food. He was a holy man, firm in his holiness. Francisco found himself respecting him—never liking him, but respecting him nonetheless. The fact that he had ridden to Dos Rios instead of walking, as was the custom of the Franciscan Order gave Francisco an inkling that his errand was important.

"Now," the priest said as soon as the door was shut, "I would speak to you of something that is of utmost seriousness to all of Mexico and California."

"Please be seated, Father. You must be terribly tired."

"I do not recognize fatigue," the priest replied sitting down, but not comfortably. He sat on the edge of the hardest-looking chair in the room, and began abruptly. "Francisco, my son, I understand that you seldom indulge in political machinations with other Californians. Is that correct?"

"That is correct," Francisco replied becoming wary.

"May I ask why, Francisco?"

"Certainly, Father, I see no reason to run about looking for trouble. If I have all I need, and everything is running smoothly, I am not disposed to tamper with the existing administration of government. Revolutions bore me. Politics amuse me."

"Concisely put. Patricio told me I might count on your integrity. I had hoped he was right. It brings us then to this point: What have you heard or thought about the movement regarding the missions?"

A guard snapped shut in Francisco's brain. So that was it. He said carefully, "I have heard a good deal, Father. There has been talk of it for years."

"What is your stand?" The question was rapped out in the same tone he might have used in addressing an Indian neophyte, but Francisco allowed no annoyance to show.

"Father Gabriel," he said smiling politely, "that is an extremely forthright question. At the risk of being discourteous I would suggest that you have little right to ask it."

"I am a priest, Francisco. Since when may a man not confide in his priest?"

Francisco was tempted to answer bluntly, but refrained, saying, "You are a priest, true, but at the moment you are acting in the capacity of a politician. I intend nothing derogatory by that statement. I utter it in all respect. You are a priest, and in confessional I would speak out to you."

Father Gabriel stood up, the scanty color ebbing from his face, his eyes dark and intense. "You are mistaken, Francisco," he said thinly. "There is nothing of the politician in me. I think I have been a priest from the day of my birth. Now I am working, in that capacity, for the good of my Church and my charges. I have every right to use whatever weapon is at hand to further my cause. What these land-grabbing settlers are trying to do is ruin the mission system, render useless all the labor of countless men like me." He stopped with an effort, trying to retain his poise, wiping with a suddenly unsteady hand the film of moisture that appeared on his face.

"Father, I'm afraid you are ill," Francisco said gently. "Please allow me to get you something—a glass of wine, even a cup of coffee."

"I am fasting. I thought I told you." The priest sat down in his chair and Francisco could see the muscles in his thighs jerk from weariness. "You have not answered me," he said after a moment.

"About the missions?" Francisco was on guard. "As you say, there has been talk—but there is always talk, Father. I ask this in all respect: aren't you perhaps attaching too much importance to the legal secularization of the missions?"

"Too much importance!"

"Father, many believe that the mission has served its purpose here. You know that it is one type of colonization. It is never thought of except as a temporary measure, a measure to civilize a place until colonists arrive and establish themselves. They have arrived, sir. California is established."

The priest rose to his feet, his face working. "And those who were here first?" he asked. "Those, my charges, what of them?"

"There are provisions for them," Francisco answered deliberately. "They will be given land as we have been—"

"Provision on paper," Gabriel interrupted scathingly. "And what use is that. I know Indians, Francisco."

"Do you think I don't, Father? I've been in this country for more than twenty years. I've had hundreds of Indians working for me."

"Working *for* you," cried the priest. "That is the key. Of course you have. They have always labored *for* you. They've been the labor that carved this land from a wilderness, and you Spaniards sit back and reap—"

"I have labored, Father. I know what work is."

"Granted, Francisco. You do know what work is—for yourself. The difference is that while you Spaniards have worked for yourselves, the Indians have not been able to work for themselves."

"Well, now they will," Francisco said with some sharpness. "They will be given land and the same chance we all have had to become self-supporting—" Something in the priest's face caused him to stop. "Father, you are ill."

"I am not ill," the priest said faintly, swaying a little. "Perhaps I was foolish to choose a fast day on which to take a long ride but I had a disturbing letter and I had to see you. You are an extremely influential man——" His voice dwindled, seemed to have no strength behind it.

Francisco felt acutely sorry for him. "Will you rest—sleep for a while, Father?" he asked.

"No, I cannot. I have not slept for two nights. Estrada, you cannot be as blind as this. You cannot think that any land given the Indians will remain very long in their possession. You know it will not. My mission consists of eighty-five thousand acres of tillable land and pasture. It is in bearing orchards, fields and pasture. Our herds of cattle, small and large, are the third largest among missions and private ranchos. Who will get it all, Francisco?" The priest's face gleamed in the light from the window. "Who, Francisco?"

"The Indians, Father. They will work as a community. They will be self-sustaining. They will be individual people instead of neophytes of the Church."

"But Indians are children, Francisco. Why do you carry a whip? You carry one because you sometimes have to lay it on the back of an Indian, because they are childish and stubborn and sometimes very stupid. You have to *make* them work, Francisco. If there is no one with authority to make them work, they do not. If they are freed and given the land, they will run riot. They will not think to make any effort until they are hungry and they discover there is no food left."

"Father, please. You excite yourself."

"I know. I excite myself, madden myself, over my children. These are my children whom I see on the brink of being cheated out of everything we have labored to give them."

"Father, no one wants to cheat them."

"You liar!" The priest leaned heavily on the table, his frame shaking. "You are a liar, Francisco Estrada. You know what will happen. You and every other land-seizing ranchero. You know that the Indians can't hold the land. They will run away, become renegades, because that is easier than working. They will die like flies. They will be enslaved. And then all the land will lie fallow and useless. The mission will be nothing but an empty building for field mice. And then who will get the land, Francisco?"

"Father, please! You are ill."

"Who will get it, Francisco?" The priest tried to shout, but his voice failed him and was little more than a cracked whisper. "You will get it. You will step in and take up the land, the planted orchards, the fields, the stock. Efficient, capable, intelligent—Indians will be no match for you and your kind. What can't be got legally will eventually be got illegally."

"That will do. There is no point in this harangue. You are a priest and a sick one, or I wouldn't stand here and allow you to fling recriminations at my head—recriminations for something which has not occurred yet and which—"

"But it will, Francisco," the priest said with an effort. "It will!" He sat down on the chair again, apparently unable to stand. "You aren't a fool. You know what will happen."

"But you have done your work, Father," Francisco said gently. "The mission has served its purpose. The country is growing. The land must pass from Church control, and along with it those Christianized Indians—"

"Control? Perhaps control is the word. But control is still needed."

"There have been abuses, Father."

"There are flaws in everything. If there were perfection, there would be no need to strive for perfection. Francisco, I can tell you the Indians are not ready to pass from Church jurisdiction."

"Domination you mean."

"Domination perhaps. But while they are being dominated, their bellies are full and there is a minimum of lawlessness and crime."

There was silence in the sunlit office.

"Since you have refused to state your stand," Gabriel said finally, "I may assume that you are in accord with the wolf pack."

"No, Father, I am in accord with no wolf pack. I am in accord only with Francisco Estrada. The function of the mission here is finished. The land is colonized and established. If the land passes from the Church to the Indians and then passes from the Indians, there is no reason why it should not pass to me."

The priest regarded him through a long silence. He spoke slowly and carefully, as if he couldn't quite hear his own voice. "You are a grasping, evil man." He stood up, although it would seem impossible for him to, he appeared for a moment so fragile. He raised his bony hand and brought it down with a hard blow against Francisco's face. It cracked out like a shot.

Francisco's face remained expressionless. "I am sorry, Father," he said. "The law is the law and I shall do nothing to stem its course."

The priest left like a gaunt and hurried shade, scarcely speaking to Petra who met him at the door, ignoring the courteous words of Enrique Padilla. Pulling his thin body onto his horse caused sweat to spring again from his face. His sandaled foot kicked the animal's side and made it start at full gallop. He sat his horse badly, awkwardly. Those watching him winced at the jars his body received. They would seem to shake the bones loose from one another.

Chapter 3

The American Takeover

The American Takeover

California under Spain and Mexico grew slowly, and no more than a thin strip along the coast was settled. As a result other nations cast covetous eyes at this potentially rich area. The Americans entered into competition for this important prize in large numbers because of the lure of four animals. First to attract the attention of Yankee ship captains was the sea otter. Skins from this lovely animal brought 100 dollars or more on the China market. Soon enterprising traders were scouring the waters of the California and Northwest coast, and, in a single season, 17,000 pelts were taken. Overtrapping ended the sea otter trade by 1820, and American ships began seeking whales and seal pelts which were also found along the California coast in abundance, at least for a time. When these animals thinned out, New England traders sought cow hides to supply leathermakers and provide tallow. Mountain men came overland in search of beaver. Jedediah Smith's party was the first to find its way over mountains and across deserts, but countless others soon followed. All of these intruders reported, in one way or another, on the beauty and richness of the region. They also noted the sparse population and the poor defenses. Such a state of affairs could not continue indefinitely, and it didn't.

Overland settlers from the United States began entering Mexican California in 1841 to join American businessmen residing in the province as traders. By 1846 approximately 750 Americans were mingled with the native population. Dissatisfaction with Mexican rule was common, and many Californios would probably have accepted transfer to United States rule. Unfortunately, the Bear Flag uprising in June 1846, possibly encouraged by the controversial John C. Frémont, prevented a peaceful transfer. Even then there was little bloodshed in the first phase of American conquest. One soldier observed, "we simply marched all over California from Sonoma to San Diego and raised the American flag without opposition. We tried to find an enemy, but could not."

The second phase of the takeover saw greater bloodshed, mainly as the result of arrogance and intolerance on the part of the American occupying force in Los Angeles. This garrison was forced to retreat to San Pedro only to return to fight (and lose) a skirmish at Dominguez Rancho. A Californio army inflicted the only defeat of the Mexican War upon an American force at San Pasqual. But this detachment, under General Stephen Watts Kearny, quickly recovered and pursued the Californios until they surrendered to Frémont's forces, marching toward Los Angeles as a result of the celebrated ride of John Brown.

14 Mountain Men

The first Americans to come overland into California were the mountain men who trapped for beaver all over the Rocky Mountain West. The following selection deals with the remarkable career of James P. Beckwourth, a mulatto from Virginia. He was, at various times, a trapper, guide, Indian-fighter, chief of the Crows, and horsethief extraordinary. He first came to California in 1844 and fought against Micheltorena at the "Battle" of Cahuenga in 1845. He "acquired" horses to drive to New Mexico in 1846. Returning to the state in 1848 he discovered the pass which now bears his name. In 1852 he opened a hotel and trading post in Beckwourth Valley, but in a short time renewed his wandering all over the West.

Dappled sunlight fell through the vine leaves. It touched Amelita's high Indian cheekbones and made bright moving patches on her glossy hair.

"Are all Yankees so full of the wandering sickness?" she asked. "Don't you ever want to stop?"

"When we get old," Jim told her, in his just-adequate Spanish. "Don't you want to come with me and see what's on the other side of the mountains?"

"I do not!" she said, and laughed. "And I feel sorry for the woman who is ever foolish enough to say yes." She looked at him, up and down, from a little distance. "But not too sorry." She kissed him. "Good-bye, Yankee." She walked away from him, out into the clear sunlight and across the courtyard.

Jim watched appreciatively the free and graceful swing of her bare brown legs. Her skirt was short enough to show them halfway to the knee. The skirt itself was a poppy red, making a pretty splash of color against the baked hardpan of the ground and 'dobe walls with the whitewash crumbling off them. He watched her until she passed through a low doorway and was gone. Then he went down to the corrals, where Rich was waiting for him.

"Someday," he said, "I'm going to marry one of these girls and settle down."

"I'd thought of it myself," Rich said, "but I ain't sure how one of 'em would get along sharing the lodge with Grass."

Jim grinned and shook his head. "They're strong like the Indian women, and they've got the dignity, but they seem to be kind of lacking in patience. I'd hate to try lodgepoling one of 'em." He had never lodgepoled Cherry, but theirs had been an unusually good relationship.

"I would reckon," said Rich, "if you was to try it on Amelita, she'd have your gizzard out and thrown to the cat before you knew what happened."

From *Follow the Free Wind* by Leigh Brackett. Copyright 1963 by Leigh Brackett. Reprinted by permission of the author's agent, Lurton Blassingame.

He looked to see if the wranglers were ready to turn out their little cavallada of twenty-eight horses. Jim swung into the saddle of the claybank stallion he was riding, and all the *vaqueros* around the lower corral shouted and laughed at him. Jim rode Indian-style, or mountain-style, which was the same thing, with short stirrups. These *Californios* liked to ride standing on their toes with their legs at full stretch. They thought Jim was very amusing, even though he had shown them he could do one or two things they couldn't.

It worked both ways. "Come on," they shouted, waving coins in the air. "Once more, Yankee! Try once more."

"I'll be along in a minute, Rich," Jim said, and went over to the *vaqueros*. He made the stallion prance, and that made the half-broken colts in the corral shy stiff-legged and snorting from the fence. Some of the *vaqueros* were pure Indio, scattered out from the missions that had no further use for them after the Secularization. They were all superb horsemen. They were good-natured, proud, high-tempered, and tough as their own *reatas*.

One of them placed a coin with great care under each of Jim's knees, where they pressed against the saddle housing.

Jim asked, "Does anybody wish to bet that I don't lose them both?"

They said he was insulting their mothers by implying that they had given birth to idiots. He had been here ten days and they knew him. Jim laughed and kicked the stallion into a gallop. The course was improvised. Over the tongues of three wagons parked beside a wall, thread a row of tall sycamores like a needle going through cloth, turn three times tightly around the well, and then back to the start at a dead run and bring the horse up rearing. Jim had lost both coins.

They were happy. They told him to go with God, and he thanked them and wished them well, and rode off after Rich. On the way he saw the *hacendado* Menendez coming from his house, a lean, straight-backed man walking like a king with a coiled whip in his hand and his huge spurs ringing. They exchanged courteous salutes at a distance. Jim reined up beside Rich at the head of the cavallada.

"I think these people are going to fight," he said.

Rich looked back at the sprawling, whitewashed buildings of the rancho as though he were thankful to see the last of them. "If they'd ever suspicioned for a minute what we were up to we'd have found out what they could do. I felt my hair turning white day by day."

Ostensibly they had been trading for horses, and if the *Californios* fought as hard as they bargained Jim thought that nobody could stand against them. He and Rich had been in California a month with their breed wranglers, traveling from the Santa Ana River up to San Luis Obispo and down again, and twenty-eight head was the best they had been able to do. They had lost money on the goods they brought in over the Spanish Trail from Sante Fe.

They expected to get it back.

The valley was wide under the peaceful sky. Low mountains closed it in on the west, and sometimes the wind that blew through the passes brought with it the smell of the sea. To the east the land lifted into rough hills cut with deep arroyos, and then into the foothills of a higher range with bare peaks of gray and sandy pink. Winter never troubled these inland valleys where the grapes and the olives grew. It was November and still warm. The sun had burned the grass to a rich dark gold, clumped with blackish-green live oaks. Beautiful country, Jim thought. A good place for a man to come to when he felt himself getting old. Right now, though, his eyes were less concerned with beauty than with horses.

Alta California was one vast range where the cattle and horses were so thick that in drought years thousands of them had to be slaughtered to save the grass. And from the Santa Ana River to San Luis Obispo and back, Jim and Rich knew exactly where the best horse herds were pastured, which ones were held in the open and which ones were corralled at night.

"I might," said Rich slowly, "feel a mite more guilty if these self-same *Californios* had been a mite more friendly when I was here before. As it stands, I got to admit that all I can think of is it serves 'em right."

The traders and the mountain men had a long, old score against the Spanish settlements. Jim had no personal grudge himself but he had heard enough stories from others, including even the almighty Bents. Individual Mexicans and Californians might be your faithful friends. They might love you, marry you, die for you. But the men who made the rules and signed the papers were a different matter. Bribery and extortion were a way of life. One time you might be given permission to trade or trap, the next time you got thrown into jail and all your possessions were confiscated. Sometimes you got shot. Imperial Spain had always claimed everything right up to the Arkansas and she tried her best to keep a stranglehold on it. Finally she strangled her own colonists into a revolution but it hadn't changed things too much for foreigners. A Yankee was still taking a risk, particularly since the *Texians* had tried the revolutionary shoe on the other foot and won their independence from Mexico, and the Mexicans didn't like it at all. California, being more remote, was less involved in these matters, but Jim knew what Rich meant. He would breathe easier when he saw Cajon Pass ahead of him.

He said cheerfully, "They've got so many horses here they throw 'em away when they get dirty. It won't hurt 'em to lose a few." He was feeling a pleasurable excitement that he had not felt since the last time his scouts came back and reported that they had found the enemy, and he began to plan the raid.

Rich said, "I hope Walkara don't mess things up again."

"He won't. He's smart, he won't make the same mistake twice." Jim laughed. "Besides, he got Pegleg so mad at him he wouldn't speak for three years, and he loves Pegleg better than he does his brothers. He won't do *that* again."

Once before, in the same guise of peaceful traders, they had come down

the Spanish Trail to California—Jim and Rich and Pegleg, Walkara the
Ute chief and two of his brothers, Arrapeen and Sanpitch. The third one,
Tobiah, stayed with Walkara's braves in the outer canyons where they
could wait unseen. Pegleg was thinking large thoughts. Jim had
discovered that Walkara did not at all feel that he had had a poor day when
he ran off four hundred head, or even one hundred. But Pegleg was
thinking in thousands, and not just any horses, but the best. This was
going to be a real expedition, carefully planned. Everything went well
until the Hawk of the Mountains got impatient with the slowness of the
white man's methods and whistled his Utes down out of the hills for a raid
of his own.

He got a little over two hundred head. A hard-riding group of
Californios got some of those back. The expedition went up in a cloud of
dust, and Pegleg, Jim, and Rich went flying out through the Tehachapis to
save their necks. When they got back to Walkara's windy roost on the
Spanish Fork, Pegleg packed up his squaws and moved out. Walkara was
brokenhearted. But it was three years before he saw Pegleg again.

Jim and Rich trailed with Pegleg for lack of anything more pressing to
do. They wintered at Santa Fe and then worked the southwestern country
which was Pegleg's old stamping ground. They didn't do well. They
moved north again, into the valley of the Green and on, ranging the
familiar mountains and trapping the familiar streams, but it was not the
same. Beaver was scarce. The mountain passes and the camping places in
the "holes" were full of strangers, and many of the old acquaintances were
gone, killed and scalped, frozen, starved, drowned, gone under.

Even the old enemies were gone. Smallpox had swept the lodges of the
Blackfeet. Many of the young men lay dead, with no one to bury them, and
the war parties no longer harried far and wide as they had used to. And
farther down the Big River, the Arikara towns were also desolate.

Jim felt a strong yearning to go home. Several times he saddled his
horse, and once he actually rode for half a day toward the Wind River range
and the passes he had first seen so many years ago. He never made it.
Something in him had been broken and was not yet healed. The time for
going home would come, he knew that, and he knew that he would
recognize it when it came. This was not it.

He returned to Rich and Pegleg and plunged into the icy streams
again, setting his traps and noticing in a vague sort of way that when Rich
came out of the water after hours of work he had trouble walking, as
though his joints had stiffened.

The summer rendezvous were still wild, loud, and drunken, but they
were like something hanging on after the need for them was over. There
were new trading posts everywhere now, in business all the year round. And
all of a sudden Jim found that he and Rich and Fitzpatrick and Bridger,
who was now known as Old Gabe, were of a different generation, and there
was a whole new young breed to sit at their feet and listen to how it was in
the old days before the Platte trail was a beaten highway.

There was something else different from those old rendezvous, when Jim had envied Fitz and Bridger their fame. He was famous himself now. Beckwourth, they would say, and look at him, the milky green-horns. The name had stories to go with it, and Jim heard them, though not often to his face. Beckwourth the runaway slave who had tried to murder his master. Beckwourth the renegade, who set his Indians onto white traders. Beckwourth the horse thief, who put Fitzpatrick and Stewart helpless on the prairie and then stole their watches too. Beckwourth who had a hundred scalps in his tipi and over half of them white, and there's plenty of men in St. Louis can swear to it because they saw them.

15 The Donner Tragedy

American emigrant parties began making their way to California in 1841. All of them suffered hardship, but the disaster which befell the 1846 Donner Party was one of the worst. Of the eighty-seven in the group, only forty-seven reached California. Trapped in the snow-clogged Sierra, some survived only through cannibalism. This incident has attracted more authors than any comparable tragedy in the state's history (recently there was an epic poem published about it). The best of several novels on the subject is by Vardis Fisher. He argues in *The Mothers* that it was the strength of the women protecting their children that saved the party from an even worse fate. In this excerpt he demonstrates how lack of experience and leadership among the men of the party contributed to its grave problems.

When Charles Stanton awoke he was cold, and he realized he had been cold all night. His bed was only two blankets on the hard earth with his trousers laid on top of his boots for a pillow. Around him was a saltbush desert, and for a few moments after awaking he breathed deeply, relishing the smells of the cool morning. Stanton was an amateur botanist, and western deserts for him were excitingly fragrant.

There were better beds than his in this company of emigrants. Some slept in their wagons, under canvas tops that shut out the brilliant night sky; and some, like the Reeds and Donners and Wolfingers, all of whom seemed to be wealthy, had bedsprings. But the Reeds, he now remembered, had lost their springs, as well as their cattle and most of their provisions, in crossing the blinding salt flats of the Great Salt Lake. Their oxen, crazed by thirst, had wandered off in the waterless wastelands and had perished. The Reed family itself had almost perished because the other emigrants, nearly as maddened as their beasts, had pushed on ahead, even though Jim Reed was the one who had ridden alone into the mirages in search of water.

Well, it had been like that, Stanton reflected, ever since the train had left the banks of the Missouri. There had been no leadership. There had been disputes and quarrels, hot tempers and angry words, distrust and spite and wild fears; until more and more, as they all pushed desperately toward California, each family had drawn apart in isolated and frenzied efforts of its own.

Back at Fort Bridger they had spent several precious days trying to decide whether to take the longer route by way of Fort Hall or to follow a short-cut that had been urged upon them. Most of the train had gone by Fort Hall, but a few families had resolved to try the Hastings cutoff across wild mountains and the Salt Lake valley. Stanton would have chosen the longer and safer route; he had come with these people because among them there were some whom he loved. There was Tamsen Donner who shared his interest in wild life and was a better botanist than himself. There were Jim Reed and his wife Margaret and their two remarkable daughters, Virginia and Patty. There was the gay and irresponsible Irishman, Pat Dolan. And there was the Graves family, including Mary, who reminded Charley Stanton of his mother.

But from the day they took the cutoff, there had been delays and disasters. They had almost perished in the mountains east of the lake; and even now, weeks later, Stanton shuddered when looking back to that time. With superhuman strength, born of desperation, every able-bodied man, woman, and child had harnessed themselves with ropes and drawn their wagons across mountain torrents or up over ledges of stone. They had been a month covering fifty miles; and hardly had they escaped from the prison of mountains when they saw before them the broad expanse of salt flats. There they had buried one of their members in a grave chiseled out of salt, and there they had sacrificed or consumed most of their provisions. There every one of them had come within an inch of dying of thirst.

Now, with hundreds of miles still between them and their goal, their beasts were so starved and gaunt that they could hardly draw the wagons, and the food rationed to each person barely sustained life. It was early in September. Not until late November, they had been told, would snow fall on the Sierras. They had two months to cover six hundred miles. That, Stanton figured, meant ten miles a day—and they could do it if they had forage for their beasts and food for themselves. They could do it if they would stop their senseless bickering and unite under a single command.

This thought led Stanton to some wry reflections. He had known none of these persons before he joined their expedition last spring. Emigrant trains heading westward always moved, he had supposed, under an able leader. There was no leader here. The two Donner families traveled apart and usually encamped some distance in advance of the main group. Tamsen Donner, the guiding spirit there, distrusted all the Germans, including a lean and furtive young man named Reinhart, a tall bearded fox named Keseberg, and a family named Wolfinger. As a matter of fact, nobody seemed to like the Wolfingers. Mrs. Wolfinger had worn costly clothes and jewels and had affected a grand manner; and Stanton had almost smiled to see her perched haughtily in the wagon, with dust heavy on her clothes and jewels. When she walked she had the air of a princess; and when she spoke in German, she seemed to expect persons to obey. With her, besides Reinhart, were two other young Germans who appeared to be her chore boys.

The Reeds had also lived apart from the others—and so, for that matter, had Franklin Graves and his large family. With the Graves family was John Snyder, by far the handsomest young man in the train. He was tall and dark and athletic, and like Mrs. Wolfinger he had an air. John was a show-off who liked to humiliate the other young men by besting them in wrestling or jumping, or by throwing down the endgate of his wagon and entertaining the girls with clog dances and Irish jigs. Stanton disliked the man and he had reasons. Snyder was six feet tall and superbly muscular; Stanton was seven inches shorter and in comparison looked like a boy. He was not the kind to catch the fancy of Mary Graves, who stood a queenly two inches above him.

Sitting up in bed, Stanton looked over at the Graves camp, wondering if the family was up. He saw no sign of life there; but a hundred yards away, kneeling to light a sage fire, was Jim Reed. Poor Jim, he thought. Poor, proud Jim who had been forced to abandon most of his stuff in the salt flats and was now largely dependent on the charity of others. Graves had lent him an ox, Pat Breen had lent him another, and he now had two yokes, but they were old and feeble. When Jim had left Illinois, he drove a fine herd of cattle and had several wagons piled high with furniture and provisions. None had been so prosperous and none more generous. But now, forced upon charity, he was a silent and unhappy man who seldom spoke.

Stanton was about to call a greeting when something unusual caught his eye. It was a gray brightness upon a saltbush. Quickly he reached out and touched the bush, and was astonished. The brightness was frost. More alarmed than he would have been by the sight of Indians, he drew on his trousers and boots and rolled up his bed. Then, doubting his senses, he went to other bushes and closed his hand on frost. He stared at the wetness on his hand. Turning to the west, he looked at a range of mountains there and was again startled. Upon their summits was an unmistakable whiteness. He hastened across the sand to Jim Reed.

"Good morning, Jim!"

"Good morning, Charley."

"Jim, have you noticed it?"

Before answering, Reed laid more sage on the fire. "Yes," he said.

Stanton looked at the distant mountains. In a voice that was hardly more than a whisper he asked: "Is it snow?"

"It looks like snow to me."

"Maybe it's just another mirage. In this desert you never can tell what you see or don't see."

Reed straightened and looked at the mountains. "It's snow, I guess."

Margaret Reed came to the fire and Jim turned to her. "Margaret, doesn't that look like snow to you?"

"Yes."

"Who would know?" asked Stanton.

"Well, Frank Graves used to live in the Green Mountains. He might know."

"Snow in September? My God, Jim, it can't be!"

"Well, Charley, I hope it isn't."

Stanton crossed the hundred yards between the Reed and Graves camps. Franklin Graves was bringing his oxen in and his wife was rationing the breakfast.

"Frank, can you tell us? Is that snow?"

Franklin Graves squared his big shoulders and looked at the summits. The peaks were gray in the morning dusk.

"Yes, Charley, it's snow."

"But this is only the middle of September. How could it be?"

"The hair on the cattle is begun to thick up. I figger it'll be an early winter."

"If that's snow, then snow fell on the Sierras last night."

"That's how I figger it too."

"Then we can't make it—not at the rate we travel and with the food we have."

"It's our livestock," said Graves, and looked at his gaunt oxen. They had spent the night cropping saltbush. "Our beasts, they're plumb tuckered out."

The two men looked into the west. Squarely across their course stood the pile of mountains, but they knew their trail went far into the south around them and then ran north to find Mary's River. They knew that for four or five hundred miles across this part of the Great Basin they could hope to see only the interminable desolation of alkali. Day after day and camp after camp they would see around them only what they saw now. The beasts would grow steadily weaker while winter filled the sky.

"I think," said Stanton at last, "someone should go for help. I'll see what Uncle George says."

George Donner was regarded by some as the leader, but he was neither bold nor farsighted. Under his broad breast was a gentle and indulgent heart; instead of cracking the whip and driving these people to their goal, he yielded to their weariness or their whims. Again and again he had allowed them to remain in a camp for two or three days to rest themselves and their beasts. After they had emerged from the terrible salt flats, he had paused for six precious days while Reed hunted in vain for his lost cattle. Throughout the long journey Uncle George had been like that.

Stanton found him with his wife Tamsen, yoking their beasts. They and their five daughters had eaten breakfast and were ready to march.

"Uncle George," said Stanton, "that's snow on the mountains."

"I wondered about it," said George in the slow, calm way of the man. In perception and fiery resolve Tamsen had everything that her husband lacked. The ninety-six pounds of her were vital, and highspirited and alert. She now came over and stood by Stanton and looked with him at the mountains.

"Charley, are you sure?"

"Frank Graves says so. He once lived in mountains."

"I thought it was low-hanging clouds."

"Didn't you notice the frost this morning?"

"Yes. Well, we'll have to hurry along. I've told George we are laggards, but he will take his time. Winter for him is like the millennium—it is certain but very remote."

"We have over six hundred miles. At ten miles a day that is two months—and snow already falling!"

"What do you think we should do?"

"Send for help."

"George, Charley thinks we should send for help."

"But who would want to go?"

"Call for volunteers," Stanton said. "Somebody must go."

The word snow ran from tongue to tongue through the camp, and families gathered to look at the mountains. Snow for these people was a more terrible word than Indian. In their clumsy and faltering way they had been racing against time and a Sierra winter. Through April and May, through the whole summer, the word snow had been in their minds, because along their route, trappers, scouts, and frontiersmen had warned them that they must cross the Sierras before late November or they would be doomed.

And now, in September, here they were in a vast and friendless desert, far from their goal; and the first snow had fallen. For those of weak heart the sight of it was like a sentence to death. For the stout and bold it was an ominous warning. But even with that dreadful threat above them in the sky, these people spent most of the forenoon giving voice to anxiety and despair. They gathered in groups to talk about the snow, to gesture at it, to exchange fears and doubts. Children questioned parents and parents answered children, but no bold spirit rose to electrify and lead them.

Some of them were so upset and dismayed that they yoked and unyoked beasts without realizing what they did. Baylis Williams, a Reed teamster, stood by his half sister Eliza and shook as if suffering extreme chills. Joe Reinhart was so scared he looked yellow. Noah James sat by a saltbush and whittled shavings and never looked up. Stanton watched these young unmarried men and pitied them, and wished for a rugged frontiersman to guide these people. But there was none. Some had come from Illinois, some from Missouri, and some from Tennessee. A few, among whom was Pat Breen, had come from Iowa. But not a single one of them had ever braved and conquered the hazards of an American frontier. They were a bunch of greenhorns, embarked on a great adventure that was as dark and uncharted for them as death itself.

This, Stanton reflected, was the kind of adventure that reached to the depths of character and made men or broke them. These men would probably make or break before this trip was done. These women, too, would show their real colors before they ever looked upon the golden valleys of California. Mrs. Wolfinger would shed her jewels and silks, if her soul was not made of such things. Joe Reinhart would lose his yellow pallor and be a man or he would slink off like a coyote and die. . . .

Then Stanton thought of the children. There were eight or ten babies nursing at mothers' breasts. There were thirty or more children under the age of ten. Half the persons here were dependent on others; and among the adults, Keseberg had a thorn imbedded in one foot, Pat Breen was crippled or pretended to be, Jake Donner was old and feeble, and a lonely old stranger named Hardcoop looked as if he were already dying. With starved beasts and only a little food, these people would never reach California without aid, even if no snow fell.

Never had a group of frightened emigrants, lost upon the broad face of a continent, stood in such dire need of an able and resourceful leader.

Morning passed and noon came before Uncle George had the gumption to call them together. He was trembling when he turned to face them, and his voice shook when he spoke. At his side, barely reaching to an armpit, stood Tamsen, his wife.

"Friends," he said, his voice shaking more from grief than fear, "we all know that it snowed last night. Frank Graves has lived in the mountains and he says all the signs point to an early winter, and a hard one. We've been told snow falls on the Sierra passes in late November, and I guess we thought we had plenty of time. But our food is almost gone and our animals are dog tired; and I've talked with some of you and you think we should send to Sutter's Fort for help."

He paused and looked at the faces. They all knew what his next words would be; and Charles Stanton, apart and watchful, was studying the faces of the young unmarried men. There were a dozen of them besides himself, but none of them were looking at Uncle George.

"So I guess," Uncle George went on, "we better send for help. We want someone to go and then come back and meet us with food. Otherwise, it looks like we'll all starve."

Again he paused. George Donner, too, was studying the faces and wondering if there was a man before him who would volunteer.

"Someone must go," he said, his voice pleading rather than commanding. "I'm asking for volunteers."

There was silence. Young men looked at the earth, and mothers with babes in their arms looked at the young men. Stanton waited. He intended to go, but he wanted to see if John Snyder, the handsome athlete standing by Mary Graves, would volunteer. Snyder's gaze was on the ground.

"I'm asking for volunteers," said George Donner's trembling voice. "We'll give them their pick of the horses and guns, and all the food we can spare."

Out of the silence came Stanton's high voice. "I'll go," he said.

"Thanks, Charley," said Uncle George. Again his gaze searched the faces of the young men. "Charley Stanton says he'll go, but there must be two men. They will go through Indian land. One man will have to stand guard while the other one naps. It's a dangerous trip, I don't have to tell any man that. The men who go will risk their lives and we all know it."

Again he waited. Stanton saw Mary Graves cast a sidelong look at the dark face of John Snyder. He saw Margaret Reed looking at Milt Elliott. He saw Pat Breen look up at the Irishman, Pat Dolan, who stood by him. Eyes searched faces and turned from face to face, but nobody spoke.

16 The Frémont Fiasco

The role of John Charles Frémont in the American takeover has long been a matter of controversy. He entered California in 1845 with approximately sixty men on what he claimed was a scientific expedition. Scholars are still not sure why he defied the Mexican authorities and seemingly tried to goad them into attacking his small force. In this fictional account Thomas Larkin, the American consul at Monterey, asks a former mountain man turned rancher to act as intermediary in an effort to avoid hostilities. After three days Frémont thought better of fighting off all of California with only sixty men. He then made his way "slowly and growlingly northward," returning a short time later.

Andy reached Monterey in mid-afternoon and rode at once to Larkin's house. The consul had evidently watched for his arrival. He met the *ranchero* at the foot of the garden.

"Thank God you're here!" he cried. "Hell's popping!"

"What is it?" asked Andy. "They talk of an army—toward San Juan. What army? Is it war?"

"War? No: that's it. It's Frémont."

"Frémont! What about Frémont? Is he back?"

Larkin stared at him incredulously.

"Do you mean to say you didn't know that! Haven't you heard that—"

"I've heard nothing; nothing at all, I tell you," said Andy.

"Oh, Lord!" Larkin threw out both hands. "And you not twenty leagues away! What can a man expect!" His shoulders stooped. "Come, get down," said he briskly, after a moment. "I suppose I've got to tell you the whole thing from the beginning!"

"I suppose you have," assented Andy. He swung from the saddle and dropped the reins of his wearied horse over its head. The two men wandered slowly up the garden path toward the veranda.

They stood there for a while, too absorbed to think of sitting down.

From *Folded Hills* by Stewart Edward White. Copyright © 1934, 1961 by Stewart Edward White. Reprinted by permission of the Trust Office, Crocker National Bank Santa Barbara, Ca.

Finally they sat, without knowing that they did so. Andy was astounded at his news. The isolation and self-absorption of Folded Hills were borne in on him as never before.

Yes, Frémont was back. He had appeared suddenly at Sutter's Fort, in December. He had with him only a few men, and had entered California over the Sierra. The main body of his company had turned south. Joe Walker was in charge of them. Joe was to bring them in by the easier route he had himself discovered years ago. The two parties were to rendezvous at Tulare Lake. After a short stay at Sutter's, Frémont had gone south to meet them. So far everything was all right, though naturally Castro and the authorities were uneasy and wanted to know why he had returned, and why he had brought so many men.

"How many did he bring?" asked Andy.

"Somewhere about sixty or seventy or eighty," said Larkin.

"Well, that's no great army. What did he come for this time?"

"Surveying a route for a wagon road, he says. I managed to smooth it over. If he'd stayed over across the Valley, it would have been all right. Maybe he intended to; I don't know."

But things broke badly. Joe Walker mistook the forks of the Kern for Tulare Lake and waited there. Frémont found the right lake but no Walker. So after two weeks he returned to Sutter's. Along the last part of January he left his party there and came alone to Monterey.

"I had him here at the house; took him to see Castro," said Larkin. "The situation was ticklish, but I managed again to smooth things over. Castro was personally inclined to be reasonable, but he has pretty positive orders about foreigners. Frémont insisted that all he was doing was to establish routes the other side of the mountains, that his men were not soldiers, that all he wanted was to winter somewhere across the Valley, and perhaps refit. Castro could not give him official permission; but I got him to say he'd offer no formal objections. It was a long session. I turned in that night feeling pretty good. When I saw Frémont off a couple of days later I felt not quite so good. Talk! Talk! Talk! Why can't people keep their mouths shut! I began to hear all sorts of things that Frémont had been telling. So did Castro. He came to see me. His friends had been telling him that Frémont had bragged that ten thousand men were starting for California from Missouri in the spring! Naturally he was all on edge again. I told him flatly it wasn't true; and I told him flatly I didn't believe Frémont had said any such thing. Of course he wasn't by any means satisfied; but I got him to let it go. But I was mightly glad Frémont was gone so he couldn't do any more talking."

"Drank too much?" surmised Andy.

"I don't think so. That fellow doesn't need drink to talk," said Larkin dryly. "Well," he went on, "I thought that was all settled. And the next thing I knew I heard that the whole kit and caboodle of them were over somewhere in the Santa Clara valley. That is a long way the wrong side of the fence."

"It sure is," said Andy.

"I began to feel like a man in a bad dream. But it wasn't so raw as it sounded. Seems the men at Sutter's got tired of waiting and started out to find their commander; and Joe Walker heard where they were heading and turned off to join them; and they got together. Bad luck it turned out that way. Looked bad. But it could be explained. It was explained. If Frémont had marched right on back to Sutter's as soon as he had joined them, everything might have been all right in spite of it."

"Didn't he?" asked Andy.

"He did not," stated Larkin emphatically.

To understand, as Andy did, what Larkin now told him of Frémont's movements, one would have to know the topography of the country. It is sufficient to say that a direct return to the Valley, and Sutter's, would have taken him east and north, his back turned to the Salinas Valley and Monterey. In place of that he marched his whole force on a wide circle, across the Santa Cruz Mountains, into the Salinas Valley, and to within seventeen miles of Monterey! And he had taken his time about it; a week for a normal day's journey!

And if this were not bad enough, he was conducting himself with an incredible arrogance.

"I warned Frémont against buying horses from anybody and everybody," said Larkin, "but evidently he paid no attention. At any rate, Sebastian Peralta—you know Peralta, a most reputable *ranchero*—thought he recognized three horses that had been stolen from him a while back, and asked Frémont for them. Frémont denied they were Peralta's. Perhaps they weren't; but he insulted Peralta and ordered him out of camp. Peralta complained to the *alcalde* at San José. The *alcalde* wrote to Frémont about it. Frémont answers—no, wait a minute, I want you should get this. I have a copy." He darted into the house, to return with a slip of paper. "Here's how he answers: 'The insult of which he complains consists in his being ordered immediately to leave camp. After having been detected in endeavoring to obtain animals by false pretenses, he should have been well satisfied to escape without a severe horsewhipping,' and he adds later that he can't be bothered appearing before any magistrate 'on the complaint of every straggling vagabond who may visit my camp.' "

"Polite cuss," observed Andy.

"And for God's sake!" cried Larkin exasperatedly, "why did he have to go out of his way to be so insulting? Here he is, in a friendly country, with an armed force, where he has no right to be. He gets permission to rest and recuperate two hundred miles away in an unsettled part of the country where he'll disturb nobody. And he comes deliberately into the most thickly settled part, and then says he's too busy to give the lawful authority any attention. And he uses conduct and language one would hardly use to a gang of genuine horse thieves, let alone a man of Peralta's standing!" He struck the arm of his chair. "And about what? Three horses! Peralta would have given him the horses if he'd asked for them! Or he could have bought any number for a few dollars at most. Unless the man is crazy or deliberately trying to provoke trouble, I cannot understand it!"*

"Perhaps he was," surmised Andy thoughtfully. "If he could get himself attacked—and hollered loud enough—"

"What's on your mind?" Larkin urged him.

"You know he's Senator Benton's son-in-law. Well—this is probably foolish—but ain't it possible the Senator's looking for a good excuse, and this feller's trying to make it? An excuse for taking over California, I mean."

"But I have very explicit instructions from the government. We've talked of that. They certainly do not jibe with any such performance as this!"

"I didn't say gov'ment," said Andy. "I said Senator Benton. When I was a kid I saw him once. Oh, yes, I told you about that! Well, from what I hear he ain't shifted his ideas. And that girl of his, from what I hear of her, is his own daughter. You heard how she held up Frémont's orders not to go on that last trip and sent him word to hustle up and get out of reach? How did that come out, anyway?"

"It raised considerable of a stink. But Benton handled it. By the time Frémont got back it was all smoothed over; and they gave him medals instead of a courtmartial."

Andy nodded. "Benton's pretty powerful then, I take it?"

"About the most powerful, I should say; at least about matters to do with the West."

"Well, there you are!"

"There I am what?" demanded Larkin impatiently.

"If you mean that Benton is resolved on the acquisition of California, I agree. Expansion westward has always been the passion, the obsession, of his whole career. But we shall have California; peacefully; with the full approval of the people. The administration has its plans all made, definite plans." He checked himself, then went on, overmastered by long-pent impatience: "I shouldn't be talking these things to you, or anybody else. But the thing is all arranged. Every navy commander on the Pacific has his orders. In case of war with Mexico they are to seize and occupy the ports. Occupy them: that's all—to keep other nations from occupying them. That's the whole idea. Then they are to use every means to conciliate the inhabitants. A land conquest would gain nothing. And if the inhabitants won't be conciliated, nothing is to be done about it for the present. That can be attended to later. If the ports are safe, there can be no trouble that can't wait. I don't know why I'm telling you these things. I ought not to. They are confidential."

Nevertheless Larkin felt no real compunction. It was a curious fact that everybody talked to Andy freely. There was something fundamentally trustworthy about the man. Vallejo had felt this same quality.

"So why," Larkin concluded, "should the government countenance

* Larkin shared that inability with future historians.

this man doing exactly the opposite?"

"I didn't say the government," Andy repeated dryly. "I said Senator Benton." He shrugged at Larkin's expression. "Go on. What's the situation?"

"That's why I sent for you. Naturally Castro sent him notice to clear out, that he must retire out of this department. I saw it; and I must say I think Castro was very restrained—for him. Frémont did not even bother to answer it in writing. He sent back word to the general effect that Castro could go to hell. Then he moved his whole force up to the top of Gavilan Peak where he's hoisted the American flag and put up breastworks. The whole country is aroused. They're mad; and I don't blame 'em. They're coming in to Castro. He has two or three hundred already. It's got me worried; worse than worried. I sent Frémont a letter telling him the people are very much surprised and excited; and I told him I thought I could fix it so that he would not be attacked if he'd pull out, and that he'd be allowed to remain if he'd behave. It would be a job, but I think I could have done it. Castro doesn't really want trouble, and sixty riflemen behind breastworks atop Gavilan would be a tough proposition. Frémont answered that 'we will fight to extremity and refuse quarter, trusting to our country to avenge our deaths.' What can you do with a man like that?"

17   The Dons of the Old Pueblo

On July 7, 1846 the American navy took possesion of Monterey and in the following weeks California was conquered with little difficulty. The truth was that most people were disenchanted with Mexico's rule and welcomed the Americans. Unfortunately, this state of affairs was rudely ended by the arrogance of some American officers. The worst of these was Captain Archibald Gillespie, referred to in the following as Gillie.

Captain Archibald Gillie, left by Stockton in command at Los Angeles, was a man whose every thought and action was regulated by a straight line. He arose at the same moment every morning, and punctually retired at the same hour every night, with religious regularity. Every hour of the day was devoted to some specific duty, and to no other. Born and raised in a little New England town, of stern old witch-burning stock, he had all their ancient narrowness but none of the facile quality of ready adaptability that has been the saving grace, in all lands and in all times, of the sons of the Puritan and Pilgrim. To him the silent, poiseful dignity of the men of the gente de razon was but the sulkiness of a conquered race, and their colorful garb but pretty childishness. Like the average man of the English-speaking world, he despised and distrusted those of a darker race, and to him there was but little distinction between the Dons in the pueblo, who proudly

From The Dons of the Old Pueblo by Percival J. Cooney. Published 1914.

traced their descent from the *conquistadores* of Cortéz, and the blanketed Indian herders from the sunburnt plains.

Much to his gratification, two of the guns concealed by Castro before his hurried flight were recovered. The former officers of Castro's little army, all residents of the pueblo, who had been in hiding at their *ranchos* in the country, returned one by one and without any objections gave their paroles not to bear arms again against the United States. In charge of the taking of the paroles, thus bringing him into touch with all the leading men of the pueblo, was Lieutenant John Carroll, formerly of the Marine Corps. Between the sensitive dignity of the people and the gruff brusqueness of Captain Gillie, Carroll's tactful personality and his command of Castilian, acquired during many years' residence in Cuba, stood always as a buffer, though of this fact the captain, with his customary obtuseness, was utterly unaware.

Gillie's first official act was the posting of a proclamation demanding the surrender of all arms and ammunition to the American authorites. Gatherings of people, either public or private, were forbidden, save where a special permit had been given. The inhabitants were warned to keep within doors after sunset, and the proclamation ended with a sweeping injunction against any "conduct prejudicial to good morals." Proclamations, however, were nothing new to the people of the pueblo. They read, smiled amiably, and went their ways much as usual.

As the captain sat at a paper-strewn table in his office in one of the rooms in the long adobe to the right of the open stockade, his tight-fitting blue jacket buttoned close, though the day was sweltering, his narrow back stiffly erect, the single lock of graying hair carefully smoothed across his bald head, he was the very embodiment of military exactitude. As he wrote, his hand plucked restlessly at his nervous underlip. Suddenly he put down his pen, glanced at his watch, and stepping to the door, spoke to the sentry:

"It is ten o'clock. Brooks, notify the sergeant to bring from the guardhouse the prisoners arrested last night."

The marine saluted, marched across the sunny square of the stockade, and in a few minutes returned with a score of prisoners. Lieutenant Carroll appeared from the next room and, pen in hand, took his place at the table. He was followed in a moment by Second Lieutenant Somers, a somber-faced man with a bushy head of ruddy hair, and a world of melancholy in his deep-set gray eyes. Here, daily, Captain Gillie, as provost marshal under military rule, disposed of the numerous cases brought before him.

Among the accused were young men who, guitar in hand, had been arrested under the windows of their señoritas; others, whose sole offense was that they had attended a family gathering for the celebration of a christening; *vaqueros* from the ranchos, absent from the pueblo for months, who had innocently ridden into town with pistols in their sashes; Indians, picked up intoxicated on the street by the provost guard; and peons, their eyes still red from last night's debauch.

Captain Gillie's interpretation of the proclamation was harsh and literal, his penalties prompt and severe. Dumb with amazement, the prisoners were led away to serve their sentences in the guardhouse of the post.

When the last of the list was disposed of, Lieutenant Carroll sat moodily silent, staring at the opposite wall and biting the ends of his heavy mustache. For some days he had been seriously considering the advisability of boldly suggesting to Captain Gillie the wisdom of modifying his stringent regulations for the governing of the pueblo. But between the hard coldness of the New Englander and Carroll's warm-hearted Celtic temperament there was not only slight sympathy but an unbridgeable chasm. Such action, moreover, would have been a most flagrant breach of military etiquette. The captain was a man who never dreamed of asking for advice, and all of Carroll's many delicately veiled suggestions had not even impinged on his consciousness. Lieutenant Somer's mournful gray eyes looked long and steadily at the captain, but he said nothing. He was a strangely silent man. During his two weeks' association with Gillie and Carroll he had never addressed them, except in regard to necessary matters of military routine.

The morning had seen but the average grist of petty offenders of the lower class, but several days before a score of the principal Dons of the pueblo had been haled before the captain's court and fined heavily for some trifling infractions of the ordinances. The fines were paid with proud promptitude, but the Californians had left the court room, their eyes flashing with rage, their lips white with suppressed indignation. That the attitude of the people toward the Americans had changed in the last ten days, Carroll was well aware. Their surly demeanor and averted glances told only too plainly that they had come to regard their conquerors with aversion and distrust.

There was trouble, too, within the stockade. With the exception of a dozen marines, the fifty men of Gillie's command were the former Bear Flag rebels; men whom the lure of the Wanderlust had drawn to this western coast; men who had fought the wild Indians of the plains, trapped the wily beaver on the lonely reaches of unnamed streams, and faced death in a hundred forms in distant mountain cañons. Poor material were they for the rigid military discipline so dear to the captain's heart. His efforts to impress them had been to him a long-drawn agony and to the men a roaring farce. When off duty they were to be found in the low dives and wine shops in Nigger Alley at the southeast corner of the plaza, and hardly a day passed but a dozen or more were dragged, fighting furiously or soddenly stupid, to the guardhouse in the stockade.

Carroll knew something of the Spanish character, its capacity for patient endurance, its easy indolence, and its unspoken contempt for the man of unnecessarily violent speech and action. As he stepped out into the morning sunshine the sound of a roaring, drunken chorus came to him from the direction of the plaza, and he sighed wearily.

As if in echo to his own unspoken thoughts there drifted to him, through an open window across the stockade, the strident voice of Jim Marshall.

"I tell ye, fellahs, the captain don't understand the greasers none,—he don't understand nuthin' but orders. Spanish folks ain't much on startin' a stand-up fight, but they is sure bad medicine if ye rub them the wrong way long enough. If this 'ere thing keeps on, thar'll be hell apoppin' in this old pueblo inside of a month. Good-by, fellahs, I'm goin'!"

18 The Battle of San Pasqual

The battle of San Pasqual was the only significant battle fought in California during the Mexican War and its results are so much a matter of controversy that the following fictional account is as accurate as any other. Brigadier General Stephen Watts Kearny, marching overland after conquering New Mexico, learned that California had been won. This force was mounted on recently acquired horses and mules which were not properly trained. Then too, the Americans went into battle with their ammunition wet. As a consequence they had to rely on the sabre against the lance of the superbly mounted Californios. The result was that twenty Americans were killed to a single Californio in the only battle the United States lost in the Mexican War.

General Kearney and Lieutenant Beale walked rapidly up and down before the tents of the wretched remnant of United States troops with which the former had arrived overland in California. It was bitterly cold in spite of the fine drizzling rain. Lonely buttes studded the desert, whose palms and cacti seemed to spring from the rocks; high in one of them was the American camp. On the other side of a river flowing at the foot of the butte, the white tents of the Californians were scattered among the dark huts of the little pueblo of San Pasqual.

"Let me implore you, General," said Beale, "not to think of meeting Andres Pico. Why, your men are half starved; your few horses are broken-winded; your mules are no match for the fresh trained mustangs of the enemy. I am afraid you do not appreciate the Californians. They are numerous, brave, and desperate. If you avoid them now, as Commodore Stockton wishes, and join him at San Diego, we stand a fair chance of defeating them. But now Pico's cavalry and foot are fresh and enthusiastic—in painful contrast to yours. And, moreover, they know every inch of the ground."

Kearney impatiently knocked the ashes out of his pipe. He had little regard for Stockton, and no intention of being dictated to by a truculent young lieutenant who spoke his mind upon all occasions.

"I shall attack them at daybreak," he said curtly. "I have one hundred

From The Splendid Idle Forties by Gertrude Atherton. Published 1902.

and thirty good men; and has not Captain Gillespie joined me with his battalion? Never shall it be said that I turned aside to avoid a handful of boasting Californians. Now go and get an hour's sleep before we start."

The young officer shrugged his shoulders, saluted, and walked down the line of tents. A man emerged from one of them, and he recognized Russell.

"Hello, Ned," he said. "How's the arm?"

"'Twas only a scratch. Is Altimira down there with Pico, do you know? He is a brave fellow! I respect that man; but we have an account to settle, and I hope it will be done on the battle-field."

"He is with Pico, and he has done some good fighting. Most of the Californians have. They know how to fight and they are perfectly fearless. Kearney will find it out to-morrow. He is mad to attack them. Why, his men are actually cadaverous. Bueno! as they say here; Stockton sent me to guide him to San Diego. If he prefers to go through the enemy's lines, there is nothing for me to do but take him."

"Yes, but we may surprise them. I wish to God this imitation war were over!"

"It will be real enough before you get through. Don't worry. Well, good night. Luck to your skin."

At daybreak the little army marched down the butte, shivering with cold, wet to the skin. Those on horseback naturally proceeded more rapidly than those mounted upon the clumsy stubborn mules; and Captain Johnson, who led the advance guard of twelve dragoons, found himself, when he came in sight of the enemy's camp, some distance ahead of the main body of Kearney's small army. To his surprise he saw that the Californians were not only awake, but horsed and apparently awaiting him. Whether he was fired by valour or desperation at the sight is a disputed point; but he made a sudden dash down the hill and across the river, almost flinging himself upon the lances of the Californians.

Captain Moore, who was ambling down the hill on an old white horse at the head of fifty dragoons mounted on mules, spurred his beast as he witnessed the foolish charge of the advance, and arrived upon the field in time to see Johnson fall dead and to take his place. Pico, seeing that reinforcements were coming, began to retreat, followed hotly by Moore and the horsed dragoons. Suddenly, however, Fernando Altimira raised himself in his stirrups, looked back, laughed and galloped across the field to General Pico.

"Look!" he said. "Only a few men on horses are after us. The mules are stumbling half a mile behind."

Pico wheeled about, gave the word of command, and bore down upon the Americans. Then followed a hand-to-hand conflict, the Californians lancing and using their pistols with great dexterity, the Americans doing the best they could with their rusty sabres and clubbed guns.

They were soon reinforced by Moore's dragoons and Gillespie's battalion, despite the unwilling mules; but the brutes kicked and bucked at every pistol shot and fresh cloud of smoke. The poor old horses wheezed and panted, but stood their ground when not flung out of position by the frantic mules. The officers and soldiers of the United States army were a sorry sight, and in pointed contrast to the graceful Californians on their groomed steeds, handsomely trapped, curvetting and rearing and prancing as lightly as if on the floor of a circus. Kearney cursed his own stupidity, and Pico laughed in his face. Beale felt satisfaction and compunction in saturating the silk and silver of one fine saddle with the blood of its owner. The point of the dying man's lance pierced his face, but he noted the bleaching of Kearney's, as one dragoon after another was flung upon the sharp rocks over which his bewildered brute stumbled, or was caught and held aloft in the torturing arms of the cacti.

On the edge of the battle two men had forgotten the Aztec Eagle and the Stars and Stripes; they fought for love of a woman. Neither had had time to draw his pistol; they fought with lance and sabre, thrusting and parrying. Both were skilful swordsmen, but Altimira's horse was far superior to Russell's, and he had the advantage of weapons.

"One or the other die on the rocks," said the Californian, "and if I kill you, I marry Benicia."

Russell made no reply. He struck aside the man's lance and wounded his wrist. But Altimira was too excited to feel pain. His face was quivering with passion.

It is not easy to parry a lance with a sabre, and still more difficult to get close enough to wound the man who wields it. Russell rose suddenly in his stirrups, described a rapid half-circle with his weapon, brought it down midway upon the longer blade, and snapped the latter in two. Altimira gave a cry of rage, and spurring his horse sought to ride his opponent down; but Russell wheeled, and the two men simultaneously snatched their pistols from the holsters. Altimira fired first, but his hand was unsteady and his ball went through a cactus. Russell raised his pistol with firm wrist, and discharged it full in the face of the Californian.

Then he looked over the field. Moore, fatally lanced, lay under a palm, and many of his men were about him. Gillespie was wounded, Kearney had received an ugly thrust. The Californians, upon the arrival of the main body of the enemy's troops, had retreated unpursued; the mules attached to one of the American howitzers were scampering over to the opposite ranks, much to the consternation of Kearney. The sun, looking over the mountain, dissipated the gray smoke, and cast a theatrical light on the faces of the dead. Russell bent over Altimira. His head was shattered, but his death was avenged. Never had an American troop suffered a more humiliating defeat. Only one Californian lay on the field; and when the American surgeon, after attending to his own wounded, offered his services to Pico's, that indomitable general haughtily replied that he had none.

Chapter 4

Gold

Gold

As Professor John Walton Caughey has so ably put it, "gold is the cornerstone of California." It was gold which triggered one of the greatest migrations in the history of man. The mass influx of people between 1848 and 1860 pushed California's population from 14,000 to 300,000. The gold rush brought instant statehood (without territorial status) and the triumph of Anglo values over those of the native Californio. Without the magnet of gold the Golden State would have experienced the slow but steady growth of Oregon or New Mexico, but quite possibly would not have become the leading state on the Pacific coast. Without the populace drawn by gold, it is also hard to imagine the building of the transcontinental railroad in the 1860s and its ultimate location. And without the great wealth found in the gold fields, California would not have symbolized the place where the great American dream of success could be fulfilled.

Nowhere else in the world has so much gold been laid out for the taking—and take it the Argonauts did! In the halcyon years of 1848, 1849, and 1850 many participated in the mad scramble for gold and many were successful. One lump of gold found near Sonoma weighed twenty-eight pounds. The first five prospectors in the Yuba River area made $75,000 in three months. A boy of fourteen cleared $3400 in a few weeks mining. Most unskilled miners averaged $30 a day in the first three years of mining—at a time when skilled laborers in California were lucky to be earning $3.00 a day. Such earnings and the dream of "striking it rich" prompted men to endure the physical drudgery of mining.

By the end of 1848 miners were prospecting from the Feather River to the Tuolumne River along the western slope of the Sierra, and by 1850 there was hardly a canyon or small valley in central California that didn't have a miners' camp. The area known as the "Mother Lode" began north of Sutter's Mill and continued as far south as Mariposa. The term possibly originated from the reference of Spanish-speaking miners to the *veta madre*. It rested upon the assumption that there was one great vein from which all of the gold originally came. As the Mother Lode country was the first to be mined, the name has become synonymous with the gold mining region. However, some of the richest mines were north of the Mother Lode in Nevada, Placer, and Sierra counties. An important but separate gold field was located north and west of the Sacramento Valley. In this area streams such as the Klamath, Trinity, Shasta, and other tributaries were the locales of productive mines.

The gold rush period of California was characterized by constant change as new fields were discovered. There was a stampede to each new area, the hasty building of a tent city followed by the erection of more durable buildings, and the influx of a large number of people. When initial high hopes were dashed, there was a rush to greener pastures and the process was repeated. Dame Shirley lamented: "Our countrymen are the most discontented of mortals. They are always longing for 'big strikes!' If a claim is paying them a steady income, by which, if they pleased, they could lay up more in a month, than they could accumulate in a year at home, still, they are dissatisfied, and, in most cases, will wander off in search of better 'diggings.' "

19 The Lure of Gold

At first there was no great rush to the gold fields because the discovery was new to the American scene—nothing like it had ever happened before. As late as May 1848 (gold had been discovered around January 14, 1848) a San Francisco newspaper saw nothing in news of the discovery, stating "a few fools have hurried to the American River, but you may be sure there is nothing in it." But by the end of the month ships were abandoned by their sailors and shops by their owners as a mad stampede to the gold fields began. Once President Polk made the discovery official in his message to Congress in December 1848, gold fever seized men throughout the country. The following selection tells what happened to a family in one Ohio town afflicted with gold fever; it was a scene repeated the length and breadth of the land. Note that the men were drawn to the adventure within the framework of American tradition while the women rebelled at leaving the world they knew. Many miners came to California as members of the kind of company described.

Until the discovery of gold ours had been an ordered household and the town in which we lived a quiet, regulated, unhurried community. I don't recall that there had even been many political differences, since almost everyone was antislavery and most favored the Mexican War.

But it seemed that an unseen force erupted from the center of the earth, changing men and women overnight from their contented daily norm to a fevered restlessness.

Several of the young unmarried men took off for the East seeking ships to take them to the gold fields, but for the most part the town's imagination was caught up in George Muller's gold company.

Our shop printed up the stock certificates. I came in to find Old Ike running them off carefully from the plates he had laboriously carved. They weren't fancy, just sheets of stiff, coated paper printed with black ink. They showed a miner with a pick on his shoulder, and the fine print stated that in

From *Gold in California* by Todhunter Ballard. Copyright © 1965 by Todhunter Ballard. Reprinted by permission of Doubleday & Company, Inc.

return for ten dollars the holder was granted a one thousandth interest in the gold discovered by the Clinton Mining Company.

The company had been organized the week before, with my uncle as president and George Muller manager. Their purpose was to raise ten thousand dollars, the sum to be used to outfit a party of ten volunteers who would be sent westward to the gold country.

These ten were to keep one half of the gold they found. The other half was to be shipped east and divided among the investors. It was also understood that any investor who chose, after the company was established, would be free to go west himself and take his place in the diggings.

To cinch his argument George Muller had built a mining machine. He had gotten the idea from his uncle who had done some mining in Georgia. It was an ingenious affair with a screen to take out the larger rocks, and a tray beneath it, mounted on leather straps, which was moved back and forth in a small tank of water by means of an eccentric and a hand crank.

Ike shut off the press and slowly filled his pipe.

"What do you think of them, Austin?" He indicated the pile of still damp stock certificates with a wave of the pipe stem.

"They're right pretty," I said.

"Um."

"Don't you think so? You made the plates."

"Best I could do with what I had. Still, I don't cotton much to the idea."

"What's wrong with it?"

He took time to light the pipe. "Well, several things. First off, who are the ten men they're going to send?"

I hadn't heard. After that first meeting at our house the group had gathered at George Muller's, and neither Dave nor Tommy had been able to listen in.

"Second, how they going to make certain them fellows will send back that half of the gold?"

I didn't know that either.

"Third, how they going to get there?"

I had the answer to that one. I mentioned the eight routes across the country, naming the mountain passes.

Ike grunted. "I went out to Santa Fe in thirty-one and it was a rough trip, and the men I was with knew what they was doing. There ain't no one in this town who does. And the trail north of that, the one the folks for Oregon have been using, is a lot worse from all I hear."

"Then you aren't going?"

He grunted again. "Oh, I'll probably go, when I have a mind. But then I never did have much sense nohow."

I heard my aunt saying almost the same thing that night at dinner. Relations between her and my uncle had become more strained each day as the agitation for the trek increased.

"I simply cannot understand you," she said as she placed the boiled dinner on the table. "Here you have about the best house in town. And the county newspaper. You are looked up to and respected, and why you should lend your name to anything as wild as this scheme of George Muller's is beyond me."

Uncle Ben was spreading freshly churned butter on a thick slice of new bread. He laid the knife and the bread down on the red-checkered tablecloth.

"Please, let's not discuss it in front of the children."

"They're going to know soon enough. I was talking to Rebel and Ephraim this afternoon. They are very concerned."

My uncle said dryly, "Your brothers live in a state of constant concern. They are a little conservative, don't you think?"

"If you call showing good sound sense being conservative, they certainly are. As they point out it was rather absurd for us to take California in the first place, and perfectly idiotic to think that people will want to stay in that Godforsaken land once they have dug up all the gold."

My uncle picked up his bread slowly. He spoke mildly but I was not deceived, he always spoke mildly when he was making a telling point.

"I seem to remember that your grandfather came out to Virginia with the shirt on his back and no baggage."

Aunt Emeline flushed. "What's that to do with it?"

"And your father came over the mountains, settled first in Kentucky and then moved on up here."

"So?"

"If your grandfather had stayed in England where would you be? If your father had stuck there in Virginia where he owned not one acre of ground what would you and your brothers have now?"

"But they didn't."

"So"—Uncle Ben leaned forward—"let's not let the spirit of adventure die in two generations. There's a lot of interesting land between here and California, but before Austin dies most of it will be filled up."

"Now I know you are insane. And about this gold company: Who are the ten men you intend to send?"

"We haven't chosen them yet."

"And what makes you think that if they find any gold at all they will ship it three thousand miles back here?"

He looked up at her then and I saw a look on his face that I had never seen there before, a tight strain.

"We've taken care of that. It was decided this afternoon. George and I are going with them."

Goose pimples raised the hair on my arms, but before I could let out a whoop the sudden chill silence of the room stabbed me. Then came Aunt Emeline's long, ragged gasp.

"Ben Garner. You don't mean it."

My uncle bowed his head. "I certainly do."

She sat in a state of shock, unable to find the words she needed, the words which were trying to thrust out of her.

"You would go away and leave me?"

He looked at her, harried. "I am not leaving you. I'll send for you and the children as soon as we get established, as soon as I find a proper place for you to live."

She rose and left the table and the room. Later I heard her crying in the darkness of her bedroom. Caroline heard it too. Caroline came and crawled into bed with me. Her nightgown crept up to her skinny knees and her feet were like lumps of ice as she pressed them against mine.

"Austin, I'm scared."

I was scared too, but I couldn't admit it to a seven-year-old girl.

"What are you scared of, sissy?"

I knew, although I did not know the proper words at the time. She was scared for her security, of the crumbling of the family structure which had made us immune to the doubts and fears that harassed some of the kids we knew.

My uncle had gone downtown, and when he came back I heard his feet on the uncarpeted stairs. Caroline had gone to sleep in my arms. I could feel the bones of her thin body through the flannel gown. I knew that she was not supposed to be in bed with me. My aunt had not let us sleep in the same bed for the last three years, but I didn't want to make any noise.

My uncle's steps were uncertain and he bumped into the doorjamb as he turned into the main bedroom. I heard the scratch of the match and saw the quick light reflected in the hall, and heard my aunt's horrified voice.

"You've been drinking."

I couldn't make out the mumbled answer at first, then he said, "It's enough to make a man want to drink, Emeline, when his wife sets herself against him."

"Ben."

"It's something I've got to do, Emmy." His voice broke and I knew that he was crying, and that was as great a shock to me as anything else. "You've got to understand, Emmy. I wasn't meant to just sit here all my life and write how many hogs Silas Appleby raised, or how Mrs. Sommers won the prize at the church supper."

"Ben Garner."

"Please understand. I'm thirty-one, Emmy, and I've never been anywhere or seen anything."

"Let's talk about it in the morning."

"No. I've got to talk about it now."

"I've never seen you drunk before. What will I tell the ladies at the . . ."

"To hell with the temperance women."

Silence.

"I sold the paper. Sold it to Malcolm Reed."

"You didn't."

"I did. We went to Fellow's saloon and sealed the bargain. He's going to take over the first of February."

She began to cry again. I heard him trying to sooth her. Then he blew out the light and I heard him try to comfort her, but the sobs continued until I went to sleep.

In the morning Aunt Emeline was unusually silent, but by then I hardly noticed. I couldn't wait to get to school and spread the news. My uncle Ben was going to California and so was I, as soon as he found us a home there.

By the time the bell rang I had the whole place in an uproar. Dave and Tommy Muller resented the attention I was getting, claiming rightly that their father had originated the idea of sending a company of men West, but nobody really listened to them.

After school I raced to the print shop, expecting to find Old Ike as excited as I was. Instead he looked as if the press had just fallen apart.

"What's the matter with you?"

He rubbed the side of his head with an ink-stained hand, leaving black streaks across his ear.

"Your uncle shouldn't have done it."

"Say he was going to California?"

"No. Sold his paper. Some of the men who pledged money to the gold company are already backing out."

I stared at him, stunned. "But why?"

"Your aunt's brothers. They've been busying around town all day, talking to one man after another. They're calling it a golden bubble, hollering that it's going to bust."

"But what for?"

Ike looked both ways to make sure he wasn't overheard.

"Your aunt," he said, "she doesn't want your uncle to go."

"I know that, but . . ."

"So she's got her brothers doing everything they can to stop him."

"Nobody listened to them before."

"They wasn't really fighting it then, just being cautious. But they're the bankers. They got a mortgage on about half the houses in this town, and most of the businessmen owe them money. And when you owe a man money you'd maybe better heed him."

This was a new idea to me, the power of money.

I said, "That's a mean trick."

"Don't you ever tell your uncle," he warned.

"Why not, if it's a mean trick?"

"You ain't old enough to understand," he said. "Women got their own method of doing things, their own way of figuring what's right and wrong. Ain't one woman in a thousand thinks her husband has got real good sense. They connive to catch a man and once they got him they ain't satisfied with the way he is. They can't leave him the way the good Lord made him, they got to plump for an alteration job." . . .

I didn't tell my uncle what the Wards were doing, but it wasn't surprising that he found out. Very little goes on in a town the size of ours that most people don't know about shortly.

It happened three nights later. I'd been out milking the cow and feeding old Jimmy, our carriage horse. It had been a warm day and the snow had nearly vanished. I went through the back porch and into the summer kitchen. In winter my aunt used this for a cold room, since there was no heat, and the milk crocks were lined up before the tin bathtub which we used only during the summer months.

I had begun to fill the crocks from the bucket of warm milk that steamed lightly in the chill air. I heard them come into the kitchen from the dining room. Caroline was spending the night with one of her friends and I suppose they thought I was still in the barn.

"Why did you do it to me?" It was the first thing I heard my uncle say. "How could you do such a thing behind my back?"

My aunt's tone was too low to hear but I realized that something terrible was the matter. Uncle Ben sounded like a small child, not angry but hurt, puzzled, completely unbelieving and bewildered.

"Everyone in town is laughing at me."

"Ben"—I now had no difficulty in hearing her—"you are acting like a fool."

"Sure, he said bitterly. "Your two brothers have gone from one end of the county to the other telling everyone that I am a fool. So why shouldn't I act like one? Tell me why?"

"You'll thank them and me once you've had time to think it over."

"I'm not going to have time."

"What do you mean by that?"

"I'm going to California. I said I would and I am going."

"You can't go. Why, everyone has deserted that crazy company, everyone but George Muller."

"That makes no difference. I am going." I heard him cross the kitchen and pull open the back door.

"Ben, if you leave this house . . ."

She did not say what would happen. She didn't have the chance for he slammed the door and I heard his boots as he stamped away.

He didn't come home until late. My Aunt Emeline fed me in stony silence. I don't know whether or not she knew that I had overheard them. I ate rapidly and then ducked up the back stairs to my room. For a long time I heard her moving around in the kitchen below me, and then the house grew still.

20 The California Dream

Most of the Argonauts made their way overland to California simply because it was the cheapest and most convenient way to go. They assembled at Independence, Missouri and formed wagon trains for the

five-month, 2,000-mile journey to the land of promise. The following
selection stresses the way in which the average citizen had been
captivated by the dream of California and its gold. Young men like
Christopher Strange were buoyed up by the image of this new land so
they could endure the hardships of the journey westward. But for those
who created a fantasy-land, the actual California must have been a bitter
disappointment.

Left to mount guard over the household goods and baggage just
unloaded from the river steamer at the landing for Independence,
Christopher stood with his back to the morning sun and looked down
the muddy road that was taking the other members of the Bascom
Company. How out of place they looked in their city clothes, he
thought, and smiled to observe that even Susie, the misanthropic
Bascom cow, gave the impression of being too gently reared for this raw
land.

A chorus of shouts made him whirl on his heel toward the river.
The steamer had shoved away from the landing and was pushing its
blunt nose upstream. Those passengers whose rendezvous was St Joseph
or Council Bluffs were screaming their farewells to him. He pulled off
his hat and waved it, shouting, "Good-by! Good luck! See you in
California!"

Just saying the words made his blood leap. *This* was the real
beginning of adventure, here where all was new and strange, where
civilized modes of travel ended. On this last frontier between East and
West, between known and unknown, he had a sense of solemnity warred
on by growing excitement. Ahead of him lay a journey, probably a
perilous journey, and he whose life had been singularly free from physical
perils knew a sudden eagerness to encounter them. He would live through
all hazards; he would live for a thousand years!

And after the journey? California! His face grew rapt at the word.
Absent-mindedly he dropped down on one of Mrs. Bascom's flour
barrels, regardless of the mark it would leave on his black coattails.
California! The word had a bell's tonality. Fit name for a fabulous land,
a land that had given rise to legends before it had been seen. A bare
century since men—Spaniards, English adventurers, Russians—hoped to
find there that elusive Strait of Anian; two centuries ago and were not
the conquistadors seeking California as a curious island inhabited by
Amazons, the streets paved with gold? And now was the reality of
California any less fabulous than the dream of it? Where else, except
California, in this humdrum modern world could a penniless young
man seek and also find fortune—perhaps honor and glory, too—as
miraculously as the youngest son of the fairy tales?

The doctor told him how Stephen J. Field, brother of the renowned
Eastern jurist, had reached California late in 1849 with ten dollars in his

pocket and how less than a week later that enterprising young man found himself magistrate, or *alcalde*, and foremost citizen of a thriving town that had not been in existence when he arrived in the state. Where but in California could such a thing happen?

Christopher's shoulders drooped. But if such an opportunity presented itself to me, could I grasp it? Would I not be far more likely to blush miserably and flee from the honor, fearing my lack of experience and wisdom? Surely somewhere between arrogance and timidity there is self-reliance, but I miss it forever and ever, shifting from one extreme to the other! No longer conscious of his surroundings or of the loiterers who were eying him with mild curiosity, he flung out one arm in an involuntary, broad gesture of despair. His lips moved silently. Practically twenty years of life and so little to show for them. I've been deaf to "Time's winged chariot drawing near." I've squandered my youth on daydreaming, on pointless musings. My father's dreams lead to virtue and truth, for he is a philosopher. I am not; therefore, dreams are my nemesis. I shall dream no more! I will be a man of action!

The loiterers had come closer, and their interest was rapidly growing, but for Christopher they had no substance: he looked through them at a vision of himself rising in a rough frontier court to champion the wronged. It was characteristic of him that in his fancy he was invariably the attorney for the defense, never for the prosecution.

"Hi! Christopher!" The doctor's roar echoed over the river, shattering the boy's dream. "Come out of your trance and give us a hand!"

Christopher leaped to his feet, his earns burning, aware now of the small group of grinning, bearded onlookers. How had the big covered wagon with its six-mule team come up behind him without his noticing it? He rushed at the labor of loading, pulling and lifting and shoving at the barrels, chests, mattresses and boxes belonging to the small company, working with such fury that the doctor was led to remonstrate, "No need to kill yourself, my boy! We've most of the day ahead of us, and we'll overtake the others before they've reached Independence."

The loading finished, Christopher climbed up beside the doctor on the high seat of the covered wagon. Fourteen-year-old Peter Bascom proudly bestrode the black horse his father had bought that morning. The doctor gathered the lines into his hand and yelled to the mules. As they lunged forward he burst into a fragment of song,

> *"Oh, I'm off to California*
> *With my washbowl on my knee!"*

"California!" said Christopher in a hushed voice. " 'The very word is like a bell!' "

"Huh?" ejaculated the doctor, startled. "Oh!" He shot a quizzical glance at his companion. "And how does the word 'San Francisco' strike you?"

Christopher turned an unseeing gaze toward the doctor, his eyes dazzled with the vision of his dreaming. "It is a city of hills over blue water," he said slowly. "Seven hills—Rome had seven hills, but Rome is dying, and San Francisco is just born. I can see the way the moist, chill wind from the sea curls fog about those hills and sends tendrils of mist up the long arms of that great bay. The new city is quickened with the sea wind and shielded by the ribbons of fog, and it sends up gleaming spires, white, tall reachings into the sky, catching the sun above the mists; and all the nations of the earth come seeking fortune through the gateways of that city veiled in mist, where the bells of St. Francis sound muted and sweet."

The doctor pushed his hat back on his head and gaped at the speaker. "You're crazy!" he muttered after a dazed silence. "You're raving! Listen to me, and take in a few *facts* about San Francisco! It's got seven hills all right! They get in the way of every street you try to run through the city. There's wind, plenty of it, knocking the poor, stunted trees flat against the hills, blowing sand in your eyes. There's fog, more than you'll like. But where in creation do you get the idea of white spires reaching skyward? It's *raw, crude*, with most of the buildings shacks. We have fires a couple of times a year that turn the whole place to ashes. Then they build again overnight, flimsy contraptions that burn like kindling in a few months. The people are mostly roistering, swaggering youngsters, ready to shoot at the drop of a hat. Sunday is a day of gambling, music-hall entertainment, bull and bear fighting, whoring. When I left you could count on nine out of every ten women you saw on the streets being prostitutes. You're crazy as a loon! You're seeing mirages before you've reached the right spot to be seeing them."

Christopher looked steadily over the backs of the mules into the distant West. "She's a young city yet, sir," he said with self-conscious diffidence, feeling that he had been a fool to let go that way to the doctor. "She's been badly treated, but she's got beauty and enchantment in her that nothing can kill. I know it!"

"Mirage!" said the doctor and shook his head pityingly. "And one of the things you can count on with those things is that whatever you see reflected in a mirage is a hundred per cent more beautiful in the mirage than it is in reality. You see a broad river, clear and shining like silver with trees beside it, and the whole thing keeps ahead of you, however fast your travel, till suddenly it vanishes. Then later you may come on the stream responsible for that mirage, and it'll be a muddy mess full of mosquitoes, with a scant growth of scrub and willow on its banks." He lifted the reins and clucked to the mules. "I'll be happy to know what you feel when you see the real city of San Francisco," he remarked dryly.

21 San Francisco in '49

The Argonauts who came by sea first saw California when they landed at San Francisco, "Baghdad by the Bay." Its picturesque setting enchanted the new arrivals, but its crudity and squalor repelled them. Overnight this sleepy Mexican village became a bustling metropolis crowded with people en route to, or returning from, the mines. But an even greater number located in San Francisco to handle the goods shipped from all over the world to be sold to the miners, or to serve the needs of the miners, real or fancied. Virtually all of those who came through San Francisco described this most unusual of American cities. The following is one account.

Nothing in the history of America since its discovery has equalled the magic by which the city of San Francisco grew in the single year 1849 from a handful of tents or slight structures of wood and cloth sheltering perhaps a thousand people to a commercial metropolis covering miles of territory, with blocks of substantial buildings, and containing a population of thirty thousand souls. As seen from the deck of the steamer by Linn Halstead, in the early sunlight of a bright May morning, the embryo city presented a most unique and picturesque appearance; but it was that of a temporary encampment rather than of a permanent settlement. One brick store, a score of adobe buildings, a hundred frame houses, and a confused jumble of tents, shanties, huts and makeshifts of every description were scattered for a mile along the shore of the cove. From here they were just beginning to climb the sandy hill-sides beyond it, and to push straggling arms into the hollows between them. The frame buildings were the merest shells, with inner walls, ceilings, and partitions of tightly stretched white muslin or brown calico. More than one half of the business establishments were simply sheds of rough boards, with canvas roofs, and open in front. In these a couple of planks laid across barrels formed the counters; the proprietors lived and slept amid the promiscuous assortment of goods heaped behind them, and every available inch of exterior space was covered with flaming advertisements, that would have shamed a circus poster, of what was to be found within. Two or three streets, or rather roads, ran parallel to the bay, and a dozen more had been laid out at right angles to them. In many cases these had been cut into the hill-sides ten or twelve feet below the original surface of the slope, so that the houses lining them could only be reached by ladders.

The city could as yet boast no wharves, and the steamer's passengers, with their baggage, were landed by small boats directly on the beach. Here Thurston left his partner seated on Moore's tool-chest to look out for their effects, while he went into the town, which during his six weeks of absence had changed almost beyond his recognition, to hunt up old friends and a boarding place.

From *The Golden Days of '49* by Kirk Munroe. Published 1889.

As Linn sat there he gazed about him in curious bewilderment. On all sides were hurrying, excited throngs of people, representing more nationalities than were ever before assembled within a similar limit of space. There were Americans from every State and Territory in the Union. The cleanly shaved individual, dressed in broadcloth and just arrived from New York, jostled the tangle-bearded, long-haired miner, fierce of aspect and loud of voice, just in from the diggings, and clad in tattered flannel, shirt, and buckskin, but perhaps counting his dollars by the thousand, while the new-comer had expended his last cent in getting there. Excited Frenchmen, phlegmatic Germans, swarthy Spaniards smoking cigarettes, blue-eyed Scandinavians, pig-tailed Chinamen, Kanakas from the Sandwich Islands, Mexicans wearing gay serapes, Peruvians and Chilians with their heads thrust through brown llama wool ponchos, burly Englishmen, canny Scotchmen, convicts from Australia, devil-may-care sons of the Emerald Isle, Italians, Greeks, and Portuguese—all were there, drawn from the remotest corners of the earth by the irresistible attraction of the golden magnet.

Halstead wondered, as he listened to the medley of voices that rose from this human pot-pourri, if the confusion of tongues about the Tower of Babel could have been any greater.

Each man in the throng was too intent upon his own affairs to take notice of his neighbors, and all were hurrying, perspiring, and working, as though conscious that they had a city to build, and that it would be as well to complete the job that day if possible. Every now and then a pistol shot rang out from one or another of the numerous drinking and gambling dens that seemed to occupy some part of nearly every other establishment in the town, and perhaps a bullet would whistle over the heads of those in the street. New-comers would duck instinctively; but the old residents, who had been there a month or so, paid no more attention to such trifles than they would to the hum of a mosquito. A temporary excitement would be created by the reckless dashing through the crowd of some drunken, yelling, pistol-firing horseman, or of a wild steer just escaped from its corral; but it would quickly subside as the former either broke his neck or came to grief in some other way, and the latter, captured by lariat-swinging vaqueros, was dragged off to slaughter.

In many of the vacant spaces near him Linn saw the booths of coffee, pie, and cake venders, at which newly arrived miners were eagerly drinking coffee at half a dollar a cup, or buying pies at a dollar apiece. He also became interested in a rude stand constructed from two boxes and a board, at which newspapers published in the principal Eastern cities two months before were selling readily at a dollar and in some cases at two dollars each. This sight suggested an idea to him. Why should not he begin at once to accumulate his fortune? He remembered that all the vacant space in the chest on which he was sitting was stuffed with newspapers to keep the tools in place and prevent their rattling about.

Stimulated by the excitement and bustle about him, to think was to act, and in less than five minutes Linn had smoothed out the twenty or more papers of various dates that he had found in the chest, and was established in business as a San Francisco merchant. In less than five minutes more he had sold one New York paper of a later date than any in the stock of his rival for two dollars, and several others at from half a dollar to a dollar each. At the end of half an hour, when Thurston returned, his partner had sold out his entire stock of goods, and retired from business with a fortune of sixteen dollars in his pocket. He had also received and promptly refused an offer of $500 for his chest of tools. In doing so he had considered that such an offer probably meant that they were worth much more than that sum, and also that in the undertaking upon which he and his partner had embarked tools might be even more valuable to them than money.

22 The Big Strike

Throughout history man has sought precious metals. The seeking of gold and its final discovery remains one of his most exciting activities. Many individuals are more enthralled with the search for gold than they are with what it will buy. In its pursuit, home, family, and established businesses have been abandoned. This selection depicts the reaction of two boys when they (as frequently happened) accidentally make the big strike.

The sun rose high overhead, and we thought we ought to start back to camp. But we sat down a second to rest up and fix my slingshot, which had become unraveled from the forks. It was pleasant here, no lessons to learn, no chores around the house, not even any dirt shoveling for a change, and we made a bargain that we'd never go back to school, ever. If they started to put us back, we'd run off and go to sea, knowing considerable about the water from living on the rivers. Then I said I'd like to see my mother sometime. He fell silent at this, and I felt bad I'd said it, because I knew he was thinking about his folks.

I stared at the opposite side of the creek bed, where the sun was brightest, and spoke up: "That's funny."

"What?"

"Those glints in the wall. It almost looks like—" I got up and went over. "Holy, jumping Jerusalem!" My head spun around so I got almost faint, out of excitement.

There were crevices there that had hunks of gold, solid gold, in them, as big as marbles. They were all up and down as far as you could

From *The Travels of Jamie McPheeters* by Robert Lewis Taylor. Copyright 1958 by the author. Reprinted by permission of Robert Lewis Taylor.

see, in streaks that ran slantwise from nearly the top to the bottom.

"I never seen anything like it," the boy said. "What do you suppose we ought to do?"

"We'd better fetch the others as fast as we can, before somebody comes along and grabs it. You go, and I'll stand guard. Here, take these hunks, tell them to drop all holds."

I was so nervous, I could hardly get the words out.

As soon as he left, running as hard as he could, I examined the bed in both directions, to see how far the vein went. There was gold plain to the naked eye on around the next bend, thirty yards or so, and no telling how much more farther on. It was a wild and woolly section of country, nothing that the average miner might be attracted to. That is, there were no promising ravines or gullies, and the total absence of water would discourage you from trying anyway. It was desert, and pretty far out, too. Still, you never could tell.

My heart was bumping around again, knocking up against my liver and my lungs, I was in such a sweat to get staked out. I hadn't any pencil, no chalk, nothing. There wasn't even a piece of slate to scratch on bark with.

So, to keep busy, I tried gouging out nuggets with the handle of my slingshot. I got two or three, but it was mighty slow going. What I needed was a metal thing like a spoon or a knife, and I'd mislaid my knife, confound the luck.

It should take an hour before Todd got back. By and by, worn out for the moment, I sat down to think things over, and then I heard something, clumpety-clump, a whole scattering of beats, off to the left, toward the high mountains. And when I ran over, keeping down, to peer through some weeds at the top, sure enough, it was a party of horsemen, five altogether, ugly and rough-looking, too.

I was so sick, I wanted to cry.

"Hold up!" I heard the first one cry, reining in with a jerk. "Have a look in the creek bed for water, Phelps. The horses is lathered up to the busting point."

My palms were so wet I could hardly hang onto the rocks. I believe if I'd had a gun, I'd a shot him.

The others hauled in their mounts, raising a cloud of dust, and the second man, the one called Phelps, said, "There ain't any water over this entire stretch. You could drill to China and raise nothing but sweat for your pains."

"Let's push on," said another. "It couldn't be over three or four miles at the outside."

"Well, I don't like it," said the first man. "Horses don't grow on trees, and I laid out fifty dollars for this one."

"You mean *some*body did," one of them said, and everybody but the first man laughed. He looked sore for a second, then yanked his horse's head around with an oath, and they clattered off.

"I hung on, feeling dizzy. It was about the closest call I could remember, and the most luck we'd had in a long time.

Half an hour later I heard another commotion, downstream, and this time it was my father and the others. They were half running and half walking, beat out but all a-twitter. The raggedy tails of my father's black coat streamed away behind, and he held his hat on with one hand while carrying a light pick in the other. Mr. Kissel had an armful of tools, and so did Uncle Ned.

"My boy," cried my father when he saw me, "is it true? Is it Golconda? Out of the mouths of babes and sucklings—"

He was all but babbling in his excitement, and his voice sounded odd-pitched, high and thin.

"For God's sake," I said—something my mother would have boxed my ears for—"cut out the yammering and get some claim signs up."

"To be sure. Correct in every detail. But be calm, stay calm and collected. You have a tendency to fly off the handle in a crisis. Always remember—"

I didn't pay any attention. I never saw anybody so unstrung. But when Uncle Ned and Mr. Kissel laid into the signs, he quieted down and began to make sense again.

You could hardly blame him. This was what he had quit his practice for, upset his family, dodged his creditors, and toiled away over three thousand miles of wilderness, filled with misery and danger. This, we hoped, was the end of the rainbow, and in about five minutes we meant to open the pot of gold.

23 Supplying the Miners

The rapid increase in population created an ever-growing market for consumer goods and some means of contact with the outside world, and the miners' ability to pay exorbitant prices stimulated commerce. Wagons laden with merchandise made their way to the mines. In the country around the northern mines, only sure-footed mules could be used on the treacherous mountain trails, and only the native Californio *arrieros* knew how to pack and handle mules. The following selection discusses this activity and how the individual miner participated in this complex trade network.

The packtrain, seventy Missouri mules long, stretched out of Sacramento City, left the shade of those great oaks, and lined out up the flood valley, up the hard-caked flood valley, bound northward to the junction of the Yuba. That was August. Fields were sear: weeds dry, brown and crumbling back into dust whence they came; the bare foothills were

From *The Pardners* by John Weld. Reprinted by permission of Charles Scribner's Sons. Copyright 1941 Charles Scribner's Sons.

brown, burned dry, the rocks hot, the trail deep in hot, heavy dust. Slowly, under creaking packs, the mules plodded up that scorched lowland, pausing every mile or so to crowd under a lone, inexplicable oak, only to be beaten back into the sun again—mules laden with food and drink and tools and clothing for the hundreds of hopefuls back in the golden hills. Captain of the train was Daniel Dancer, a thick-torsoed hombre with a red, hard-drinker's face, bright blue, moist eyes, and a slump-shouldered, lazy, nonchalant way of sitting a horse. There were seven muleteers—one to every ten mules. . . . Each mule was loaded with three hundred pounds. In that day a good Missouri mule cost from five to seven hundred dollars. Freight rates from Sacramento to the gold camps along the Yuba were from seventy-five cents to two dollars a pound, according to the distance traversed and the nature of the article being packed in. Thus, in two trips a mule could earn its cost. Muleteers got ten dollars a day and their keep but even so they were hard to find. Impatient, proud, domineering Anglo-Saxons could not be induced to take such menial work. They would rather grub in ditches than work for any man; they would rather take a thousand-to-one chance of making a ten-strike than drudge along on a measly eagle a day. Too, the work was hard—hard and dangerous. Indians, highwaymen, bears, rattlesnakes, fevers and crumbling trails along precipitous mountainsides—these and the scurvy and the monotony were hazards you had to take in your stride.

From the junction of the American and the Yuba rivers to Purdy's Camp, in Sycamore Flat, was sixty-one miles—over hills, up canyons, and along dipping ridges—miles of cutback, don't-slip trail originally laid out by nimble-footed elk and deer. A half dozen mining camps were spread along the way: Ole's, Texas Tent, Tennessee House, Bellyache, Sucker's Hole, Oregon Hill, Dobbins, Crabtree, Bullard's Bar, where Cut-eye Foster had his store, thence up Middlefork Ridge and down into Sycamore Flat. And as the train passed through these camps the unpacked mules were left behind to be picked up on the return journey, reloaded with gold for San Francisco and the States. By the time the train came down Middlefork into the deep canyon of the Yuba—1000 feet in five miles—following the narrow trail with its unnumerable cutbacks, there were but thirty-one of the seventy mules left in the train—thirty-one mules, four muleteers, Dan Dancer and his horse.

"Bunch your heels, God-dam yer hides!"

"Sacré Dios, you sons-o'-beeches!" And the muleteers dug their own heels into the trail's deep dust, hanging onto the short-haired handlelike halves of the mules' tails.

"Git in thar an' dig, dam you!"

And the mules, imbued with a philosophy which would shame Christianity, gathered their hooves and thrust their awkward legs foreward, balancing the heavy packs on their ridgy backs like tightrope walkers; and the wobbly line came sliding down the mountainside, clawed at by the brush on one side and sucked at by a sheer drop on the other.

Gawk-faced Knute Poole was lying in his tent, his guts watered by diarrhea, was lying there in the heat of that August afternoon thinking of home, when he heard the music of the lead mare's bells. And ailing though he was, Knute responded as if it were a woman's voice, responded as he would not have responded to any medicine—jumped up and staggered out of the tent, went running crazily down the trail to meet the train, his long, swivel legs flying loosely as he ran, his high nasal voice carrying like a clarion: "Packtrain's a-coming! Packtrain's a-coming!"

And General Lafayette, the "Johnny Crapaud," which meant Frenchman, dropped the cradle he was repairing and came running down the path after Knute; and Link Purdy burst out of his store, stood there, account book in hand, pencil behind an ear, stood blinking against the sunlight; and from the river came slight Sandy MacBain, followed by Jeff Wilkes, the preacher, and Willie Higbee, the concertina player, and old Cyclops Skinner, and Judge Atkinson, and Tex Tremaine and the King of Siam—all came a-humping and a-hollering, came like pigs to slop, came a-snortin and a-puffing and a-grunting.

Dan Dancer, riding ahead of the lead mare, had topped the knoll and was riding, stiff-legged and jolting, down the slope, while behind him came the mules, their hooves bunched, now sliding, now stepping, ludicrous-looking under their immense tarpaulin packs. And the train came swaying down through the sweet afternoon bringing tidings and whiskey and provender.

Knute reached Dan as that florid-faced packer rode down onto the flat, his heavy body riding easily, slumped in the saddle. "Glory be t' God! You've come at last!"

"Howdy, pard'," the packer said, and drew up his horse and stood half-twisted in the saddle, a hand on the saddlebags, looking back. The lather-covered horse was breathing hard through wide, dilating nostrils.

"What in th' name of Jesus kep' you s' long, Dan?"

The packer slumped back in the saddle. "Well, to tell you th' truth, son," he said, wiping his forehead with a bandana, "we was held up by th' snowdrifts down at Marysville." He laughed at his joke, heeled his horse; and the mustang broke into a weary walk, his head down.

Knute strode along beside the horse, walking gawkily, toes pointed outward, his sick bony face upturned. "Bring me any mail?—Knute Poole's th' name."

"Now jes' hold yer horses. Lemme get this load in, will you?"

"Been 'spectin' er letter from m' maw. Been six months, now." A look of pain suddenly came on the man's bony face and as he tightened on his intestines he said, "Bring any lime juice? I got th' runs bad."

"Sure. We got lime juice. Pickles, too. Fix you right up. Just lemme get this load in."

Knute crouched slightly, then suddenly turned off the trail and ran, bent down, behind a clump of chaparral. The packer looked after him, laughing. Other members of the community stood scattered along the trail shouting like schoolboys. And Dan, flashing his store teeth, bowed and removed his sombrero, and said, "Howdy, boys," and nonchalantly hooked a heavy leg over the saddlehorn, rode on toward the cabin. His head was flat and scantily haired.

As he rode up to the cabin, followed by the news-hungry miners, Link advanced to meet him. "Wal, it's high time!"

"Howdy, Link."

"You ain't only three weeks late."

The red-faced man threw the reins over his horse's head. "Sorry," he said, and the saddle squeaked under his weight as he swung down, "but to date I ain't figured no way t' rush fate or fortune." He put out a rough, knot-jointed hand. Link grinned and accepted it.

Link said, "What kept cha?"

"Couldn't get no grub. There jest warn't none t' be had. Men's pourin' in s' fast there ain't hardly enough t' go around."

"How 'bout whiskey?"

Dan turned to see the progress of his mules. The lead mare was halfway up the trail. "Don't think I'd come without it, do you?" He caught his horse's bridle, started for the corral.

"How 'bout bustin' open th' mail?" some one hollered.

"Now don't rush me, boys. Lemme get th' saddle off Pimiente here. Poor critter's plumb wore out."

Impatient hands helped him tether the horse. Lafayette pulled back the sapling gate and slapped the mustang as he went into the corral. Inside, the mules and jackasses were standing, heads over the railing, ears pricked up, watching their brothers, sisters and first cousins come up the trail. The packmules looked pitiably small beneath their bulky loads. The lead mare's bells clanged beautifully, nostalgically as she plodded her way, her stoical head rising and falling with each lift of a foreleg. One of the mules in the corral lifted his head, curled his lips, and blasted forth a welcoming bray.

The packer unstrapped his saddlebags, swung the saddle up onto the railing, and with saddlebags over a shoulder, led the anxious miners back to the cabin. Every one crowded about him as he opened one of the bags and drew forth a sheaf of letters. "Now there ain't no need of crowdin'," he said, turning around. "If there's a letter here fer you, you'll get it, so gimmie elbow-room." He tapped the pack of letters on the bench, straightening them, taking plenty of time; now he put a foot on the bench, leaned forward, an arm on his knee; he took a boodle from his pocket and set it down on the bench beside the saddlebags. "As you come get your letters, don't fergit t' feed th' kitty," he said, indicating the deerskin sack. "Fer them that don't know—postage is two bucks a letter. Now then—Carl Anderson!"

"Ain't here," Link said. "Last I heered of him, he was down to Dobbins."

"Edward Atkinson, Esquire!"

Every one laughed. Old Cyclops said, "Will ya listen t' that, now— Esquire!" The Judge's face was a rich mixture of joy as he accepted the letter.

Dan said, "That'll be two bucks, brother," and the Judge dropped in two good pinches.

"Ira Allen."

Every one looked around to see if the Virgin were anywhere about, and one or two miners called his name aloud. Link said, "Reckin he ain't here. I'll see he gets it."

The packer looked meaningfully at the boodle and Link sprinkled two pinches into it.

"Noah Gilroy!"

Link said, "He ain't here no more. Went upcountry coupla weeks back."

Knute Poole had come up and was standing, weak-kneed, his hands in his hip pockets.

"Jacques Fournier!"

Lafayette said, "Si, si," and put out an eager hand. "Leenk—you pay for me, no?"

Dan said, "Funny writin'," as he handed the letter to the Frenchman.

Link looked doubtfully at the Frenchman and then said, "Yeh, I reckon so."

"Amos Jenkins!"

Link said, "Lives over t' Coyote. I'll take it."

Dan was regarding the next letter quizzically. "Can't make head nor tail of this one," he said, and handed the letter to Link. "See kin you."

"Mus' be fer Nigger Steve," Link said, and laughed, accepting the letter. "Sure," he said readily, looking at the soiled envelope, "it's fer the' Nigger." He looked around. "Wonder where th' hell he's at?" Then he looked back at the envelope and said, "Jesus! what a handle!" and sprinkled two more pinches in the packer's poke.

Tex said, "Lemme see," and gawked at the envelope. It bore a half-dozen lavender stamps and was addressed to Sztefan Korzeniowski. Tex shook his head. "Wal, I'll be God-dam."

"Wilbur Higbee, Esquire!"

Willie caught the packer's hand in both his own, pressed it gratefully. "Gee, thanks, Dan!"

Dan said, "Mind you don't forget th' kitty, son."

Now the last mules were plodding up the trail toward the corral, were moving toward rest and shade. The half-breed muleteers were lining them up near the corral.

"Tom Henderson!"

Link looked around and hollered, "Hey, Tom!"

The Judge looked up from his letter and said, "I ain't seen him all day. I'll see he gets it."

"Lemuel Collins!"

"Ain't here."

"Jeremiah Ellis!"

Tex said, "Ain't that Buck's name?"

"B'lieve 'tis," Link said.

Willie looked up from his letter and said, "He was through here last week. Went on down the hill."

"Doctor John Middleton?"

"Ain't here."

"Salvadore Fernandez!"

"Likely to find him at the greaser camp, up above."

"Abraham Schultz."

"Ain't no Jews 'round here."

"The Reverend Jefferson Wilkes!"

"God be praised," the parson shouted, and pushed his way through the crowd.

Knute Poole watched the parson tear open and unfold the message; and there was such a rare brand of happiness on the preacher's face that Knute turned back eagerly, hopefully to the mailman.

Dan read off several other names no one had heard before. He found a letter for Link Purdy and a second for Willie Higbee. He then ran through those addressed to Goodyear's and The Fork, looking for any that might have become misplaced. Then, having run through them all, he flipped the letters, slapped them against a thigh, and said, "Well, boys, I reckon that's all th' bad news." That was his standing joke; he never failed to say it.

Chapter 5

The Indians

The Indians

The Spanish found a relatively large concentration of Indians, perhaps as many as 275,000, when they arrived in 1769. Over 135 different languages were spoken, which included twenty-one or twenty-two different linguistic families. Most natives lived in villages (or rancherias) with a maximum population of 1,000. The majority were food-gatherers, with acorns as the basic staple. Some fishing and small game supplemented the acorn. Only the Yuman Indians cultivated the soil extensively.

The presence of these Indians was the principal reason for the Spanish colonization of California. The Franciscans were eager to convert them to Christianity and used missions for this purpose. After ten years at the mission, the natives were to be released to be productive tax-paying citizens of the Spanish crown. This ideal was not realized, and few Indians made the transition into Spanish society. The role of the mission remains one of the more controversial topics in California history. Defenders of the institution stress that the mission made possible Spain's settlement of the province and that most Indians preferred mission life. Opponents argue that the clergy stripped the native of his cultural heritage and did not properly train him either in Christianity or in assuming the responsibilities of freedom. In any event, Indians fled the routine of the mission at every opportunity. The ongoing failure of the missions was reflected in the falling birthrate and a tremendous disparity between births and deaths among the Indians. Between 1769 and 1833 there were 62,000 deaths and only 29,000 births in the missions. Of those born, approximately three-quarters died in infancy. The harsh penalties meted out to runaways and the seizure of infants in campaigns against the wild tribes were considered necessary to prevent the mission from collapsing.

The missions were secularized in the 1830s and the Indians either rejoined their tribes or went to work on the ranchos, where they found it hard to adjust to the white man's world. Their numbers continued to decline, due to their inability to cope with their new condition and their susceptibility to diseases. The gold rush and the arrival of the Anglo accentuated the sad plight of the Indians. There was now no place to hide as gold seekers invaded even the most remote haunts, and farmers or ranchers destroyed Indian refuges. The number of California Indians declined to 15,000 in 1900 despite some efforts to assist them on reservations. The tragedy which befell these "first" Californians is a common subject for novels.

24 The First Californians

Much of our knowledge about the Indians of the era before 1769 remains
speculation. Their numbers have been estimated to be as low as 133,000
or as high as 275,000. It is certain that there was great diversity among
them and that being isolated geographically made their culture
somewhat different from other native tribes of North America. This state
of affairs lends greater credence to the following selection which depicts
what life may have been like for one California Indian group at some time
in the past.

After the lake had shrunk back and the Old People had gone away, the
place lay uninhabited, and during many centuries no man, unless some
wanderer, stooped to drink where the trickle of warm water ran out from
the pool. Then at last came a tribe that took the place at its own terms,
and lived there.

Why they came there, we cannot know, but can only suppose that
some hard pressure coerced them from their home in better country, for
there is no worse country where men can live at all.

There by the spring we find their little arrowheads mingled with the
heavier spearpoints, and in them perhaps we find the answer why they
could live there and the Old People could not—for, with bows and
arrows, they could be more skillful hunters.

Who they were, who were their kinsfolk, that we know surely from
the testimony of language. They were the ultimate fringe, the poor
relations, of all that farflung group of peoples who hold the mountains
and plateaus and desert-basins—Shoshone, Ute, Hopi, Pima and
Papago, Yaqui—from where Snake River cuts its canyon through the
lava-beds until at last one comes, by a far cry, to the conquering Aztecs
of Mexico.

They called themselves "Numu," meaning "The People." The
whites most often called them Diggers, because they grubbed for roots,
unlike the horse-loving buffalo-hunters of the plains.

Their different bands bore different names, ending with a suffix
meaning "eater," evidence that mere existence was their chief problem
and concern. Thus there were the Woodchuck-eaters, and Tuber-eaters
and Jackrabbit-eaters, and Ground-squirrel-eaters—curious names, in
that they all imply a certain restriction or fastidiousness in diet, whereas
these bands were equally ready to eat jackrabbits or tubers or
woodchucks or ground-squirrels, or anything else on which they could
lay hand.

They had no taboos of food; only a tribe that has grown fat can say
luxuriously: "We shall not eat pig!" Or, "We shall not eat rats!"

They kept a few dogs, generally half-starved. When the master himself is eating guts and all, what shall he throw to his dog?

They had no sure traditions of when they first came into this desert country, but perhaps it was not more than a few centuries ago. This we should judge to be true because their traditions, more than those of most peoples, tell of change, as if they were still adapting to the country, and when one of their old men talks, he says, "We did it in this way when I was a boy, before the white men came, but before that, when my grandfather was young, we did it differently."

As to where they came from, we would say, "From the south," for in their customs they hark back to some land of mild winters. They had no fear of heat and the fierce sun, and even in summer often walked without head-covering. They were not skilled at fashioning warm clothes, so that in frost and snow they wore only short cloaks of rabbit-skins. Their houses, moreover, were often mere circles of brush thrown up as windbreaks, with a fire burning in the middle about which they huddled.

They feared snow, and hated it. What little magic they practiced was mostly to break the grip of winter.

"Yes," said one of them, "in the old days my grandmother could make the snow melt. She cried like a buck-antelope at rutting-time, and took a firebrand of greasewood, and pointed it at the south, saying, 'Come on, rain! Come on, rain!' "

Thus they lived stoically, almost as strangers, in a hard country of bitter winters, suffering and going hungry often, and not thinking that anything except suffering and going hungry often was to be expected of life. Yet they lived, and every year the children were born, and a few of them grew up, and even thus to maintain the generations in that country was no mean achievement.

An anthropologist wrote of them stiffly: "Their economic life was difficult because of an unfavorable environment and only through unceasing and assiduous toil could it be made to supply a livelihood." But one of the old men, sitting on the steps of the store at the reservation, put it more eloquently, remembering the days of his youth: "We used to dig food all summer—until it was gone. We gathered seeds and roots, and buried them. In winter we stayed at one place till the buried food was all gone, and then moved on to the next place. Besides, we hunted every day, all year."

Thus we may write generally of The People, but of all their bands none lived worse than the Kotisdoka, the Rat-eaters, who wandered in the midst of the desert, along the dry mountainsides and across the salt-flats, and came often to camp by the spring beneath the high black rock. To be sure, they were called Rat-eaters, not by any derogation, for among all The People, the rat was held a delicacy. Nevertheless, the other bands had better supplies of food. Compared with the Rat-eaters, the Woodchuck-eaters lived almost in comfort, for they could now and then kill a deer or a bear, and could dig camas-roots. And the Seepweed-seed-eaters had a few oak-trees in their country and made acorn-mash. Those who lived near some lake could catch fish, and those who lived south of the river had pinyon-nuts. But the Rat-eaters had the least of all.

This was the rhythm of the year, among the Kotisdoka, being determined mainly by eating. . . .

In the summer the women and children gathered seeds. They worked hard every day and all day, for there was no thick growth to be harvested like a field of grain, and the seeds of the desert-plants were tiny, not like wheat or barley. So the women and children wandered about, and each conical carrying-basket grew slowly heavier as they shook out and beat out here a few seeds and here a few more, having to go out week after week ranging widely, long hours daily, since the seed of the different plants ripened at different times and most of it fell to the ground quickly.

They gathered seed from the bulrushes that grew around the spring and from the seepweed that grew among the hummocks and from the shad-scale that grew on the old beaches and from the little scattered tufts of bunchgrass that grew on the mountainsides. After they had brought the seed into camp, they dug holes and stored much of it in the baskets, against the winter.

While the women and children gathered seeds, the men worked just as hard at hunting. Now and then one of them put an arrow into a mountain-sheep or an antelope, but such hunting risked much time. A man might disguise himself in a sheep- or antelope-skin and go stalking for a week, and then come back empty-handed. So, more often, for smaller but surer profit, they set snares across rabbit-trails or lay in wait there with throwing-stick or bow-and-arrow.

But, in the summer, rats were even more the staff of life. The men were clever at thrusting a flexible stick into a rat-hole, and when they felt a softness against the end of the stick, they twisted suddenly, and caught the stick in the hide, and then quickly drew the squeaking rat out. Sometimes when one of them was hunting rats, he came upon a badger similarly engaged. Then if the man rat-hunter could put an arrow into the animal rat-hunter the man ate the badger too.

In the summer also there was always the chance to pick up tidbits such as quail or a blackbird that came to drink at the spring, or some mice or a big lizard, or some ants or crickets. If a horde of locusts descended, this was not a disaster, but the occasion of a feast.

In autumn the seeds had all fallen to the ground, but the hunting was better. By now all this year's young rats and rabbits were being forced out from the old foraging-grounds to seek new homes for themselves; they were inexperienced and ignorant of runways, and dug holes in conspicuous places, and so were easily killed. Now was the time for two or more bands of The People to gather together and organize a big drive for rabbits or antelope. At such times, when there was extra food, they played games of hand and of hoop-and-pole, and held tribal festivities, but they had no elaborate rituals and dances, for when a man throughout most of the year must work all day and every day merely to keep from being hungry, he has no time or spirit for dances and rituals.

Soon the winter descended, and then they were all hungry and cold most of the time. They dared not, in fear of a late spring, eat heavily of the little stores of buried seeds. The insects had vanished; the lizards were in hibernation; even the rats lived deep within their burrows, eating the food that they themselves had stored up during the summer. In the bitter cold a hunter would freeze if he tried to spend long hours slowly stalking antelope or sheep. Only the rabbits remained, and the hunters followed after them ceaselessly, and set many snares and deadfalls. Now, when a man saw a rabbit disappear into a hole, he thought it worth his time to kindle a fire and blow the smoke into the hole, fanning with a bird-wing, and force the rabbit out into his hands.

When the store of seeds at one spring had been exhausted and the rabbits had grown scarce, eveyone had to go off to the next spring, no matter how cold the weather. If some old woman grew feeble and halted and froze to death on the march, that was something that no one could help, and a part of life. In the winter they were glad when it came time to camp by the big hot spring, for by building their shelter close to it, they found that the warm column of rising steam moderated the cold a little.

But the springtime, especially if the cold weather held on long, was the worst of all. By then the stored food had been exhausted or nearly so, and the rabbits had been hunted down and were fewer. Everyone was weak with long hunger and cold, and was always hungry. Then they began to look each at the other questioningly. Then as a hope they made their snow-melting magic. Then, sometimes, when one among them was growing weaker and was soon to die, they quickened the death by hitting him over the head, and they ate his body, so that the children might live. But this was something that they did not do willingly, but only because logic dictated. Sometimes, in that starving time, a man would have the luck to come upon a wild-cat that had just struck down a rabbit. Perhaps the wild-cat, itself half-starved, did not run, but stood snarling to defend its prey, and the man might have the luck to put an arrow into it. Then he carried back both wild-cat and half-eaten rabbit, and the people would gladly eat both, and also that part of the rabbit that was already in the wild-cat's stomach.

At last, however, the south wind blew again and the snow melted under a meager rain, and the rats came out of their holes. Then the sun grew hot, and the first seeds ripened, and thus was completed the cycle of the year. . . .

When the first emigrants came, though they themselves may have been long unbathed, they held their noses at a Digger camp. "Their children run naked," wrote one. "Their women wear nothing above the waist, and their men little either above or below it. They are all dirty, and smell. They eat jackrabbits, rats, reptiles, insects, roots, and grass-seed, and they are more filthy than beasts, and live in habitations which are nothing more than circular enclosures of brush against the wind. Their feces are piled up outside, and these are copious and large in diameter, doubtless because of the coarseness of their food." And another wrote: "Rats, unskinned and unopened, are thrown into the fire, and when they seem to be roasted, they are drawn out and eaten, entrails and all, the children in particular being very fond of the juices, which they lick in with their tongues and push into their mouths with their fingers." But another, more charitable or more philosophical, noted, "They, like other mortals, have their tastes. Some eat their locusts in soup, and some boiled, others crush them and make a kind of paste which they dry in the sun or before the fire. And others, who doubtless are their gourmets, spit a number of locusts upon a stick, and roast them delicately in the fire, and eat them *en brochette*."

All of them spoke of the Diggers as cowards, and only to be despised in comparison with those war-lords, the Sioux and Cheyenne. And certainly the Diggers, who had no luxuries, could not afford war, which is the greatest luxury of all. Still, they were not cowards. When pushed too hard, they fought bravely and shrewdly. In the willow-brakes of the Truckee they routed the white men, for all their rifles. But the bow and stone-tipped arrow could not hold out against the rifles for long, and soon the cavalry and the posses did the work. Those that the soldiers did not kill were herded into the reservations. There you will find their grandsons now, not unskilled as cattle-breeders, as unknowing as you or I of how a rat tastes or how it may be drawn with a stick from its hole.

25 Indian Runaways

A continuing problem of the mission era was that the Indians fled to rejoin their own people at every opportunity. To recapture these runaways, armed expeditions were sent from the coastal area into the interior. The "heathen" Indians were at first friendly and receptive to those expeditions; however, their early hospitality waned as Indian children were forcefully taken for the missions, Indian women were abused, and as stories of mission life, told by runaway neophytes, became widespread. Worst of all, the soldiers attacked any Indians they met, thus punishing the innocent as readily as the guilty. In this selection, an American mountain man entering California becomes involved in the defense of Indians attacked by brutal Mexican soldiers.

From *Ranchero* by Stewart Edward White. Copyright 1933, 1960 by the author. Reprinted by permission of the Trust Department, Crocker National Bank, Santa Barbara, California.

To the mountain man, new come from a long sojourn among the warlike tribes of the plains and ranges, from the winter blizzards and summer "dry scrapes" of the wilderness of the "Great American Desert," riding about in this lovely land in pursuit of such simple savages as he had seen looked more like a picnic than a campaign. But he agreed politely.

"These Indians make war on your people?" he asked.

The Mexican explained. The missions and ranches of the Spanish occupation were all near the coast. The Indians there were Christians, civilized by the efforts of the *padres*.

"A cattle, señor," said the officer contemptuously, "but useful."

Back of this narrow strip lay the broad valleys and the Sierra, a wild country visited by no man in his senses except at the call of duty. Here dwelt the wild tribes, the "gentiles." They were lower than cattle, mere beasts. No one disturbed them.

"Save when the good *padres* need converts, señor."

But these gentiles would not stay put. Every so often they made raids. Then they must be pursued. And the duty of pursuit fell upon him, Jesús María Corbedo de Cortilla. It was a hard life.

"You have not a large force, señor," observed Andy.

"Stout hearts! Strong arms!"

Nevertheless, thought Andy, these gentiles could not be very formidable. He questioned. It developed that the warfare was not a matter of much bloodshed. The Indians raided with one object in view, to steal horses. This they accomplished at night, without attempting to come in conflict with the *rancheros*, indeed with a very successful determination to keep out of sight. Then the soldiers were sent out in pursuit. Ordinarily they succeeded in recovering most of the stolen animals, for the trail was easy to follow, driven animals moved more slowly than mounted men, and the raiders scattered without resistance when overtaken.

"Like quail, like rabbits, señor," complained the lieutenant, "in the bush, the *barrancas*, in the mountains where horses cannot go."

Nevertheless, he talked largely of doughty deeds, trying to convey the impression of terrible slaughters and reprisals. Andy's shrewdness and experience read between the lines. He began to be slightly amused. These excursions to him took on more and more the character of picnics. Andy was tough and hard from his ten years in the trapping country. About the only hardship he could discover in the situation was the necessity of wearing the many-plied *cueros* of antelope skin—if it was a necessity. They must be very hot. Sometimes the raiders managed to get clear away with their booty. Then, it seemed, they did not ride the horses, they ate them! This was the culminating grievance.

That was the present case. Don Sylvestre Cordero had been relived of a whole *manada* of breeding mares. The savages had managed to confuse their trail and had wholly disappeared. It developed that some of the mares belonged to Cortilla himself! So he had pushed on in hope of vengeance, much farther to the north than he had ever been before.

"I circle wide to cut the trail," he cried. "My men are expert at tracking. Soon I shall meet with these *roto cabrones!* And they shall learn that it is not well to affront Jesús María Corbedo de Cortilla—and the Mexican government!" he added. "You encountered no such people?" he asked.

"Oh, I met some Indians," said Andy carelessly, "but they were not the people you are looking for. They were friendly. I don't think, by the way they acted, they had ever seen a white man before. They had no horses."

The young officer brooded darkly for a moment, then turned upon Andy a countenance beaming with friendliness. Andy had listened well, and it was evident that Jesús María had talked himself into a liking for so respectful an audience. And he still had an eye on the long rifle lying in apparent carelessness across the young man's lap.

"As for this present difficulty," said he, "I should, as I said, escort you to the capitol. But I am on other duty, and Jesús María Corbedo de Cortilla never shrinks from duty. I will take your word. You will ride to the Governor. You will report to him. You will say that I have sent you. Thus all will be regular."

"I have never had other intention," said Andy simply.

"*Bueno!*" cried the officer gayly. "Then, señor, we shall meet again. And know this, I, Jesús María Corbedo de Cortilla, am an intimate of the new governor who comes, Figueroa. We are like that, " he laid his two forefingers side by side. "A word in his ear, eh? We shall see!"

"Thanks, señor," said Andy. "*Vaya con Dios.*"

He mounted and drew aside to watch the little cavalcade pass. The soldiers, he thought, were rather stupid looking, though they sat their horses gracefully and well. They glanced at him sullenly as they passed, lowered resentfully at their officer's sharp command. They, too, wore the antelope skin *cuero de gamuza* and the glazed flat hats. They too carried swords, but no pistols. But they were armed further with long lances and short guns slung under the leather skirts of their saddles, and swathed heavily in fox skins, the tails dangling. It crossed Andy's mind that the battle would be about over before they could bring these clumsy smoothbores into action. As additional defense each bore a round rawhide shield. These had been varnished and painted with the arms of Mexico. They presented a very gay but not particularly warlike appearance.

"I think, señor," Andy called after them, "that you will do better to swing to the east. I saw no sign in the north."

The Mexican waved his hand gayly and rode on.

Andy too went his way. But not for very long. Within the half mile an uneasiness overtook him. It was a mental—or rather a psychic—

condition with which past experience had made him familiar. In externals and in most essentials Andy was a direct, matter of fact, rather slow bit of efficiency, but he possessed spiritual perceptions, antennae, which worked mysteriously below his knowledges. Sometimes they helped him, as when they enabled him to smell out hidden danger; sometimes they disconcerted him—as when they forced him too clearly to see the other fellow's point of view. But he had learned never to ignore them. So he reined in his horse and sat relaxed in his saddle, his eyes roaming the surrounding prospect for sign of life, his inner ear cocked for a whisper.

Then, unquestioning, he turned back on his trail. He did not yet know why, but that was the thing to do. When an hour's travel had returned him to the top of the butte-like hill where he had spent the night, the reason was revealed.

From the elevation he could see ahead for a long distance over the plain. About half a mile distant Andy saw Cortilla and his four men gathered in a compact group. The lieutenant was holding out something in his hand and apparently making a speech. In a moment Andy saw why. A dark head appeared above the grass, then another and another, until a dozen were in sight. They were at some little distance from the Mexicans. Cortilla was evidently trying to coax them nearer but was having difficulty in doing so. They seemed shy, and at a sudden movement of one of the horses dove out of sight like scattering quail. But Cortilla persisted. Finally one of the savages, bolder than the rest, perhaps the chief, plucked up courage enough to take the object that Cortilla was offering. He examined it; others drew near to look. Soon the Mexicans were surrounded by a dark crowd of savages; as Andy had been surrounded the day before. Now, Andy reflected, if Cortilla knows their language, he may get some information. But as yet he did not know why he had come back. It was none of his council.

But suddenly Cortilla arose in his stirrups. The sun caught a flash of his sword as it leaped from his scabbard. The bright pennoned lances of the troopers dipped. The horses plunged, rearing high, striking down viciously. The black mass of the savages held for an instant's astonishment, then broke into flight. The dark figures dove into the grass in all directions. A few stood, apparently paralyzed with fear. Andy saw these pierced through by the soldiers' lances. Then all five men, holding together in a compact group, set their horses at speed through the high grass, ranging like bird dogs, hunting down the fugitives, flushing them from their concealments or overtaking them as they ran.

26 The Fate of Mission Indians

The missions were secularized between 1834 and 1836, and the resident Indians were given title to land. Some did not know how to adapt to their new status and lost their land because of an inability to pay taxes or because they abandoned it or failed to care for it properly. Unfortunately, more of the Indians had their land taken from them by unscrupulous means. The following selection tells how this was accomplished in one instance and also relates some of the difficulties Indians faced after secularization.

The long spell of foggy weather was broken at last, and hot California sun once more warmed the Valley of the Carmelo.

Loreta Prealta sat on the ground beside her tule hut. As her hands worked at pulling husks from yellow ears of corn, she lifted her eyes to the golden hillside, and wished that San Carlos, the Patron Saint of the Mission, could have made just one more sunny day for her father, before Juan O-nes-e-mo's bones were taken over the hill to Monterey, so far away from the Mission he had helped to build on the Carmelo. Her father longed for one last warming by the sun on his poor, old body, and he would have liked to be put away near the beautiful tower he had built; the tower where swallows flew in and out, showing green-tinted wings, and where the wind made sighing noises when there was a storm at sea. Loreta had begged them to let Juan's body stay near the work of his hands, but now that the Spanish Padres were gone and the Mission deserted, and only a Mexican priest in Monterey, there were no ears open to hear the words of an Indian woman.

She looked at her brown son as he made his way to her on unsteady legs. He was busy trying to pull a bit of duck down from a finger sticky with honey. When the feather stuck to the finger of his other hand, and was changed back and forth several times, José gave up trying. He sat his bare little behind on the ground and roared with anger.

Loreta went to the baby, pulled away the feather, and was pouring water on his hands to wash off the honey, when she heard the clatter of horses' hoofs on the other side of the hut. Could this be *another* Mexican for taxes? She had already paid Alvarado's man twenty hides, and another man before him ten hides! Her father had helped her scrape the fat hides for taxes just before he died!

She walked around the hut. Two Mexicans were sliding off their horses. One, a small fellow with a wrinkled face and crafty eyes, saw Loreta as she looked at him.

"Here you, Indian," he called in Spanish. "You're on my land, and I've come to tell you to move off of it."

Loreta drew herself up as became an Indian woman who was eighteen years old, and taught by the Padres at the Mission; then she walked slowly to where the men stood. Wind from the sea blew her brown cotton dress tight against her straight young body. Her bare feet made no sound on the hard-baked yellow ground.

"This land belongs to Loreta Prealta," she said quietly, when she was near to them. "When Padres left the Mission on Carmelo they gave this land to Loreta and Antonio, because we were Mission Indians." She took her stand by the oxcart that Antonio had made such a short time ago. "Taxes have been given already to the Mexican Government."

The man came closer to her. His face had a worried look to it now. "Who is Antonio," he asked, "and where is he?"

"Antonio was the father of my boy, and husband to me. We were married by the Padres," Loreta told these Mexicans, who were looking around anxiously. "He was killed by savage Indians at Los Laureles, the rancho of the Spaniard Don José Manuel Boronda, so now his share too belongs to me."

"Well, you don't own the land," the man glared and pushed a paper toward her. "Governor Gutierrez signed this paper of mine. It says that the land belongs to me. You have no paper telling about your land. You don't belong *here*."

Her father, Juan O-nes-e-mo had often told Loreta that an Indian woman must never change a muscle of her face to give away the thoughts in her heart, for a face can tell to another, things that the mouth does not say. "Governor Gutierrez is no longer governor. How can a paper from him be good, when Alvarado is the governor now?"

"Can't you read?" he shouted. "This paper is dated 1836, before Governor Gutierrez left Alta California for Mexico. The land is mine. Alvarado and his crowd may think that they are rulers, but Chico and Gutierrez have sailed back to Mexico for five thousand soldiers and will bring them to fight Alvarado and the Californians who want to rule over Mexican country. This land is mine and is Mexican. Indians get off it."

Loreta sighed and looked over at the hills beyond the river. "So many governors have come here and taken land and taxes away, and never come back. Indians lived here in the Valley of Carmelo before Mexicans came, or even Spanish and Padres. Loreta Prealta is the one who *belongs* here. In the Padre's book, is written down the land given to Loreta and Antonio. That is all the paper Loreta had, but the priest in Monterey will know. Padre Real will tell you. It is written in a book covered with rawhide and tied together with thongs. They wrote it down the day stock and Mission implements were given out before Padre Abella and Payeras left. Loreta and Antonio saw them write it."

The man set his jaw. "This bottom land belongs to me. Get your animals off. I'm going to burn the tule huts and all the vermin along with them." He pointed to the hills at the north. "Up there is where your land is. You can't read." He tapped the paper again. "I'm not going to argue with a squaw. The huts are to be burned tonight."

"But I cannot grow corn for us to eat on poor hill land," Loreta told him. "There is no water except the spring of Weeping Eyes, and that is not enough for growing food."

"I'll give you work. You can wash for us and have food and a place to sleep. It will be better than hill land."

Loreta shook her head. "I will move the stock, and go to the hills—for a while," she told him. "It is time the huts were burned—time for new ones." She walked up close to this Mexican. "But the land is mine, and Father Real, the Mexican priest in Monterey, will give Loreta a paper, too."

"They still have faith in a sinking ship, don't they? Don't even have sense enough to know that Padres are less than nothing now," the man said, and turned to his comrade and laughed a laugh that did not bring happiness to Loreta's ears. "She'll be harmless enough—alone as she is," he added as they both mounted. "Handsome squaw too, with a straight back and a small bottom—and firm young breasts. Who knows? She may come in handy one day." He put a spur to the belly of his horse and was off.

Loreta watched the Mexicans ride toward Los Beracos, the little town of tule huts along the river, where some of the Indians had settled after Padres left the Mission. . . .

Later, as she made things ready for the night, Loreta heard fiesta music and singing in the valley below. There was the crackle of flames, and she saw that Los Beracos was burning!

A prayer went from her lips for the kind-hearted fandango girl from the dance house there. She who had come in her high heels and purple satin dress and played the Christmas song on the Padre's fiddle so that Loreta's father could die in peace and happiness.

Loreta could not take her eyes away from the bright glow, as fire burned up the house she had helped Antonio to build. Her bones ached with weariness from the moving. She had paid out so many hides in taxes and yet here she was on the hillside, homeless and alone, with only her little son to comfort her. The story was always the same, fighting between governors and hides and tallow taken from Indians to pay for the fighting. In Monterey she heard how Gutierrez and Chico, the Mexicans, had sailed with a special boat to carry hides and tallow stolen from the Missions. With this they would buy soldiers to come back and fight the Californian Alvarado. Only sleep could take away the sadness.

José was very much excited over the trip to Monterey the next day. He seemed to like things that were different. Father Real was working among the flowers around the governor's church when they arrived. He was kind to the little boy and gave him a holy picture to look at while Loreta talked.

"No, my child," Father Real shook his head. "I have no book with entries in it. It was here for a time, but so many people were looking at it, governors, and secretaries, and alcaldes and others. One day I came from prayers and it was gone."

"Then there is nothing to show? Loreta has no land that the Padres gave her?" She could hardly believe that the loss of a book, a book made by Padre Payeras, could make so much difference to an Indian woman.

"I will go to the alcalde, to the other proper people and tell them about you," Padre Real said. "I will tell them I was there when the land was given to you and swear to a paper. Everything will be all right." He patted her shoulder. "Now go into the church, child, and calm yourself with prayer. I will watch the boy while I garden here."

Loreta felt quieter and more at peace in the church with the little altar light glowing through the dimness. It was cool here and she was tired. Her prayers—she couldn't think of the words.

"Wake up, my child. You must be exhausted." Father Real's voice came to her. He was standing by her side, and looked tenderly at her. "Come and eat, and you will feel better."

After the food was blessed and eaten, José went to sleep, and then the priest told Loreta about the graveyard lot.

"You must bring some hides to pay for Juan O-nes-e-mo's grave in the cemetario," he said.

Loreta didn't understand. "My father must buy a little land to lie down in and rot?" she asked. "Indians never bought land to bury in at Carmelo. I did not buy land for Antonio who lies beside the Mission."

"That was different. Juan is over here in Monterey, in a graveyard with Spanish and others. It is like a pueblo for the dead, and lots must be bought for graves."

Loreta nodded, but she didn't really understand. "Juan would have liked to be where he could see the beautiful tower of Carmelo, with no Spanish and Mexicans. Juan did not want to rot in Monterey."

The Padre sighed. "But Carmelo is no longer a place to bury. We must all do as we are told, Loreta. Things have changed now."

"Things have changed now," she repeated. "What do I pay for this ground for Juan?"

"Two cow hides will do."

Loreta nodded.

Before she left Monterey that afternoon, Father Real went with Loreta to the alcalde and got a paper that was signed and had a seal on it. He gave it to her. "Keep this always. It is called a deed, a right to your land."

Such a lump went away from Loreta's heart. "Then I can go and tell the Mexican this is my land, and build again on the flat where Antonio and Loreta made their first house?"

The alcalde shook his head. "Gonzales is in possession now. We can't do anything about that. We can't take it away from him. This paper gives you the rest that Father Real heard Padre Payeras give you."

Loreta was bewildered. Mexicans could take away from her, and from dead Antonio, and Juan, who had lived there a long time, but they could not take away from the Mexican who had been there only one night. She wished hard that she could ask the Spanish Padre Payeras and Abella about all this business of different kinds of papers.

27 Ramona

The most famous novel based in California undoubtedly had been
Ramona by Helen Hunt Jackson, first published in 1884. Mrs. Jackson
became interested in the sad plight of the American Indians of that day
and sought to write a book which would help them in the way *Uncle
Tom's Cabin* had aided blacks. Her work did help bring attention to the
dismal state of the "first Californians." This was accomplished, however,
more through the emotional impact of the story than by a realistic
portrayal of Indian life. This excerpt shows why the novel succeeded as
propaganda but had shortcomings as historical literature.

There was no real healing for Alessandro. His hurts had gone too deep.
His passionate heart, ever secretly brooding on the wrongs he had borne,
the hopeless outlook for his people in the future, and most of all on the
probable destitution and suffering in store for Ramona, consumed itself
as by hidden fires. Speech, complaint, active antagonism, might have
saved him, but all these were foreign to his self-contained, reticent,
repressed nature. Slowly, so slowly that Ramona could not tell on what
hour or what day her terrible fears first changed to an even more terrible
certainty, his brain gave way, and the thing, in dread of which he had
cried out the morning they left San Pasquale, came upon him. Strangely
enough, and mercifully, now that it had really come, he did not know it.
He knew that he suddenly came to his consciousness sometimes, and
discovered himself in strange and unexplained situations; had no
recollection of what had happened for an interval of time, longer or
shorter. But he thought it was only a sort of sickness; he did not know
that during those intervals his acts were the acts of a madman; never
violent, aggressive, or harmful to any one; never destructive. It was
piteous to see how in these intervals his delusions were always shaped by
the bitterest experiences of his life. Sometimes he fancied that the
Americans were pursuing him, or that they were carrying off Ramona,
and he was pursuing them. At such times he would run with maniac
swiftness for hours, till he fell exhausted on the ground, and slowly
regained true consciousness by exhaustion. At other times he believed he
owned vast flocks and herds; would enter any enclosure he saw, where
there were sheep or cattle, go about among them, speaking of them to
passers-by as his own. Sometimes he would try to drive them away; but
on being remonstrated with, would bewilderedly give up the attempt.
Once he suddenly found himself in the road driving a small flock of
goats, whose he knew not, nor whence he got them. Sitting down by the
roadside, he buried his head in his hands. "What has happened to my
memory?" he said. "I must be ill of a fever!" As he sat there, the goats of
their own accord, turned and trotted back into a corral near by, the
owner of which stood, laughing, on his doorsill; and when Alessandro

From *Ramona* by Helen Hunt Jackson. Published 1884.

came up, said good naturedly, "All right, Alessandro! I saw you driving off my goats, but I thought you'd bring 'em back."

Everybody in the valley knew him, and knew his condition. It did not interfere with his capacity as a worker, for the greater part of the time. He was one of the best shearers in the region, the best horse-breaker; and his services were always in demand, spite of the risk there was of his having at any time one of these attacks of wandering. His absences were a great grief to Ramona, not only from the loneliness in which it left her, but from the anxiety she felt lest his mental disorder might at any time take a more violent and dangerous shape. This anxiety was all the more harrowing because she must keep it locked in her own breast, her wise and loving instinct telling her that nothing could be more fatal to him than the knowledge of his real condition. More than once he reached home, breathless, panting, the sweat rolling off his face, crying aloud, "The Americans have found us out, Majella! They were on the trail! I baffled them. I came up another way." At such times she would soothe him like a child; persuade him to lie down and rest; and when he waked and wondered why he was so tired, she would say, "You were all out of breath when you came in, dear. You must not climb so fast; it is foolish to tire one's self so."

In these days Ramona began to think earnestly of Felipe. She believed Alessandro might be cured. A wise doctor could surely do something for him. If Felipe knew what sore straits she was in, Felipe would help her. But how could she reach Felipe without the Señora's knowing it? And, still more, how could she send a letter to Felipe without Alessandro's knowing what she had written? Ramona was as helpless in her freedom on this mountain eyrie as if she had been chained hand and foot.

And so the winter wore away, and the spring. What wheat grew in their fields in this upper air! Wild oats, too, in every nook and corner. The goats frisked and fattened, and their hair grew long and silky; the sheep were already heavy again with wool, and it was not yet midsummer. The spring rains had been good; the stream was full, and flowers grew along its edges thick as in beds.

The baby had thrived; as placid, laughing a little thing as if its mother had never known sorrow. "One would think she had suckled pain," thought Ramona, "so constantly have I grieved this year; but the Virgin has kept her well."

If prayers could compass it, that would surely have been so; for night and day the devout, trusting, and contrite Ramona had knelt before the Madonna and told her golden beads, till they were wellnigh worn smooth of all their delicate chasing.

At midsummer was to be a fête in the Saboba village and the San Bernardino priest would come there. This would be the time to take the baby down to be christened; this also would be the time to send the letter to Felipe, enclosed in one to Aunt Ri, who would send it for her from

San Bernardino. Ramona felt half guilty as she sat plotting what she should say and how she should send it,—she, who had never had in her loyal, transparent breast one thought secret from Alessandro since they were wedded. But it was all for his sake. When he was well, he would thank her.

She wrote the letter with much study and deliberation; her dread of its being read by the Señora was so great, that it almost paralyzed her pen as she wrote. More than once she destroyed pages, as being too sacred a confidence for unloving eyes to read. At last, the day before the fête, it was done, and safely hidden away. The baby's white robe, finely wrought in open-work was also done, and freshly washed and ironed. No baby would there be at the fête so daintily wrapped as hers; and Alessandro had at last given his consent that the name should be Majella. It was a reluctant consent, yielded finally only to please Ramona; and, contrary to her wont, she had been willing in this instance to have her own wish fulfilled rather than his. Her heart was set upon having the seal of baptism added to the name she so loved; and, "If I were to die," she thought, "how glad Alessandro would be, to have still a Majella!"

All her preparations were completed, and it was yet not noon. She seated herself on the veranda to watch for Alessandro, who had been two days away, and was to have returned the previous evening, to make ready for the trip to Saboba. She was disquieted at his failure to return at the appointed time. As the hours crept on and he did not come, her anxiety increased. The sun had gone more than an hour past the midheavens before he came. He had ridden fast; she had heard the quick strokes of the horse's hoofs on the ground before she saw him. "Why comes he riding like that?" she thought, and ran to meet him. As he drew near, she saw to her surprise that he was riding a new horse. "Why, Alessandro!" she cried. "What horse is this?"

He looked at her bewilderedly, then at the horse. True; it was not his own horse! He struck his hand on his forehead, endeavoring to collect his thoughts. "Where is my horse, then?" he said.

"My God! Alessandro," cried Ramona. "Take the horse back instantly. They will say you stole it."

"But I left my pony there in the corral," he said. "They will know I did not mean to steal it. How could I ever have made the mistake? I recollect nothing, Majella. I must have had one of the sicknesses."

Ramona's heart was cold with fear. Only too well she knew what summary punishment was dealt in that region to horsethieves. "Oh, let me take it back dear!" she cried. "Let me go down with it. They will believe me."

"Majella!" he exclaimed, "think you I would send you into the fold of the wolf? My wood-dove! It is in Jim Farrar's corral I left my pony. I was there last night, to see about his sheep-shearing in the autumn. And that is the last I know. I will ride back as soon as I have rested. I am heavy with sleep."

Thinking it safer to let him sleep for an hour, as his brain was evidently still confused, Ramona assented to this, though a sense of danger oppressed her. Getting fresh hay from the corral, she with her own hands rubbed the horse down. It was a fine, powerful black horse; Alessandro had evidently urged him cruelly up the steep trail, for his sides were steaming, his nostrils white with foam. Tears stood in Ramona's eyes as she did what she could for him. He recognized her good-will, and put his nose to her face. "It must be because he was black like Benito, that Alessandro took him," she thought. "Oh, Mary Mother, help us to get the creature safe back!" she said.

When she went into the house, Alessandro was asleep. Ramona glanced at the sun. It was already in the western sky. By no possibility could Alessandro go to Farrar's and back before dark. She was on the point of waking him, when a furious barking from Capitan and the other dogs roused him instantly from his sleep, and springing to his feet, he ran out to see what it meant. In a moment Ramona followed,—only a moment, hardly a moment; but when she reached the threshold, it was to hear a gun-shot, to see Alessandro fall to the ground, to see, in the same second, a ruffianly man leap from his horse, and standing over Alessandro's body, fire his pistol again, once, twice, into the forehead, cheek. Then with a volley of oaths, each word of which seemed to Ramona's reeling senses to fill the air with a sound like thunder, he untied the black horse from the post where Ramona had fastened him, and leaping into his saddle again, galloped away, leading the horse. As he rode away, he shook his fist at Ramona, who was kneeling on the ground, striving to lift Alessandro's head, and to stanch the blood flowing from the ghastly wounds. "That'll teach you damned Indians to leave off stealing our horses!" he cried, and with another volley of terrible oaths was out of sight.

With a calmness which was more dreadful than any wild outcry of grief, Ramona sat on the ground by Alessandro's body, and held his hands in hers. There was nothing to be done for him. The first shot had been fatal, close to his heart,—the murderer aimed well; the after-shots, with the pistol, were from mere wanton brutality. After a few seconds Ramona rose, went into the house, brought out the white altar-cloth, and laid it over the mutilated face. As she did this, she recalled words she had heard Father Salvierderra quote as having been said by Father Junipero, when one of the Franciscan Fathers had been massacred by the Indians, at San Diego. "Thank God!" he said, "the ground is now watered by the blood of a martyr!"

"The blood of a martyr!" The words seemed to float in the air; to cleanse it from the foul blasphemies the murderer had spoken. "My Alessandro!" she said. "Gone to be with the saints; one of the blessed martyrs; they will listen to what a martyr says." His hands were warm. She laid them in her bosom, kissed them again and again. Stretching herself on the ground by his side, she threw one arm over him, and whispered in his ear, "My love, my Alessandro! Oh, speak once to Majella! Why do I not grieve more? My Alessandro! Is he not blest already? And soon we will be with him! The burdens were too great. He could not bear them!" Then waves of grief broke over her, and she sobbed convulsively; but still she shed no tears. Suddenly she sprang to her feet, and looked wildly around. The sun was not many hours high. Whither should she go for help? The old Indian woman had gone away with the sheep, and would not be back till dark. Alessandro must not lie there on the ground. To whom should she go? To walk to Saboba was out of the question. There was another Indian village nearer,—the village of the Cahuillas, on one of the high plateaus of San Jacinto. She had once been there. Could she find that trail now? She must try. There was no human help nearer.

Taking the baby in her arms, she knelt by Alessandro, and kissing him, whispered, "Farewell, my beloved. I will not be long gone. I go to bring friends." As she set off, swiftly running, Capitan, who had been lying by Alessandro's side, uttering heart-rending howls, bounded to his feet to follow her. "No, Capitan," she said; and leading him back to the body, she took his head in her hand, looked into his eyes, and said, "Capitan, watch here." With a whimpering cry he licked her hands, and stretched himself on the ground. He understood, and would obey; but his eyes followed her wistfully till she disappeared from sight.

The trail was rough, and hard to find. More than once Ramona stopped, baffled, among the rocky ridges and precipices. Her clothes were torn, her face bleeding, from the thorny shrubs; her feet seemed leaden, she made her way so slowly. It was dark in the ravines; as she climbed spur after spur, and still saw nothing but pine forests or bleak opens, her heart sank within her. The way had not seemed so long before. Alessandro had been with her; it was a joyous, bright day, and they had lingered wherever they liked, and yet the way had seemed short. Fear seized her that she was lost. If that were so, before morning she would be with Alessandro; for fierce beasts roamed San Jacinto by night. But for the baby's sake, she must not die. Feverishly she pressed on. At last, just as it had grown so dark she could see only a few hand-breadths before her, and was panting more from terror than from running, lights suddenly gleamed out, only a few rods ahead. It was the Cahuilla village. In a few moments she was there.

It is a poverty-stricken little place, the Cahuilla village,—a cluster of tule and adobe huts, on a narrow bit of bleak and broken ground, on San Jacinto Mountain; the people are very poor, but are proud and high-spirited—veritable mountaineers in nature, fierce and independent.

Alessandro had warm friends among them, and the news that he had been murdered, and that his wife had run all the way down the mountain, with her baby in her arms, for help, went like wild-fire through the place. The people gathered in an excited group around the house where Ramona had taken refuge. She was lying, half unconscious, on a bed. As soon as she had gasped out her terrible story, she had fallen forward on the floor, fainting, and the baby had been snatched from her arms just in time to save it. She did not seem to miss the child; had not asked for it, or noticed it when it was brought to the bed. A merciful oblivion seemed to be fast stealing over the senses. But she had spoken words enough to set the village in a blaze of excitement. It ran higher and higher. Men were everywhere mounting their horses,—some to go up and bring Alessandro's body down; some organizing a party to go at once to Jim Farrar's house and shoot him: these were the younger men, friends of Alessandro. Earnestly the aged Capitan of the village implored them to refrain from such violence.

"Why should ten be dead instead of one, my sons?" he said. "Will you leave your wives and children like his? The whites will kill us all if you lay hands on the man. Perhaps they themselves will punish him."

A derisive laugh rose from the group. Never yet within their experience had a white man been punished for shooting an Indian. The Capitan knew that as well as they did. Why did he command them to sit still like women, and do nothing, when a friend was murdered?

"Because I am old, and you are young. I have seen that we fight in vain," said the wise old man. "It is not sweet to me, any more than to you. It is a fire in my veins; but I am old. I have seen. I forbid you to go."

The women added their entreaties to his, and the young men abandoned their project. But it was with sullen reluctance; and mutterings were to be heard, on all sides, that the time would come yet. There was more than one way of killing a man. Farrar would not be long seen in the valley. Alessandro should be avenged.

28 Indian Slaves

The lot of the Indian under Spain and Mexico was harsh. Mission life weakened indigenous cultural values and dramatically changed the "heathen" tribes. The Anglo invasion completed the destruction of the very fabric of Indian life. Matters worsened under the Yankees because they came in such numbers and speeded cultural change. The gold rush meant that there were no longer any places for the Indian to retreat. Disease had taken a horrible toll in mission days but it was worse under the Americans. The most blatant of all injustices was the widespread cheating of these once proud people. "If ever an Indian was fully and honestly paid for his labor by a white settler, it was not my luck to hear of it," commented one observer. The following scene was an all too common one in Los Angeles in the 1850s.

From *This Land I Hold* by Virginia Myers. Copyright 1950 by Virginia Myers. Reprinted by permission of the Bobbs-Merrill Company, Inc.

Gerald stood on the warm dusty road and gazed at the Indian corral. It was Monday afternoon and, although the crowd was thinning out, the corral showed evidences of having been packed full the night before. The space was littered with refuse, broken bottles, rags, paper, excretion from both man and beast over which large green flies buzzed frantically. And in and out among everything roamed weary emaciated vicious dogs, mongrels of a hundred breeds and mixtures. They snuffled at some offal here or worried a bone there or deftly dodged a hurled stone or a kick.

Gerald's eyes flicked from sight to sight, seeing a woman, unnoticed and in apparent pain, vomiting by a fence post. There was a man whose thigh was bandaged with a brown-encrusted rag. There was another who sat motionless in dust with his head in his hands. Becoming more accustomed to the melee, Gerald discerned a prone figure the color of ground on which it lay.

Gerald removed his hat and blotted his face with his handkerchief. The man was dead, he felt sure. Grimly, almost wishing he had not passed this way, he put his hat on again. He would go for Father Ignacio. If the man were dying or dead, the need for a priest was indicated. Two men in the corral started to quarrel halfheartedly as Gerald turned away and started down the dusty road.

Father Ignacio would be unhappy. He detested the alcalde system of attempting to preserve order, for a week end rarely passed when at least one dead Indian was not found in the crowded corral Monday morning.

Approaching Father Ignacio's door, Gerald grinned to himself at the dignified term "alcalde." The Indians who rounded up and herded the disorderly from the Street of the Maidens at sundown Sunday were sober and lawful only because they had been locked up during the week end with that result in view.

Monday was a busy day, for those who had broken the law must be sentenced and fined. Those who could not pay their fines—and none could—were sentenced to labor on the public works. And since there were never enough public works to keep them occupied, their labor was sold to private individuals with funds to pay the fines.

All day rancheros and mayordomos had been arriving to buy up the Indians for work on the ranches and in the vineyards. At the end of the specified term, Gerald knew, the Indians would be given some additional money or aguardiente. Then they would return to Los Angeles and disappear into the Street of the Maidens, only to be rounded up and herded into the corral Sunday evening. This insured an ever-ready supply of cheap labor.

The Indian in the corral was not dead, but dying, when they returned. Father Ignacio knelt in the filth of the corral to administer the rites. Gerald, hatless, bowed his head, more because he didn't care to look than because he was devout. The somber beautiful words of the ritual fell in the hot dusty air.

When the priest had finished, the Indian was carried away.

Chapter 6

The Americanization
of California

The Americanization of California

Under American sovereignty the sparsely inhabited and isolated pastoral Mexican province of California became transformed overnight into a bustling American state. The gold rush was the major cause of this rapid change-over and triggered a rise in population from 14,000 in 1848 to 300,000 in 1860. The distinctly American form of government provided by the constitutional convention resulted in a slow but steady decline of Hispanic traditions. Admission to the Union was accomplished despite the growing national tension over slavery and dispute over the question of California's status as a slave or free state. The state's new political system reflected the national political scene. The Democrats dominated local politics with their two powerful adversaries battling each other for leadership of the party: William Gwin, a pro-slavery advocate came to California from the South; his opponent, David Broderick, was anti-slavery and from New York City. Both served in the United States Senate.

Although the new state had all of the political trappings, it suffered from growing pains. The highly mobile and restless (and predominantly male) population which thronged to the gold fields included a large number of social misfits. Official law enforcement agencies were lacking and the essential police and judiciary didn't expand fast enough to keep up with the mushrooming population growth. Then too, many police and judges were incompetent or corrupt. The result was a breakdown of law and order in many areas and the creation of vigilante groups by which the citizenry sought to protect itself. Many scholars have praised the work of the vigilantes of the 1850s. Some contend, however, that there was no justification for such extra-legal agencies and claim they did more harm than good. Fiction writers are about as evenly divided over this as are historians.

One of the saddest results of the Americanization was the destruction of the Californios. These people found themselves in a strange and chaotic world which only a few could adjust to. Not accustomed to a money economy, they borrowed at extortion-level interest rates. Many went bankrupt trying to prove the legality of land grants which had been in their families for years. Making matters worse, the insecurity of land titles drove away prospective purchasers and pushed interest rates up for the local inhabitants when they were forced to borrow. Lawyers were as expensive then as they are now, and the cost of successfully proving a title often caused bankruptcy. It is impossible to estimate the number of rancheros who were bilked of their land by crooked lawyers or dishonest officials, but fiction writers would have us believe that it was a frequent occurrence.

29 Constitution Making

Peace with Mexico made necessary a more formal government for California. When Congress adjourned without providing for a territorial government, Governor Bennett Riley called for a constitutional convention. Of the forty-eight delegates, eight were Spanish speaking; and an official translator had to be used. Only fifteen were immigrants from the slave-holding South. It was a young convention with an average age of thirty-six. The Iowa and New York constitutions were liberally copied by the delegates. This reading gives some of the background of the convention and discusses the most important matters decided by its members.

The heavy fog persisted all through the next morning and was as thick as ever at noon when Shane, Halleck, and Colonel Stevenson walked up toward Colton Hall.

"It's a good-looking building at that," Shane exclaimed. "I don't blame Colton for being proud of it."

The hall was built of gleaming white stone, two stories in height, with a pair of large colonial pillars holding up a rounded portico in front, and with a flagpole in the center.

"The children are all happy as can be because school has been let out for the convention," Halleck said. "They're hoping that we'll get deadlocked here and the session will last the rest of the year."

"What session?" inquired Shane. "It doesn't look like we're going to have enough people here to get deadlocked over anything."

Halleck glanced around.

"You're right," he admitted. "There isn't much chance of the *Frémont* coming in through this fog. But there's Semple anyway. If we could just put a light on his head, he's tall enough to act as a lighthouse."

Semple was leaning out of an upstairs window, and now he called down: "Where is our quorum?"

"Still lost," Halleck responded. "I just hope we get enough people here by Monday so things can get under way."

"You certainly can't start anything without Dr. Gwin," Colonel Stevenson added. "It's an open secret up in San Francisco that he's got the constitution all written out in his pocket, and all you fellows are going to have to do is just sign it."

"The hell we will!" Halleck declared. "There are a lot of points that I want cleared up before I sign anything!"

A little group of men came out of the fog, and Shane ran forward to greet one of them. They shook hands, and then Shane brought the man to their party and said: "Halleck, this is J. McHenry Hollingsworth, one of the men in our regiment. He's over here for the San Joaquin district."

From *Eagles Fly West* by Ed Ainsworth. Copyright 1946 by the author. Reprinted by permission of Mrs. Katherine Ainsworth.

"I understand there are going to be six or seven of my boys in this meeting if they ever get here," Colonel Stevenson added.

Shane was introduced to the men with Hollingsworth: Antonio Pico from San Jose, and Henry Tefft from San Luis Obispo.

"Come on upstairs," called Semple. "We might as well sit down and wait."

They tramped up the stairs. Shane looked curiously at the auditorium. It was about seventy feet long and possibly thirty wide, with a railing across the middle and a dais at the far end. Ten or twelve persons were sitting in the space provided for spectators, while the seats inside the railing were reserved for the delegates.

The whole room was decorated with American flags. A Bible was on the rostrum.

"Looks like a church," Colonel Stevenson muttered.

"It probably won't sound like it for long, though," Shane responded.

The delegates congregated in a little group inside the railing and talked for a while. They looked hopefully at the door each time someone entered, but only three other delegates arrived—Kimball Dimmick, another member of Colonel Stevenson's regiment, J.D. Hoppe, and Joseph Aram, all from San Jose.

"This looks like all," Larkin finally said. "Why don't we organize at least enough so that we can adjourn?"

Dimmick was elected chairman pro tem, and Tefft secretary; and then Halleck moved an adjournment until Monday noon.

They all filed out again and began speculating as to when the fog would lift sufficiently for the San Francisco and Sacramento delegations to come in.

By noon Monday, the heavy mists had relented sufficiently for the *Frémont* to arrive with its representatives from the north. Others from the mining districts and the south came Sunday or Monday morning. . . .

Hour after hour, day after day, the long-winded wrangles over minor points, over seating of delegates and rules of order, went on. Finally, the convention decided to admit forty-eight delegates, seven of them Shane's companions in the regiment. Then it took up the matter of electing a permanent chairman.

The whole assemblage suddenly came to life, delegates and spectators alike. Mrs. Gwin and Jessie Frémont craned their necks. The members who had been lolling in their seats or talking in bored whispers on the balcony outside the door at the back of the rostrum, now sat expectant of fireworks.

Everyone knew Gwin expected to be president. Had he not told everyone that he had given up "the most lucrative political post in the United States," at New Orleans, to come to California? Had he not promised Stephen A. Douglas on the streets of Washington the very day of Zachary Taylor's inauguration that he would return from California within a year as a United States Senator? Was he not regarded in all informed circles—including Jessie Frémont's house here in Monterey—as the most experienced and competent political figure in the convention?

And did he not, by common repute, have the new constitution for California in his pocket merely waiting for the signatures of the delegates?

This last statement was the only one he had not publicly avowed. But every delegate was sure of its truth.

Tentatively, the maneuvering began. . . .

In the next few days the three main questions of the convention took form. If they were not yet apparent on the floor, they were demanding and receiving more and more attention behind the scenes, where so much of the real work was done. Hazily, at first, and then more and more definitely as events focused attention upon them, the three Big Issues emerged.

First, of course, and most obvious was the question of slavery. Second, and tied in with the first was the issue of permitting persons of color in the state at all.

Third was the matter of the boundary, this likewise being interrelated with the first two.

A minor preliminary dispute was over whether a state should be organized at all, or whether it was better to form a territory. This was quickly settled, however, in favor of a state over the objection of nearly all the Southern California delegates, who feared heavy state taxes might ruin their livestock business.

. . .

As the first week ended, it was obvious that some of the real issues would come up Monday.

The first issue moved to a vote with such abruptness that both the convention members and the spectators were left breathless.

The Monday session started off in approved fashion, with Rev. Señor Antonio Ramírez, who was alternating with Rev. Mr. Willey, offering a prayer. Then the drab procedure of the reading of the journal and the approval of the rules for the convention was got through with, amid yawns and fidgeting.

The convention resolved itself into a committee of the whole, and Captain Lippitt took the chair. Shane's mind flashed back to the night on the ship just out of New York when Colonel Stevenson, Dr. Perry, Captain Lippitt, and he had talked over the question of California and slavery and the grim prospect of possible civil war.

Now, here was Lippitt in a place of honor in a decisive gathering on the far-reaching issues involved in that whole discussion.

A debate started over a section which would bar anyone from holding office in the state if he participated in a duel. It was finally beaten after a whimsical speech by President Semple, who intimated his huge frame offered too good a target for him to wish to go upon the field of honor.

Others were adopted:

"The military shall be subordinated to the civil power . . ."

"No soldier shall, in time of peace, be quartered in any house. . . ."

"No person shall be imprisoned for debt . . ."

Then Captain Shannon from the Sacramento district arose and in a matter-of-fact voice moved to insert an additional section in the California law:

"Neither slavery nor involuntary servitude, unless for the punishment of crimes, shall ever be tolerated in this State."

This was it, Shane realized with a start. This was the crux, the climax of the entire discussion of California and slavery both nationally and locally—all in eighteen simple words. It dawned on him too, that three members of Stevenson's Regiment were responsible for midwifing this historic pronouncement—Shannon as its author, Lippitt as the chairman, and Marcy as secretary.

"General" McCarver proposed also to forbid the introduction of free negroes, but action on this was postponed.

Shannon's proposal was put to a vote.

It was passed unanimously.

Slavery was forbidden in California! The state now a-borning would become the sixteenth free commonwealth and thus leave the slave states in a minority of fifteen.

Calmly, the convention went on with its work, apparently hardly realizing the monumental nature of the decision it had just made. Shane could hardly believe that even Gwin had failed to vote against the antislavery measure.

But it was done, and the members lapsed into such trivialities as the issuing of instructions for the exact manner of the printing of Spanish copies of papers before the convention.

After adjournment, the real significance of the vote began to penetrate. All over Monterey—at the Larkin home, in Jessie's salon, at the little Mexican cafes, in the Washington Hotel, and even on the street—small groups gathered to discuss the decisive vote.

"But I'll bet they have a real fight over the free-nigger question," said Crosby to Shane.

Indeed, attempt after attempt was made to insert some sort of clause in the constitution designed to prevent the entrance of negroes into California at all.

Young Jones from San Joaquin flamed into speech one day to epitomize the miners' views:

"There is now a respectable and intelligent class of population in the mines, men of talent and education, men digging there in the pit with spade and pick, who would be amply competent to sit in these halls. Do you think they would dig with the African? No, sir, they would leave this country first."

Ed Gilbert from San Francisco, in the most powerful and logical argument of the whole discussion, pointed out that any such prohibition undoubtedly would be held unconstitutional because it was in conflict with the United States Constitution, and that therefore California would

be throwing away all chance of recognition in Congress if it adopted an
antinegro clause.

When the showdown ballot finally came, only McCarver and seven
others voted for the exclusion of negroes while thirty-one voted against
it. . . .

The convention, once over the free-negro hurdle, proceeded toward the
danger signal hoisted on the boundary question.

All of Monterey was trying to crowd into the spectators' seats now.

The delegates, once fresh and full of enthusiasm, were growing tired
and touchy.

The furrows in the brow of unfortunate Chairman Semple became
deeper and deeper as tempers became shorter and shorter.

"Now we get down to the meat of the whole business," Colonel
Stevenson predicted to Shane. "I don't think the possibility of creating
slave states out of all this extra territory east of the Sierra is really the main
trouble at all. That is, I don't believe there's any 'Southern plot' such as
some of these fellows are talking about. I believe it's mostly an honest
difference of opinion on which boundary will give us the best chance of
recognition from Congress. I hate to admit that I agree with this ass of a
King on anything, but I believe he's on the right track in this."

Shane knew the man's sentiments only too well, having been
introduced to him at Larkin's. King had shaken hands, smiled woodenly,
and gone on with a remark which everybody was to hear over and over
again before the convention was finished:

"For God's sake leave us no territory to legislate upon in Congress!
The great object in our formation of a state government is to avoid further
legislation. By adopting this course, there can be no question as to our
admission, and all minor matters can be settled later."

As the boundary dispute developed, King buttonholed more and more
delegates and poured out his plea, his beaver hat on one side of his head
nodding with almost comic earnestness as he sought to stave off the
horrible possibility of Congress having millions of acres of new territory
dumped in its lap with an African question mark in every acre.

And the boundary dispute was threatening to incinerate in one fiery
upheaval all the noble sentiments and happy compromises which had
gone before.

Gwin and Halleck were teamed up on this particular issue, Halleck
supporting Gwin's proposal for an immense state more than twice the size
of the one wanted by another group in the convention. McDougal wanted
the eastern boundary to run along the One Hundred Fifth Meridian beyond
Santa Fe.

Halleck's mind, trained in the technicalities of military science,
leaned to the idea that a boundary should embrace as large a territory as
could be construed to be the spoils of war. In this case, "California" very
readily could be considered to run to the Rocky Mountains.

But young Jones, who had spent so much time with the Frémont-

Preuss maps at the Castro house, was likely to spring a surprise because of
his intimate and fuller knowledge of the whole subject. Shane had been
amazed in talking with him to discover how minutely he had dissected the
maps and interpreted the geographical conclusions to be drawn from them.

It became obvious very soon that the discussion was not going to be
confined to a gentlemanly debate upon geographical matters.

Both sides carefully lined up their oratorical "big guns."

Sherwood and Halleck proclaimed in impassioned speeches that
Congress would more surely admit the new state if the larger boundary
were chosen and slavery thus excluded from the whole vast territory
reaching to the Rocky Mountains, rather than in the narrow strip
reaching merely along the eastern base of the Sierra Nevada.

Botts of Virginia leaped to his feet and cried:

"I can hardly keep cool—sirs, I can tell you this will not be the
means of your admission. You will never get into the Union with this
boundary. Or, if you do, it will be only to sit amongst its ruins, like
Marius among the ruins of Carthage!

Shane glanced back and saw the tense faces of the spectators. Jessie
Frémont was leaning forward with her lips parted and her eyes upon the
speaker. Mrs. Gwin, the famous hostess of many a Louisiana dinner,
showed a forehead puckered in displeasure at this assault upon her
husband's cherished dream. Señora de la Guerra was drinking in every
word with the avidity she showed in reading a new book. Around them
were the intent, sometimes wondering faces of the native Californians.

Still young Jones was not heard from. He continued silent as the
tempestuous debate moved toward a vote.

Finally, the question was called, and the votes were counted.

The Gwin-Halleck proposal for the larger boundary was announced
as carried by a majority of seven.

Immediately in front of Shane a table was flung upward, and
overturning, crashed to the floor. Every delegate sprang to his feet. Cries
of rage arose on every side. Another table was overturned. Botts was
shaking his fists in the face of Gwin.

Screams of "Cheat!" and "Fraud!" dinned in Shane's ears.

Semple's voice boomed above the clamor, calling for order. Getting
no order, he screamed "Adjourned" in a voice so loud the whole
building seemed to tremble.

Some of the spectators started scrambling down the stairs to avoid
the riot. Shane stayed hopefully. But no blood was spilled.

Everybody finally went home to build up a grudge for the morrow.

The next morning the strategy of young Jones's persevering silence
became apparent.

With all the delegates fresh and watchful, he arose to make a new
proposal.

"I will move a reconsideration of the vote of last night for the express purpose of offering this proposition to the House: that we shall take the Sierra Nevada line," he said. "But, if Congress will not admit us with that line—if it is an insuperable barrier to our admission—then we provide for this difficulty by saying we will take a larger—we tell the Congress of the United States what our choice is. We tell them what we want. If we cannot get in under that line, we say, in order to conciliate the opponents of the smaller line, 'You may admit us under the larger line.'

"We give them no choice besides the two. We do not give them the right to carve out the territory here as they please. We tell them precisely what the alternative is. There is nothing indefinite about it . . . .

"If they contend that we cannot divide the territory, if they compel us to come in with the large boundary, where are the great and 'insuperable' difficulties which will fall upon the unrepresented inhabitants?

"We could, within one or two years, or even six months, divide them off, and put them into a separate state—a Mormon state."

Gwin himself was so impressed, he immediately announced he would accept the Jones plan, if need be.

The backers of the smaller boundary saw their chance of victory slipping, for it was feared Congress might really adopt the larger area if the choice were left to it.

Botts leaned toward Shannon and asked in an agonized stage whister: "Where in the hell is Lippitt?"

Shannon craned his neck and shook his head.

"He's home sick," Shane told Botts in a low voice. "He's got one of those awful headaches that come on him once in a while."

"We've got to get him," Shannon said. "He's the only one who can make a speech good enough to stop this thing from going through."

"Well, let's go!" exclaimed Botts.

They ran out of the hall, and returned, each supporting an elbow of Lippitt, who seemed to be in pain, although he walked almost like one in a trance.

He was supported to his seat, where he regained some animation from the lively scene around him. Botts hovered near, but Shannon came over and sat down beside Shane.

"We had to dope him up with laudanum to get him here at all. He was nearly crazy with the pain."

At this very moment Lippitt arose and began quite rationally:

"I beg leave, Mr. President, to explain the reason which will induce me to vote against the proposition of the gentleman from San Joaquin [Jones]. I am in favor of the Sierra-Nevada line, and most decidedly against the proposition to extend the boundary to the Rocky Mountains . . ."

More and more eloquently he proclaimed his position, and impressed many of the delegates.

"One of the best speeches I ever heard," grunted Halleck

grudgingly.

Still, this was far from the end.

Ed Gilbert tried persuasion. General McCarver got up but was howled down and strode angrily out of the building to the accompaniment of loud applause after screaming:

"I will not be insulted! If this house is to stamp me down and allow other individuals to speak as long as they please, I shall no longer remain here."

Ultimately, when sheer weariness forced the convention to make some decision, the honor of having proposed the actual boundary fell upon young Jones, for the first half of his proposal, limiting the state to the Sierra-Nevada line, was approved without the second, dealing with the discretion of Congress. His long hours with the maps of Frémont and Preuss had paid dividends.

"Whew!" whistled Shane, after it was all over. "So this is the way constitutions are made. By the way, Lippitt, you really made a mighty good talk."

"Did I?" Lippitt rubbed his forehead perplexedly. "I can't remember saying a word. It must have been the laudanum talking."

30   Gwin and Broderick

California politics were dominated by William Gwin and David Broderick, two of the most talented and colorful personalities the state has produced. Gwin, a member of the constitutional convention of 1849, was a southerner, pro-slavery, close to the national Democratic administration, and the leading figure in state politics during the 1850s. Broderick, who challenged Gwin's leadership of the Democratic party, was from New York City and violently anti-slavery. The battle between these two strong men and their followers was waged fiercely until Broderick's death in a duel in 1859. The following describes the details of the sensational deal between the two which saw Broderick help his political enemy, Gwin, obtain a United States Senate seat.

The big Negro George hulked in the kitchen doorway, filling it up almost to the top. "Whyfo you wanta see Mista Broderick?"

"It's Gwin," I said. "Bill Gwin wants to have a conference—a strictly private conference. That's why I came to the kitchen door."

"What Gwin?" The Negro peered into the empty darkness behind me.

"You take my word for it, nigger, he's around. You fix things up and I'll have him here within five minutes."

This was Saturday. From Monday until Saturday, ballot after ballot had placed the count at Gwin 26, Latham 21, McCorkle 15, and Critenden 2, for that unexpired vacancy of four years. As he had promised, Broderick had let them fry in their own juices. By a word, a nod of his head, he could have forced the election of any except Critenden. Everybody believed McCorkle his probable choice.

"We'll make a few concessions," Gwin had said to me. "You gotta do that in politics, young fellow. Make a few concessions, get his support, and later in Washington I'll smear him and ride him on a rail; I'll make him yell. I'll break him. President Buchanan will support me. He'll blackball every Broderick appointment. We'll break him. Promise him everything now. Political promises, hah."

"So that's the way you play it?"

"That's the way."

"No rules."

"Rules of rough-and-tumble. Everything dirty."

I didn't like it, but there didn't seem to be any help for it. Without Broderick's cooperation, Gwin was licked.

After while the Negro came back to the kitchen door and said that Broderick would see Gwin. I went out to the alley where Gwin waited, tall thin figure of a man in a black cloak, part of which he used to mask his face. Had anyone seen him come here to connive with Broderick, his sworn enemy, he was ruined. As I boosted him astride the fence and the wind caught the tails of his cloak, he looked like Ichabod Crane. I handed his walking-stick to him.

When we reached the kitchen the Negro was gone, but the door remained open. I led the way upstairs.

Broderick sat at a table, a clutter of papers before him, stocky and solid, giving the impression of great nervous stamina packed tight in a strong container, and his dark color, faint pink in his cheeks, made him look very healthy. He smoked a cigar.

The Negro barred the way between us and Broderick. He wanted to search us. Bill Gwin thrust ahead of me. "Out of the way, nigger." And when George didn't budge, Gwin swatted him sharply with the walking-stick. The Negro didn't even blink. Broderick bounced out of his chair, crossed the room, yanked the cane from Gwin, and raised it to strike Gwin. Like taking a stick from a child, the Negro pulled the cane from Broderick's hand. "No use, boss," the Negro said.

"Out of my way, Rastus." Bill Gwin wasn't ruffled.

"His name is George," Broderick said, "George Sylvester, and he's a free man. You strike him, you strike me."

Broderick went back and sat down. I was surprised at this outburst. I'd never seen Broderick worried about anybody's comfort and well being heretofore, not even Hester's.

Jake bumbled out of the shadows with a tray, a bottle, and five glasses. Jake poured the brandy. He and the Negro stood up with theirs;

we sat.

Bill Gwin wiped his glasses clean, not touching the drink, and peered upward at the wet, tobacco-colored face of the Negro, the sweat having burst out on the Negro at what had happened, and now there was the faint and different smell of his sweat in the room, even though he looked like a clean Negro. Their sweat smells a little different is all.

Gwin said, "I don't drink with niggers."

"You're a Northerner, ain't you?" Broderick said.

"I don't drink with niggers. Where in the Constitution does it mention a nigger? I say damn a nigger. Where it says about men being free and equal, does it mention a nigger? Damn a nigger. Was George Washington a nigger? Or General Putnam? Only Benedict Arnold was, under the skin. I say damn a nigger. Let them as loves niggers go to Africa." It was the kind of talk going the rounds.

"You through?" Broderick asked. He was very softspoken.

"I've had my say."

"Shall we drink?" Broderick asked. "Shall we drink to my success in the United States Senate?"

Hand upraised, Gwin watched the Negro. He was beating that man's hide with the fury of his eyes and the hatred of his eyes and the pinched and angry mouth. The Negro set down his glass.

"Take that up, George," Broderick snarled. George picked it up again.

"Shall we drink, Senator?" Broderick asked. His sneer was sawtoothed.

"I don't drink with a goddamned—"

"Shall we drink?"

"Yeah. Oh, yes. Sure. Here's to your success, Senator, and colleague."

"Colleague?"

"Colleague. That's what I said. It's a good toast."

"On my terms?"

"On your terms," Gwin agreed.

"Let's drink, gentlemen." We downed the drink. The Negro didn't drink until we had downed ours, and then he drank his alone.

Broderick dictated, and Gwin wrote, the most infamous document in California political history, the Scarlet Letter: 'The Right Honorable Senator David C. Broderick. Esteemed Sir, I am likely to be the victim of the unparalleled treachery of those who have been placed in power by my aid and exertion. The most potential portion of the federal patronage is in the hands of those who by every principle that should govern men of honor should be my supporters instead of enemies; and it is being used for my destruction. My participation in the distribution of this patronage has been a source of numberless slanders upon me that have fastened a prejudice in the public mind against me and have created enmities that have been destructive to my happiness and peace of mind for years. It has entailed untold evils upon me; and while in the Senate I will not recommend a single individual to appointment to office in this state. Provided I am elected, you shall have exclusive control of this patronage, so far as I am concerned; and in its distribution I shall only ask that it may be used with magnanimity and not for the advantage of those who have been our mutual enemies and unwearied in their exertions to destroy us. This determination is unalterable; and in making this declaration I do not expect you to support me for that reason or in any way to be governed by it; but as I have been betrayed by those who should have been my friends, I am in a measure powerless myself and depend upon your magnanimity. Your sincere friend and admirer . . .'

That last, that *your sincere friend and admirer,* Broderick dictated with ironic relish, watching the beaklike big-pored nose and winglike protuberances of the shoulder blades as Gwin hunched over his writing.

Gwin laid down the pen. "It's hard terms, a hard bargain, sir."

"Sign it. I am giving you much in return. I am giving you back your seat in the United States Senate. Otherwise you're through, and you know it."

"It's asking a good deal."

"Sign it."

"It stinks," I said. "It stinks to high heaven. Don't sign it."

"Sign it."

Then I thought maybe it would be a good thing if he did sign it, so I didn't say anything else, and he scrawled his name at the bottom of the document: 'William M. Gwin, Junior.'

Again I glanced out of the windows, I studied the situation of the room, a door on each side, and I fixed the location of the furniture sharp in my mind. Broderick filed the letter away with some other papers in a cardboard box which he left on the table. He would hide the box somewhere, but was likely to leave the letter in it. That letter would make a powerful weapon for Broderick's enemies, I thought. With his bodyguard always around him, though, it would be practically impossible to steal it.

They shook hands. I shook hands with the Negro and with Jake, but I ignored Broderick's outstretched hand. However, I took a drink with them, a nightcap. I never turn down a drink.

31 The Decline of the Californios

While Yankees were organizing and directing a state government, there was also a slow but steady transition to an economy that was distinctly American. The friendly easy-going Hispanic ways of conducting trade were replaced by a two-fisted, harsh business atmosphere that was not readily grasped by the dons. Thus, it was easy to take advantage of them.

This reading outlines the clash between the old and the new; the clash
between two cultures.

After his first anger Gerald went grimly about the business of
discovering the amount of Agustín's indebtedness to Yount. He returned to
Estrella Grande as soon as his business in Los Angeles was taken care of.

"It was not quite so bad as I feared," he told Agustín. "It was a note,
payable on demand, but it bore interest only at ten per cent a week,
compounded weekly."

"And the amount?" Agustín asked blandly, while Magdalena felt
herself becoming sick.

"The amount is already over two thousand dollars."

The hundred dollars had become two thousand! Incredible!

"And you advise?"

"Pay it, Agustín," Gerald said bitterly. "I could say fight it, but we have
no evidence of fraud. If you said it was your understanding that it was
simply an order on your cattle, the court will wonder why you did not read
the paper. The court will assume that if you signed your name to it you
knew what it contained. It seems a bitter alternative, but if we take it to
court it will probably cost more in the end—and you will still have to pay
it."

"I see," Agustín said slowly. "In that event . . . there is no other way."

It cost him more than two thousand dollars, Magdalena knew. It cost
him much in loss of face. Out of simple courtesy he had let himself be
tricked and cheated as if he were stupid, completely without intelligence.
The humiliation was galling to him.

While Gerald remained at Estrella Grande, Agustín sent word
summoning both Refugio and Rafael. When the sons came he questioned
them about any debts they had in town, any papers they had signed. Both,
sobered and anxious, went back minutely over their actions during the past
year or so. In the end there was much to pay. Rafael had borrowed twice,
totaling, with interest, some twenty-five hundred dollars. Refugio had
purchased a horse which his eldest son had fancied. Magdalena clenched
her hands. A horse! There were hundreds of horses on Estrella Grande!
Refugio and Rafael also owed one or two bills here and there. With the two
thousand that Agustín owed Yount, the complete total of all of the
outstanding interest-bearing papers amounted to seven thousand dollars.

The old days were passing away. The days when a Californian could
enter a store and order what he pleased, signing nothing, knowing that
when the traders came up and down the coast to pick up the hides and
tallow he could pay; knowing that the simple giving of his word was
enough for any merchant or ship's captain. Now it was different. Now even
the merchants in the stores and shops got the ranchero's signature for this
or that. Interest was charged on everything possible. Then, of course, it

From *This Land I Hold* by Virginia Myers. Copyright © 1950 by Virginia Myers.
Reprinted by permission of The Bobbs-Merrill Company, Inc.

seemed foolhardy to collect immediately when a bill was due. Let it wait, let it slide. The ranchero had land and money. He was careless. He forgot. Let him forget. Then, when the bill had doubled or trebled, present it and demand payment. If the Californian was short of cash, pressed for funds, take another note—better yet, get a mortgage on his land. That could be recorded, put into the public records. Then if feeling became high and you were forced to leave for a while, the notes and mortgage still worked for you, eating up the ranchero's land and assets, and when you chose to return you might be a wealthy man.

"Pay him," Agustín said, assigning the task to Gerald. "Give this to Narciso for his alertness and friendship. Extend to him my thanks, which I shall deliver in person when I am in Los Angeles."

They learned with unhappiness that Adam had not paid his loan either. "I have lived too long in California," Adam said when next they met him. "I have grown careless. I used to be as shrewd as the best of them. I am not any longer." So Adam paid, too, and Magdalena knew it cost him dearly, for Adam's beginnings had been as poor as hers and, for all his lavish California ways, he knew the value of money and appreciated it.

Security was like sand slipping away, running out. She felt powerless to stop it or hold it or gather it up again. The valley was lost. The rancho was partitioned to permit Refugio to be his own master. Los Peñascos was gone. There had been all the draining expenses of defending their titles. And here and there along the borders of the land cattle seeped away in the night, cut away from the edges of the big herds or siphoned off in groups of four or six or a dozen if the cattle ranged widely. It mounted up. Agustín could discover the cost of it at the rodeo when the new calves were branded. Totaled, the yield was not what it should be. Long years of cattle raising had taught the Pereas how to compute almost to the exact figure what the increase should be. The result fell short of this and they knew the difference had gone to cattle thieves. Bands of renegade Indians, outlaws, Mexicans, Californians and Americans knew the big stock ranches and made periodical raids on them.

Sometimes they were caught. Some were shot. Some were hanged. But outlaws did not expect to live long—more were there to fill their places. It was vicious, insidious. It seemed the Californians were surrounded, beset, bedeviled. No matter what precautions they took, what efforts they made, the laws and usages conspired to confuse and defeat them.

They cannot, thought Magdalena in desperation and rage, they cannot. There are ways to circumvent these things. One must be careful, intelligent, prudent. We cannot lose what we have left! And as the time for the baby's birth approached she found herself passing her hands over the polished furniture as she had done just after her marriage, finding it valuable and beautiful. Often she lightly kicked the side of the wicker basket to assure herself that it was still heavy.

32   The Gathering of Grapes

The conflict between Hispanic and American cultures often took place within families, as many Yankees married the lovely California senoritas. In some instances a son-in-law even repossessed the rancho of his father-in-law. In this selection a dispute between brothers-in-law typifies the cultural warfare which plagued California in the first decades of statehood. The native Californio, resenting the suggestion that modern machinery be tried for harvesting grapes, claims that "this method was good enough for my father and it's good enough for me."

Francisca felt Manuel's death keenly, yet at the same time was relieved because she had always feared his revenge. Little was said between her and Philip regarding it. Tía Ysabel, however, voiced her feelings to Francisca. She felt no sadness over it; only regret that it should have happened in such a manner and at such a time. Now that the baby had come and the christening was over she talked of returning to Mexico but Philip urged her to remain. She did not need much persuading.

The harvest that May was satisfactory, the five hundred acres of barley yielding fifteen thousand bushels. By the following harvest they hoped to have double the number of acres under cultivation. With the machinery now in operation, the yield should be multiplied several times.

The gathering in of the grapes and the making of the wine began in September. Shortly before, a group of Mexicans, men, women and children, arrived at the ranch offering their services for the harvesting. Philip learned that these itinerant groups came year after year.

Philip took no part in the harvesting, feeling that he should leave it entirely to Carlos and keep out of the way. Each day, however, he rode over to watch, fascinated by the continual stream of Mexicans carrying the baskets of luscious Mission grapes to be made into wine. Each basket was filled with large bunches, many of them weighing two pounds or more. Carlos directed the work with an experienced, though often a harsh, hand. He ignored Philip, sitting there on his horse, and probably resented his watching.

There was no machinery for handling the grapes and turning them into wine. It was still all done by hand as it had been in the early years when first the vines had been planted. Indians or Mexicans brought in the grapes and tossed them into the large hopper, dusty and unwashed. Then they climbed into the hopper and trampled the juice from them with feet that were likewise dusty and unwashed. No one apparently questioned the unhygienic practice. To an Indian washing was considered effeminate.

The juice was carried in buckets to large casks, each holding a

From *Against the Tide* by Muriel Elwood. Copyright 1950 by Muriel Elwood. Reprinted by permission of The Bobbs-Merrill Company, Inc.

hundred gallons, and this was made into white wine. The residue of skin and pulp was taken from the slats of the false bottom of the hopper and put into a great vat to ferment into red wine. The vat had a trap door which served two purposes. It permitted the fermenting gases to escape and also made possible the stirring of the mash. During the fermentation period a man would get down through the trap door and stir the mash with his bare feet. The natives liked this part of the procedure, for the rising fumes induced a glorious state of intoxication, so glorious that often the men had to be replaced two or three times.

Philip watched and wondered, but said nothing. After that, every time he drank wine, he thought of those dirty feet. But common sense overcame fastidiousness, for he had to admit that the taste of the wine was uncommonly delicious.

He talked to Dan Freeman about the method. The Centinela ranch did not have vineyards, but Dan knew about the modern machinery used and as always was helpful with suggestions. Philip waited until the harvesting was over and the wine sold before mentioning the matter to Carlos. Since Manuel's death Carlos had been very morose. At mealtimes he seldom talked and after supper remained in his room or went out. Even when Philip shared the wine profits with him he said little. He accepted them reluctantly, making Philip wonder what was working in his strange mind.

On the afternoon that Philip rode over to talk with him about the machinery, he found him sitting idle, staring into space. "Have you a moment, Carlos?" he asked cordially. "I'd like to talk to you about the vineyards."

"What about them?" Carlos asked suspiciously.

Philip tied Ebano's reins and left him to graze. Then he sat down beside Carlos, offering him a *cigarito* which he refused.

"I'm thinking of buying some modern machinery for harvesting the grapes. Dan Freeman tells me that you can now get some that will crush the grapes and carry the juice to casks by a system of pumps and hoses."

The look Carlos gave him was one of disdain. "You gringos and your modern methods!" he sneered.

Philip felt his temper rising but controlled it. The use of the word "gringo" he let pass. "Don't you want to make a larger profit?" he asked sharply.

"Why should I? This method was good enough for my father and it's good enough for me. We Spaniards aren't always trying to squeeze the last dollar out of everything."

"Since the vineyards belong to me I shall use my own judgment as to what is best."

"Oh, yes, everything belongs to you. You own the land, you own us, body and soul! Someday I suppose you Americanos will own the world! You've stolen our land—"

"I *bought* this land, Carlos, with money that I earned by hard work."

"Money, money! That's all we hear these days! We didn't have to have money when this land was granted to us, granted to us for *services* we had rendered, not for how much money we had made or stolen."

Philip's eyes blazed. "I didn't notice you refusing the money I handed you the other day as your share of the profits," he snapped. "If you despise money so much why did you take it?"

"So that someday I won't have to be dependent on you!"

"And so that you can squander it on drink as you have been lately. You've hardly done any work since the harvest. You're no better than your worthless brother."

"Leave Manuel alone! If it hadn't been for you and your money, he would never have behaved the way he did. You gringos drove him to drinking and gambling, you with your money always thrust under his nose. We'd never have lost the ranch if things had continued as in the early days. My father was warned of the crafty ways of your people. Now I'm expected to be subservient to you because you own his land."

Philip gave him a long, steady look, then got up, untied Ebano and rode away. He rode around the ranch for more than an hour, seeing nothing. He was seething. He had thought he had done a generous thing by giving Carlos a share in the vineyards and now it had been flung in his face. He wondered how long he could put up with Carlos.

33 Land Titles

Stewart Edward White told the early history of California in a remarkable series of books—*The Long Rifle, Folded Hills, Ranchero,* and *Stampede.* In the following he writes of the contemptuous attitude of the conquering Anglo towards the native Californio landholder and explains why land titles were so widely challenged. Boundaries were often poorly marked, land titles were improperly recorded by Mexican authorites (and often not recorded at all), the requirements of land grant law were not followed, and actual titles were even lost by rancheros. Such deficiencies were not important until the legal-minded Yankees insisted that land ownership had to be proved.

"No right to the land!" the rough-looking customer was saying incredulously. "Haven't we taken the country?"

"That fact hardly gives title over those who already owned it," suggested the other, but lazily, without conviction.

"Own it, hell! Who are they? A passel of greasers too lazy to make any use of it. What right has any one man to own fifty thousand acres? I ask you that."

"Don't ask me." The smaller man waved a hand in disclaimer.

"Well, I'll tell you!" returned the other. "They got it by cheating and false swearing and just plain bribing. Micheltorena issued land grants after he was kicked out from being governor. Pico sold 'em fast as he could as soon as he seen the country was going to be American. Way I look at it that all these old grants just plain lapsed when the country was took over. You mean to tell me different?" He thrust his face forward truculently. The little man seemed unalarmed.

"Not at all," he said amusedly. "But I still am inclined to speculate on what the law is going to say finally to these squatters—for that is exactly what they are. And how they expect to get title."

"Law! title!" The other spat contemptuously overside. "The boys across the Bay's got the right idea. They've took up their hundred and sixty acres apiece, like they got a right to anywhere—"

"On public land, not private land," murmured the small man.

The other paused to glare but made no direct answer.

"And they're raising crops. Danged good crops, too! I tell you, there's a heap of land in Californy, and there's a passel of folks coming across the plains looking for it. And when anyone asks them where's their title, they got a cannon, and they point to that and tell 'em there's their title, and it's good enough."

"Let's see, what's the name of the man the land belongs to—is supposed to belong to?" the small man corrected himself.

"Oh, an old greaser named Peralta. He claimed to own the whole shore and way back into the hills. We showed him better."

"We? You claim land there?"

"I sort of got the boys settled."

"Peralta; that's it. I remember. Put him in jail, didn't you, and fined him—for attempting to put off trespassers—what he called trespassers, that is? Isn't that pretty rough?"

"I'd like to know why. He's got to be l'arned. Don't waste no tears on that old son of a bitch. He'd steal you blind. He's a greaser, I tell you, and I never seen one yet that wasn't a dirty liar and a thief."

The young man on the front seat turned his head, gravely surveyed the speaker for a moment, and turned back again.

The stage rounded the last of Visitacion's shoulders and came out upon a wide plain between the Santa Cruz mountains and the Bay. Here were spaced live oaks and ripening grasses that bent in the breeze, and bands of cattle here and there, and watercourses with sycamores voiced with the soft mourning of doves. The coolness of the upper end of the peninsula gave way to the power of the sun, so that the dust of the road awakened from its damp sleep and enveloped the vehicle in a cloud. The stage driver and the other passengers produced wide bandannas of cotton or silk, which they tied loosely across the lower parts of their faces. The small man buttoned his long linen coat to his chin. Leslie, inexperienced in this sort of travel, had provided no such protection. The dust was powder fine. The slightest wind current lifted it. A ground squirrel, scampering across, raised a cloud of it that hung in the air and resettled slowly and reluctantly.

"I suppose," the bigger man continued the conversation in muffled tones, "that you figger good American citizens are agoing to pack up and git off'n their own property just because a lot of lawyers tell 'em to!"

"I wouldn't dare guess."

"Wouldn't you fight ef'n somebody tried to put you off yore farm that you'd t'iled and sweat over to make yourself a home in the wilderness?" insisted the other oratorically.

"Probably! Probably!" conceded the small man. "And," he added, "I'd probably do a little fighting if a gang of cutthroats came and sat down on land I'd always owned and declined to get off."

"Hell!" said the other man contemptuously. "That kind ain't got no fight in 'em!"

. . .

Leslie and Djo, and later Panchito, rode the *rancho* for several days, trying to identify landmarks, to establish the boundaries. It was impossible to do so with any accuracy. "A white-oak tree," "a curious rock," "a mound of earth." Many of them, apparently destroyed or disappeared. Others existing in bewildering duplication. Distances and compass directions sometimes flatly contradictory. The whole thing was a mass: a jumble. Leslie could make no head or tail of it. Panchito, though he had been present, was not of much help. Except that he could, under close questioning, give Leslie some idea of how this extraordinary hodgepodge had been accomplished. The whole survey had been done on horseback, generally at a lope.

"But how could measurements be taken?" cried Leslie.

By a *reata*. A horseman dropped one end and paid it out until he reached the other. At full gallop? But of course; how else? And how about while the rider was recovering and recoiling the *reata*? Oh, allowance was made for that. But how? By guess? But surely; how else?

Leslie looked about him in despair. He reapplied himself to the terms of the grant. It was an impressive document, on parchment, with a great seal and the signature of the governor, Figueroa, in a fine flourish. It read well and fluently. "South three hundred and fifty *estradas* to a large live-oak tree, thence a hundred and twenty-five *estradas* to a white oak riven by the wind," and so on, from one point to another. It was all very clear, except for one thing: there was rarely by any chance a live oak or a white oak or a curious rock or whatever within any reasonable distance of where it ought to be. The indications—or rather those Leslie guessed at as being the nearest to description—led them on and on until even Djo stopped, bewildered.

"But this is not the boundary of Folded Hills!" he cried. "Folded Hills extends way over the hills yonder!"

"Let's go back and try again," said Leslie. In spite of the fact that he seemed the volatile, and Djo the steadfast, character, it was Leslie who stuck to the task obstinately long after Djo's patience was exhausted. But Djo did not as yet take the matter very seriously. Leslie's mind had been educated to a more formal politic. He was appalled.

The day was strong with the dry heat of interior California that smells hot and tastes hot in the nostrils, but in which is no prostration. They drew up finally in the shade of a wide live oak and dismounted for a little, while Panchito squatted apart, holding the horses. Djo was chuckling at their discomfiture.

"Well, are you licked, old stick-to-it?" he asked affectionately.

Leslie had difficulty making him see the gravity of the situation, or rather its grave possibilities. As the matter stood right now, it would be entirely possible for any stranger to file on at least the outlying acres of Folded Hills, with a very fair possibility that he would, in fact, be taking up legally public land. As a usual thing, legal remedying of defective titles were so long drawn out and involved and expensive that, when the smoke had cleared away, it was likely that nothing remained. Leslie was eloquent with examples; the result of his week's investigation. Few of these large landholders had any ready money with which to pay lawyers or taxes or the expense of defense. To raise such funds they had often to sell part of the land. Land whose title was clouded fetched only a fraction of its real value, for only speculators would buy it—or the sharper lawyers, who were on the inside. If the case was decided in the landowner's favor, it was almost invariably appealed to the higher local court, thence to Washington. There was no end to it. More and more fees and costs. The necessity of raising more money. Generally the lawyers were willing to take their fees in land and cattle; and so gradually they and their clients changed places, and the lawyers became the *hacendados*. That's the way it had happened, was happening about the Bay.

"We don't want your father to get into that kind of a mess," said Leslie.

"I should say not!" cried Djo . . . .

"Get the title straight," said Leslie promptly. "That's why we've got to trace out this boundary if we can. So I can make a good report. If I can't report everything in order, don't you see what will happen? As soon as it got out, they'd be down here like a swarm of locusts."

"Who?"

"The squatters. The least little rumor that the title of any land might turn out to be shaky and they come arunning. Those are mostly the sort that squat and hang on long enough to sell out to someone really looking for a farm. They sell out cheap and move on. They only try it where the title is in doubt. The real squatters settle down anywhere, regardless."

"How do you know so much about all this?" Djo looked at him

with an admiration that brought to Leslie's spirit a comforting glow. Leslie had been, at Folded Hills, the humble greenhorn.

"Part of my job," said he.

Of course Folded Hills was a long distance back, still . . .

"Let's go back to the *mojonera* and start over again," said Djo, rising.

They mounted and rode back to the *mojonera*, the official starting point of Casteñares' original "survey." It was clearly identifiable, "a monument of rounded stones in which is planted a wooden cross." The wooden cross had long since disintegrated, but the pile of stones was still there. But the fresh start gave no better result. The original inaccuracies of measurement and direction would probably have been sufficient. But additionally—and neither Djo nor Leslie could know that—the very location of the *mojonera* was fictitious. It was supposed to abut a corner of El Rancho Soledad. But Señor Casteñares had been unable to find monuments of the latter. He did not look long.

"Ah, well," he had said comfortably, "it is undoubtedly somewhere in this valley," and had wasted no more time in the matter, but had built himself a new one.

34 The Californians

While Gertrude Atherton wrote numerous volumes on the glories of the Spanish Arcadia which had been destroyed by her fellow Americans, she had little sympathy for the "old grandees" who had lost. In addition to championing the cause of women's rights, her writings stress that California was created for the strong. Her ideal was a "Hamiltonian" man who could overcome all difficulties. She writes here of the kind of don she applauded—one who worked with the greedy Yankee and became his partner.

Don Roberto Yorba had escaped the pecuniary extinction that had overtaken his race. Of all the old grandees who, not forty years before, had called the Californias their own: living a life of Arcadian magnificence, troubled by few cares, a life of riding over vast estates clad in silk and lace, botas and sombrero, mounted upon steeds as gorgeously caparisoned as themselves, eating, drinking, serenading at the gratings of beautiful women, gambling, horse-racing, taking part in splendid religious festivals, with only the languid excitement of an occasional war between rival governors to disturb the placid surface of their lives, —of them all Don Roberto was a man of wealth and consequence today. But through no original virtue of his. He had been as princely in his hospitality, as reckless with his gold, as meagrely equipped to cope with the enterprising United Statesian who first conquered the Californian,

From *The Californians* by Gertrude Atherton. Published 1898.

then, nefariously, or righteously, appropriated his acres. When Commodore Sloat ran up the American flag on the Custom House of Monterey on July seventh, 1846, one of the midshipmen who went on shore to seal the victory with the strength of his lungs was a clever and restless youth named Polk. As his sharpness and fund of dry New England anecdote had made him a distinctive position on board ship, he was permitted to go to the ball given on the following night by Thomas O. Larkin, United States Consul, in honour of the Commodore and officers of the warships then in the bay. Having little liking for girls, he quickly fraternised with Don Roberto Yorba, a young hidalgo who had recently lost his wife and had no heart for festivities, although curiosity had brought him to this ball which celebrated the downfall of his country. The two men left the ball-room— where the handsome and resentful señoritas were preparing to avenge California with a battery of glance, a melody of tongue, and a witchery of grace that was to wreak havoc among these gallant officers,—and after exchanging amentities over a bowl of punch, went out into the high-walled garden to smoke the cigarito. The perfume of the sweet Castilian roses was about them, the old walls were a riot of pink and green; but the youths had no mind for either. The don was fascinated by the quick terse common-sense and the harsh nasal voice of the American, and the American's mind was full of a scheme which he was not long confiding to his friend. A shrewd Yankee, gifted with insight, and of no small experience, young as he was, Polk felt that the idle pleasure-loving young don was a man to be trusted and magnetic with potentialities of usefulness. He therefore confided his consuming desire to be a rich man, his hatred of the navy, and, finally, his determination to resign and make his way in the world.

"I haven't a red cent to bless myself with," he concluded. "But I've got what's more important as a starter,—brains. What's more, I feel the power in me to make money. It's the only thing on earth I care for; and when you put all your brains and energies to one thing you get it, unless you get paralysis or an ounce of cold lead first."

The Californian, who had a true grandee's contempt for gold, was nevertheless charmed with the engaging frankness and the unmistakable sincerity of the American.

"My house is yours," he exclaimed ardently. "You will living with me, no? until you find the moneys? I am—how you say it?—delighted. Always I like the Americanos—we having a few. All I have is yours, señor."

"Look here," exclaimed Polk. "I won't eat any man's bread for nothing, but I'll strike a bargain with you. If you'll stand by me, I'll stand by you. I mean to make money, and I don't much care how I do make it; this is a new place, anyhow. But there's one thing I never do, and that is to go back on a friend. You'll need me, and my Yankee sharpness may be the greatest godsend that ever came your way. I've seen more or less of this country. It's simply magnificent. Americans will be

swarming over the place in less than no time. They've begun already.
Then you'll be just nowhere. Is it a bargain?"

"It is!" exclaimed Don Roberto, with enthusiasm; and when Polk
had explained his ominations more fully, he wrung the American's
hand again.

Polk, after much difficulty, but through personal influence which he
was fortunate enough to possess, obtained his discharge. He immediately became the guest of Don Roberto, who lived with his younger
sister on a ranch covering three hundred thousand acres, and, his first
intention being to take up land, was initiated into the mysteries of
horse-raising, tanning hides, and making tallow; the two last-named
industries being pursued for purposes of barter with the Boston skippers.
But farming was not to Polk's taste; he hated waiting on the slow processes
of Nature. He married Magdaléna Yorba, and borrowed from Don Roberto
enough money to open a store in Monterey stocked with such necessities
and luxuries as could be imported from Boston. When the facile
Californians had no ready money to pay for their wholesale purchases, he
took a mortgage on the next hide yield, or on a small ranch. His rate of
interest was twelve per cent; and as the Californians were never prepared to
pay when the day of reckoning came, he foreclosed with a promptitude
which both horrified Don Roberto and made imperious demands upon his
admiration.

"My dear Don," Polk would say, "if it isn't I, it would be someone
else. I'm not the only one—and look at the squatters. I'm becoming a
rich man, and if I were not, I'd be a fool. You had your day, but you
were never made to last. Your boots are a comfortable fit, and I propose
to wear them. I don't mean yours, by the way. I'm going to look after
you. Better think it over and come into partnership."

To this Don Roberto would not hearken; but when the rush to the
gold mines began he was persuaded by Polk to take a trip into the San
Joaquin valley to "see the circus," as the Yankee phrased it. There, in
community with his brother-in-law, he staked off a claim, and there the
lust for gold entered his veins and never left it. He returned to Monterey
a rich man in something besides land. After that there was little
conversation between himself and Polk on any subject but money and
the manner of its multiplication; and, as the years passed, and Polk's
prophecy was fulfilled, he gave the devotion of a fanatic to the retention
of his vast inheritance and to the development of his grafted financial
faculty.

Between the mines, his store, and his various enterprises in San
Francisco, Polk rapidly became a wealthy man. Even in those days he
was accounted an unscrupulous one, but he was powerful enough to
hold the opinion of men in contempt and too shrewd to elbow such law
as there was. And his gratitude and friendship for Don Roberto never
flickered. He advised him to invest his gold in city lots, and as himself
bought adjoining ones, Don Roberto invested without hesitation. Polk

had acquired a taste for Spanish cooking, cigaritos, and life on horseback; his influences on the Californian were far more subtle and revolutionising. Don Roberto was still hospitable, because it became a grandee so to be; but he had a Yankee major-domo who kept an account of every cent that was expended. He had no miserly love of gold in the concrete, but had an abiding sense of its illimitable power, all of his brother-in-law's determination to become one of the wealthiest and most influential men in the country, and a ferocious hatred of poverty. He saw his old friends fall about him: advice did them no good, and any permanent alliance with their interests would have meant his own ruin; so he shrugged his shoulders and forgot them. The American flag always floated above his rooms. In time he and Polk opened a bank, and he sat in its parlour for five hours of the day; it was the passion of his maturity and decline.

Chapter 7

The Development of an American Economy

The Development of an American Economy

The population influx effected by the gold rush rapidly transformed California into an area where Anglo values dominated. This was especially true in the evolution of an economy which, although peculiar to the Golden State, was dominated by recently arrived Yankees. Only in the sparsely settled southland did the ways of the Hispanos linger. A series of disasters in the 1860s hastened changes even there, and the advent of the railroads completed the transformation.

In the process of developing an American economy between 1850 and 1900, gold continued to be mined in scattered areas, although the total never approached the amount taken in the early years of the 1850s. Some of the mining was done by hydraulic means with a resulting ruin of farmland. In 1884, after a long and bitter conflict, the courts forced hydraulic miners to curb their most destructive practices.

In the main, however, the new economy was agricultural. Farming was initially slow to develop as most Anglo newcomers were convinced that California was a desert half the year and flooded the other half. Exorbitant prices for produce led a few adventurous souls to plant crops, and their financial success encouraged others. Experimentation and irrigation led to the growing of citrus fruits, walnuts, grapes, olives, and numerous other crops. In the late 1850s, wheat became the first important commercial crop. The high prices paid for grain during the Civil War led to a rapid expansion of acreage planted with this crop in the San Joaquin Valley. California was an ideal place to raise winter wheat. Sown in the fall, it could profit from the winter rains and ripen in the dry period of late spring and early summer. Wheat production reached its peak in 1879 and began a decline after this date, but it is still an important crop where irrigation is not feasible.

Lumbering was another major contributor to the development of an American economy. Redwood had been used for building as early as 1776 by the Spanish; the processing of wood products flourished in the Mexican period; and it was the building of a sawmill at Coloma which led to James Marshall's discovery of gold. But it was the rapid population increase of the Anglo era which caused lumbering to emerge as one of the state's leading industries—one which has continued to be significant to the present.

An indispensable ingredient in the evolution of an American economy was the completion of the transcontinental railroad and the building of numerous spur lines in the state. There was now an effective means to get crops to market and for people to migrate to the state. However, the railroads also brought problems. The imported Chinese workers competed for jobs once the railroads were completed. In the lean times of the 1870s efforts to drive these hard-working Orientals from the state resulted in an outburst of racial demagoguery. The railroad owners also attempted to fleece innocent small landowners, thereby triggering the Mussel Slough tragedy.

In Southern California the railroads brought in a flood of migrants between 1884 and 1886, helping this once sparsely populated area to catch up with the more densely settled central area of the state. The boom of the eighties was followed by bust, but it left a lasting impact upon the Southland.

35 Gold Is Where You Find It

A bitter confrontation took place between California farmers and gold miners during the years from 1873 to 1884. Once the placer deposits were depleted, it became necessary to use hydraulic pressure to mine gold. This technique was first used in 1853, but twenty years passed before the technology was sufficiently advanced for extensive use. Conflict arose as tailings or debris from washed-away hillsides choked the streams, causing them to overflow their banks and deposit a slimy sediment called "slickens" which ruined cropland. Many farms were destroyed before hydraulic mining was curtailed by court action in 1884. The conflict between the *laissez faire* attitude of the miners and the efforts of the farmers to defend their interests is expressed in this dispute between two brothers.

The candles guttered low in their sockets. Ralph poured the dregs of the first decanter of brandy into his glass, unstoppered the second, and filled it. He pulled his coffee-cup nearer and knocked the ash off his cigar . . . . "Trouble with you is, 'Gin, you're fifty years late."

The Colonel raised his brows. "Still know enough to know that when you knock off a cigar-ash, the flavor's gone. Here—take a fresh one and treat it mo' respectful. It's got a name as old as yo' own."

"God almighty!" Ralph laughed shortly. "Can't even smoke a cigar my own way!"

The Colonel exhaled a lingering puff. "Couldn't treat a fine cigar like a plug of nigger-twist fifty years ago, and you can't to-day. Some things don't change, Bud. Quality's one."

It was the old argument. But to-night Ralph had a reason for getting to it in his own way. Deliberately, he ignored the fresh cigar. "'Gin, you're an anachronism. Like those dogs. Probably aren't a hundred men alive today

From *Gold Is Where You Find It* by Clements Ripley. Published 1936.

who'd know that about a cigar. Or bother about it."

"Only one Robert E. Lee," the Colonel pointed out. "Maybe you'd say he was an anachronism, too?"

Ralph nodded cooly. "Yes," he said. "I would."

If he had blasphemed against the Holy Ghost (whom the Colonel in his heart would probably have put in second place) he couldn't have been more startled. But Ralph was going on—

"Your hard-headedness is costing us money, 'Gin . . . . Now wait—I know what you're going to say. The Yankees overran Mississippi. You set out to make a gentleman's empire, wheat-raising in California—"

The Colonel's hand hit the table. "And it'll stay a gentleman's empire while I've got any strength! I and others like me—"

Ralph leaned back. "No, it won't stay a gentleman's empire, 'Gin, and I'll tell you why." His forefinger tapped the table. "Wheat is done. There's stuff in the ground of California you never planted there—and it'll swamp you. . . . You never liked my saying this, but the time has come when you've got to look at the facts. The Comstock's played out—"

"Thank God!"

"All right. But men who see things are turning to the California side again. The hydraulic process'll let them work the low-grade ore. Stuff the old cradle and Long Tom couldn't touch. You're going to see things that—"

"Decision against 'em in the courts last year," the Colonel reminded him with calculated mildness. "Filling the rivers with rocks and silt— slickens all over the river fields—"

"I tell you, 'Gin, that decision'll never stand. There's too much money backed up against it. There are profits in hydraulicking, and where there are profits, men are going to get 'em. Gold production's jumped 25 percent in the last five years. No court and no legislature is going to try to stop that. This is a democracy—"

"Way you talk, it might be a hog-pen!"

"Well, did you ever see a hog-pen where all the hogs were the same size? The big ones get big because they shove the little ones away from the trough."

The Colonel dipped the end of his cigar, the ash carefully guarded, into his coffee. He took a sip of brandy. "Bud," he said, "Lord knows I've got no call to love a Yankee government, but I won't believe—"

"Seeing's believing!" Ralph leaned forward earnestly. "'Gin, you're licked! You and Robert E. Lee and Bedford Forrest, too. There's a new era coming. Wheat's done—the mines'll cover every foot of land we've got with slickens in another ten years. Ever seen a hydraulic monitor running full blast? It'll plaster a man against the wall so flat you'll have to scrape him off with a hoe. It'll rip down a mountain and toss it into the river before you can figure what's happened. And every foot of bedrock they hit's got a workable amount of gold—"

"Court decided against 'em just the same," the Colonel insisted stubbornly. "Even a Yankee court knows plain common law. You can't throw dirt in another man's face—ruin his land—cover his crops with rocks and slickens and mess."

Ralph picked up another cigar. He bit the end. . . .

"Here! That's no way to cut a cigar!" his brother interposed. "You want to —"

"It's my way!" Ralph lit the cigar, got it between his teeth, and set the candle back. . . . "That decision's been appealed," he pointed out. "Those folks have money behind them. They've got the smartest lawyers in the state—"

"Smartest lawyers in the world won't prevail against decency. Not in the long run. That case was open and shut. They can't run over us!"

Ralph smiled. "That's what you said in '61, 'Gin. Sutter thought the same. Thought the law would protect his planting against the gold rush."

"Sutter was a damned Dutchman." (To the Colonel, all Europeans not of the British Isles were either Dutchmen or Frenchies.) "Even so, he was a gentleman. He saw California for what it is, and ought to be—the finest planting country on earth."

"All right, take a look at Sutter now. How long did his farming empire last against gold? What courts they couldn't buy, they scared— and they didn't take much scaring either. And I know something about what's behind this hydraulic crowd, 'Gin—yes, old Slippery Harry McCooy. I tell you, ten years from now Bannockburn won't even be a wheat-ranch. It'll be three feet deep in mine debris. You know what comes down the rivers now—what it cost us last year building levees—"

"And what—" the Colonel's face hardened—"d'you propose doing?"

"I'd propose selling. Get out of wheat. Get into gold."

The Colonel puffed his cigar—twice. "You'd sell your land?" . . . The question was rhetorical. Naturally, no gentleman would sell his land. "Bud," he said, "you' drunk! Talkin' wild!"

"If you think so," Ralph said deliberately, "make me an offer for my share of Bannockburn."

The Colonel drew a slow breath. Then he smiled indulgently. "Sho', Bud, get on up to bed! Rosanne's waiting—oughtn't to have kept you this long. . . . Why, Bud, in two hundred years no Ferris has sold land except to buy more land. You talkin' like some Yankee, dealin' in city lots!"

He stoppered the decanter. He gripped Ralph's shoulder affectionately. "Come on, Bud! Yo' kind of excited. And you tell Rosanne I never meant a thing—"

Deliberately, Ralph knocked the ash off his cigar. "I've asked you to make me an offer, 'Gin. . . . Good Lord, it isn't as if this hadn't been coming for a year! I'm fond of you—you know that. It's just a difference of opinion, that's all. You simply won't see it my way—"

The Colonel was staring at him. Ralph's eyes were hard and level. They were not hostile, but suddenly they were the eyes of a stranger.

"I'm no child, you know, 'Gin!" he was saying. He sat back and drew on his cigar. "Go on—offer. That is, if you mean what you say."

Colonel Ferris gripped the chair back. His high cheekbones whitened. "I—I reckon yo' funnin', Bud! I reckon—well then, by God, a hundred thousand dollars!"

It was once and a half what Ralph's share was worth. Wheat land somehow wasn't selling for so much at the moment. But something had to be done right now to bring Bud to his senses!

Cooly, Ralph finished the brandy in his glass. "It's a trade," he said.

"It's—it's—why, listen, Bud, you wouldn't sell yo' *land!*"

"I said it was a trade. Cash, of course."

"Cash—" The Colonel, breathing heavily, seemed to tower. "I had figured my check would be good with you. Howsoever, if—"

" 'Gin!" Ralph was on his feet. "Don't talk like a fool! Of course, your check's good! I only meant—oh, good Lord, man, don't take it so hard!"

The Colonel's lips were a straight line that ran into deep dents at the corners of his mouth. A muscle twitched in his forehead. "Cash," he said slowly. "Or certified check within forty-eight hours. I—by God, all I ask is you'll be gone by then."

Ralph's face burned a slow red. "Don't worry," he said. "I'll be gone."

36 The Chinese Must Go!

In the 1870s the California dream was corroded. San Francisco attracted working men seeking high wages; and when there was no work, they failed to understand all of the forces behind the Panic of 1873 and looked for scapegoats. The most convenient of these were the Chinese, "Crocker's Pets," whose labor had built the Central Pacific Railroad. Confined to ghettos contemptuously called "Chinatowns," they were attacked by hoodlums with monotonous regularity, one of the worst assaults coming in 1871 in Los Angeles. But the most concerted drive against them occurred in San Francisco in the late 1870s when Denis Kearney excited the masses on the sand-lot with his cry, "The Chinese Must Go!" In this selection, Mrs. Fremont Older, wife of the famed newspaper publisher and an author in her own right, writes of Kearney, giving him the name Paul Stryne.

During the seventies nothing was extraordinary in San Francisco because everything was extraordinary. . . .

San Francisco was a drunk, delirious city. The population was divided into two classes, millionaires and those who hoped to be millionaires.

There is no hunger when thousands feast upon hope. A prospective owner of a bonanza could not make himself absurd by complaining of no breakfast. Amidst the sweat and smell of the workshop laborers

From *The Socialist and the Prince* by Mrs. Fremont Older. Published 1903.

considered the cut of their lackeys' livery.

The working man was never more prosperous. The working man was never more discontented. He had seen his companions close their eyes and open their hands. Directly the tail of a comet showered precious stones. These men gathered their treasures indifferently, drifted away from toil, spoke like gentlemen, looked like gentlemen, and were gentlemen.

Presently the working man believed something wrong when Seal Rocks did not nourish roses, and strawberries refused to thrive on sand-lots.

In the middle of the seventies came a cataclysm that changed the surface of San Francisco. A great bank failed.

That such an event could occur was a shock to the hope of the city. It was a hard world of reality after all. One could be sad in California as well as in the East, South, or across the seas from whence these adventurers came.

Even those who had not lost by the failure of the bank felt hungry after the occurrence.

Another catastrophe befell the city. Gold had been gushing from the veins of the gigantic Mazeppa mine. It was strange that none recognized the arterial blood flooding the State. The Mazeppa was dead.

Some dreamer had believed that still another heart of treasure might be found in this mine of Ophir. At one time quite probable, now it was as remote as the rainbow's base or Aladdin's lamp.

The peach-blossom hue left the air. Joy, youth, hope, ambition perished. Men, women, and children were hungry. They were even reduced to wishing that two "bits" might be changed into nickels. Many laboring men were idle.

The middle classes felt the pinch of need. The millionaires went back to the bar or sluice-box. To this day their descendants boast of the sums their grandfathers lost, and thus alleviate their present poverty.

There are still extant the deserted foundations of vast buildings begun at that period, but never finished.

Nickels were seen in currency. Values assumed rational form. The boom had burst.

It was not until then the laborer realized that, while he had allowed himself to become intoxicated by the aroma of his harvest, thousands of yellow, insignificant worms had curled into the blossoms and destroyed them before the fruit came. These were the Chinamen.

If a cook was out of employment she was told that a Chinaman had taken her place. Laundrymen lost their clients because the Chinamen underbid them. Seamstresses famished while Chinamen performed their work. It was unfortunately true that the Chinaman usually labored more conscientiously than the Caucasian.

The Chinamen spent nothing for necessities or luxuries. None but California, the fabled land of riches, could endure the outflow of gold sent to China. There was no return from it except more Chinamen.

They came by every boat. They came over the borders. When news arrived of the plague in the Orient, the working man cried, "There is no plague but Chinamen."

Railroad builders, capitalists, fetched them by the hundred, and grew rich from the putrid social conditions of the rotting empires of the East.

There was no one to protest but a few politicians during campaigns. Objections ceased with election. The Chinaman promised to be a serviceable political issue of perennial utility.

Idle men huddled together and discussed their wrongs in the squares, parks, and on street corners. Often moved by their passions they swept into the Chinese localities, set fire to buildings, and killed the occupants as they fled from the flames.

After the tempest of wrath subsided, nothing decisive or effective was done.

Sometimes San Francisco had a presentiment that it was to be destroyed by fire. This premonition seemed about to be fulfilled one evening. While the safety committee was discussing how to protect property and life, a cry went up the throat of the city that the Pacific Mail dock had been set on fire. It was thought to be the beginning of a general conflagration, and rioting began. In the struggle to suppress the rioters several laborers were killed.

The following day in every workshop and factory circulars were distributed. On them in black letters was printed:

This Evening

At GOLDEN GATE TEMPLE

A Working Man

WILL SAY

SOMETHING TO WORKING MEN

. . .

"Ladies and gentlemen: I have the pleasure to interduce to ye a brother working man, Mr. Stryne—Mr. Paul Stryne, the distinguished traveler and social philosopher. You all know of him."

None of them had heard his name before. McCann made his acquaintance but that morning. Yet they all applauded and cheered as Stryne bowed his acknowledgements.

There was something in the speaker's salutation which irritated the audience. His heels almost came together and the bow was that of a man of rank. For a moment the audience was chilled. They felt that he was not one of them, and that they were about to be lectured.

The people were reassured by Stryne's clothing, for a handkerchief, knotted loosely about the neck of his blue flannel shirt, took the place of a collar. As he arose to the height of five feet ten, he seemed like a boy prematurely old. He was not more than thirty.

After the applause subsided, Stryne began in a low, deep voice, which was but a whisper of the reservoir of tone from which it was drawn:

"MEN AND WOMEN: How many are there present who want to hear lies? Hands up. Good! None. How many here want to listen to the truth? Everybody! Everybody! This is God's country after all. Very well, men and women, if you have the truth, remember it is not my fault. It is yours. You have voted for it. You shall have it."

These first few words convinced that he was an American working man. As Stryne continued his voice lost its music. The notes broke into discord, but they shrieked into the listeners' ears and held the thought.

"I have been introduced as a traveler and philosopher. Let me disabuse your minds. I am a laborer, a working man, like yourselves, and when I die I want no other obituary—An American, a working man.

"To be sure, I have seen more countries of the globe than this. I will tell you why. In the beginning I was a seaman. When I left my ship, want drove me from England to France, France to Germany, Germany to Italy, and from Italy back to the United States, my home. I can paint you no brilliant picture of my travels, for I saw only the poverty and misery of those countries.

"Which is the best government, you ask? Which is the worst? God knows. Everywhere it is the same story of protecting those who have and taking from those that have not. This crime has been seared into my eyes. Even in the United States, the Utopia of Jean Jacques, the ideal of Jefferson, the poor man is begging for work and the rich man is saying: 'You can't have it. I will go to Asia for laborers. Starve. I must grow richer.' In the United States this happens, and we, you and I, fools, allow it."

When the applause forced Stryne to cease speaking he said in somewhat lowered tones . . .

"If any man has a right to talk at a time of depression like this, it is I. Let me tell you, want rocked my cradle and I sucked the teat of hunger. I cried to my mother for bread and she gave me tears. I have trod the thorny valley of pain. Ever at my side was the black shadow of misery, the companion who never deserted me. The only philosophy I understand is that of grief.

"My friends, do you know why I am here speaking to you this minute? It is because of a sight I saw last night. Four poor young men, laborers, were shot down while defending Chinamen for a corporation of millionaires. They were volunteers who perished as nobly as any soldier. Where were the men whose property was attacked? At their clubs; in their houses on Nob Hill, eating ten-course dinners with their mistresses; in their yachts on the Mediterranean—in any place but where they should be.

"Was any capitalist, bloated from the blood of the people, killed? Was any son of the plutocrat shot? No. Last night, as always, it was the poor man's son, the poor mother's son who died. My impulse, friends, was as generous as yours. I, also, was there defending the property of the Pacific Mail. When a nineteen-year-old boy fell over into my arms dead, I left you all.

"I said, 'Here we are dying for the rich and their Chinamen. Men, women, I've not slept since. One thought, one purpose has frenzied me, to arouse you to the use of the power that is in your hands, the ballot."

Perhaps it was not so much what Stryne said as his vehemence of utterance that held the audience dry-lipped awaiting more words. Greater approbation than applause came—silence.

"In the beginning I was asked the difference between the United States and the countries across the Atlantic. It is this: Here it is possible for each of us to have as much power in election as a Vanderbilt, a Gould, or an Astor. We all have reform in our hands. Let the laboring men organize into a solid mass which no charge from capital can break, and I tell you we will force justice from the gullets of the men on Nob Hill."

Stryne mopped his brow and the cords of his thick neck stood out like pencils. He realized that these simple impressionable beings before him had surrendered their souls to him, and he went on as if inspired by it. A smile crept about his lips at times as he spoke, and beautified his countenance. It broke the straight line of his mouth and gave it a gentle expression. The smile was doubly effective since for the most part his features were grim, determined, and sad. What the smile betokened no one could explain. To the audience it was the promise of hope, a rainbow illumining the world.

"Now, men and women, I want you to talk. Are we to keep on defending Chinamen? Are we to keep on defending Nob Hill, or are we to work for ourselves and the right?"

The audience failed not to respond with its brassy shrieks of "Yes!" Hats were thrown into the air, and the speaker realized that they and their passions were under his control.

"Good, my friends. You have decided it. You have voted.

"Men, working men, I appeal to you. Let me hear your voice again. How many present want to see your honest wives in rags that the capitalists may have harlots?

"Not one!

"How many have the heart to tell their children that there is no bread to be had because there is no work?"

Stryne's audience was growling with him. He shook his head and waved his fist until he was like a madman—to all but the reporters. The men had reached the point where he could have issued any commands and they would obey.

"Mothers, women, when you go to your homes tonight and find no food for your babes, it is not your fault, it is not your good man's fault. It is because it has been shipped across the seas to China. It has been stolen from you by great railroad builders, by great capitalists. Those jewels on my lady's bosom are yours. They belong to your hungry children. Are you willing to give up your food, women of the people of San Francisco, that those haughty dames who are no better than you may blaze at the opera?"

The flame of youth and energy leaped from his lips and enkindled them all.

"I put it to you together, are you going to have liberty, or are you going to be chattels? I ask the great common man, the people—the word that next to liberty smacks the sweetest."

Stryne's soul was in his mouth and he launched forth into a review of California as he had learned it in a few weeks. Not a man present could have given it more accurately. He spoke of the present and the future as it might be at the working man's behest.

"I warn you, men, that we can not live with these yellow creatures. We are in a cage of reptiles and the white man or the serpent must die. Am I going to help you drive them out? Shall we vote to ship them back to China? If they refuse to go, shall we drive them down into the sea? If the ballot fails, let it be the bullet. Shall we throw down the gage of battle to the lions of corruption? Shall we make the vow?"

Then the whole assembly arose and took the oath of allegiance to the principle.

"Remember, men and women of San Francisco, the law is our father and mother, but liberty is our soul. Our oath, whatever happens, *The Chinese must go!*"

Stryne raised his right arm with the gesture of a sword as he uttered the last word. It seemed that his voice was the heart and voice of the multitude. He expressed the innermost soul of the audience.

Before the echo of the speaker's words had died, the hundreds present took up the shout, "The Chinese must go!" It was on the street and the ragged rabble everywhere was repeating it as a battle-cry.

"The Chinese must go!" took the place of bread and butter. It was the panacea for all ills and evils.

37   The Saga of Wheat

The first dominant commercial crop of the state was wheat. It was easily grown in a climate which received most of the rainfall in the winter, and it was especially adapted to the San Joaquin Valley with its vast expanse of relatively level land. Highly prized on the world market, this California staple declined with the advance of irrigation. Frank Norris, whose career as a writer was cut short by an early death at the age of thirty-two, was fascinated by man's struggle with the elements to produce this basic food. In *The Octopus* he wrote the finest description of the process ever penned.

The day was fine. Since the first rain of the season, there had been no other. Now the sky was without a cloud, pale blue, delicate, luminous, scintillating with morning. The great brown earth turned a huge flank to it, exhaling the moisture of the early dew. The atmosphere, washed clean of dust and mist, was translucent as crystal. Far off to the east, the hills on the other side of Broderson Creek stood out against the pallid saffron of the horizon as flat and as sharply outlined as if pasted on the sky. The campanile of the ancient Mission of San Juan seemed as fine as frost work. All about between the horizons, the carpet of the land unrolled itself to infinity. But now it was no longer parched with heat, cracked and warped by a merciless sun, powdered with dust. The rain had done its work; not a clod that was not swollen with fertility, not a fissure that did not exhale the sense of fecundity. One could not take a dozen steps upon the ranches without the brusque sensation that underfoot the land was alive; aroused at last from its sleep, palpitating with the desire of reproduction. Deep down there in the recesses of the soil, the great heart throbbed once more, thrilling with passion, vibrating with desire, offering itself to the caress of the plough, insistent, eager, imperious. Dimly one felt the deep-seated trouble of the earth, the uneasy agitation of its members, the hidden tumult of its womb, demanding to be made fruitful, to reproduce, to disengage the eternal renascent germ of Life that stirred and struggled in its loins.

The ploughs, thirty-five in number, each drawn by its team of ten, stretched in an interminable line, nearly a quarter of a mile in length, behind and ahead of Vanamee. They were arranged, as it were, *en échelon*, not in file—not one directly behind the other, but each succeeding plough its own width farther in the field than the one in front of it. Each of these ploughs held five shears, so that when the entire company was in motion, one hundred and seventy-five furrows were made at the same instant. At a distance, the ploughs resembled a great column of field artillery. Each driver was in his place, his glance alternating between his horses and the foreman nearest at hand. Other foremen, in their buggies or buckboards, were at intervals along the line, like battery lieutenants. Annixter himself, on horseback, in boots and campaign hat, a cigar in his teeth, overlooked the scene.

From *The Octopus* by Frank Norris. Published 1901.

The division superintendent, on the opposite side of the line, galloped past to a position at the head. For a long moment there was a silence. A sense of preparedness ran from end to end of the column. All things were ready, each man in his place. The day's work was about to begin.

Suddenly, from a distance at the head of the line came the shrill trilling of a whistle. At once the foreman nearest Vanamee repeated it, at the same time turning down the line, and waving one arm. The signal was repeated, whistle answering whistle, till the sounds lost themselves in the distance. At once the line of ploughs lost its immobility, moving forward, getting slowly under way, the horses straining in the traces. A prolonged movement rippled from team to team, disengaging in its passage a multitude of sounds—the click of buckles, the creak of straining leather, the subdued clash of machinery, the cracking of whips, the deep breathing of nearly four hundred horses, the abrupt commands and cries of the drivers, and, last of all, the prolonged, soothing murmur of the thick brown earth turning steadily from the multitude of advancing shears.

The ploughing thus commenced, continued. The sun rose higher. Steadily the hundred iron hands kneaded and furrowed and stroked the brown, humid earth, the hundred iron teeth bit deep into the Titan's flesh. . . .

At intervals, from the tops of one of the rare, low swells of the land, Vanamee overlooked a wider horizon. On the other divisions of Quien Sabe the same work was in progress. Occasionally he could see another column of ploughs in the adjoining division—sometimes so close at hand that the subdued murmur of its movements reached his ear; sometimes so distant that it resolved itself into a long, brown streak upon the grey of the ground. Farther off to the west on the Osterman ranch other columns came and went, and, once, from the crest of the highest swell on his division, Vanamee caught a distant glimpse of the Broderson ranch. There, too, moving specks indicated that the ploughing was under way. And farther away still, far off there beyond the fire line of the horizons, over the curve of the globe, the shoulder of the earth, he knew were other ranches, and beyond these others, and beyond these still others, the immensities multiplying to infinity.

Everywhere throughout the great San Joaquin, unseen and unheard, a thousand ploughs up-stirred the land, tens of thousands of shears clutched deep into the warm, moist soil.

It was the long stroking caress, vigorous, male, powerful, for which the Earth seemed panting. The heroic embrace of a multitude of iron hands, gripping deep into the brown, warm flesh of the land that quivered responsive and passionate under this rude advance, so robust as to be almost an assault, so violent as to be veritably brutal. There, under the sun and under the speckless sheen of the sky, the wooing of the Titan began, the vast primal passion, the two world-forces, the elemental Male and Female, locked in a colossal embrace, at grapples in the throes of an infinite desire, at once terrible and divine, knowing no law, untamed, savage, natural, sublime.

. . .

Then, at length, Annixter's searching eye made out a blur on the horizon to the northward; the blur concentrated itself to a speck; the speck grew by steady degrees to a spot, slowly moving, a note of dull colour, barely darker than the land, but an inky black silhouette as it topped a low rise of ground and stood for a moment outlined against the pale blue of the sky. Annixter turned his horse from the road and rode across the ranch land to meet this new object of interest. As the spot grew larger, it resolved itself into constituents, a collection of units; its shape grew irregular, fragmentary. A disintegrated, nebulous confusion advanced toward Annixter, preceded, as he discovered on nearer approach, by a medley of faint sounds. Now it was no longer a spot, but a column, a column that moved accompanied by spots. As Annixter lessened the distance, the spots resolved themselves into buggies or men on horseback that kept pace with the advancing column. There were horses in the column itself. At first glance, it appeared as if there were nothing else, a riderless squadron tramping steadily over the upturned plough land of the ranch. But it drew nearer. The horses were in lines, six abreast, harnessed to machines. The noise increased, defined itself. There was a shout or two; occasionally a horse blew through his nostrils with a prolonged, vibrating snort. The click and clink of metal work was incessant, the machines throwing off a continual rattle of wheels and cogs and clashing springs. The column approached nearer; was close at hand. The noises mingled to a subdued uproar, a bewildering confusion; the impact of innumerable hoofs was a veritable rumble. Machine after machine appeared; and Annixter, drawing to one side, remained for nearly ten minutes watching and interested while, like an array of chariots—clattering, jostling, creaking, clashing, an interminable procession, machine succeeding machine, six-horse team succeeding six-horse team—bustling, hurried—Magnus Derrick's thirty-three grain drills, each with its eight hoes, went clamouring past, like an advance of military, seeding the ten thousand acres of the great ranch; fecundating the living soil; implanting deep in the dark womb of the Earth the germ of life, the sustenance of a whole world, the food of an entire People.

When the drills had passed, Annixter turned and rode back to the Lower Road, over the land now thick with seed. He did not wonder that the seedings on Los Muertos seemed to be hastily conducted. Magnus and Harran Derrick had not yet been able to make up the time lost at the beginning of the season, when they had waited so long for the ploughs to arrive. They had been behindhand all the time. On Annixter's ranch, the land had not only been harrowed, as well as seeded, but in some cases, cross-harrowed as well. The labour of putting in the vast crop was over. Now there was nothing to do but wait, while the seed silently germinated; nothing to do but watch for the wheat to come up.

. . .

There it was, the Wheat, the Wheat! The little seed long planted, germinating in the deep, dark furrows of the soil, straining, swelling, suddenly in one night had burst upward to the light. The wheat had come up. It was there before him, around him, everywhere, illimitable, immeasurable. The winter brownness of the ground was overlaid with a little shimmer of green. The promise of the sowing was being fulfilled. The earth, the loyal mother, who never failed, who never disappointed, was keeping her faith again. Once more the strength of nations was renewed. Once more the force of the world was revivified. Once more the Titan, benignant, calm, stirred and woke, and the morning abruptly blazed into glory upon the spectacle of a man whose heart leaped exuberant with the love of a woman, and an exulting earth gleaming transcendent with the radiant magnificence of an inviolable pledge.

38 Millionaires of a Day

The history of California has been marked by cycles of boom and bust. None was more spectacular than the boom which occurred in Southern California in the 1880s. A rate war between the Southern Pacific and the Santa Fe railroads triggered the boom which was fueled by one of the most successful promotional campaigns in history to sell the attractions of Southern California to the rest of the nation. The population of Los Angeles jumped from 12,000 to 100,000 in two years, and the rest of the area grew proportionately. In this reading, two participants reminisce on the meaning of the era's prosperity and the future of the region.

The silvery strip that marked the watery horizon on the distant west was brightening under the declining sun when the Major remarked:

"Tough! isn't it, to have to come down the way we have?"

"Not half as bad as it might have been if the boom had gone on a year or two more until all the money was owed to outsiders instead of at home. I think, considering the fools we made of ourselves, that we are in big luck," said the General. "The boys are hard up for coin, of course; but every one has enough to eat and drink and wear. There is no such thing as suffering or destitution anywhere. It would be impossible anyhow in California. The only thing to suffer much is pride, and I have mighty little of that left. I am not kicking any. I made a big fool of myself, but nobody else is to blame. All that I have been buying was stuff fit only to sell to tenderfeet, who wanted it only to sell to other

From *Millionaires of a Day* by T.S. Van Dyke. Published 1890.

tenderfeet. I didn't have sense enough then to see the folly of it. But what a piece of stupidity! For a country that can raise what Southern California can and in the quantities that it can, and get the prices for its products that it can, to be making itself dependent for its happiness on selling dry land and town-lots to a lot of crazy greenhorns is positively disgraceful. Every man that has even five acres of good bearing orchard or vineyard is making money now, while we are scratching up here for grub. Here the country is walking off with the markets of the world, its produce is bringing the very top price and the world is crying for ore, and we have been overlooking all this and trying to get rich by selling unproductive stuff to a lot of asses years ahead of any possible legitimate demand for it. For one, I deserve all the punishment I have got. And yet I did only what the great majority did, and a majority too of people who had ten times my opportunity to know better."

The Major took a long whiff of his five-cent pipe, and, deeply meditating on the twenty-five-cent cigars he used to smoke, replied:

"Yes; single-handed and alone, with all the world apparently against her, Southern California has gone through the decline with flying colors. It is all over now, and although there is some trash that will fall still lower in value, the whole country is on the up-grade again. We are about the last of the lame ducks, the liquidation is about all over and the country is making more money out of the ground to-day than any other equal acreage in the Union. But where do I come in on the new racket? That's the question. The country right now is on the eve of the biggest boom it ever had—a boom of raising good stuff and plenty of it to sell to those who can't raise it. The money is pouring in already everywhere where the orchards and vineyards are old enough. But where am I coming in? is the question that worries me. It looks most mightily as if the only satisfaction I am to get out of it will be the satisfaction of being proud of my new home. That is a trifle thin for a steady diet. The country is now where it should have kept itself all the time—independent of the 'tenderfoot;' for the surest way to command his respect and make him crazy to buy is to show him a country independent of him. But I am afraid that I am dependent on him yet. About all I am adapted for is selling town-lots to greenhorns. That's been my business always, and I don't understand any other work. I am afraid I am going to make a failure of farming, and I don't know anything about speculating in outside property here. At the foot of that great snowy mountain in sight sixty or seventy miles away there in the north, you can almost see a piece of land that would have made me rich if I had known enough to buy it when I came here and bring water on it from that long, deep canyon that you see running into the heart of the mountain. The money I then had would have bought it and put the water on it, and left me considerable over. But I hadn't sense enough to see it; and because the soil looked thin and rough, I laughed at the man and asked him if he saw anything green in my eye when he offered it to me for one twentieth of what it is selling for like hot cakes to-day. It is not once in a lifetime that such chances strike man as I have thrown away there, and I feel clear out discouraged. I feel as if I had lost my grip, and never should make anything again."

The General made no answer, and both sat for a while in silent thought as they looked down upon the vast expanse of land and sea before them. . . .

A strange land, where the breeze never rests, yet rises never in anger; where all the conditions of the cyclone seem present, yet cause nothing but occasional little whirls moving gently over the plain; where the clouds gather as heavily as anywhere, over a land as heavily charged with electricity as any, yet cause no thunder-storms worthy of the name. A strange land, where all the vegetation of the temperate zone and tender plants from the tropics with exotics from every clime reach perfection side by side; a land where almost every bird and animal, and tree and grass, and flower and shrub, is different from any of its genus on the Atlantic coast; where annuals become perennials, herbs become shrubs, and shrubs trees; a land where trees and vines and nearly all deep-rooted plants stand green, and the wells show no sign of failing, and the springs pour out a steady stream through periods of drought that would kill all vegetation in any Eastern State and dry up the wells and springs in half the time; a land where nearly all rules of farming are reversed— where the poorest-looking soil needs only water to make vegetation overleap the bounds of propriety, and where land deemed worthless to-day is found the most valuable to-morrow.

"Well," said the General, finally, "the boom will come again. Not so wildly as before, but perhaps strong enough to suit you. Like causes produce like results; and this country sets a certain proportion of people crazy, and always will do so. There will be chance enough for you to follow your profession and sell lots again to greenhorns; but as for me, I am quite sufficiently amused, thank you. This quiet life suits me first-rate for a change. It takes me back to my early days, when I was raised in the woods of Michigan and roamed them half the time with a rifle, and was happier than I have ever been since. I have made such a fool of myself I don't dare trust myself in a boom again. I had made enough money to think I was mighty smart, and had seen just enough booms and made enough on them to make me think I knew all about them. It is not an easy matter to get such a start in the world again as I had when I came here; and if I didn't have sense enough then to keep what I had, what is the use of trying again? The more booms you see the less you know about where the top of the next one is. They change your nature, and make you think you see different conditions in each one that will make it impossible to collapse. You grow so that you don't know money when you see it. You think when you start in that you know what enough is and will be satisfied with that; but the amount necessary even for a competency keeps growing every day, and the longer it lasts the bigger fool you become, and the more impossible it is to get out and stow away a reasonable sum. I am done with all ambition. The only prominent part I will ever play in this world will be at my own funeral. Life is but a game anyhow, and he beats it best who plays for the smallest stakes. For years I have been playing for big stakes, and when I win it is all staked on another big play, and I don't enjoy a cent of it. I am more happy right here now with plenty of time to read and hunt than I have been for fifteen years, and I don't care whether another boom comes or not, or whether another tenderfoot comes or not, or whether anybody buys anything or not, or whether the country goes ahead or not." . . .

The Major knocked the ashes from his pipe, and with a long sigh said:

"Yes, we all thought we were mighty smart. But the only smart ones were those that paid their debts and lived as they always had before until they saw the game through. Every one that did that is now away ahead of the rest. But the fellows that thought themselves big operators like we did—where are the most of them now? You remember perhaps in the last years of the war how lots of little country shopkeepers thought themselves big merchants because they were making money while prices were all the time going up? But when prices began going down they all went to the grass mighty quick. We were just like them. We thought ourselves great financiers. But we were simply *chain-lightning on a rising market.*"

"Worse than that," replied the General, with an air of disgust. "We were a lot of very ordinary toads whirled up by a cyclone until we thought we were eagles sailing with our own wings in the topmost dome of heaven."

39 The Octopus

The California farmer faced many problems, the most important being the difficulty of getting his produce to market. The state's farmers eventually came to view the railroad as a great exploiter, blaming it for high shipping rates and fraudulent land deals. The conflict between the ranchers and the railroad men has been ably depicted by Frank Norris, who saw the iron monster as an octopus in its relations with man. In the following selection, the tranquil atmosphere of the wheat ranching country is disturbed by the railroad engine which spreads destruction and ruin as it hurtles by.

As from a pinnacle, Presley, from where he now stood, dominated the entire country. The sun had begun to set, everything in the range of his vision was overlaid with a sheen of gold.

First, close at hand, it was the Seed ranch, carpeting the little hollow behind the Mission with a spread of greens, some dark, some vivid, some

From *The Octopus* by Frank Norris. Published 1901.

pale almost to yellowness. Beyond that was the Mission itself, its venerable campanile, in whose arches hung the Spanish King's bells, already glowing ruddy in the sunset. Farther on, he could make out Annixter's ranch house, marked by the skeleton-like tower of the artesian well and, a little farther to the east, the huddled tiled roofs of Guadalajara. Far to the west and the north, he saw Bonneville very plain, and the dome of the courthouse, a purple silhouette against the glare of the sky. Other points detached themselves, swimming in a golden mist, projecting blue shadows far before them; the mammoth live-oak by Hooven's, towering superb and magnificent; the line of eucalyptus trees, behind which he knew was the Los Muertos ranch house—his home; the watering-tank, the great iron-hooped tower of wood that stood at the joining of the Lower Road and the County Road; the long wind-break of poplar trees and the white walls of Caraher's saloon on the County Road.

But all this seemed to be only foreground, a mere array of accessories—a mass of irrelevant details. Beyond Annixter's, beyond Guadalajara, beyond the Lower Road, beyond Broderson Creek, on to the south and west, infinite, illimitable, stretching out there under the sheen of the sunset forever and forever, flat, vast, unbroken, a huge scroll, unrolling between the horizons, spread the great stretches of the ranch of Los Muertos, bare of crops, shaved close in the recent harvest. Near at hand were hills, but on that far southern horizon only the curves of the great earth itself checked the view. Adjoining Los Muertos, and widening to the west, opened the Broderson ranch. The Osterman ranch to the northwest carried on the great sweep of landscape; ranch after ranch. Then, as the imagination itself expanded under the stimulus of that measureless range of vision, even those great ranches resolved themselves into mere foreground, mere accessories, irrelevant details. Beyond the fine line of the horizons, over the curve of the globe, the shoulder of the earth, were other ranches, equally vast, and beyond these, others, and beyond these, still others, the immensities multiplying, lengthening out vaster and vaster. The whole gigantic sweep of the San Joaquin expanded, Titanic, before the eye of the mind, flagellated with heat, quivering and shimmering under the sun's red eye. At long intervals, a faint breath of wind out of the south passed slowly over the levels of the baked and empty earth, accentuating the silence, marking off the stillness. It seemed to exhale from the land itself, a prolonged sigh as of deep fatigue. It was the season after the harvest, and the great earth, the mother, after its period of reproduction, its pains of labour, delivered of the fruit of its loins, slept the sleep of exhaustion, the infinite repose of the colossus, benignant, eternal, strong, the nourisher of nations, the feeder of an entire world.

Ha! there it was, his epic, his inspiration, his West, his thundering progression of hexameters. A sudden uplift, a sense of exhilaration, of physical exaltation appeared abruptly to sweep Presley from his feet. As from a point high above the world, he seemed to dominate a universe, a whole order of things. He was dizzied, stunned, stupefied, his morbid supersentitive mind reeling, drunk with the intoxication of mere immensity. Stupendous ideas for which there were no names drove headlong through his brain. Terrible, formless shapes, vague figures, gigantic, monstrous, distorted, whirled at a gallop through his imagination.

He started homeward, still in his dream, descending from the hill, emerging from the cañon, and took the short cut straight across the Quien Sabe ranch, leaving Guadalajara far to his left. He tramped steadily on through the wheat stubble, walking fast, his head in a whirl. . . .

By now, however, it was dark. Presley hurried forward. He came to the line fence of the Quien Sabe ranch. Everything was very still. The stars were all out. There was not a sound other than the *de Profundis*, still sounding from very far away. At long intervals the great earth sighed dreamily in its sleep. All about, the feeling of absolute peace and quiet and security and untroubled happiness and content seemed descending from the stars like a benediction. The beauty of his poem, its idyl, came to him like a caress; that alone had been lacking. It was that, perhaps, which had left it hitherto incomplete. At last he was to grasp his song in all its entity.

But suddenly there was an interruption. Presley had climbed the fence at the limit of the Quien Sabe ranch. Beyond was Los Muertos, but between the two ran the railroad. He had only time to jump back upon the embankment when, with a quivering of all the earth, a locomotive, single, unattached, shot by him with a roar, filling the air with the reek of hot oil, vomiting smoke and sparks; its enormous eye, Cyclopean, red, throwing a glare far in advance, shooting by in a sudden crash of confused thunder; filling the night with the terrific clamour of its iron hoofs.

Abruptly Presley remembered. This must be the crack passenger engine of which Dyke had told him, the one delayed by the accident on the Bakersfield division and for whose passage the track had been opened all the way to Fresno.

Before Presley could recover from the shock of the irruption, while the earth was still vibrating, the rails still humming, the engine was far away, flinging the echo of its frantic gallop over all the valley. For a brief instant it roared with a hollow diapason on the Long Trestle over Broderson Creek, then plunged into a cutting farther on, the quivering flare of its fires losing itself in the night, its thunder abruptly diminishing to a subdued and distant humming. All at once this ceased. The engine was gone.

But the moment the noise of the engine lapsed, Presley—about to start forward again—was conscious of a confusion of lamentable sounds that rose into the night from out the engine's wake. Prolonged cries of agony, sobbing wails of infinite pain, heart-rending, pitiful.

The noises came from a little distance. He ran down the track, crossing the culvert, over the irrigating ditch, and at the head of the long reach of track—between the culvert and the Long Trestle—paused abruptly, held immovable at the sight of the ground and rails all about him.

In some way, the herd of sheep—Vanamee's herd—had found a breach in the wire fence by the right of way and had wandered out upon the tracks. A band had been crossing just at the moment of the engine's passage. The pathos of it was beyond expression. It was a slaughter, a massacre of innocents. The iron monster had charged full into the midst, merciless, inexorable. To the right and left, all the width of the right of way, the little bodies had been flung; backs were snapped against the fence posts; brains knocked out. Caught in the barbs of the wire, wedged in, the bodies hung suspended. Under foot it was terrible. The black blood, winking in the starlight, seeped down into the clinkers between the ties with a prolonged sucking murmur.

Presley turned away, horror-struck, sick at heart, overwhelmed with a quick burst of irresistible compassion for this brute agony he could not relieve. The sweetness was gone from the evening, the sense of peace, of security, and placid contentment was stricken from the landscape. The hideous ruin in the engine's path drove all thought of his poem from his mind. The inspiration vanished like a mist. The *de Profundis* had ceased to ring.

He hurried on across the Los Muertos ranch, almost running, even putting his hands over his ears till he was out of hearing distance of that all but human distress. Not until he was beyond earshot did he pause, looking back, listening. The night had shut down again. For a moment the silence was profound, unbroken.

Then, faint and prolonged, across the levels of the ranch, he heard the engine whistling for Bonneville. Again and again, at rapid intervals in its flying course, it whistled for road crossings, for sharp curves, for trestles; ominous notes, hoarse, bellowing, ringing with the accents of menace and defiance; and abruptly Presley saw again, in his imagination, the galloping monster, the terror of steel and steam, with its single eye, Cyclopean, red, shooting from horizon to horizon; but saw it now as the symbol of a vast power, huge, terrible, flinging the echo of its thunder over all the reaches of the valley, leaving blood and destruction in its path; the leviathan, with tentacles of steel clutching into the soil, the soulless Force, the iron-hearted Power, the monster, the Colossus, the Octopus.

Chapter 8

The Turn of the Century

The Turn of the Century

Californians contemplated their world with satisfaction as the twentieth century began. The hard times of the 1890s were a memory and the state's citizens, along with the rest of the nation, were enjoying prosperity. But the Golden State had many problems, and the first of these was unexpected. The San Francisco earthquake and fire of 1906 devastated the state's leading city and left a heritage of uneasiness which still prompts people to question whether such a catastrophe could happen again.

The first two decades were also a period in which labor sought to obtain a larger share of the California economic pie. Wages had been high in the early period of statehood but had fallen after the railroads brought more and more workers. The blowing up of the Los Angeles *Times* building in 1910 cost twenty lives, and the resulting trial damaged the image of organized labor in Southern California for years to come. In San Francisco the sensational Mooney-Billings affair was a divisive force nationally and remains a black mark upon the state's judicial system. The Industrial Workers of the World (IWW), an anarchosyndicalist-oriented radical group which sought to organize field hands, miners, and lumber hands, had little success; but it kept labor relations in turmoil for more than a decade.

Much of the continual growth of the state's economy resulted from the ability of talented and ruthless men to bring water to the major cities of San Francisco and Los Angeles. Others found ways to irrigate the ever-expanding crop acreage by taming minor rivers as well as the mighty Colorado. The steadily growing citrus industry solved complex production problems and evolved marketing techniques which made California oranges and lemons dietary staples throughout the nation. Petroleum had been produced since 1855, but it had made slow progress until the 1890s, when production increased and it was used for generating power and for street surfacing. By 1903 California led the nation in production, and the birth of the automobile age caused its importance to increase every decade.

40 San Francisco—1906

The San Francisco earthquake and resultant fire was the most spectacular disaster in the history of the state—and perhaps of the nation. More than 450 lives were lost, four square miles of the city were destroyed, and damage was estimated as high as $500 million. Countless books have been written about this tragedy, some of them arguing that it was divinely ordained to punish a modern Sodom and Gomorrah. Royce Briar, a San Francisco newspaperman, assigns his own occupation to the main character in this selection, who vividly describes the events of the first day.

Poole was awakened by a gentle joggling, which had the outlandish property of amusing him. He thought in his first half-conscious moment that some celebrating reporters had got into his room and were shaking the foot of his bed.

He opened his eyes, but the reporters were not there, and he saw the gray-green light of dawn, soft and furtive. The joggling persisted, about five movements a second, with rhythmic rise and fall, and he thought of the earthquake last year, and of Phronsie. He thought of the Antipodes Bank, and he wondered if this would halt the run, and this thought also amused him.

He could not understand why his last thought was for Cyr and the baby absent from her, somewhere with its father. He wondered if Cyr were afraid. Probably not, but he would telephone her in a little while.

Ten seconds had gone, and the movement died abruptly. Poole looked up at the chandelier, observing that it trembled slightly, that one of the bell-shaped shades was sounding with some high note which was sensuously almost imperceptible. He had one more instant for thought, that an earthquake was the deepest experience man knew in his outer world, freeing him from the dull prison of his ego. Poole had always vaguely delighted in them.

As he watched the shade, trying to understand its singing, almost forgetting the twelve seconds past, the chandelier leaped sidewise, and insanely started swinging like the clapper of a bell. His bed moved with a whip of vicious life, his whole room swayed sickeningly, as though it were pendent, some car of a ferris wheel.

He had one flash of supernal incredulity. The sway, the lightning sense of being caught in a cosmic and ungovernable power, preceded by a twinkling in his perception, the sound.

There was a ripping, like lightning at close quarters, and above it the tinkle of falling glass, which had the quality of pattering rain, and there was a creaking and crying of wood and steel on wood and steel, as though a thousand wagons with dry wheels were in the street. Pitched lower than these sounds was a measured grinding, like a hand coffee-mill magnified a

From *Reach for the Moon* by Royce Briar. Published 1934.

thousand times, and beneath it all was a booming like big guns, yet deeper than any possible massing of man-made ordnance.

The violence and the sound ceased abruptly, and there was a gentle rocking which to Poole was inertia. He was out of bed now, pulling on his underwear and his socks. He was shaking with excitement and he was afraid, he was thinking of Cyr as much as he could fix his thought on anything.

He was afraid for himself, too, afraid of instant and untimely death.

He was putting one leg into his trousers, when he was hurled across the room. He stumbled over a chair, plunging headlong to the radiator in the bow window. From the radiator pipe came lukewarm water, tickling his outspread fingers like crawling insects. He lay prone, and the floor beneath him boomed with sledge-hammer blows. He had a thread of thought that there was no hope for the world. The earth had collided with another body in space.

From where he lay, pondering this with a critical faculty of which he was inordinately proud, having lost his fear of personal death, he saw through half-opened eyes a crack from the lower sill of the window to the floor, a wedge-shaped crack with the green light of morning beyond.

Astounded at light in chaos, he got to his knees, biting his lip as nausea came to him. There was a cut on the back of his hand, and he smeared the blood on his underwear. He looked up the street.

A church steeple a block away was disintegrating like brown sugar in a pan of water. Sections of the steeple fell away, one after another, leaving a stark skeleton against the pale sky. The mound of bricks below was growing, and a white dust, like a big balloon at a county fair, hovered before the church.

And all this disintegration was from movement less violent than had been; some pecular tortion was demolishing the church facade at this stage, and it was all in silence, because deeper sounds smothered the sound of falling material, and the silence made it seem unreal. He had seen such destruction in a moving picture, and this also seemed contrived.

As he knelt there the subterranean booming, to which he had become inured, ended. The shocks fell away to a violent trembling, which seemed anodyne to Poole. He had no hope for it, however, he was confident the next shock would make an end of things. He had a sick longing to reach Cyr, but he did not perceive it as a remote possibility. He blinked in some wonder to see the ranks of buildings still standing in Sutter Street. One had a gap in a brick wall, exposing a white bedstead, but most of them were unchanged save for sheered cornices and staring windows without panes.

The trembling continued at an even tenor; there were several hammer-blow shocks, and then the independent undercurrent of trembling grew steadily feebler. Poole crossed the room, clinging to the foot of the bed and awaiting another great impact. The one shade of the chandelier resumed its singing vibration. Poole sat in a chair, putting on his shirt, looking idly at the cut on the back of his hand.

In the sixty-five seconds of the earthquake he had not heard a human voice, and now he heard a voice whimpering beyond his open window.

"It's—it's a great disaster," he muttered aloud, to himself. "By golly, it's come," as though he had forseen it.

A shock knocked any further words from him, and again came a shuttle-like movement of the hotel building. He stopped buttoning his shirt, with a kind of fortitude awaiting the outcome of this temblor, as though it were useless to button a shirt if the task were never to be completed.

He heard the clang of a fire-engine bell, and he laughed. He supposed fire bells were ringing all over the world. Of what use, he wondered, were fire departments. He gave thought again to a planetary collision, perhaps a body had upset the earth's orbital movement, or there had fallen some vast meteor. He could not conceive this as casual fault-slipping; the orbital deflection seemed the most logical. The earth was shaking now like jelly. There were occasional lulls, and one came to dislike them, and to prefer the steadfast agitation.

Four or five minutes had passed. Poole had resumed dressing, and he methodically hunted a clean collar in the commode, which was covered with plaster from the ceiling. Beside the commode was a Chinese chest, and he suddenly jerked open the lid and peered quizzically at his manuscripts.

The sound of stirring life came to him. He heard running in the hall, and muffled pounding on a door. There was a distant shout, and the high music of a hammer on iron, and the far clanging of a church bell, and the fairly irritating toots of a factory whistle. A small dog yelped. An automobile horn honked.

At first Poole could not relate these sounds to the earthquake, each had an origin both obscure and aberrant. Perhaps a demented sexton rang the bell, a drunken night-watchman blew the whistle, the dog was being bullyragged by a boy. Then Poole was arrested by the sound of an approaching horse. He stepped to the window. It was coming at breakneck speed, trailing a fragment of harness, its bay shoulders flecked with foam. It fled as though all the world but it had stiffened in death. It passed, and far down Sutter Street its shoes rang with terrible periodicity.

Poole related all the sounds to the earthquake, and he knew how completely he had been dominated by a sense-world for seven or eight minutes. He was delivered suddenly into a world which had a touch of rationality. He knew himself for a newspaper man, and he knew it was hell to pay for him.

And he knew beyond all, beyond work and life, that he must find Cyr Baskerville. He looked at his watch. It was twenty-one minutes past five o'clock.

He tried to open his door, but the floor had sunk, the door-frame was splintered, and each panel bellied outward like a full sail. As he crossed the room for a chair, he saw a woman in a bathrobe descending a fire escape across the street. He suspected that every door in town was jammed. This, he thought, grinning over his sagacity, was not so sublime a conception as one of colliding planets.

When he struck his door with the chair, the panels exploded into the hallway. Exploding doors were the greatest hazard of the morning, he concluded, having wholly forgotten the fallen church. He stepped into the corridor. A woman waddled by, speaking to herself with the curious abstraction of the White Rabbit.

The hotel lobby was already filled with guests, some in absurd garb or lack of it, all in obtrusive emotional states, calm being the most obstrusive of them all. Many of the resident guests, knowing Poole, rushed to him for information. He shook his head, but such trust cleared his thought. He took the receiver from the desk telephone. The clerk spread his hands, and Poole spread his own and replaced the receiver.

There was a heavy shock, and a rolling motion of the hotel building. The clatter of voices ceased. A wisp of thought drifted in Poole's head: he loved cigars at a three-alarm fire.

"Gimme a few cigars."

"Cigars?" The clerk's face was like whitewashed stone.

Poole raised the glass lid of the cigar case and chose ten Owls and gave the clerk fifty cents. A man who wore no necktie, and who had pinned to his lapel a slip of paper bearing his name, gazed at Poole.

"You—buy—cigars?" he muttered.

"Sure—have one," and Poole thrust a cigar into the other's vest pocket. The man stared down at it.

"Thanks."

Poole nodded and went to the front steps of the hotel. He felt the jelly trembling of the board beneath his feet, but he didn't mind it. After all great earthquakes came after-shocks; he forsaw a score of them in a few hours. Feeling wise, he lighted a cigar.

"Now, for a hack," he spoke aloud, and then he laughed at himself for it.

He cocked his cigar at a Speaker Cannon angle. There were no hacks to be had. He sauntered up the street. A small crowd was gathering at the wrecked church, and some boys were poking about among the bricks, looking for copper. Down the street, as Poole looked, there was debris from cornices, and glass littered the sidewalk as far as he could see, like spume along a straight beach.

He looked again at the church, at the gold cross askew on its steeple skeleton, gleaming in the first rays of the rising sun. The air was soft and warm, and hazy with dust. The sunlight lay in pale bronze squares against the higher buildings, but had not yet reached into the street. A trace of green dawn still lingered in the sky.

As Poole glanced east again, his eye caught a white mushroom, almost perfect in symmetry beyond the skyline. He was certain it had not been there a moment before. At first he thought it was a cloud, but it seemed to throb like a heart, and it was licked by a long tongue of darker smoke.

Poole noted that several others had espied this splendid plume in the morning sky, and he waited for them to say something, but they said nothing.

He went down the street, watching for a fire-engine which would take him across town. The street was filled with increasing traffic, which was beginning to snarl at intersections. There were shouting drivers, but the sidewalks were deserted. People had already learned to walk in the street. A sharp shock at this moment confirmed them, but they were going downtown anyway. Some were laughing and some were grave. Some made jokes and some stared stupidly at the jesters, but excepting these interludes, they were all gabbling like fowls.

A little old woman in a deaconess's cap plucked Poole's sleeve. She pulled him down, as though he, too, were deaf.

"It hain't much," she shouted.

Poole shook his head and smiled. "No—not much."

"That's what I said!" She triumphantly marched away.

Poole thought perhaps she was right. The entire city was thoroughly frightened, but it would be forgotten in a week. It was a great morning for plate-glass setters. Oh, it was a good story—the best story to crack in this town in five years.

And when he reached Powell Street he saw a crowd, and policemen's gray helmets, and ambulances, and he pinned on his police badge and struggled through to a drug store, and on the linoleum floor lay five dead, one a little girl. . . .

He strode on down to Market Street. A cable car was standing on its track, deserted. There was a prevalent flow of traffic toward the Ferry Building, wagons and buggies piled high with household goods. Some of the horses were jogging, some were walking, led by their drivers. From this throng came no talking and no laughter. It was like an army on the march, a bleak and endless army. The women had lost the identity of sex. It was like the forlorn cavalcade in the painting of Napoleon's retreat from Moscow.

The hands of the Ferry Tower clock stood at sixteen minutes past five. There was something unearthly in the minute hand traveling on a few minutes before failing, even though Poole knew it was electricity which had failed. He looked at his watch. It was eight minutes after six o'clock.

Black smoke was rising south and north of Market Street, and the Ferry Tower pointed a gray finger between the darker clouds. Above the street to the west were two more great fires. One of them was probably the white mushroom, now brown, a column churning like a tornado he had once seen south of Saint Paul.

As he hastened down Sansome Street, another shock shuddered through the city, seeming to carry with it a silence.

Men were moving to and fro without many words. Automobiles and victorias were arriving in the financial district, bringing bankers and brokers to their places of business. Down to see if the money-bags are safe, thought Poole, striding along. Near the Scimitar Building, another building had collapsed, but the Scimitar Building was apparently undamaged.

Poole climbed the narrow, unlighted stairway. Old Broom was sitting with his feet on the city desk. Kincheloe was there, but the room was otherwise empty.

"Looks like a page one story, Harp," mocked Broom, jovially.

"Yeah. A cop told me there're twenty dead at the Mechanics' Pavilion. I've got the names of three out of five dead in a drug store, that is, brought in from somewhere."

"You won't need names," sniffed Broom. "San Francisco is doomed."

"Four fires."

"Four? Eighteen! Barney was in here a minute ago. Police have runners out. Barney's drunk, but he's got it written down—eighteen."

"Anybody seen Walter Cheyne?"

"Not I. . . . . Say, there's a fire down here on Davis Street that's a lulu! You won't even be sitting here a few hours from now. The pressmen out there're cleaning up their machines, but there's no water, and no gas to heat the metal, so if you'll tell me how we're going to get out a paper, I'll tell you how to jump over the City Hall."

"You can climb over the City Hall with a good Alpine outfit right now," said Kincheloe.

"You didn't see Walter Cheyne, Kinch?"

"Nope."

"Walter Cheyne," remarked Broom, "is probably so drunk by now that a copy boy is carrying him around in a bucket. . . . Listen to that switch board buzz. Got a short."

"Any word from Clack?" Poole asked.

"Nope, nothing ever happens on the morning side, as I've ofttimes remarked," cackled Broom. "If we could get a staff here, we could do some circulating."

"It's going to be a whopper to cover, all right."

"Whopper? Listen, kid, this is going to be the biggest concentrated disaster story in the history of the world, understand? Not in dead. A Chinese famine kills a million, don't it? That beats Lisbon and Mount Pelée. But this is going to be the biggest, and no exceptions."

41 Labor Conflict

Most laboring men failed to find California the promised land in the early twentieth century, but workers in the forests, fields, and mines were the poorest. Attempts to organize these forgotten people were made after 1906 by the Industrial Workers of the World (IWW or Wobblies). The best known member of this radical union today is Joe Hill. His legendary fame began only after he was executed for the murder of a Salt Lake City grocer in a hold-up. He went to his death pleading his innocence and became a world-wide martyr to the union cause. His folk songs were set to popular melodies and inspired union men in their struggle—thereby adding to the Joe Hill myth. Few facts exist about him that can be accepted (even including his correct name), but it is known that he was a dockworker in San Pedro in 1910, and he is reputed to have done some organizing for the IWW in California. The following description of how the IWW organized a ranch in the Sacramento Valley has a striking similarity to a riot on the Durst ranch near Wheatland in 1913.

The sun came up over the brown hills, hot from the moment of its rising, and it grew hotter with every quarter-hour of its climb. By the time the six had finished breakfast and were scattering through the camp to line up every man they knew and could trust, even the dogs were hunting shade, and the first dense twittering of birds in the pepper trees had died away to an occasional cheep.

Art Manderich remained behind with Fuzzy, ostensibly to protect Fuzzy from Hale's finks, but also for the influence he would have in keeping Fuzzy from the temptation to stool if he were inclined that way. Manderich himself had thought the precaution unnecessary; it was Joe who insisted on it.

Now as he worked through the camp listening to the talk, waiting in backhouse lines, passing the time of day with men along the canal, there was none of the mystery that night had thrown over the tents and shelters and the red wink of fires. Under the unblinking sun the exposure of the camp's poverty was pitiless and complete. Blankets, quilts, discarded clothes, trailed over the tent ropes and stumps, or lay in the dust. In some camps there were cots, and these stood up above the dust with a kind of arrogance. Tent flaps were open, tent walls rolled up to let in air, and the contents of the tents bulged and slid out into the dust outside—water cans and jugs, baby buggies, lanterns, suitcases and telescope bags. He saw lizards dart dust-colored across dust-colored bedclothes. And everywhere he found people jumpy, already irritable from the heat. At the slightest noise or movement they looked up as if expecting something. Without any of the mystery, without any of the obscurely ominous air as of a sleeping army that it had worn last night, the camp was still full of that sense of waiting.

Two Mexican boys broke into a fist fight: within a matter of seconds men, women and children had thronged around to see what was happening. Further down the camp, a picker's child fell into the irrigation ditch: instantly there were two dozen hands there to pull her out, and for ten minutes afterward people kept coming to see what the excitement was. There was a good deal of talking, a good deal of spanking of children. In the space of a half-hour he heard a dozen different languages spoken. It was a slovenly, heat-tired, irritable, hopelessly mixed crowd; whatever they made of it—and he went carefully, making what he could—would have to be made by pure will and determination, and held together against all the disintegrative weaknesses of the mob. They would take a lot of talking to.

And there were also the finks to think about.

He was up on the ditchbank, looking over the shelters and waiting for the Kirkhams and Virtanen to appear, when he saw the little flurry over by the packing sheds. A man's bald pink head rose up above a group, mainly women, and the noise that at first had been only a gabble of voices paused and steadied and became singing. Under the big thin-leaved pepper, with the road's empty width between him and the sheds, the pink-headed man bawled above the thinner voices of the women. They were singing "From Greenland's Icy Mountains." The baldheaded man rotated so that his voice went off almost inaudibly in other directions and then bellowed like a megaphone. Between verses he made sweeping come-all-ye motions with his arms, beckoning people in.

Joe's first reaction was a pulse of rage. The preaching fool would block everything. He was right in the spot they had picked for their own meeting, and he would probably go on for an hour or two. He would use up all the restlessness and all the patience to stand in the sun and listen that the camp contained, and he would send them home with the promise of pie in the sky.

Or was the preacher a plant of the boss's? Nothing would suit the purposes of Hale better than a Jesus-meeting. It would pay him to hire a preacher at a hundred dollars a Sunday to bring the slaves the gifts of the spirit.

He swung around, furiously intent on rounding up the boys and breaking up the meeting, at whatever cost to their own plans, but as he turned he saw the fink who last night had cased their camp. The fink was leaning against a tree, his booted foot braced back of him against the trunk, and he was idly peeling a green twig with his thumbnail while he watched and listened. Joe hesitated. Already people were coming from every direction like workers streaming into a factory gate in the morning. They picked their way between tents and shelters, crossed the plank bridges across the ditch, stood up from their sloven campsites and craned to see and hear. They were thickening by the minute around the bald-headed preacher at the road's edge. And the fink was casually peeling a twig. It was that which made Joe's anger back up and make way for a plan. One of the best ways to get a big crowd together without trouble from the finks was to let this preacher do it. . . .

Ahead of him, not very far now, the preacher was loud, and Joe listened consciously for the first time as he slid and wormed and worked his way forward, making a path for the others.

". . . If you haven't known Jesus! Oh, brothers and sisters, I can't possibly tell you the joy I felt in my heart when I first knew Jesus was my friend! I been carrying a millstone around my neck all my days and never knew it. I was weighted down with sin, oh I confess it, brothers and sisters, I confess it gladly, I've had my soul washed clean and that old burden of sin don't bother me any more. But I carried it around till I was bowlegged with it, I carried a pack of sin like a peddler's, brothers and sisters, and all because I didn't know Jesus was my friend, all because I didn't know where to go to get my burden lightened. Now I've laid it down, and I tell you one and all, I'm a new man. You'll never know what living can be until you come to Jesus and have those sins forgiven. You've all got 'em, brothers and sisters, everybody's got 'em. Just make up your mind to come in and lay that burden down. . ."

The three were near the heart of the crowd, where a little breathing space had been left around the preacher's backless chair on which he stood and shouted. Joe looked around. There were too many women; in close the crowd was two-thirds women, yet even they did not seem to be taking in what the preacher said. Some were Mexican women he was sure did not understand one word in ten.

Once more he looked carefully around, tiptoeing to see better, but he spotted no finks whose faces he knew. The heat of the crowd packed him in; he wanted to break away and fight himself free and into the open. The red-faced preacher roared on, streaming sweat. *"Jesus,* my friends. Keep that name in mind. When He first visited this sinful world, coming from the city of jasper and pearl and pure gold, He stepped down out of that glory just to save sufferin' humanity, just out of the pity of His great heart, and I want to say to you, brothers and sisters, He's still ready to save, He's still got His hand stretched out to the poor and needy. . ."

The eyes of the three met. In two smooth steps Joe and Manderich were beside the preacher's chair. Joe took hold of the preacher's pocket and yanked, tearing the seam so that the white lining showed; instantly the preacher's hand shot down to grab his wrist, the preacher's hot face turned down on him, glaring. Then Manderich reached, and together they yanked so that he had to hop off backward to keep from toppling. His hoarse roar of anger was chopped off short as he leaped, but he was threshing his arms free as soon as his feet hit the ground. Manderich's heavy clutch pinioned one arm, but he broke the other free from Joe's lighter weight, and as he did so Joe grabbed a handful of the man's wet shirt with his left hand. His right dove halfway under his own coat, and held it there on the gun butt, his eyes inches from the preacher's furious face, until the man's eyes chilled and understood and the furious threshing of his arms quieted. With a final cautious half-meant twist he freed himself and stood still. Joe slipped around behind him, next to Manderich, his eyes swooping in one comprehensive glance across the faces near at hand. They looked merely astonished. A couple of the women had begun to edge away. But no trouble, not a peep. Ahead of him the preacher stood, breathing hard, his blue shirt wet and dark. Sweat ran as Joe watched down the pink scalp under the thinning fringe of hair, a crooked drop crookedly running until it came to the roundly shaven neck, and then it skidded and disappeared under the wet collar. Art Manderich, breathing formally through his nose, his face set like the face of a hussar at inspection or an usher in a church, stood with his arms folded.

Up on the chair Fuzzy Llewellyn was shouting in the preacher's place—a sharper, more cutting voice, saw-edged and nasal and penetrating. "We're takin' over this meeting right now! Why are we takin' it over? I'll tell you. Because we all got more important things to meet about than the size of somebody's private pack of sin. We got a lot of grievances in this camp, and a lot of conditions have to be improved. How do you get a drink of water in this stinkhole? You've tried it down at the field. You've hit up the stew-wagon guy. What'd it get you? And how long did you stand in line by one of those backhouses this mornin'? There was a line of twenty-six people waitin' when I came down. Just put your mind for a minute on what you was linin' up for. Waitin' in line to use a thing like that. I don't know how yours was, but mine would've made a hyena throw his lunch. That's what we're takin' over this meeting for. To see if anybody here agrees with us something ought to be done about it." . . .

Two days ago three other guys and I got sick of the filth in this camp and we squawked. We went over to the super and we raised some hell. You know what happens after that? Just by accident we all have callers that night. They take us out on the south road and beat hell out of us and make us run the gauntlet while a dozen of them whale away at us with barrel staves. Just a great big Hallowe'en party. Then they point us down the road and invite us not to come back."

He paused, his squirrel teeth exposed by the back-drawn lips. For a moment it was so quiet Joe heard his breath hiss, and heard the sound of a motor starting on the other side of the sheds. He looked for anger in the sheep faces of the crowd and saw none, only the alert, half-expectant listening look.

"But I come back!" Fuzzy shouted. "By God I doubled around and I limped back in that same night, and I been here ever since. You want to know why I came back? I'll tell you. I came back because I knew if enough of us squawked it wouldn't be possible to take care of us with barrel staves. Let just a hundred of us out of this whole mob get together and stand together, and they ain't goonin' us off the ranch. They ain't doin' nothin' then. They're listenin', because they'll have to listen."

The last faint lingering suspicion that Joe had had of Fuzzy was gone now. Fuzzy was going good. He was militant and he had guts and he could pour it on from up on the box. And no matter how his eyes and ears searched the crowd, he could catch no premonition of trouble, no shouldering stir of deputies coming in, no sound of heckling, no fighting. Nothing but this waiting.

. . .

Fuzzy Llewellyn looked out over the heads, his arms still wide in the gesture of leading the singing. For one flicking instant his one good eye dropped to meet Joe's, then Manderich's. His mouth formed a sidelong word. "Law." Joe made a motion to Kirkham to come in closer, to help form a ring around the box.

Now Fuzzy let out his voice again, and the nasal, penetrating half-whine seemed twice as loud and twice as penetrating as before. "They're comin' in here right now!" he shouted. "What are they comin' for? To stop me from talkin'. To run me into the calaboose and stop my mouth, or knock it off. They don't want any meetin's like this, and you know why? Because they work you like horses and pay you starvation wages and don't give a good god damn whether you live or die. Because they want that last bloody nickel you sweat out for them out in the sun. They want that last nickel even if it comes to them red with the blood of your children! And if you squawk, here come the finks and the deputies with pick handles and barrel staves. HERE THEY COME RIGHT NOW!"

The peremptory authoritative voice shouted again. Joe could see the crowd buckling and swirling compactly out in the sun of the road, and as the swirl came inward Joe saw the red head of Russ Kirkham coming with it, backing before it. Other men, four or five, seemed to be doing the same.

"They're comin' in right now!" Fuzzy yelled. "What I want to know is what you're gonna do about it. Do they shut us up? Do they bring out their dirty hired law and do we knuckle under? Do we submit to their god damn gunmen OR DO WE STAND UP TO THE SONSABITCHES? DO WE CLOSE RANKS AND FIGHT FOR OUR RIGHTS? I'M ASKIN' YOU, FELLOW WORKERS, AND YOU AIN'T GOT LONG TO DECIDE!"

Manderich looked at Joe, and they shoved the preacher forward a step so as to be free. Joe made sure the automatic was loose in the holster. Manderich's grim smile deepened the creases in his face; for the first time Joe noticed that his hair was thin, that in his neck there was the beginning of an old man's dewlap of sagging skin. Pushing the preacher again, they moved out another step or two to meet the incoming disturbance of the law. Women were clearing out; there was a quick, hurried, anxious pressing-away from the direction of the disturbance as Fuzzy, useless now and unlistened to, kept shouting from the elevated chair.

The swirl of the in-pressing law was close now. Into the space the women had left, Kirkham and four others were thrust suddenly, retreating ahead of a solid group of more than a dozen. The deputies were sweating, their shirts sticking to them, their nickeled badges sagging the wet cloth. All had guns buckled around them. With them was one dressed like themselves but wearing a tie and a white stetson. Joe guessed him to be the sheriff. And behind the sheriff was a man in a Panama hat and an alpaca coat, smooth-faced, pink with heat—boss or lawyer, a different breed, and wearing no gun.

Kirkham's group fell back with Joe and Manderich and the others.

A narrow lane formed itself between them and the tightly grouped law. Back of him Joe felt the continuous stir of people getting out of the way; what should have been a silence as the men faced each other was full of a steady, ponderous rumble, a heavy stir in the air like the sound of wagons crossing a plank bridge.

The sweating deputies were looking at the sheriff, but they were nervous and their heads kept turning and their hands stayed close to the guns on their hips. They braced a little against the curious weight of the crowd.

"Llewellyn!" the sheriff said. "I've got a warrant for you. You're under arrest."

Joe was up on the balls of his feet. He watched the sheriff and the man in the Panama hat, and he heard the rumble of the crowd closing in like silence after the sheriff's words. Behind him Fuzzy Llewellyn screeched in a cracking voice, "WELL, FELLOW WORKERS, HERE THEY ARE! I'M UNDER ARREST, THE SHERIFF SAYS. OKAY, I'LL LET MYSELF GET PINCHED. I'LL GO WITH THIS BUNCH OF GOD DAMNED LAW WITH THEIR SAPS AND SIX SHOOTERS. THAT'S ALL I CAN DO, ALONE. BUT IF YOU'RE WITH ME I CAN DO SOMETHING ELSE. I CAN TELL THIS SHERIFF THERE ARE ALMOST THREE THOUSAND WORKERS HERE THAT WON'T . . ."

It came as both a sound and a thrust of movement, a slow crescendo coming inward from the far edges of the crowd. Joe heard it rising and growing; he saw it take hold on the clustered deputies and saw them brace against it. He saw fear leap into the face of the pink-faced man in the Panama and saw with sharp clarity how the deputies elbowed and hampered each other, half turning to resist the pushing from behind. They shouted; one drew his gun half out.

He had completely forgotten the preacher who stood beside him, and only the flickering impression he caught from the corner of his eye of some danger, some blow, kept him from being taken completely unaware. He ducked, crouching, so that something came over the top of him and bore him down with a mauling weight. But even as he went down he heard the three quick shots and the terrible cresting roar of the crowd.

For a minute he was utterly helpless, tossed under trampling feet, smothered and squashed under struggling bodies. A shoe came down on his hand and he rolled, trying to break free. Blows were landing on him, and he struck back and kicked and rolled again until the feet thinned and he made his feet, throwing the long hair out of his eyes as he came up, his right hand diving for the gun. A bullet went past his cheek so close that he felt the wind of it and heard the soggy *puk* it made as it hit something behind him. But as he turned the crowd picked him up like a chip and carried him along. His feet tangled in the yielding mass of a body so that he almost went down again. The noise of the crowd now was an unbearable tense continuous stream.

He was borne struggling against the trunk of one of the pepper trees, a tree where children had made a ladder out of the stubs of old branches. As the pressure swirled past on both sides he caught one of the stubs and pulled himself up out of the tumult, the gun ready in his hand.

But already the thing was over. He saw fierce-eyed men whirl in the choking dust, fearful of enemies, but there were no enemies, only pickers like themselves. They fell back warily, mistrustful of everyone else, many of them nursing hurts, away from the soapbox where miraculously Fuzzy Llewellyn still stood, and as they fell back and the dust cloud stilled and cleared Joe saw the bodies on the ground, the bloodied, dirtied white shirts patched with adhesive dust, the fallen hats, the darker curving figures of fallen men.

At the first opening below him he jumped and landed running, coming up beside Fuzzy. One of the Kirkhams was there, blood streaming from his nose. Twenty feet away, one across the other, lay the pink-faced man and the sheriff, and near them a picker. Joe could not see his face, but his hand was brown. Still beyond, doubled up with his face against his knees, was a deputy. The rest of the deputies, as well as the preacher, had disappeared. And close up against the backless chair where Fuzzy stood, his dead face tramped and smashed by the fury and panic of the crowd, lay old Manderich.

Kirkham's teeth were chattering. He looked at Joe and shook his head and wiped his streaming nose with the back of his hand.

Up on the chair Fuzzy stood with his hands at his sides, his squirrel teeth bared, looking out almost abstractedly across the road. The short, savage flare of mob anger had lasted only a matter of minutes, the surge inward upon the deputies had been a reaction as sudden and automatic as impulse and blow. Now men were sneaking away, retreating from both instigator and result of their fury. The few who stayed stayed with an awed, scared look on their faces. A hush was over the whole meeting place, the whole camp.

42 Battling with the River

Economic opportunity continued to be the basic magnet drawing people to California. And the key to continued expansion in this area was water. The cities had to have this life-giving fluid in order to grow, and more and more water was needed to continue expanding crop acreage. Irrigation of the Imperial Valley began in 1901, utilizing the bountiful waters of the Colorado River. But, as previously noted, wherever man has tried to tame nature a struggle has ensued. The peculiar geology of the Imperial Valley described in the following was understood by experts, but real estate promoters did not take their warnings seriously. Rapid growth in farm acreage led to demands for more water, and when an additional intake was cut to the river without the construction of proper flood control gates, the Colorado River spilled into the Imperial Valley. The river soon flooded 488 square miles of farmland; it took two years and six attempts before the river was returned to its former channel to the sea.

Some day, perhaps, the history of that River war will be written. It can only be suggested in my story.

It was a war of terrific forces waged for a great cause by men as brave as any who ever fought with weapons that kill.

The attacking force was the Rio Colorado that with power immeasurable had, through the ages past, carved mile-deep canyons on its course and with its mountains of silt had built the great delta dam across the ancient gulf, thus turning back the waters of the sea that sun and wind might lay bare the floor of the Basin and work the desolation of the desert.

Using the Seer's open hand for his map of La Palma de la Mano de Dios, Jose, the Indian, had traced the course of the river along the base of the fingers flowing toward the gulf which lies between the edge of the palm and the thumb—this same inner edge of the hand representing roughly the high ground that shuts out the waters of the sea. The thousands of acres of The King's Basin lands lie from sea level to nearly three hundred feet below. The river at the point where the intake for the system of canals was located is, of course, higher than sea level, for the waters that pass the intake flow on southward to the gulf.

It was the river flowing thus on higher ground that made irrigation and reclamation of the desert possible. It was this also that made possible the disaster that was now upon the hardy pioneers, who had staked everything in their effort to realize the vast potential wealth of the ancient sea bed. The grade from the river at the intake to the lowest point in the bottom of the Basin is much steeper than the established fall of the river from the intake to the gulf. The water in the canals on this steeper grade was controlled by headings, spillways, gates and drops, while the structure at the intake, with gates to regulate the flow into the main canal, prevented the river from leaving its old channel altogether, pouring its entire volume into the Basin and in time converting it again into an inland sea.

The dangerously cheap and inadequate character of the vital parts, built by the Company upon the usual promoter's estimates, had led Abe Lee to protest against the risk forced upon the settlers and had finally caused him to resign. Later, as the Company system of canals was extended and more and more water was needed to supply the rapidly increasing acreage of cultivated lands, Willard Holmes came to appreciate the desert-bred surveyor's view of the danger and insistently urged his employers to supply him with funds to replace the temporary wooden structure with safe and lasting works of concrete and steel.

From *The Winning of Barbara Worth* by Harold Bell Wright. Published 1911.

But the hunger of Capital for profits forbade. Someday the work would be done, the directors promised. In the meantime, without increasing the original investment by so much as a dollar but with the revenues derived from the sale of water rights, they were extending the system to supply the ever increasing fields of the settlers, thus shrewdly forcing the people, who were ignorant of the terrible risk they were carrying, to supply the funds to build the canals and ditches that belonged to the Company; while for the water carried to the ranches the farmers continued to pay the Company large rentals. The original investment of the Company was very small compared with the thousands invested by the pioneers who had been induced to settle in the new country. And yet from every dollar of the wealth taken from the land the Company would receive a share.

But the Rio Colorado gave no heed to the decree of the New York financiers. The forces that had made La Palma de la Mano de Dios are not ruled by Wall Street.

Willard Holmes, who had come to understand that his work was not alone to safeguard the property of his employers but to protect the interests of the pioneers as well, had been discharged because he would not deliver the people wholly into the hands of the Company. A new engineer out of the East, as faithful to the interests of Capital as he was unfamiliar with conditions in the new country, was placed in charge.

It was as if the river, in the absence of the man whose constant readiness held it in check, saw its opportunity. Swiftly it mustered its forces from mountain and plain. Hundreds of miles away it gathered its strength and hurried to the assault. The sources of information established by Holmes on the tributaries and headwaters wired their reports: a foot rise on the Gila; three feet coming down the Little Colorado; two-feet rise in the Salt; five feet on the Grand. The New York office engineer received the messages with mild interest. The daily reports from the weather bureau covering the countries drained by the Rio Colorado lay on his desk unnoticed.

Mr. Burk warned him, but the thoughtful Manager of the Company was not an engineer. Willard Holmes tried to help him, but Holmes had been discharged by the Company, and the words of discharged men have little weight with those who succeed to their positions.

The daily reports from the gauge at Rubio City showed an increase in the river's volume of twenty thousand second feet; then thirty thousand more; and on top of that came another twenty thousand. The assistants of the new chief engineer tried to tell him what it meant, but the assistants were subordinates and friends of Willard Holmes. The man from New York, who was privileged to write several letters after his name, was supposed to know his business.

Then the assembled forces of the river reached the intake, and the trembling wooden structures that stood between the pioneers and ruin, besieged by the rising flood, battered by the swirling currents, bombarded by drift, gave way under the strain and the charging waters plunged through the breach.

Too late the Company's forces were rushed to the scene. Before their very eyes the roaring waters, as if mad with destructive power, wrenched and tore at the Company's property, twisting, ripping, smashing, until not a trestle, plank or stick was left in place and the terrific current, rushing with ever increasing volume and power through the opening, plowed into the soft, alluvial soil of the embankment, undermining and carrying it away until nearly the entire river was admitted.

As quickly as men and material could be assembled, the Company's chief engineer began the battle to regain control of the mighty stream. The warfare thus begun meant life or death to the greatest reclamation project in the world.

Millions already invested by the settlers in farms and towns and homes and business enterprises were at stake. Many more millions that were yet to be realized from the reclaimed lands depended upon the issue of the fight.

Against the efforts of the engineers and the army of laborers the river massed from its tributaries in the regions of heavy rains and melting snows the greatest strength it had assembled in many years.

Five times, with piling and trestles and jetties and embankments, the men who defended The King's Basin were in sight of victory. Five times the river summoned fresh strength—twisted out the piling, wrecked the trestles, undermined the jetties and embankments and swept the nearly completed structures, smashing, grinding, crashing, away—a twisted, tangled ruin.

While the engineers and men of the Company were waging this war with the river, the situation of the pioneers in the Basin grew daily more perilous. Without a well-defined channel large enough to carry the incoming stream, the flood spread over a wide territory in the southern and western portions of the Basin, filling first the old channels and washes left by the waters ages ago, forming next in the areas of nearly level or slightly depressed sections shallow pools, lakes and seas, out of which the higher ground and hummocks rose like new-born islands, growing smaller and smaller as the rising tide submerged more and more of their sandy bases. Meanwhile the whole flood, eddying slowly with winding sluggish currents in the shallow places, moving more swiftly in the deeper washes and channels, swept always onward toward the north where, miles away, lay the deepest bottom of the great Basin.

Many of the settlers in the flooded districts were forced to abandon farms they had won with courage and toil, for the sweeping waters covered alike fields of alfalfa and grain and barren desert waste. The towns of Frontera and Kingston were protected from the inundation by earthen levees, in the building of which men and women toiled in desperate haste, and night and day these embankments were patrolled by watchful guards, who frequently summoned the weary, besieged citizens from their rest to protect or strengthen some threatened point in their fortifications.

The eastern side of the Basin being higher ground, the settlers in the South Central District and east of Republic, with the two towns built by Jefferson Worth, were in no immediate danger, but the old Dry River channel became a roaring torrent, bank-full; and it was only a question of time, if the river were not controlled, when every foot of the new country with its wealth of improvements and its vast possibilities would be buried deep beneath the surface of an inland sea.

The situation was appalling. The remarkable development of the new country, the marvelous richness of the reclaimed lands, with the immense possibilities of the reclamation work as demonstrated by The King's Basin project had attracted the attention of the nation. The pioneers in Barbara's Desert were, in fact, leaders in a far greater work that would add immeasurably to the nation's life—that would, indeed, be worldwide in its influence. Because of this, the attention of the nation was fixed with peculiar interest upon the disaster that had fallen upon The King's Basin.

. . .

The complete destruction of all that the settlers had gained and the utter desolation of the land was now a question of weeks.

The Company town of Kingston was directly in the path of that moving Niagara. While the Company's men were making a last desperate effort to close the break, the great falls were eating their way nearer and nearer the little city. When the roar of the water and the crashing and booming of the falling banks could be heard on the streets and in the offices of the Company, the people left their homes, their stores, and their shops; the town realizing that no human power now could avert the disaster.

Heroic efforts were made to direct the course of the new river away from the little city, but the waters with savage, resistless power chose their own way. The pioneers, who built the first town in the heart of The King's Basin Desert, saw that mighty, thundering cataract moving upon the work of their hands and felt the earth trembling under their feet as they watched homes, business blocks, the hotel, the opera house, the bank and finally the Company building undermined and tumbled, crashing into the deep canyon.

In a few short hours it was over. The falls moved on and where Kingston had once stood was that great gorge, with a few scattered houses only remaining on each side.

That same day the last attempt of the Company men to close the break failed. . . .

A little apart from Jefferson Worth and his two companions, Willard Holmes stood alone on the brink of the broken embankment looking down into the swirling muddy water. He knew that his time had come. He knew that at that moment the railroad officials were concluding a deal with The King's Basin Land and Irrigation Company through its president, by which the S. & C. would assume control of the situation and attempt to save the work. His chief had told him to be ready. He was ready.

In the railroad yards at Rubio City and on every available side-track for several miles east and west were standing trainloads of ties and rails. In the yards at the Coast city were cars loaded with machinery, implements, and supplies. In the yards at the harbor were other train loads of timber and piling. With the readiness of a perfectly equipped and organized army, the forces of the S. & C., backed by the resources of that powerful system, waited the word, while every moment the disaster that threatened the pioneers drew nearer. From the roaring river at his feet Willard Holmes turned to look toward the tent. Why were they so slow?

Then his face lighted up and he took an eager step forward as the private secretary of the general manager came out of the tent and hurried toward him.

"They want you, Mr. Holmes," said the young man. The engineer went quickly to answer the call.

When he entered the tent every man in the party turned toward the engineer. "Holmes," said his chief, "we will attempt to close the break. You will take charge at once."

Within an hour the forces of The King's Basin Land and Irrigation Company already on the ground were set to work under the Seer preparing the grade for a spur track that would leave the main line near the river fifteen miles north of the break, and Holmes, with Abe Lee, set out on horseback for Rubio City.

With the return of the general manager and his party to their train, the movement already planned began. Without hurry but with ready promptness the orders, voiced by the hundreds of clicking telegraph instruments covering the district affected by the operations, were obeyed. Special trains carried Jefferson Worth's force of railroad builders with teams and equipment to the point at which the spur track would connect with the main line where, under Abe Lee, they began pushing the grade southward to meet the forces that, under the Seer, were working northward from the front.

Throughout the Basin the call for men and teams was issued by Jefferson Worth, and the pioneers, answering as the Minute Men of old, were hurried to the scene where they found trainloads of equipment waiting ready for their use, while every hour brought reinforcements— laborers of many nationalities gathered in the cities of the coast by the agents of the railroad company.

The waiting trains loaded with ties and steel began to move and the construction gangs followed close on the heels of the graders. And when the last spike in the track to the scene of the decisive battle was driven, the trackmen with their sledges stepped aside to clear the way for the panting engines that drew the first train loaded with piling and timbers for the trestle.

Hour by hour now, without pause or halt, the men under Willard Holmes working in shifts met the Rio Colorado in a hand-to-hand fight for The King's Basin lands. By day under the white, semi-tropical sun, by night in the light of locomotive headlights that gleamed strangely over the dark swirling floods, the trestles were forced farther and farther out into the plunging current that wrenched and twisted and tugged with terrific strength in a mad wrestle with those who dared attempt to check its sullen destructive will, while steadily, irresistibly, the canyon-cutting falls drew nearer and nearer. It was not alone the magnitude of the task directed by Willard Holmes that made the work heroic. It was that this seemingly impossible work must be accomplished against time. In his fight with the river the engineer raced against a destructive force which, if it reached the scene of the struggle before the battle was won, would make final defeat certain and place the Colorado, so far as The King's Basin reclamation was concerned, beyond control of men.

43 The Orange

The most typical California agricultural product was the orange. The pioneers in citrus were frequently men who had earned substantial money in other enterprises. They usually were not farmers and thus were prepared to innovate in this new endeavor. This was of lasting importance as they had to use trial and error in evolving their own system of irrigation, pruning, cultivation, treatment for diseases, harvesting, and marketing. Many a man went bankrupt before these problems were solved. This passage tells how a New Englander developed an approach to the frost danger.

The states to the north and east were already in the grip of winter, with temperatures abnormally low for that time of year. What if these high western winds should shift to the north? It was a question some asked, and others dismissed with a laugh.

Towards the end of the first week in January, however, a high wind sprang up, suddenly one day at noon, carrying the usual amount of dust. But it blew from the north, a cold dry wind, which searched out the cracks of ill-fitting casements, and chilled where it went. Still, the temperature was not too low. Another night passed. The hill ranches at least were uninjured, if there was a little too much frost down below. Men were watchful, but confident. California had existed for a generation, and nature had never deserted the orange ranches; besides, Escalona was sheltered. There were high mountains all around to guard its groves from destruction.

It was Sunday. The sun shone. But the wind still blew, and that day also it came from the north. The women were glad of their furs, the men

From *Jacob Peek, Orange Grower* by Sidney Herbert Burchell. Published 1915.

of their warmest clothing. Those who had to be in the open, sought the most sheltered places. On the mountain tops there was a good deal of snow. But the wind was not high, and there was still some hope that the worst was known, and that the wind would change.

But it did not. The night came. But still the wind blew, and as darkness fell it increased, and carried with it an icy coldness, that seized on the orange and lemon ranches with death-dealing intensity. There had hitherto been confidence in wind, for moving air meant safety from frost. But experience availed nothing this night.

Wind, or no wind, the temperature began to fall. At seven o'clock it stood in the neighborhood of forty degrees, at ten it had fallen to twenty-six. Here was the danger point for oranges.

But long before this latter temperature was reached, Jacob's automatic thermometers were ringing their bells in Prosper's little shed. . . .

Every detail of the night's struggle had been discussed and arranged. Little need was there for Jacob's interference. The men engaged were all used to the work. But they had never taken a hand in smudging where it was done so thoroughly, with such a seeming disregard of cost. Jacob spent his time, unmindful of the smother, in making the round of a series of thermometers that had been placed in various positions about the ranches, including Prosper's. Armed with pencil, note-book, and lantern, the old man visited them one after another, taking note of time and temperature.

The effect of the labors of himself and assistants was quickly seen. At first stationary, the temperature began to rise, until the danger point was left some degrees behind. But this was only accomplished by an unusual number of smudge pots, and a high grade of oil. There were many difficulties to contend against, the cold wind and the cold surroundings. Especial reinforcements at some points were found necessary, around the boundaries of the ranches. And had it not been that the groves concerned adjoined one another, the chances for raising the temperature would have been slight.

It was yet early in the night. Jacob had visited his thermometers more than once already, and had had the satisfaction of observing that the fall of the mercury had been arrested.

The scene was a weird one. Clouds of smoke rolled from the hundreds of smudge pots around, illuminated by the flames of the burning oil. Only the trees in the immediate vicinity were to be seen, standing like shadowy presences, helpless, perhaps a prey to the coldest weather known to living memory in that part of Southern California. Jacob's tall thin figure, appearing and disappearing in the shadows and heavy vapors from the smudge fires, lantern in hand, seemed, from a distance, like that of the evil genius of the place, superintending some demoniacal rites of a nether world.

. . .

Sunrise brought but little relief to the frozen land. Irrigating and storm ditches, the gutter of the streets, where water had flowed the previous day, were now solid ice. And the frost, though but a few degrees, lasted all day. But the cold north wind continued to blow, and that night the thermometer registered fourteen or sixteen degrees of frost. Fruit that had previously escaped, was frozen Monday night. The loss to Escalona was complete, overwhelming, running into millions of dollars. Hill ranches and those in the valleys suffered alike, and lost their entire crops. Only one man on the hills put up a fight, and he alone came off victorious.

All through this time, indeed for a day or two, Jacob kept his smudge-pots going. No matter what the sun was doing up above, he shut it out with his clouds of smoke. Never once did he relinquish his efforts. It was a big battle, but he was the very man to take hold of such a situation, and he refused rest and sleep.

"If I go home," he told his wife, who came out to the ranches more than once in her anxiety for him, "if I go home, it'll be for a couple of baths. I never was so dirty in my life. But I reckon the dirt'll wait."

But it was during that Monday night that the fight became the sternest. Ranchers saw the crisis coming, and were helpless in their despair. Warnings were out. But they could do nothing, but stand shivering in the pitiless wind, and see their fruit becoming balls of solid ice, and the leaves of the trees curling up against the frozen stems.

During the day Jacob had caused Reginald Smith to 'phone to Los Angeles and elsewhere for more pots.

"I must have more pots!" he shouted. "I don't care what kind of pots! Only get me more pots, and plenty of 'em."

The lad did his best. He kept the exchange girls busy for an hour. But not a single pot could he procure. Oil there was in plenty. So he impressed into service all kinds of old cans. It delighted Mr. Peek every time a wagon load of them made their appearance at the ranches.

"I don't care what it costs!" he exclaimed. "I'm going to save that fruit."

And he did. Never surely in the history of smudging, was there such an array of fires, and such a pall of smoke, as enveloped Jacob Peek's orange trees. The frost literally could not make an impression. But another day, and another night, followed of more or less frost, during which time he continued his efforts. By the middle of the week, however, he had come off victorious. A change in the weather had set in. The thaw, a slow one, was general, and continued. Rain, too, was not far off. Not, however, till he was quite sure that the frost had gone, did he quit his post, leaving Prosper on guard, to sound an alarm in case the enemy should make its reappearance. . . .

So the great frost—great for Southern California—became a thing of the past, but was not to be easily forgotten. The destruction it had wrought was visible for scores of miles, in the great valleys of the south. No ranch escaped, although in some places location led to less destruction. Not even the hill groves were spared. Some declared that they had suffered even more severely than those in lower places, but, generally speaking, that was not so. But the destruction of nursery stock was practically complete, perhaps a more significant loss than that of fruit, for it implied a set back to the development of land, and a certain curtailment of the output of citrus fruits, for some time to come; perhaps no disadvantage to the country, and the ranches that remained.

One thing became self-evident too, that hundreds, perhaps thousands, of acres would have to be abandoned for orange growing, by a process of elimination, which would have an important bearing upon the future of the industry; again, perhaps, not without its benefit to the state at large, and to those who were courageous enough to grow the fruit.

"I tell you, Smith!" exclaimed Jacob one day, shortly after the freeze, "I ain't convinced that Californy has seen the last of these freezes. I don't believe it. Men don't know much about Californy. It's all guess-work. Their knowledge goes back only a little ways. My experience is that in matters of climate the years are bunched together. This is the third anyway, with a good sting in the tail."

But there were many in Escalona who did not take the situation so philosophically. They little regarded what the next winter had in store for them, the disaster of the present one was more than enough. It reached the very hearths of their homes. If the fruit crop had vanished, where was the money coming from, not alone to pay off indebtedness, but to provide the necessaries of life! In a district where the people depend upon one great industry for support, and which suddenly vanishes, what can they turn to for a living! Some fruit might go out, but the very heart of the trade, the busy effort of a score of packinghouses, must of necessity be crippled. Consternation was depicted upon nearly every face during these early days. Strange as it may seem, a land where such exuberant irrepressible optimism prevailed, which no ordinary buffet could diminish, was now the scene of the very opposite quality, an almost morbid pessimism.

Groups of men invaded the city, and stood at the business corners, as though stunned by the calamity that had befallen them, to discuss the situation. Many families packed up their belongings, and left the city, to seek work elsewhere. This immediate action was seen, too, in others than the workers. People that had spent money freely, and who owned fine automobiles, partly paid for, shut up their houses, stalled, or surrendered their cars, withdrew their sons from the universities, and began to practise the utmost economy. Church music was put down with a ruthless hand, and superfluous ministers had to seek fresh pastures. And many of these things happened while the ice had hardly melted in the gutters and frozen solar-heaters.

When Jacob heard of some of these things, he sat in amazed silence. "Is this a city of gilded gingerbread?" he exclaimed. "Have all these folks been livin' from hand to mouth, or on credit, all these years? We don't live in that way in Maine."

"But this is a new country, father," Jane pointed out. "Maine is an old one."

"No, Jane Samantha!" he returned sharply. "That ain't the reason. These people have had it too long their own way. The climate has favored them for years, until they've got to believe that it'd never fail them. So bang went their money, and when they wanted more, they traded on the future. But they've traded once too often. Nature has given them a sharp rap over the knuckles. I tell you, Jane, altho' I'm no better myself 'cause I been a fool to buy those ranches, this lesson is a mighty good thing for Californy. It's goin' to bring some saneness back to the people, to put values where they should be, and to force truth into their dealin's. But I'm mighty sorry all the same for the pinch it's goin' to mean to them and to me.

44 Black Gold

Petroleum has justly been labeled "black gold" and its value in California has exceeded gold several times over. Originally used by the Indians, its use grew slowly after 1855 when Andres Pico collected tar seepings from a well near Newhall, until in 1903 California led the nation in production. This position was held until 1936. The automobile helped increase the need for oil, especially in the southern part of the state. Upton Sinclair, the state's famed muckraking novelist, attacked man's abuse of his oil resources. In the following he discusses the digging of an oil well in the 20s.

Far down in the ground, underneath the Ross-Bankside No. 1, a great block of steel was turning round and round. The under surface of it had blunt steel teeth, like a nutmeg-grater; on top of it rested a couple of thousand feet of steel tubing, the "drill-stem," a weight of twenty tons pressing it down; so, as it turned, it ate into the solid rock, grinding it to powder. It worked in the midst of a river of thin mud, which was driven down through the center of the hollow tubing, and came up again between the outside of the tubing and the earth. The river of mud served three purposes: it kept the bit and the drill-stem from heating; it carried away the ground-up rock; and as it came up on the outside of the drill-stem, it was pressed against the walls of the hole, and made a plaster to keep the walls rigid, so that they did not press in upon the drill-stem. Up on the top of the ground was a "sump-hole," of mud and water, and a machine to keep up the mixture; there were "mud-dogs," snorting and puffing, which forced it down inside the stem under a pressure of 250 pounds to the square inch. Drilling was always a dirty business; you swam in pale grey mud until the well came in, and after that you slid in oil.

Also it was an expensive business. To turn those twenty tons of steel tubing, getting heavier every day as they got longer—that took real power, you want to know. When the big steam engine started pulling on the chain, and the steel gears started their racket, Bunny would stand and listen, delighted. Some engine, that! Fifty horsepower, the cathead-man would say; and you would imagine fifty horses harnessed to an old-fashioned turn-table with a pole, such as our ancestors employed to draw up water from a well, or to run a primitive threshing-machine.

Yes, it took money to drill an oil-well out here in California; it wasn't like the little short holes in the East, where you pounded your way down by lifting up your string of tools and letting them drop again. No siree, here you had to be prepared to go six or seven thousand feet, which meant from three hundred to three hundred and fifty joints of pipe; also casing, for you could not leave this hole very long without protection. There were strata of soft sand, with water running through, and when you got past these you would have to let down a cylinder of steel or wrought iron, like a great long stove pipe; joint after joint you would slide down, carefully rivetting them together, making a water-proof job; and when you had this casing all set in cement, you would start drilling with a smaller bit, say fourteen inches, leaving the upper casing resting firmly on a sort of shelf. So you would go, smaller and smaller, until, when you got to the oil-sands, your hole would have shrunk to five or six inches. If you were a careful man, like Dad, you would run each string of casing all the way up to the derrick-floor, so that in the upper part of the hole you would have four sets of casing, one inside the other.

All day and all night the engine labored, and the great chain pulled, and the rotary-table went round and round, and the bit ate into the rock. You had to have two shifts of men, twelve hours each, and because living quarters were scarce in this sudden rush, they kept the same bed warm all the time. A crew had to be on the job every moment, to listen and to watch. The engine must have plenty of water and gas and oil; the pump must be working, and the mud-river circulating, and the mixing-machine splashing, and the drill making depth at the proper rate. There were innumerable things that might go wrong, and some of them cost money, and some of them cost more money. Dad was liable to be waked up at any hour of the night, and he would give orders over the telephone, or perhaps he would slip into his clothes and drive out to the field. And next morning, at breakfast, he would tell Bunny about it; that fellow Dan Rossiger, the night-foreman, he sure was one balky mule; he jist wouldn't make any time, and when you kicked, he said, "all right, if you want a 'twist-off'." And Dad had said, " 'Twist-off' or no 'twist-off,' I want you to make time." And so, sure enough, there was a "twist-off," right away! Dad vowed that Dan had done it on purpose; there were fellows mean enough for that—and, of course, all they had to do was to speed up the engine.

Anyhow, there was your "twist-off"; which meant that you had to lift out every inch of your two thousand feet of pipe. You pulled it up, and unscrewed it, four joints at a time—"breaking out," the men called that operation; each four joints, a "stand," were stood up in the derrick, and the weary work went on. You couldn't tell where the break was, until you got to it; then you screwed off the broken piece, and threw it away, and went to your real job, "fishing" for the remainder of your drill-stem, down in the hole. For this job you had a device called an "overshot," which you let down with a cable; it was big and heavy, and went over the pipe, and caught on a joint when you pulled it up—something like an ice-man's tongs. But maybe you got it over, and maybe you didn't; you spent a lot of time jiggling it up and down—until at last she caught fast, and up came the rest of your stem! Then you unscrewed the broken piece, and put in a sound piece, and let it all back into the hole, one stand at a time, until you were ready to start again. But this time you went at the rate Dan Rossiger considered safe, and you didn't nag at him for any more "twist-offs!"

Meantime Dad would be spending the day at his little office down in the business part of the town. There he had a stenographer and a bookkeeper, and all the records of his various wells. There came people who wanted to offer him new leases, and hustling young salesmen to show him a wonderful new device in the way of an "underreamer," or to persuade him that wrought casing lasts longer than cast steel, or to explain the model of a new bit, that was making marvelous records in the Palomar field. Dad would see them all, for they might "have something," you never could be sure. But woe to the young man who hadn't got his figures just right; for Dad had copies of the "logs" of every one of his wells, and he would pull out the book, and show the embarrassed young man exactly what he had done over at Lobos River with a Stubbs Fishtail number seven.

Then the postman would come, bringing reports from all the wells; and Dad would dictate letters and telegrams. Or perhaps the 'phone would ring—long distance calling Mr. Ross; and Dad would come home to lunch fuming—that fellow Impey over at Antelope had gone and broke his leg, letting a pipe fall on him: that chap with the black moustache, you remember? Bunny said, yes, he remembered; the one Dad had bawled out. "I fired him," said Dad; "and then I got sorry for his wife and children, and took him back. I found that fellow down on his knees, with his head stuck between the chain and the bull-wheel—and he knew we had no bleeder-valve on that engine! Jist tryin' to get out a piece of rope, he said—and his fingers jammed up in there! What's the use a-tryin' to do anything for people that ain't got sense enough to take care of their own fingers, to say nothing of their heads? By golly, I don't see how they ever live long enough to grow black moustaches on their faces!" So Dad would fuss—his favorite theme, the shiftlessness of the working-class whom he had to employ. Of course he had a purpose; drilling is a dangerous business at best, and Bunny must know what he was doing when he went poking about under a derrick.

There came a telegram from Lobos River; Number Two was stuck. First, they had lost a set of tools, and then, while they were stringing up for the fishing job, a "rough-neck" had dropped a steel crowbar into the hole! They were down four thousand feet, and "fishing" is costly sport at that depth! Seemed like there was a jinx in that hole; they had "jammed" three times, and they were six weeks behind their schedule. Dad fretted, and he would call up the well every couple of hours all day, but nothing doing; they tried this device and that, and Dad 'phoned them to try something else, but in vain. The hole caved in on them, and they had to clean out and fish ahead, run after run. They had caught the tools and jarred them out, but the crowbar was still down there, wedged fast.

The third evening Dad said he guessed he'd have to run over to Lobos River; it was time to set a new casing anyhow, and he liked to oversee those cement fellows. Bunny jumped up, crying, "Take me, Dad!" And Dad said, "Sure thing!" Grandmother made her usual remark about Bunny's education going to pot; and Dad made his usual answer, that Bunny would have all his life to learn about poetry and history—now he was going to learn about oil, while he had his father to teach him. Aunt Emma tried to get Mr. Eaton to say something in defense of poetry and history, but the tutor kept a discreet silence—he knew who held the purse-strings in that family! Bunny understood that Mr. Eaton didn't mind about it; he was preparing a thesis that was to get him a master's degree, and he used his spare time quite contentedly, counting the feminine endings in certain of the pre-Elizabethan dramatists.

45 Golden Valley

Los Angeles has been frequently plagued by a lack of water for its steadily increasing population, and obtaining an adequate supply in the arid Southland was a major problem. At the turn of the century William Mulholland, the city engineer, determined to tap the Owens Valley, 240 miles from the city. An aqueduct was ultimately built over mountains and across the desert to carry this water to the city. The manner in which the city obtained the water rights remains a subject of great controversy. Many authors of both fiction and non-fiction contend that there was "a rape of Owens Valley." The evidence to substantiate such a claim is not available, but there is ample proof of wrongdoing by city officials. This selection describes their actions.

John told me the story of his trip as precisely as he could, pacing restlessly about the room, flinging himself down into a chair, then moving about

From *Golden Valley* by Frances Gragg and George Palmer Putnam. Copyright © 1950 by Duell, Sloan and Pearce, Inc. All rights reserved. Reprinted by permission of Hawthorne Books, Inc.

again. I tried not to let his nervousness become contagious, and followed as closely as I could.

"Frank Masters wasn't much impressed to start with," he said. "He'd heard Los Angeles had been nosing round. He didn't think that meant anything. Said they're notorious for that. Anyhow, with the government stepping in, whatever L.A. might have in mind's a dead horse."

John said he hadn't wasted time arguing with Frank. "Henry and I went on to Bishop to see Will Fiske and persuaded Frank to follow us. He didn't want to much." . . .

"He was pretty startled to see us at that time of night. A lot more so when I got through telling him what brought us. But like Frank, he was inclined to consider the whole thing moonshine."

The three had argued for a time, then John asked Will point-blank what he knew about Enderby. Will had said at once that he was all right, an A-1 engineer. Then, John said, Will had squinted up his eyes and thought for a moment and said Enderby wasn't exactly the sort of fellow one would go fishing with.

"I kept digging," John told me. "I knew that boy wasn't just gossiping the other night, Abbie. He's all right, that young Allen. I knew there was something wrong somewhere, and there was bound to be a loose clew if we could get on to it that would lead us to the hitch.

"So I took a new tack. Being after water, they'd naturally file on any that was free and buy up any water-owning land they could. I asked Will if there had been any unusual activity in land transfers lately.

"That made him sit up! He squawked right out, 'Jeerusalem—and I never gave it a minute's thought! Put 'em down to natural speculation, account of the district.'

"I asked if he meant sales, and he said, 'No—options.' Thought back and said he bet he'd notarized twenty in the past month. He was squirming into his shirt and pretty near ran us the couple of blocks to his office."

John took one of his turns about the room and I pressed my hands together in my lap and managed to sit still, though I wanted to pace with him. I knew Will's office. Dingy and dusty with books and papers scattered in every possible space.

"It was hot as a bake oven in there," John said. "And smelly. You know—dust, old tobacco smoke, musty books, moldy old carpet. The water kept dripping out of the tap over the sink and it seemed to make the heat worse than ever." John pressed his lips together, swung about, and looked at me as a thought occurred to him. "Funny," he said, "come to think of it, dripping water ought to sound cool. That didn't.

"It took us over an hour, but we ran it down. Will's notary records showed about fifteen thousand acres optioned around Bishop and another ten thousand between there and Big Pine. A few names were scattered in the lot, but most of it went to a George W. Bushnell. The name of Los Angeles wasn't anywhere."

I felt that I should make some comment, but had no words worth saying. My interest was like a pain pressing against me and holding me silent. For the first time in many years I had the feeling that our security, my world itself, was falling apart. . . . I pinned my mind to what John was saying.

"As fast as Will dug the items out of his records, Henry jotted them down and I marked them off the map. We'd just finished when Frank walked in. He looked hot and cranky. He laid his Stetson down in the cleanest place he could find on Will's desk—you know how particular Frank is about his hat, Abbie—and said, 'You boys laid your ghosts now?'

"I told him not so's he could notice it. 'Come here,' I said, 'I want to show you something.'

"I was standing at that big map of Bishop Will's got hanging in his office. 'See those?' I said, and I ticked off the optioned ranches fast as I could. I'd circled each one of 'em in red.

"Frank studied them for a minute. 'All right,' he snapped. 'What about it? What do those red circles mean?'

"I told him they meant that every one of those ranches had been optioned out in the past month.

" 'Who to?' Frank says, and I told him different people, but mostly to a fellow named Bushnell, 'George W. Bushnell,' I said.

"Frank wanted to know who he was, and I couldn't tell him, but Will explained that Bushnell was a newcomer, little nondescript chap with one of those hearing devices on his ear. Will said he hung around the saloons a lot but wasn't one to treat often. Not friendly, either. Frank just grunted and went back to studying the map. When he spoke up he sounded scared.

" 'I got a lot of money strewed around here,' he said. 'You think this might tie up with that Los Angeles business?' I said I didn't know but it didn't look good. Frank said it looked like hell to him, and he spread his big paw over the map. 'I got a lot of money strewed around there,' he said again.

"There didn't seem to be much to say to that. Frank did have money loaned out on pretty near every ranch I'd circled and a lot more besides. Bishop ranches have always been good risks.

"Will told Frank not to let it bother him. Sold or not, Will said, those ranches were all good for Frank's loans. Frank turned on him like a trapped bearcat. 'Hell,' he snarled. 'It ain't them I'm worrying about. It's these here.' He wiped his hand right over the whole district. 'The best ranches here never owned a drop o' water in their history. Been living off of seepage for fifty years. Take that seepage away and where'll they be?'

"Somehow or other, none of us had thought about that. It didn't make the picture a bit prettier, Abbie, you can see that. Henry was popeyed. He started to sputtering that they couldn't do that—you know Henry gets all riled up. 'Maybe they can't,' Frank said, dry as you please, 'but they'd bust a hamstring trying.' "

John flung himself wearily onto the sofa and rubbed his hands across his face. "That's what they'll do, too," he said, "and it'll mean ruin,

Abigail. Take it away and the desert will have the land back again inside of three years! If you doubt me, look at my abandoned homestead."

"But, John," I cried, "they wouldn't—they couldn't do that. . . ." I thought of Henry's ranch, Tom Ellison's, the Schultzes', every one of them fertile from seepage water.

. . .

MacAndrew's Ditch that was to rob us of our snow-fed waters, taking them from the brightness of sky and sun to the gloom of iron pipes under the streets of Los Angeles, crawled inexorably southward.

"Come hell or high water, my city drinks!" MacAndrew had stormed at Abby. It had not drunk yet, but each day the ditch crawled forward, bringing near that time when it would have its water. Only the magnitude of the task itself and Haiwee stood between. We who had been so certain when Abby bought Haiwee that the city's need of it for a reservoir site could be used as a club to bring decent justice to those who saw their ranches dying, began to lose some of our certainty.

Will Fiske came back from the first trial of the city's lawsuit to condemn Haiwee. Charlie Hunter had sent it over to Mariposa County, as Will had foretold. Now even he was dubious.

"I dunno," he observed gloomily. "Meredino did all he could. The record's so full of holes the case is bound to be sent back for retrial. I'm beginning to wonder if the city can't afford time better than we can. They didn't appear in any compromising frame of mind to me."

Frank Masters' bank was forced to close its doors. Disregarding all warnings Frank had gone his stubborn way, trying to fight Los Angeles with dollars—the city that had a hundred thousand dollars to his one. When Frank went down, with him went ranchers, merchants, homesteaders, prospectors, stockmen, and miners. That Frank could not survive the crash of the house he had built, passing away in his sleep before the audit was even begun, didn't shorten the line of those who waited before the doors that would never open again. I saw that line in my dreams again and again—toil-bent men, faded women. Even the children, clinging to their mother's skirts, were strangely silent, their little faces scared and defeated. I avoided that corner of the town as much as I could. The sheriff boarded up the windows and doors after someone had thrown a rock through the plate glass in which Frank had taken such pride.

Day after day tragedy stalked the valley. A Bishop rancher hanged himself in his barn. A Big Pine woman ate arsenic. Another rancher blew the top of his head off with a shotgun. A homesteader from Eight Mile shot himself beside his last dwindling haystack. Jane Calkins moved away from her dying ranch and all she had worked so hard to gain. I heard that she was cooking in someone's kitchen in Pasadena and had been obliged to put her children in a foundlings' home. I wrote to her but never got a reply to my sorrowful, inadequate letter. A young couple in Bishop were found dead in bed, clasped in each other's arms. The coroner's cold, impersonal report was the single word: strychnine.

"City's sore as hell," Little John grunted. "About the Haiwee business. Hear they're going to turn the valley back to the desert."

"But they can't! They wouldn't!" I cried.

Little John looked at me. "Tomorrow," he said, "I'll show you something."

We rode out to Fred Lindstrom's old place. With a sick heart, I looked about me. The meadow was already brown and dead. Wind rattled through the dying orchard and sent the leaves from the old cottonwoods scurrying over the ground. When it caught up a bit of dry ash from where the burnt barn had stood and sent it swirling, I made Little John take me away. I shut my eyes against the weed-grown garden and the empty house with its staring windows.

Fred had been one of the first to sell to Los Angeles. His barns and haystacks were the first to be burned. Fred was angry when he moved to Long Beach. But presently letters began to come from him. In his cramped, Old World handwriting, he begged for news of his mountains, of the valley, of his beloved ranch. Then the letters stopped, and we heard Fred had died of a heart attack. But I knew they had broken his heart.

After Frank Masters' bank failed, ranch after ranch passed swiftly into the city's hands. No longer were the dazzling prices paid. "Take it or leave it," was the city's motto. Penniless people took it, choking back unspeakable heartache. For the others, those with the seepage-fed ranches, there was nothing to do but watch the browns spread and spread, or take the pittance city land sharks offered.

Chapter 9

Cults, Sects, and Faddists

Cults, Sects, and Faddists

California is the spawning ground and incubator of more unusual religious groups than any other area in the world. This is particularly true of the area around Mt. Shasta and some parts of the desert country, but the rest of the state has also experienced its share. A week seldom passes without the birth of a new religion, philosophy, or movement. Men claiming to be the reincarnation of Christ—or John the Baptist or Buddha—petition to have their names changed to conform to their new status or run newspaper advertisements to let the world know of their existence. "Here," wrote Bruce Bliven, "is the world's prize collection of cranks, semi-cranks, placid creatures whose bovine expression shows that each of them is studying, without much hope of success, to be a high-grade moron, angry or ecstatic exponents of food fads, sun-bathing, ancient Greek costumes, diaphragm breathing and the imminent second coming of Christ." A casual glance at the newspaper advertisements of church worship services shows a mixture of churches unknown elsewhere in the United States.

Many of the unique churches profess to be Christian, but their theology, when they have any, stresses that California is the Holy Land, and the promise of the better life is now, not in the hereafter. Hell and damnation are slighted in favor of sermons designed to make parishioners feel good. "Beyond Positive Thinking," "You Can Be Greater Than You Are," "Dare to Be Healthy," and "What World Are You Living In?" are samples of sermon topics on a single Sunday. Even staid and orthodox churches in California take on a cast very different from that found elsewhere. Incidents of glossalia (speaking in tongues) are reportedly more common in the Golden State. Elaborate church structures are built, sometimes with the aid of faked membership rolls and stewardship records. The bishop of one Protestant denomination, after hearing charges of heresy in one of his congregations moaned, "Only in California could such things go on!"

Some of the non-Christian sects turn to Oriental religions for their inspiration. Others borrow from the fantasy of science fiction, and many are based, at least in part, on the ideas of theosophy. The theosophist movement was founded by Helena Petrovna Blavatsky in 1875 (women have always played a key role in California cultism), and her writings are still influential. First brought to San Diego (Point Loma) by Katherine Tingley, theosophy was eclectic in its approach; it "sought to synthesize, to include the essence of all cults." In addition, theosophists promised to bring out the latent powers of man so he could harmonize with nature. The movement splintered into many different groups, usually as a result of personality clashes, or because of some newly discovered belief.

Just why cults and fads have flourished in California remains a matter of speculation. Some attribute it to the fact that Mediterranean-like climates have always spawned new religions, while others claim that the health-seekers have created an especially fertile environment for this type of activity. Professor Robert G. Cleland believed the cause was California itself: "In a society so diverse in objectives and community of interest, so lacking in cohesion and unity of character, the quack, the charlatan, the prophet of a new cult, the advocate of a new school of healing, the spokesman for the novel, spectacular, and bizarre, whatever its nature or purpose, seldom found it necessary to search the highways and hedges to obtain a following." The idea that a rootless, mobile society is responsible is strengthened by the fact that many cults cater to the fears of people. Some groups claim that the "Hidden Rulers" are going to poison the water to keep the people docile; some believe that the good life is denied them because manufacturers keep new products off the market; others find all the problems of the day originating in Washington; and anti-semitism, perhaps mankind's oldest "red-herring," has been a facet of many of the state's cults.

Californians tend to worship the unconventional; thus, the more "far-out" a belief, the better its chances of acceptance. Just as strong personalities dominate the political arena, so also are they found in the religious realm. In fact, most sects rise and fall in accordance with the life span of their dominant leader.

The Golden State is also reputedly a place where sex inhibitions are relatively absent, and the close relationship of sex and religion, especially among the cultists, has been widely studied. Sex has always been a part of the religious experience. Historically, pagan man combined sex rites with the worship of divinities, and sex symbolism in primitive religions has been widely noted. So perhaps California's climate of sexual freedom has nourished its unbridled religious freedom.

46   The Crucifixion

An irreverent Los Angeles newsman, used to bearded men in flowing white gowns and sandals in simulation of the Nazarene, once commented sarcastically that, "the next thing you know they'll be having a fake Crucifixion in Pershing Square." The events described in the following novel are sufficiently bizarre, although the locale was not the Los Angeles abode of eccentrics. Instead, it took place in an amusement park, something of a Bible version of Disneyland in the California desert. The complex was built as a replica of the scenes of Holy Week in

Jerusalem and was intended by its promoters to lure the faithful of Southern California. The young man on the cross had played the role of Christ in the Passion Play and decided to pay the supreme sacrifice in order to publicize abuses at the park.

Nicholas Concert, a minister without particular portfolio or flock, and once, long ago, a priest of the Roman faith, awoke in a troubled dawn. It was the new day sensed rather than perceptible to him in the interior blackness of the detached truck camper. It was cold. He was tempted to huddle in his sleeping bag awhile longer, until the sun would rise out of the Mojave, climb the ridge and fill the isolated desert valley. He had not slept well. His night had been frantic with apparitions, sounds, fragments of dialogue.

It had been a long night, a terrible night, one that Concert had thought would never end or, at its worst, that it *had* ended and he had died during its passing and this was his eternal hell, to be transfixed in this night forever, kept from his tomorrow as Moses, flawed, had been kept from his. As far as he knew, there was no one but himself in all of The Valley of His Passion Park, Inc., that night. But he had heard *them* talking: Mary—the *real* one, Christ's mother—in a voice of such sweetness and sorrow Concert had wanted to go to her, console her, weep with her, though the terror that he might actually find a voice embodied rather than conjured from lines of the Passion Play or Scripture had kept him from going out there; Magdalene the whore, now blessed—how he yearned to have been the instrument of her salvation as he could never be the instrument of another's; the disciples, the Roman soldiers, crowd noises, Joseph of Arimathea, and —most terrible of all—Jesus himself crying out in his agony.

But they *were* other voices and he had shut them out, fearful to peek through the windows of the low, immobilized truck camper in which he slept; fearful to see if this replica of the Holy Land they had built in the California desert had indeed, by some transmutation, become peopled with the originals. It was too awesome a thing to witness by oneself if true. Or it would be said that he had been drinking, which he hadn't.

The sounds now were of wind rustling brush and trees, the last hoots of great horned owls sated from the night's hunting, small creatures scurrying. He separated each new noise, traced it swiftly in his mind, identified its source. The voices were gone. He decided it was weariness and anticipation that had bred his hallucination. The weariness of many months of physical and mental labor for The Valley of His Passion Park, Inc. The anticipation of their opening and the first performance of their Passion Play in the week before Easter.

Concert unzipped the sleeping bag in which he had lain fully clothed. He slid out of it, moved haltingly from window to window to door of the grounded camper body. It was said by skeptics that days and nights alone in the desert would do things to a man, would make him see and hear God. But he didn't want to think of that. A coyote howled, and while its cry was still in the air, it was joined by others, and then there was a terrible cacophony of growls and snarls and yelps, as though the pack had caught some poor helpless creature and was tearing it apart alive. He thought of Jesus and the mob, and trembled.

Concert opened the camper door. His eyes fixed upon the grouping of stark white plaster statues fifty yards away. Pending more dramatic or interesting disbursement throughout the park, these dozens of tall biblical figures were gathered in The Garden of the Saints, preaching, listening, discoursing, accusing, summoning, or reflecting degrees of beatitude. On the blackest of nights, they drew into themselves light from distant sources and emanated it as their own. Concert spent many minutes staring at them, rooting each to its place, brazenly challenging each to move or speak and then, certain that it hadn't and wouldn't, shifting his gaze to another. The darkness lightened ever so slightly as he watched.

Then the earth trembled. A distant rumbling, lessened by miles and the barrier of mountains, vibrated through the ground, came diminished over the ridges into the cup of the high valley, and was captured there to reverberate lowly. Though he knew what it was, Concert was frightened. The first time, he had thought it was an earthquake. Now he knew that rockets were being fired on static test pads to roar out their harnessed fury in another valley of the high desert. It happened often, and startled him each time. He didn't like it for what it was. He didn't like it for the threat it foretold to God and heaven. He put on his shoes and left the camper. His eyes anxiously traveled the ridge lines. To the east, the barely discernible paleness of dawn made him quicken his steps.

He took the dirt road toward Calvary Hill, stopping on the way at the latrine and washhouse. Once, Reverend Rudolf had caught him urinating elsewhere on the grounds and had severely reprimanded him for despoiling holy ground. Concert tripped on the top step. The flimsy wooden shack vibrated. There were no lights there and he groped his way in the dark. The bare enclosure was cold and it stank. It was only temporary for the workmen who filled the valley in the daytime. So much of The Valley of His Passion Park, Inc., was still temporary or incomplete that Concert worried whether they would be able to open on time. Reverend Rudolf continually assured him they would.

Concert dashed cold water on his stubbled face, dried himself on a dirty towel, and left the shack. The earth tremble stopped. He walked very quickly toward his destination so that he would be sure to be there at exactly the right moment. He passed the big signboard on which were printed SODOM and GOMORRAH. Arrows enclosed the words and pointed across a moat to two large buildings. Neon tubing overlaid the letters and arrows. Within a few days, electricity would run through the tubing, flashing its message day and night. Concert felt the strong disapproval he always felt when he passed this place or thought about Reverend Rudolf's Sodom and Gomorrah.

"We must show them sin, too—else how shall they know goodness and salvation?" Reverend Rudolf had said, in explaining to his associates and employees his reasons for this late and costly addition to the park. Concert, who was paid a small salary, provided with food—generally spartan—and given a place to sleep, though not always the same place or one to call his own, was never sure from one moment to the next whether he was an associate or an employee. His status seemed to change as the Reverend Rudolf's moods and needs changed; and his degree of protest, therefore, in this instance, as in others, had been modest and unavailing. "Think of it, Nicholas," Reverend Rudolf had expounded further, "as a dramatic presentation in which the public will be able to take part with the performers to feel the evil more deeply, to see it, hear it, touch it! A dramatic presentation, as all of The Valley of His Passion Park will be! We will be speaking to them in parables, in stories as Jesus did."

Concert recognized no need for exploiting sin. He could tell them about it. There was no need to tempt them to share in it, as Concert in his life had been tempted, and had fallen; and would be tempted again and fall again. He moved through the dark grove of eucalyptus in which picnic tables and benches and barbecue pits had been built. The air here now was heavy with the sour-sweet aroma of fallen leaves and soil dank from winter rains. He had tried to explain to Reverend Rudolf that in the searing days of desert summer, when those branches and leaves hung brittle and dry and gasping for water, the barbecue pits would constitute a serious fire hazard. But the Reverend had told him, "We will provide for them. We will bring in water sufficient to turn our desert into a veritable Eden. The shade in that grove will be blessed. You will see, Nicholas, on hot days that little grove will be the most popular spot in the park. Mothers and fathers and children will rest there. They'll eat their picnic lunches, and we'll have a refreshment stand for those who don't bring their own, and in one direction they'll look back through the trees toward The Garden of the Saints, and in the other they'll be looking on the most awesome spectacle in Christendom."

Concert dropped his eyes as he passed through the other side of the grove. He came here almost daily, in just this way. It was his habit to move with eyes downcast beyond this point, to kneel where the ground began to rise, to pray for a few moments, and then to raise his eyes to the crown of Golgotha, without yet trying to really see what was silhouetted there, and then to let the bursting dawn itself reveal to him the three crosses against the sky in all their terrible power.

At the base of the knoll, Concert dropped to his knees, and though he was no longer a priest, his lips moved in the old and familiar morning office—for it came from deep within his heart and, despite his defection, he saw no reason to forgo its salutary effect or any grace that might accrue to him for saying it.

In the first instant of looking up, he accepted without question what he saw there—for he had often conjured the bearded, dying figure on the center cross. Then he gasped, and a sound of absolute terror strangled his throat and barely escaped his lips. He struggled to his feet, trembling, his gaze locked onto the scene thirty yards from him. He shook his head, blinked his eyes to clear the hallucination that had invaded his brain. But it did not leave. It was real. There was a man nailed to the cross.

Concert backed away, stopped, moved forward. His hand raised in a gesture of anguished empathy; his lips formed words of wonder and supplication that were struck from him before they could be uttered. His legs moved to flee. His mind told him to go quickly to a place where he would find people of authority. His heart bade him rush forward and give aid. His soul cried for help from Him whom he would help. He staggered closer, shielding his eyes from the rising sun split by the silhouetted cross and figure. He came close enough to expunge any further notion of hallucination, close enough to see and smell and feel the reality of the thin white naked body, the terribly pierced hands and feet, the still wet falls of blood, and the bearded, gaunt face fixed in the distortions of pain and anguish of so horrible a dying.

"Oh, my God!" Concert cried.

He backed away again, stumbled, turned, and ran. The nearest communication with the outside world was a public phone booth on the highway two miles away, near the entry road where cars from Palestina turned toward The Valley of His Passion Park.

47   The Disenchanted

Several reasons why the unusual in religion abounds in California have been advanced. But there is a limit to the understanding of such a phenomenon by the social scientist or even the sociologist of religion. A writer can often suggest more valid explanations through fiction. Nathanael West, author of *The Day of the Locust*, one of the greatest novels ever written probing the California psyche, discusses in this selection the attraction exotic cults have for the disenchanted. The main character, Tod, is a painter who views these people with the discerning eye of the artist. The people West describes lived such boring lives, they were starved for excitement or for anything which would salvage their egos. A cause or cult was frequently the answer, and they switched allegiance as soon as their "church" lost its savor.

He spent his nights at the different Hollywood churches, drawing the worshipers. He visited the "Church of Christ, Physical" where holiness was attained through the constant use of chestweights and spring grips; the "Church Invisible" where fortunes were told and the dead made to find lost objects; the "Tabernacle of the Third Coming" where a woman in male clothing preached the "Crusade Against Salt"; and the "Temple Moderne" under whose glass and chromium roof "Brain-Breathing, the Secret of the Aztecs" was taught.

As he watched these people writhe on the hard seats of their churches, he thought of how well Alessandro Magnasco would dramatize the contrast between their drained-out, feeble bodies and their wild, disordered minds. He would not satirize them as Hogarth or Daumier might, nor would he pity them. He would paint their fury with respect, appreciating its awful, anarchic power and aware that they had it in them to destroy civilization.

One Friday night in the "Tabernacle of the Third Coming," a man near Tod stood up to speak. Although his name most likely was Thompson or Johnson and his home town Sioux City, he had the same countersunk eyes, like the heads of burnished spikes, that a monk by Magnasco might have. He was probably just in from one of the colonies in the desert near Soboba Hot Springs where he had been conning over his soul on a diet of raw fruit and nuts. He was very angry. The message he had brought to the city was one that an illiterate anchorite might have given decadent Rome. It was a crazy jumble of dietary rules, economics and Biblical threats. He claimed to have seen the Tiger of Wrath stalking the walls of the citadel and the Jackal of Lust skulking in the shrubbery, and he connected these omens with "thirty dollars every Thursday" and meat eating.

Tod didn't laugh at the man's rhetoric. He knew it was unimportant. What mattered were his messianic rage and the emotional response of his hearers. They sprang to their feet, shaking their fists and shouting. On the altar someone began to beat a bass drum and soon the entire congregation was singing "Onward Christian Soldiers."

. . .

New groups, whole families, kept arriving. He could see a change come over them as soon as they had become part of the crowd. Until they reached the line, they looked diffident, almost furtive, but the moment they had become part of it, they turned arrogant and pugnacious. It was a mistake to think them harmless curiosity seekers. They were savage and bitter, especially the middle-aged and the old, and had been made so by boredom and disappointment.

All their lives they had slaved at some kind of dull, heavy labor, behind desks and counters, in the fields and at tedious machines of all sorts, saving their pennies and dreaming of the leisure that would be theirs when they had enough. Finally that day came. They could draw a weekly income of ten or fifteen dollars. Where else should they go but California, the land of sunshine and oranges?

Once there, they discover that sunshine isn't enough. They get tired of oranges, even of avocado pears and passion fruit. Nothing happens. They don't know what to do with their time. They haven't the mental equipment for leisure, the money nor the physical equipment for pleasure. Did they slave so long just to go to an occasional Iowa picnic? What else is there? They watch the waves come in at Venice. There wasn't any ocean where most of them came from, but after you've seen one wave, you've seen them all. The same is true of the airplanes at Glendale. If only a plane would crash once in a while so that they could watch the passengers being consumed in a "holocaust of flame," as the newspapers put it. But the planes never crash.

Their boredom becomes more and more terrible. They realize that they've been tricked and burn with resentment. Every day of their lives they read the newspapers and went to the movies. Both fed them on lynchings, murder, sex crimes, explosions, wrecks, love nests, fires, miracles, revolutions, war. This daily diet made sophisticates of them. The sun is a joke. Oranges can't titillate their jaded palates. Nothing can ever be violent enough to make taut their slack minds and bodies. They have been cheated and betrayed. They have slaved and saved for nothing.

48   Prophet of the Third Revelation

This selection offers a further explanation of why cults and faddists flourish in California. It also stresses the great importance of a strong personality with which the faithful can identify. Above all, the organization depicted here allows people to become involved in the actual services, even if it is only to answer a question by raising their hands. This suggests that one reason for the multiplicity of religious groups in the state arises from the failure of conventional churches to provide a spiritually satisfying message to a mobile populace. Modern technology, in the form of radio (and later TV), expanded the arena of the powerful pastor and vastly increased his impact.

Of all the people Bunny knew, it appeared just now that only one was perfectly successful and completely happy, and that was Eli Watkins, prophet of the Third Revelation. For the Lord had carried out to the letter the promise revealed to the runners of the Bible Marathon; he had caused a great banker, Mark Eisenberg, who ran the financial affairs of Angel City, to reflect upon the importance of Eli's political influence, and to put up a good part of the money for the new tabernacle. Now the structure was completed, and was opened amid such glory to the Lord as had never been witnessed in this part of the world.

Southern California is populated for the most part by retired farmers from the middle west, who have come out to die amid sunshine and flowers.

Of course they want to die happy, and with the assurance of sunshine and flowers beyond; so Angel City is the home of more weird cults and doctrines—you couldn't form any conception of it till you came to investigate. To run your eye over the pages of performances advertised in the Sunday newspapers would cause you to burst into laughter or tears, according to your temperament. Wherever three or more were gathered together in the name of Jesus or Buddha or Zoroaster, or Truth or Light or Love, or New Thought or Spiritualism or Psychic Science—there was the beginning of a new revelation, with mystical, inner states of bliss and esoteric ways of salvation.

Eli had advantages over most of these spiritual founders. In the first place, he had been a real shepherd of flocks and herds, and there are age-old traditions attaching to this profession. Also it was symbolically useful; what Eli had done to the goats he was now doing to the human goats of Angel City, gathering them into the fold and guarding them from the cruel wolf Satan. He had taken to carrying a shepherd's crook on the platform, and with his white robes and the star shining in his yellow hair, he would call the flocks, just as he had done upon the hills, and when he passed the collection plate, they would do the shearing of themselves.

Eli possessed a sense of drama and turned it loose in the devising of primitive little tableaux and pageants, which gave rapture to his simple minded followers. When he told how he had been tempted of the devil, the wicked One came upon the scene, hoofs, horns and tail, and with a red spotlight on him; when Eli lifted up the cross on high, the devil would fall and strike his forehead on the ground, and the silver trumpets would peal, and the followers would burst into loud hosannahs. Or perhaps it would be the command, "Suffer little children to come unto me"; there would be hundreds of children, all robed in white, and when Eli lifted his shepherd's crook and called, they came storming to the platform, their fresh young voices shouting, "Praise the Lord!" And of course there was the regular mourners' bench, and the baptisms in the marble tank. You were never allowed to forget that you had a soul, and that it was of supreme importance to you and to Jesus, and that you were having it saved by Eli's aid. You were always being called upon to do something—to stand up for the Lord, or to clap your hands for salvation, or to raise your right hand if you were a new-comer to the tabernacle.

But the great advantage Eli had over the other prophets was the pair of leathern bellows he had developed out on the hills of Paradise. Never was there such an electrifying voice, and never one that could keep going so long. All day Sunday it bellowed and boomed—morning, afternoon, evening; there were week-day services every evening but Saturday, and in the mornings and afternoons there were prayer meetings and Bible schools and services of song and healing blessings and baptismal ceremonials and thank offerings and wholesale weddings and Bride of the Lamb dedications—you just couldn't keep track of all that was going on in the many rooms and meetinghalls of this half million dollar tabernacle.

Science had just completed a marvelous invention; the human voice became magnified a hundred million fold, it could be spread over the whole earth. The population of America had gone wild over radio, and everybody had rushed to get a set. The first great public use made of this achievement in Angel City was to open a new three million dollar hotel for the pleasure of the very rich, and the opening ceremonies were broadcasted, and the newspapers were full of the wonder of it; but it proved to be dreadful, because everybody in the hotel got drunk, and the manager of the institution placed himself in front of the microphone and poured out a stream of obscenities such as farmers' wives from Iowa had never dreamed in all their lives. So it was felt that the new invention needed to be sanctified and redeemed, and Eli proceeded to install one of the biggest and most powerful broadcasting stations. Through the Lord's mercy, his words were heard over four million square miles, and it was worthwhile to preach to audiences of that size, praise Jesus!

Eli's preaching had thus become one of the major features of Southern California life. You literally couldn't get away from him if you tried. Dad had been told by his doctor that he needed more exercise, and he had taken to walking for half an hour before dinner; he declared that he listened to Eli's sermons on all these walks, and never missed a single word! Everybody's house was wide open in this warm spring weather, and all you had to do was to choose a neighborhood where the moderately poor lived—and 90 per cent of the people were that. You would hear the familiar bellowing voice, and before you got out of range of it, you would come in range of another radio set, and so you would be relayed from street to street and from district to district! In these houses sat old couples with family bibles in their hands and tears of rapture in their eyes; or perhaps a mother washing her baby's clothes or making a pudding for her husband's supper—and all the time her soul caught up to glory on the wings of the mighty prophet's eloquence! And Dad walking outside, also exalted.

49 Health Faddism

Many observers claim that the arrival of health-seekers was an important prelude to religious quackery. One observer complained bitterly, "They come to California to die, and, dammit, they don't." When the climate fails to cure their many ailments they turn to charlatans. As Morrow Mayo commented, "Los Angeles leads the world in the advancement and practice of all the healing sciences, except perhaps medicine and surgery." Thus, nostrums, health cures, and freak brands of medical science abound and often cults are associated with them. This selection tells how a quack and a former medical student combine to advance the fleecing of the gullible. Note their mention of how these people move about from one purveyor of panaceas to another and their concern about legal complications.

"Sorry," Spartan repeated, knowing that, having once made the slip, he would be calling Bootmaker that in his mind, and probably half the time to his face, from there on. "Anyway, I think we can set this up in January, and have it rolling for the spring symposium. I'll have my certificate by then, and I can—"

"I don't know what you're talking about, and I doubt if you do. When you came in here Monday, you talked like a pitch man, but I felt you had something genuinely good that needed only a little working out. I liked the sound of Healthopathy—it showed inventiveness—and I was anxious to give you a chance. But now, four days later, you're in here giving me another pitch, and you haven't done a thing all week but—"

"But get you out of a jam with the Powell kid, and tell you to get rid of that poor woman with coccidioidomycosis before she died in the reception room some bright morning."

"Oh, I don't think she would have . . . I'll admit I would never had guessed she had San Joaquin Valley fever—"

"Well then," Spartan interposed righteously. "And she is going to die with the stuff. She's got the progressive form, and I don't think she has the constitution to ride it out."

"That is still neither here nor there, though. The M.D.'s lose patients constantly and there's no to-do about it."

"M.D.'s don't have to bother with cranks, either. We do. And every time one of them dies under the age of eighty, I'll bet a squawk goes up among the Faithful that you can hear clear out to Grand Street. From what I've seen of the coterie, they seem to circulate among themselves a lot more than the patients an M.D. has. And that means that a lot of gossip and comparing of notes must go on."

"Well, of course," Bootmaker said reasonably. "And that's one reason why I took you in. You had me convinced you'd stir up a little excitement, get the word going around that there's something new and titillating going on in the Bootmaker office. Instead of that, you've curbed one patient's earache and advised me to send one of my most remunerative patients away. As for the rest—any green kid out of chiropractic school could have done as efficiently, and I'd have paid him two hundred a month. If I hired him at all, that is."

"Oh, stop carping," Spartan said unwisely.

"Certainly. And I think we should stop the nonsense, too. McClintock, I'm dissatisfied. Suppose you go somewhere else with your ideas."

That's what I deserve for trying to deal with an ass, Spartan thought. He began heatedly, "What did you expect in three days? A horde of maniacs hiccuping with delight and pounding at the door because we're handing out pills to make them all eighteen again? I told you I would have to keep in the background until I got my certificate, and you seemed to agree. I was to help out with the routine stuff, do a bit of diagnosis, and damn little else until I could take the exam. That was the agreement, and here you are yapping—"

"I'm doing more than yapping. I'm demanding. Have you or haven't you something new to offer? Is Healthopathy a well-worked-out plan of attracting new patients and keeping them? Or is it just a name you stumbled across?"

Taking the gamble, Spartan decided to be honest. "Oh, hell, it was just a name. A name plus the conviction that with my background I could probably think up a better line of junk than you and Knox K. Knox put out at the symposium. I had only this much to go on: that you and all the rest were taking the negative approach. You were panning the M.D.'s and doing a bit of spinal adjustment and colonics, and not much else. And worst of all, you were fooling around with a group of sick people who needed serious medical attention. And that's as far as I had—"

"I might as well set you straight on one thing right now," Bootmaker interrupted, but not rudely. "You're right in that ostensibly we're out to cure illnesses. But what you don't know is how this crew acts. They listen to us pan the M.D.'s and they seem to gobble it up. But whenever they become desperately ill, they cross the last ditch and run to an M.D. Of course, as soon as they're cured, they come right back to us again. I can't explain the psychology behind it, but it is a fact. However, we're getting away from the point, McClintock."

"No, we're not," Spartan said, thinking rapidly, "we're right on it. As I say, you take the negative approach. The sick ones leave you anyway, and the healthy ones stay in the same condition. And by that I mean you don't jazz them up, you don't—Look, let me put it this way: A hypochondriac walks in here. You pummel her around a bit and tell her to breathe through her nostrils. Momentarily you've distracted her; but when she goes home, her imagination starts up again. The next day she's over at Knox's, and the next, she's listening to Phoebe Kidd tell her about the delights of kumiss. And that's my—"

"Like a game of musical quacks," Bootmaker said, smiling.

"A—I guess I didn't hear you."

"I said that they make the rounds, like a game of musical quacks, so to speak."

"Oh." And that, Spartan told himself, will teach you to misjudge your man. Pulling himself together, he went on, "Your point is my point. So anyone who comes up with a system that will actually perk up the hypochondriacs physically has a drop on the rest of the boys."

"He most certainly would have. Have you got such a system?"

"I think so. It was the bottle of kelp tablets that gave me the idea. But we'll have to work quietly on this, because if the rest catch on they'll be doing it, too, and the music will start all over again."

"And what is your idea?"

"Vitamins."

"Just vitamins?"

"Empirically, yes," Spartan said, slyly pronouncing the word. "The rest is predicated on garnering all the cranks away from The Boys, and handing them the dangerous cases in turn. Of course, I'll have to think up a line of patter about kinetic forces or somethng like that. And the vitamins won't be called vitamins, we'll call them Dynamics or something like that, and—"

"I don't think—"

". . . no, we won't! We'll call them Kinetabs! Just that, nothing more. We can go through a lot of hocus-pocus diagnosing them—I have an idea or two for that—and then prescribe Kinetabs to jazz them up . . ." Spartan saw Bootmaker was wincing. "What's the matter?"

"Your expression, 'jazz them up.' It irritates me."

"Oh? Well, anyway. . .the tablets will have to contain a lot of B_1 to — umm—promote a feeling of energetic well-being. But the point is this: Since they will not know what they're getting, and it's a fact that vitamins can and do—"

"I am aware of that McClintock. But as I say, I'm not a manufacturer—"

"No, but you're happy to sell kelp tablets to anyone who'll take them. Why not have our own brand of vitamins packaged and labeled for us alone. Nothing on the label to indicate what it is. And with the rigmarole about kinetics to go with it. . . . Well, can't you see what I'm driving at?"

"Yes, and it won't work. In the first place, there are legal angles—"

"There are lawyers for hire also."

"In the second, your idea isn't new enough. Kidd is always screaming her head off about vitamins."

Spartan leaned forward and said in all sincerity, "What makes you think it won't succeed? It's mediocre enough, isn't it?"

Bootmaker turned in his chair and appraised Spartan at length. "I'm afraid I've underestimated you, McClintock. But that's the first intelligent thing you've said this afternoon. If you hold your course to that line of thinking, you can make a success of anything. I know."

"Damn right."

"Since we agree on that, let's get down to the details. You must have something in mind."

50 Krotona

Theosophy furnished the core of belief for many of California's sects, and off-shoots of them are active to the present day. The most famous theosophist colonies were at Point Loma and in the Ojai Valley. The hero in the following entry was typical of cultists in that he was from outside the state and drifted to the Pacific shores in the quest for answers to the eternal questions. Originally from Detroit, he searched all over the nation for a spiritual home before finding it in Hollywood, the site of the colony of Krotona. For him, as for so many, California became the terrestrial paradise. Actually Krotona had a greater cultural impact than most cult centers. Its sponsorship of the arts led to outdoor theatrical productions and the creation of the Theater Arts Alliance in 1919, out of which evolved the Hollywood Bowl concerts of today.

To Wilton Crosby, Krotona in its circle of hills above Hollywood was like some mythical birthplace of his soul and it welcomed him like a prodigal son. He had been torn with loneliness and frustration; Krotona took him in. He had been mauled and defeated all along the line by hard-fisted materialistic cities; Krotona healed his wounds, restored to him his flagging self-confidence. It gave him platforms on which to speak and appreciative audiences, in white stockings and peculiar-looking hats, who listened with eager receptivity. Not only this: these people took him into their homes, implored him to remain, fed him fruit and nuts and suggested that he do his writing in their walled gardens, etc. Many of them had read his books and those who had not, proceeded to do so now that the great man was in their midst. They called him an "arbiter of the newer education," discussed him in reverential tones on every knoll, heeded his most trivial utterance. . . .

In the rear of Mrs. Beckner's house (she was also a Theosophist) rose the hills of Krotona where the temple was and the lotus pond and the vegetarian cafeteria. There were several smaller tabernacles as well, a metaphysical library, a Greek theater where "The Light of Asia" was being played and numerous dwellings cut into the hillside above and below the winding road. It was all very beautiful, but Paula, perversely, disliked it. Krotona gave her an indoor feeling; people's faces had a consciously sanctified look; her father's friends struck her as queer. Or perhaps it was the cold in her head and the appalling lack of Brandt. They all had colds.

"When are we going to move into a house of our own?" she asked her father as they strolled together the second morning.

Soon, Wilton replied. In fact, he and Judith were going house-hunting that afternoon. Was she anxious to move?

"Yes," Paula said. "Aren't you?"

"In a way, yes, though I have been very contented here. Mrs. Beckner has been extremely kind."

"*Natasha*, you mean."

"Paula, you must not be intolerant."

"We're not going to live in Krotona, are we?"

"Don't you like Krotona?"

"It's—it's stuffy."

Wilton was indignant. Krotona was one of the most beautiful spots on the planet and a highly magnetized spiritual center as well. The people were open-minded, intelligent. It was a privilege to be here, a glorious privilege! His voice resounded on the morning air, but Paula felt oppressed. Something's wrong, she thought.

They were walking up the white hill road through Krotona.

"There's a grove of eucalypti at the top," her father explained. "It was there alone one morning that I decided to send for you all instead of going back."

And it was there alone, though he did not speak of it, that he had lived out the strangest of his hours, sitting on a stone in a windy dappling of light and shade: an hour of self-confrontation like death, or rather, like after-life, as one might expect to see with the eye of a soul newly emerged from the bonds of flesh. In this revelation he saw himself on the bluff edge at Remsen, summoning his soul: *I am here, I am waiting, I am willing.* And he saw the answer to that cry given into his hands only to be fumbled with, mauled, destroyed. A high point had been reached in his life, a possibility of being somehow super and he had fallen into blind human ways. Only the shattered remains of his great opportunity were left him, a cloud of the unabsolved hung over and his heart was torn with the disaster of its unblooming. Judith, too, must hold the broken image in her hands. His children, his mother, even the friends about him must carry the pieces of that shattered perfection.

He spoke to Paula out of the mood of that strange morning:

"There is no failure without the sag and breakage of etheric matter," he said with what seemed to her striking irrelevance. "Human tissue rallies, only to discover some subtler essence drained from it, and twice the will is needed to go on. But so our strength is developed," he added philosophically.

Paula glanced round at him as they climbed, noticing a gray shadow across his cheek and a difference in his eye that seemed vaguely alarming at the moment.

"Is anything the matter?" she could not help asking.

"This grove is a highly magnetized spot," Wilton said. "See what impression it leaves upon you."

But Paula already had an impression: "You're not going to become a Theosophist, are you?" she asked abruptly.

Wilton halted and eyed her sternly. "My dear, what do you know about Theosophy?"

"Nothing."

"I've been urged to join the society, of course. I haven't formally, but I'm quite in sympathy with the doctrine of H.P.B.—always have been."

"I hope you don't," she said definitely, but could not explain why. The idea was urgent in her, nevertheless. "I hope you don't," she repeated, as they entered the wood.

. . .

"I don't believe you are listening," he said irritably. "Aren't you feeling well?"

"Not very."

Wilton was not one to encourage illness through pampering or over-concern. "Since you advised me so strongly against joining the Theosophical Society, I thought you might be interested," he continued with acerbity. "Intuition on your part. Sheer intuition."

"You're not going to, then?" she asked listlessly.

"No. In fact I have severed my connections with Krotona. Not that there has been any unpleasantness. I have no quarrel with Theosophy—the spirit, but only with Theosophy, the form. In following the letter too closely the spirit may be lost. Forms must remain of secondary importance. The instant they assume the proportions of a separate power, a force in themselves, their initial beneficence is lost. They may even become dangerous, for forms do not remain empty long—unfortunately." Wilton smiled at this subtlety. "Forms rendered useless to constructive force swiftly become tools of the destructive," he expatiated. "It is all in that. And yet I do not mean to infer that Theosophy has become a destructive force. Nothing so definite as that. It has occurred to me, however, that the West needs a cult of its own, unrestricted by the precepts of the ancient East, as a young man setting out to meet life, frees himself of the creed of his mother, though her teaching may form the basis of his whole equipment—" Wilton paused to make a note of this. He was writing an article on the subject designed for publication in the *Philosophical Journal.*

"As a young man setting out to meet life," echoed in Paula's brain with thrilling inference. It required a distinct effort of the will to detach herself from her present all-absorbing concern and attend to her father's words. What had he been saying? "... severed my connections with Krotona ... the West needs a cult of its own." She sat up. "Are you planning to start something?"

"Yes."

"A 'movement'?"

"It depends upon what you mean by 'movement!' "

"Like the Theosophical Society or Unity or New Thought—"

"Like none of them," he said sharply.

"A 'cult,' you said—"

"A mere expression, Paula. It will not be a 'cult' in the usual sense in that it will not separate itself from the whole. It will seek to synthesize, to include the essence of all cults. There will be no formal joining; a recognition rather. Those who answer to its vibration will automatically *belong.* There will be meetings at regular intervals, of course, a communal property later, perhaps, a monthly or quarterly magazine for the benefit of those out of direct touch—"

It seemed to Paula that all her life her father had been starting something. What would happen now that he was going to be a leader? What would Brandt think of this plan, she wondered deeper and began to worry again, so that she missed her father's next words:

" ... and it seems that just such a system of united effort has long been awaited by those who have progressed beyond the desire to join an organized society, yet who wish to co-operate in the work of spiritual unfoldment. I propose that this Western approach be based upon fundamental laws of moral rectitude, that it be first of all a character-building work, though having no taint of the puritanical; stressing the analogy between natural and spiritual laws, the deeper significance of order, the relative necessity of health and clean living. Naturally I understand the responsibility of inaugurating such a plan, which calls for exemplary conduct on the part of all concerned."

"What if we aren't that good?" Paula inquired, but her father did not smile.

51 Make Way for the Lord

A favorite topic for novelists for many years has been speculation as to how Christ would be received if He returned to earth. In the following, Sister Angela (who is strikingly similar to Aimee Semple McPherson) introduces an Australian seaman as the Lord. Another character in the novel is Caslon, a visitor from the East, who is writing a novel about California. The comments on how the world reacts to the Second Coming are obviously very cynical, but the novel does suggest the theatrical flair for which Sister Aimee was famous. Note, especially, the stress that such things could only happen in California.

When Angela kidnapped the young seaman, Milton, from the teakwood boat of the Honorable Yang Kuo-chung, she brought him to her large Georgian town house that stands by the side of her imposing Temple. She saw to it that he bathed, brushed his beard and tended his fingernails which had not been in the best of taste . . . though this is no criticism of seamen in general. She devised a costume for him which was Biblical in every sense, clean and fresh-looking white robes that did not hide his feet which were long, slim and well-shaped. Then she set him to reading the Old and New Testaments, though he had read them before and was almost letter-perfect where the parables were concerned.

The next and most important step was to prepare the world for his coming. After a decent interval, during which time Milton was coached and instructed in his duties, Angela announced to a startled audience in her Temple that Jesus had at last returned and that His first thought had been to get "in touch" with her. Sister Angela was stirred and proud that Jesus should have "looked her up" before, say, Mr. Rockefeller's pastor, but the implication was that if any minister in the world deserved this great honor, it was Angela Flower. She went on to inform her awed and open-mouthed listeners that Jesus would appear to deliver a sermon in the Temple within the next few days; He would also go out amongst His people and preach.

From *The Flutter of an Eyelid* by Myron Brinig. Published 1933.

They that fell down and worshipped Him would be saved; the others, the heretics and unbelievers, might conceivably be forgiven. It all depended on how the Lord felt about His children. So far, Angela wasn't certain.

The announcement created an even greater sensation than Angela had expected, and she was, by this time, accustomed to sensations. The audience in the Temple, caught in the flames of Angela's voice, moved by the organ which squeezed the pious juices of hymns out of tonelessness, became hysterical. Many of them were so frightened that they fell dead of heart-failure; and those who were the more fanatical, tore off their clothes and started dancing in the aisles, sufficient proof that Mr. Havelock Ellis was correct when he said that the art of dancing had its origins in religious fervor. In these same aisles there occurred scenes that will never be forgotten by those who witnessed them: for women gave themselves to men they had never seen before, in a terrible ecstasy of belief, and certain other men and women, carried away by the extraordinary news that Jesus was back at last, butted one another like goats. Still others leapt from their seats in the balcony, catching hold of chandeliers and pillars, and swung back and forth through the golden auditorium like monkeys.

Next morning, the newspapers bawled their printed words through the streets: "Jesus Returns: Rests With Angela," which, of course, was not literally true, but no one expects literal truth from the American press. There were columns and columns that told of Jesus' life when last on earth, and there were countless re-tellings of the famous Bible stories by authorities on the subject. Thus, one noted priest was quoted as saying that now Jesus was back on earth, the American people could safely look to an end of the present economic depression; and a leader of the Episcopal Church said that Jesus had shown He was a hundred-percent American by choosing California for the scene of His return. Papers that had for long been losing readers jumped their circulations into the hundreds of thousands. Arthur Brisbane wrote characteristically in his column: "So Jesus has returned! Millions all over the world will welcome the news. Other millions will wonder what He is going to do about international debts, politics, taxes, love, prohibition and the grasping public utilities. But whatever happens, you may rest assured that California, as usual, will continue to be the beauty spot of the earth, visited by millions of tourists yearly who will spend their money for California home-products and California's incomparable sunshine."

The New York Times had an entire edition devoted to Jesus, and there were special articles by noted explorers and aviators. One writer in the paper went so far as to say that the return of Jesus would revolutionize aviation. Thousands of writers moved *en masse* to California, and Sister Angela invited them, along with ordinary reporters, to meet Jesus at a tea. Angela had seen to it that the tea served to the most skeptical of the gathering was generously blended with Bacardi rum. Whereupon even the most doubting of the visitors fell to their knees and kissed the hem of Milton's robe. "Jesus was a striking figure in white," wrote Miss Lucy

Simple, fashion editor of a great series of syndicated articles. "Jesus Believes in Being Well Dressed" was one of her subheads.

Everywhere were likenesses of Jesus, in papers, on billboards, in street cars, on banners that were hung from public buildings and on motion picture screens. When Milton appeared in the films, audiences rose and cheered as they did at football contests and political conventions. Even Jews were impressed. One Hollywood motion picture magnate offered Milton two millions of dollars to appear in a single picture to be directed by Cecil B. De Mille. Angela wisely refused the offer, thinking that her protege would show to better advantage in a film that she herself would write and direct. "The whole thing must be kept on a high plane," she said. She felt that the screen was a magnificent educational force, but Hollywood was not the place to make a motion picture starring Jesus. The logical place was the Holy Land. Whereupon Jews and Arabs in Palestine formed a "Welcome Home Jesus" Committee, though Angela later denied any intention of making a picture that did not have her "beautiful California" for a background.

Angela did give her consent to Milton's appearing in short subjects that had to do with scenes from the Bible. There were also films that showed him going about the city streets healing the sick. The newspapers continued their very profitable fanfarade: "Jesus Lauds Hollywood; Lunches With Mary and Doug." Box offices that had been on the verge of bankruptcy were flooded with silver. All over the nation, Jesus was the Man of the Moment. Men discarded their ugly clothing and donned robes and went about helping old ladies to cross traffic-thronged streets. Thousands of American wives in Kansas, Iowa, Utah, Minnesota and other states journeyed to Los Angeles, each woman with a cake of soap and a wash-pan, all eager to lave the sublime feet of the man they believed to be the Lord. Little Jesus dolls and toys appeared in the windows of curio shops and department stores, some of these toys reciting the Lord's Prayer after they had been wound with a key. Jesus appeared in the popular songs written on Broadway:

"Jesus is a Pal of mine.
Rain or shine
That Sweet Somebody
Thinks I'm somebody,
My Pal, my Buddy,
My Jesus."

And what were Milton's reactions to all the publicity and excitement? He was charming, witless, lovable through it all. A peculiarly brainless man, he did all that Angela arranged for him to do with a grace and delicacy that amazed all who saw him. His slimness and exquisitely shaped head, his golden beard and sea-blue eyes were refreshing and picturesque; his hands with the long, nebulous fingers healed through some miraculous sensitivity and innocence. Cheap as were the people who became his worshippers, Milton retained his poise, nor could radio microphones, newspapers, church platforms and motion picture stages corrupt that complete and trusting vacuity which was his paramount trait. He was a human mirror, an instrument that remained unblemished and harmonious. Only one as altogether childlike as Milton could have passed through these coarse experiences without being contaminated by them.

The people who believed in Milton without being distracted by the cheapness of the passing show—and there were a few such people—were illuminated and benefited by his purity. So men and women came to Milton in the Heavenly Temple, and some were cancerous, others consumptive and crippled. And he raised his beautiful hands above their heads, an almost audible music releasing itself from his finger-tips; and the sick were made whole. And a certain man who did not believe, a man who wrote caustic articles for a "liberal" weekly in New York, came before Milton and spat upon him. And Milton raised his hands and where the discolored saliva had trickled to the floor there arose a flower. But still the man muttered, and in the next article that he wrote, he proved that any man may turn spit into flowers; it is all a question of cleverness. But the man was wrong. It is not cleverness that works miracles. It is innocence.

Who is Jesus? Where is He? Why, all about us. A piece of pie is Jesus. Every time we receive an unexpected check through the mails, there is Jesus. He is High, and yet His robes are not soiled by muck. Matter contains Him. He announces himself in the beauty of a satisfying sexual experience. He is in the air we breathe. He is in our hearts that suffer, our friends we crucify.

And that is plain enough, wrote Caslon in his novel, but could not help thinking that very few people would believe it. He wondered just how far his novel would lead him. Desperately, he strove to burst the bars in which he was imprisoned, thoughts too stiff for elasticity, images too faint for reproduction on the page. There is a kind of madness in me now, he wrote, a madness to propagate truths and untruths, scenes and abstractions, every emotion of the human race, every heartbeat, every posture. I see through everything. I am the sieve through which all experience passes.

After a month had passed, Milton was so completely accepted by the people of America that he was beginning to be forgotten. The first mighty enthusiasm that had swept the nation into hysteria, was now beginning to fade. When Milton spoke over the radio now, many listeners turned the dial to a different station, a dance orchestra, a comedy sketch, a talk on beauty preparations. While Angela's own particular following showed no loss of enthusiasm or awe, others outside this following, of a more restless, cerebral disposition, were tired. The American people tire very quickly, and when they are tired they would just as lief drink wood alcohol as a vintage dark and sweet, fragrant with its aged bouquet.

Crowds continued to follow Milton when he walked abroad. Thousands of the ailing and diseased still came to him so that he might lay his hands upon them; but it was evident that the country at large, even the world, had taken up a new viewpoint in regard to him. Now, he was a matter of course, a man who lived in the same world with them, a habit. Angela was worried. It appeared that all the various forms of publicity she had used were not enough to keep the people at a white heat of interest. It was at this point that Angela conferred with Milton in the privacy of her home; or rather, she did all the conferring, since Milton was her instrument, a perfect instrument because of his deep sincerity. She had learned that the way to make the deepest impression upon him was to be motherly, a beautiful, magnetic mother, a Grecian mother who loved her son to the very depths of her being. In ancient Greece, mothers had often cohabitated with their sons, the offspring of such a union being considered divine. So it was with Angela and Milton, who brought divinity into the world that the masses of people but dimly understood. And now Angela spoke softly to Milton, but with the kind of feminine softness that is nine-tenths allure.

"My son, I am sorry to say that we are losing ground. When you played in that Great Drama ages ago, there was the splendid climax of Calvary. Something must be done, though, of course, I would not have you crucified over again. It is much too painful an experience. Besides," and Angela lowered her voice contemptuously, "I wonder if the people are worth it." She sighed. "Sometimes I am inclined to consider the crucifixion in the light of a fruitless sacrifice."

Milton drew his thin, almost transparent fingers through the bright silk of his beard. "I don't know," he said simply. "What do you want me to do? I am your son, Virgin Mother." And he lowered himself to the floor, and with both his arms clasped Angela's knees. She wondered why he had called her a virgin mother? Certainly, she did not look virginal and despised virginity, thinking it a stupid, barren state of existence. It must have been the word *virgin*, the sound and look of it that appealed to him; for Milton had an instinctive love of beauty, and *virgin* is one of the most beautiful words in the language. The word, for some reason, perhaps its sound, made her think of water, and she asked, "Have you ever walked on the water?"

He was immediately fascinated, so that his body took on the shape, the fluidity and grace of the idea. "I should like to do that," he said quietly.

"Do you really think you can?" asked Angela. "I don't want to run the risk of losing you." She thought, Perhaps if I can follow him in a boat, there will be no danger. But then again, a boat would spoil the effect, the purity of the setting. He must walk alone, as Jesus did, his slender feet calming the ridges and eddies of the sea. If he succeeded—but how could he fail?—interest in him would be greatly revived. Stupid people! They must always be provided with sensations; they would not even accept a Saviour without the embellishments of the freakish. For a moment, Angela wondered why she preached at all; and in that short space of time, her whole being was weighed down by pessimism, and she became almost a scientist. Then she caught hold of herself and once more believed in the supernatural, the basis of all romance. When Milton walked on the water, the people would be shaken from their apathy. She would advertise the spectacle with every means at her command and there would be sure to be a huge crowd present. They would come from every point in the compass.

"Can you swim?" she asked Milton. "Not that there will be any need of swimming . . . if you concentrate and think only of me . . . as you have before." The brilliance of her eyes was a history and a future, and he was drawn up into her pupils, himself a wraith, a mist, son of woman. He could not move or think, but words came to his lips: "I will walk on the water."

"Very well. I'll inform the newspapers and talk about it over the radio. A week from Sunday, perhaps . . . yes . . . and on the beach in Santa Monica." The police would have a difficult time, but she was positive that the large crowd, sure to attend, could be managed. The weather would be sunny and fine, for it rained but rarely during the summer months in California. Angela was pleased. She wondered why she had not thought of the plan before. Truly, Milton would be a striking figure, his white robes above the green sea, a divine figure. For a minute, she wondered if it would not be best to carry Milton off so that she might always have him for herself. The thought entered her mind because of the fact that she believed, sooner or later, the masses of people would forget him, just as they had forgotten Him on the cross. Then she cut her thought short. What good will he be to me alone? Even if the world does forget him, he will, at least, have brought a minute of divinity into the lives of men and women. And a minute is often enough.

Chapter 10

Between the Wars

Between the Wars

The decade following World War I saw California seemingly fulfilling its promise. Constantly expanding economic opportunity encouraged a sixty per cent rise in population in the 1920s. The movies brought investment capital, and they also advertised the state, drawing tourists and retirees to enjoy the climate. These outsiders brought money to invest which further fueled the economy. National prosperity likewise caused the state's producers of fruits and vegetables to prosper. Affluence was widespread; bank deposits increased rapidly, factory payrolls rose, highway building expanded, and public buildings were erected with great rapidity. The boom fed upon itself and each new arrival brought with him a set of economic wants which added to the already overheated economy. The Golden State's boosters, never noted for their modesty, now trumpeted that the economic millennium had arrived. What these enthusiasts failed to realize was that the economic life of the state was shallow-rooted. It depended, to a large extent, upon the influx of investment money earned elsewhere. Even retirees who flocked in brought their pensions or "nest-eggs" from New York or Iowa.

The bubble burst, the prosperity of the twenties was succeeded by the depression of the thirties, and California's residents were as shocked as most Americans. In many respects California suffered from the economic collapse more than other areas. Investment capital from the rest of the nation quickly dried up. Those who retired to the sunshine on pensions or savings saw them wiped out in bank failures or the collapse on Wall Street. A high percentage of people, who had been independent, and upper middle-class became public charges. With one-third of the nation's wage-earners unemployed, the demand for California fruits and vegetables declined rapidly. Worst of all, the jobless from the factory areas of the East joined dust bowl victims in fleeing from the haplessness of their circumstances to the promised land on the Pacific shores. After all, California promoters had sold the state as a veritable paradise since the 1880s. Now, desperate people reacted to the long period advertising the virtues of this modern "every-man's eden." Few understood the changed circumstances and, despite efforts to keep new migrants out, they still came in large numbers; Los Angeles even had guards at the state's borders to screen newcomers.

Within California, welfare recipients were encouraged to accept a bus ticket home, wherever that might be. Mexican families were induced, and often hounded, to return to their homeland. Surplus workers competed for the few available jobs and thus drove down an already marginal wage. Labor fought back by trying to organize. Numerous efforts to unionize agricultural workers failed miserably. The greatest success of labor was realized on the San Francisco waterfront. However, most people, especially older citizens, spent their time in a fruitless search for economic panaceas.

Between the wars the making of movies became the state's leading industry. Although its origins dated back to 1908, Hollywood didn't attain its virtual monopoly of the world's production of movies until the 1920s. The movie industry was unique in that it profited from the area's sunshine (an important consideration in the days before improved lighting), needed little in the way of raw materials, and could ship its products great distances to market. Movie-making was also impervious to the nation's business cycles, as people went to the cinema in good times as well as bad. Thus, the earnings and payroll of film making helped the state weather the depression. The film colony helped advertise life in Southern California and thus attracted more people to the area. Then too, movie-making spawned a number of associated industries such as radio and TV, and the manufacture of specialty clothing. In addition, the movie industry has created a unique concentration of artistic talent, lured by the high salaries of Hollywood.

52 The Boosters

Few areas of the world have been promoted as effectively as has been Southern California. Numerous books and magazine articles trumpeted the virtues of the area. Letters from residents to relatives and friends accomplished a similar purpose. But the greatest instrument of advertising the region was the movies, and its publicity was as free as it was valuable. All of the promotion helped the population grow from 3,426,861 in 1920 to 5,667,252 in 1930. Continual growth was a mainstay of the California economy and every resident, consciously or subconsciously, realized this and encouraged the population flow into California. The boosters were often tiresome bores to non-residents, as the following relates.

The man from Los Angeles was in active eruption.

"I don't care where you go," he declared, "you can't beat Southern California. It's the garden spot of the globe and Los Angeles is the pick of the garden. She's a living proof that truth is stranger than fiction. The sober facts sound like a pipe dream. In 1880 we had only eleven thousand inhabitants. Today we've over six hundred thousand. There she sits on her rolling hills—Our Lady, Queen of the Angels—the Sierra Madre at her back, the blue Pacific at her feet, the wonder city of the world. Our people are the salt of the earth. You betcha. You'll find no starch in their manners. They're first of all Americans; second, Californians; third, Angelenos; and, fourth, boosters every minute they're awake. Want me to tell you why they're boosters? It's because Los Angeles delivers the goods. You betcha. She's happy, healthy and handsome. Our water supply comes sparkling from the mountains through the longest aqueduct ever built. Absolutely. You've read history. You know that one of Rome's chief glories was her aqueducts. Well, they weren't a patch on ours. Ever heard its capacity? It's ten times that of all the aqueducts Rome could boast. And that's not the whole story. That water also means horse power. It generates electricity. We make it work. For we're more than a pleasant loafing place for tourists, and believe me, we manufacture a lot of things besides moving pictures. Our chamber of commerce, by the way, is the livest organization of its kind in the United States. Don't get the idea, though, that we think of nothing but business. Our schools and colleges are second to none. As for homes, why, you have to come to Los Angeles to appreciate the meaning of the word home. And climate"—he reverently muted his tone—"we've got the finest climate on God's footstool."

Hammond wondered if the finest climate on God's footstool was responsible for such rhapsodies and whether one not native born might breathe its heady ozone and hope to retain a normal perspective.

. . .

"Better call it a day," he suggested. "And a year while you're about it. This lets us out of little old 1919. Some finish for Los Angeles, I'll tell the world. The one white spot on the industrial map! All the rest of the country blue as indigo and buying one-way tickets out here! The continent will get lopsided and spill us into the Pacific if the stampede keeps up. No sign yet of its dropping off. It's just gathering headway if I'm any judge. It's going to make the excitement of 'forty-nine look as tame as a strawberry festival on the church lawn."

"It's like the ancient migrations," said George. "I can't understand it."

"You can't!"

"The original impulse, I mean—the force that set the mass in motion."

"War profits," said Bundy. "That's how I size it up. A lot of folks have saved enough to afford a change of scenery. They're quitting the old farm, the old shop, the old factory. They've got the chance to do something they've been hankering for since God knows when. They're pulling up stakes and moving to Southern California."

The great hejira was still cloaked in mystery for George. "But there are plenty of places they could go," he said. "Why do they all crowd in here?"

Bundy answered with a question.

"Ever live in Kansas or Iowa?"

"No."

"Well, I have. In fact I was born back East."

"Were you?" said George, taken by surprise. "I had somehow formed the impression that you were a Native Son."

"Not me," said Bundy. "I was born about twenty miles from Topeka. When I was sixteen my old man decided to try Iowa and on my own hook I've sampled Nebraska and South Dakota. So you see I know how these people feel. California soaks into their bones long before they start, as a rule. It did in mine. I'd get letters from friends that had settled here or maybe talk with some one home on a visit, and I'd hear about the orange groves and palms and figs, and the green peas and fresh vegetables the year round, and the sunny days and cool nights, and how the only snow you saw was miles off on the mountains, and—well, I was sick of prairie landscape and stoking furnace all winter and frying all summer, and, first chance I got, I boarded a train to find out if this country came up to the brag. I've never regretted coming—not for a minute. You couldn't bribe me to live anywhere else. Last week I attended an Advertising Club luncheon and one of the speakers—he'd just located in Los Angeles—told us that if he had to go back East now he'd feel that he'd left the romance of America behind. And, by gravy, he was right!"

53   Los Angeles in the 1920s

This selection is as much promotion as the previous one but there is a difference in emphasis. This is a look at Los Angeles in the 1920s by an old man who has seen many changes in the past, can put the present era into proper perspective, and has sufficient prescience to foresee many more changes coming. Some readers may not agree with the basis of comparison, but none can question the stress upon the unique character of Los Angeles nor upon the forecast that she is the precursor of cities of tomorrow. The selection is from *The Outsiders*, a masterful saga of an Angeleno family.

Responsibility did not suit Albert, yet he had it forced upon him. Somebody had to take care of various everyday details, and he seemed to be the only candidate. A Graduate of the Westlake School for Girls and now enrolled in a business college (she had refused to go to a university), Cissie offered scant aid; she was annoyed by domestic crises and disappeared at the slightest hint of them. Grandpa was Albert's main problem; he had participated avidly in the mushrooming boom of 1923, but in the next year a prolonged sinking spell apparently robbed him of most of his powers, and he spent months confined to his room. His conversation became disordered, he could not concentrate, and even signing his name was difficult. Notwithstanding, he refused to surrender control, and Albert had to act as intermediary with Mr. Baltim and Mr. Lely, not to mention with Mrs. Godby, Mrs. Gonzales and the maid assigned to help Lagonda; it was Albert who decided on menus, called

plumbers and electricians, settled the frequent disputes between Hank
Isbrow and the housekeeper, ordered the house painted, brought urgent
bills to his drowsing grandfather, and gave consideration to the future of
Cissie.

Then, amazingly, Grandpa emerged from hibernation in 1925 and
proceeded to enjoy an Indian summer. He was approaching his eighty-
sixth birthday: walking was hard for him, he was quite deaf, and
distressingly lank, but his head grew clear again, he could see fairly well,
and his appetite for whiskey and cigars returned. The cellar had become
depleted, and his first decision was to establish relations with a bootlegger
Dr. Loren disapprovingly recommended in lieu of providing unlimited
supplies of prescription liquor. Established once more in the solarium,
bellowing into the telephone on the assumption that everyone he talked to
was just as hard of hearing, he entered zestfully on a program of harrying
the Messrs Sego, Baltim and Lely.

Though pleased by Grandpa's return to an indecent sort of activity,
and grateful for relief from household and business burdens, Albert
found there were disadvantages to a phoenix rising. The old man leaned
on him and was too demanding. He needed company, and Albert was
his mainstay. To refuse him was unthinkable. Cissie stood willing to
have breakfast and dinner with him, and no more; the remainder of her
leisure she spent by herself. Stoically, Albert resigned himself to the task
of amusing Grandpa.

Among his duties was that of driving Grandpa around in the Ford
roadster, for he had taken a liking to both the car and inspections of the
city, and declined the services of Hank. Every day Albert could spare,
until Grandpa's curiosity was exhausted, the pair of them covered a
confounding sweep of loosely joined suburbs from the mountains to the
sea. Driving was fun, and cutting classes, missing out on baseball
practice, and allowing a budding romance or two to languish was not
overly onerous, but Albert's interest in Los Angeles quickly subsided.
That the great bowl of land had been occupied and reduced to an
unappetizing conglomeration of houses, buildings, factories, stores,
streets, and traffic appeared to him self-evident and not surprising, and the
wonderment of his passenger struck him as a little crazy. Tremendous
growth had occurred during his own few years. For example, the high
school he attended was, when Cissie first went to it, far out of town, and
after the streetcars the students then used put Western Avenue behind, only
open fields and isolated dwellings met the eye; now neat residential blocks
and an array of cross streets intervened, and the rabbits and gophers had
vanished. What was so remarkable about that? Why shouldn't people move
in and settle down?

Grandpa told him, upon his venturing an opinion. "You're a
newcomer, Albert," he said, "and I've been here overlong. My God, who
would have thought it? I made a speech once, I think it was on the
hundredth anniversary of the town, and advised 'em to keep booming.

Suppose I could have told them we'd have a million inhabitants by 1925! They would have committed me to an insane asylum. I was a promoter who cashed in on the optimism of '87 and got out hurriedly. Later on ruin came. Everybody lost hope and decided the Queen was through. But 1887 didn't hold a patch to 1923. Can't you see how improbable this place is? Everything's new each twenty-five years— citizens, spread, values, the things we live with. When I came here they used adobe for buildings, open ditches carried the water, bandits roamed the highroads, a steamboat was a novelty and railroads a dream. Now we've got radio, autos, telephones, electric lights, women in one-piece bathing suits, and the Goddamned government at war with people distilling whiskey. And there's more money to be made than ever!"

"Haven't you got enough?" Albert asked.

"That's a silly remark," Grandpa said. "Nobody ever has enough. You can make me look like a piker if you have any brains. This is Golconda—it's going to be the biggest city in the country in another century. All you have to do is ride the tiger."

He marveled at the harbor where ships could bunker crude oil for ten cents a barrel, at the forest of derricks on Signal Hill outside Long Beach, at proliferating Santa Monica, at the plushy suburb of Beverly Hills, at the sweep of Wilshire Boulevard, at the southward plains still undeveloped, at the gathering decrepitude of East Los Angeles in which lived the poorer immigrants and minorities cheek by jowl with flourishing industry, at the expansion in the San Gabriel and San Fernando Valleys, and at the mansions wintered in by eastern capitalists on the rim of the Arroyo Seco on the edge of Pasadena.

"West Adams Boulevard is finished," he mused. "The potentates from the Middle West who got rich selling groceries, harness and oranges are dying off, like the *hacendados* before them. And Orange Grove Avenue can't last—a trust-busting government and taxes will take care of it. Where will the next bunch of outsiders go? West, I guess, toward the ocean breezes. Baltim says the business area won't grow past Figueroa Street, and then move south; but he's always wrong. Albert, your father had luck putting branch banks in the sticks, perhaps with a shove from me. The sticks didn't stay that way long. This isn't going to be a city on the design of any other. The Queen won't have a heart or cohesion, or the same people from generation to generation, and it'll copy the snake and grow a new skin every ten years. The center will lay wherever you persuade 'em to go, and force continually outward when men have to buy cheaper land. She's a huge, fat queen, a whore, ready to lie down and spread her legs anywhere for new lovers. She no longer needs a bed and a house and pimps to bring in the trade. Growing up late, she can afford to break all the rules. She's how cities will look in the twenty-first century, I think—a thousand villages and encampments, constructed to last out a mortgage in a mild climate—held together by telephone wires and rubber-tired wheels and entertainment sent through the air. San Francisco is pretty. Los Angeles is a phenomenon."

54   After Many a Summer Dies the Swan

Most Californians were satisfied with the life style developed in their state
between the wars and would agree with the two previous selections.
However, many visitors did not concur that California had created "the
best of all possible worlds" and penned a number of vicious attacks upon
what they observed. Two of the most competent of these were by
transplanted Englishmen, Aldous Huxley and Evelyn Waugh (*The Loved
One*). Aldous Huxley, who had so brilliantly satirized English society in
the 1920s found even less to approve in California. This excerpt
describes how Los Angeles looked to a newly arrived Englishman who
was appalled at the cultural confusion he saw.

Jeremy laughed a little uncomfortably. A week in America had made him
self-conscious about that voice of his. A product of Trinity College
Cambridge, ten years before the War, it was a small, fluty voice, suggestive
of evensong in an English cathedral. At home, when he used it, nobody
paid any particular attention. He had never had to make jokes about it, as
he had done, in self-protection, about his appearance, for example, or his
age. Here, in America, things were different. He had only to order a cup of
coffee or ask the way to the lavatory (which, anyhow, wasn't called the
lavatory in this disconcerting country) for people to stare at him with an
amused and attentive curiosity, as though he were a freak on show in an
amusement park. It had not been at all agreeable.

"Where's my porter?" he said fussily in order to change the subject.

A few minutes later they were on their way. Cradled in the back seat of
the car, out of range, he hoped, of the chauffeur's conversation, Jeremy
Pordage abandoned himself to the pleasure of merely looking. Southern
California rolled past the windows; all he had to do was to keep his eyes
open.

The first thing to present itself was a slum of Africans and Filipinos,
Japanese and Mexicans. And what permutations and combinations of
black, yellow and brown! What complex bastardies! And the girls—how
beautiful in their artificial silk! "And Negro ladies in white muslin
gowns." His favourite line in The Prelude. He smiled to himself. And
meanwhile the slum had given place to the tall buildings of a business
district. The population took on a more Caucasian tinge. At every corner
there was a drug-store. The newspaper boys were selling headlines about
Franco's drive on Barcelona. Most of the girls, as they walked along,
seemed to be absorbed in silent prayer; but he supposed, on second thought,
it was only gum that they were thus incessantly ruminating. Gum, not
God. Then suddenly the car plunged into a tunnel and emerged into
another world, a vast, untidy, suburban world of filling stations and
billboards, of low houses in gardens, of vacant lots and waste paper, of

occasional shops and office buildings and churches—primitive Methodist churches built, surprisingly enough, in the style of the Cartuja at Granada, Catholic churches like Canterbury Cathedral, synagogues disguised as Hagia Sophia, Christian Science churches with pillars and pediments, like banks. It was a winter day and early in the morning; but the sun shone brilliantly, the sky was without a cloud. The car was travelling westwards and the sunshine, slanting from behind them as they advanced, lit up each building, each sky sign and billboard as though with a spot-light, as though on purpose to show the new arrival all the sights.

EATS. COCKTAILS. OPEN NITES.

JUMBO MALTS.

DO THINGS, GO PLACES WITH CONSOL SUPER-GAS!

AT BEVERLY PANTHEON FINE FUNERALS ARE NOT EXPENSIVE.

The car sped onwards, and here in the middle of a vacant lot was a restaurant in the form of a seated bulldog, the entrance between the front paws, the eyes illuminated.

"Zoomorph," Jeremy Pordage murmured to himself, and again, "zoomorph." He had the scholar's taste for words. The bulldog shot back into the past.

ASTROLOGY, NUMEROLOGY, PSYCHIC READINGS.

DRIVE IN FOR NUTBURGERS—whatever they were. He resolved at the earliest opportunity to have one. A nutburger and a jumbo malt.

STOP HERE FOR CONSOL SUPER-GAS.

Surprisingly, the chauffeur stopped. "Ten gallons of Super-Super," he ordered; then, turning back to Jeremy, "This is our company," he added. "Mr. Stoyte, he's the president." He pointed to a billboard across the street. CASH LOANS IN FIFTEEN MINUTES, Jeremy read; CONSULT COMMUNITY SERVICE FINANCE CORPORATION. "That's another of ours," said the chauffeur proudly.

They drove on. The face of a beautiful young woman, distorted, like a Magdalene's, with grief, stared out of a giant billboard. BROKEN ROMANCE, proclaimed the caption. SCIENCE PROVES THAT 73 PER CENT OF ALL ADULTS HAVE HALITOSIS.

IN TIME OF SORROW LET BEVERLY PANTHEON BE YOUR FRIEND.

FACIALS, PERMANENTS, MANICURES.

BETTY'S BEAUTY SHOPPE.

Next door to the beauty shoppe was a Western Union office. That cable to his mother.... Heavens, he had almost forgotten! Jeremy leaned forward and, in the apologetic tone he always used when speaking to servants, asked the chauffeur to stop for a moment. The car came to a halt. With a preoccupied expression on his mild, rabbit-like face, Jeremy got out and hurried across the pavement, into the office. ...

He returned to the car and they drove on. Mile after mile they went, and the suburban houses, the gas stations, the vacant lots, the churches, the shops went along with them, interminably. To right and left, between the palms, or pepper trees, or acacias, the streets of enormous residential quarters receded to the vanishing point.

CLASSY EATS. MILE HIGH CONES.

JESUS SAVES.

HAMBURGERS.

Yet once more, the traffic lights turned red. A paperboy came to the window. "Franco claims gains in Catalonia," Jeremy read, and turned away. The frightfulness of the world had reached a point at which it had become for him merely boring. From the halted car in front of them, two elderly ladies, both with permanently waved white hair and both wearing crimson trousers, descended, each carrying a Yorkshire terrier. The dogs were set down at the foot of the traffic signal. Before the animals could make up their minds to use the convenience, the lights had changed. The Negro shifted into first, and the car swerved forward, into the future. Jeremy was thinking of his mother. Disquietingly enough, she too had a Yorkshire terrier.

FINE LIQUORS.

TURKEY SANDWICHES.

GO TO CHURCH AND FEEL BETTER ALL THE WEEK.

WHAT IS GOOD FOR BUSINESS IS GOOD FOR YOU.

Another zoomorph presented itself, this time a real estate agent's office in the form of an Egyptian sphinx.

JESUS IS COMING SOON.

YOU TOO CAN HAVE ABIDING YOUTH WITH THRILLPHORM BRASSIERES.

BEVERLY PANTHEON, THE CEMETERY THAT IS DIFFERENT.

With the triumphant expression of Puss in Boots enumerating the possessions of the Marquis of Carabas, the Negro shot a glance over his shoulder at Jeremy, waved his hand towards the billboard and said, "That's ours, too."

"You mean, the Beverly Pantheon?"

The man nodded. "Finest cemetery in the world, I guess," he said; and added, after a moment's pause, "Maybe you's like to see it. It wouldn't hardly be out of our way."

"That would be very nice," said Jeremy with upperclass English graciousness. Then, feeling that he ought to express his acceptance rather more warmly and democratically, he cleared his throat and, with a conscious effort to reproduce the local vernacular, added that it would be *swell*. Pronounced in his Trinity College Cambridge voice, the word sounded so unnatural that he began to blush with embarrassment. Fortunately, the chauffeur was too busy with the traffic to notice.

They turned to the right, sped past a Rosicrucian Temple, past two cat-and-dog hospitals, past a School for Drum-Majorettes and two more advertisements of the Beverly Pantheon. As they turned to the left on Sunset Boulevard, Jeremy had a glimpse of a young woman who was doing her shopping in a hydrangea-blue strapless bathing suit, platinum curls and a black fur jacket. Then she too was whirled back into the past.

The present was a road at the foot of a line of steep hills, a road flanked by small, expensive-looking shops, by restaurants, by night-clubs shuttered against the sunlight, by offices and apartment houses. Then they too had taken their places in the irrevocable. A sign proclaimed that they were crossing the city limits of Beverly Hills. The surroundings changed. The road was flanked by the gardens of a rich residential quarter. Through trees, Jeremy saw the facades of houses, all new, almost all in good taste— elegant and witty pastiches of Lutyens manor houses, of Little Trianons, of Monticellos; lighthearted parodies of Le Corbusier's solemn machines-for-living-in; fantastic adaptations of Mexican haciendas and New England farms.

They turned to the right. Enormous palm trees lined the road. In the sunlight, masses of mesembryanthemums blazed with an intense magenta glare. The houses succeeded one another, like the pavilions at some endless international exhibition. Gloucestershire followed Andalusia and gave place in turn to Touraine and Oaxaca, Düsseldorf and Massachusetts.

"That's Harold Lloyd's place," said the chauffeur, indicating a kind of Boboli. "And that's Charlie Chaplin's. And that's Pickfair."

The road began to mount, vertiginously. The chauffeur pointed across an intervening gulf of shadow at what seemed a Tibetan lamasery on the opposite hill. "That's where Ginger Rogers lives. Yes, *sir*," he nodded triumphantly, as he twirled the steering wheel.

Five or six more turns brought the car to the top of the hill. Below and behind lay the plain, with the city like a map extending indefinitely into a pink haze.

Before and to either hand were mountains—ridge after ridge as far as the eye could reach, a desiccated Scotland, empty under the blue desert sky.

The car turned a shoulder of orange rock, and there all at once, on a summit hitherto concealed from view, was a huge sky sign, with the words BEVERLY PANTHEON, THE PERSONALITY CEMETERY, in six-foot neon tubes and above it, on the very crest, a full-scale reproduction of the Leaning Tower of Pisa—only this one didn't lean.

"See that?" said the Negro impressively. "That's the Tower of Resurrection. Two hundred thousand dollars, that's what it cost. Yes, *sir*." He spoke with an emphatic solemnity. One was made to feel that the money had all come out of his own pocket.

An hour later, they were on their way again, having seen everything. Everything. The sloping lawns, like a green oasis in the mountain desolation. The groups of trees. The tombstones in the grass. The Pets' Cemetery, with its marble group after Landseer's Dignity and Impudence. The Tiny Church of the Poet—a miniature reproduction of Holy Trinity at Stratford-on-Avon, complete with Shakespeare's tomb and a twenty-four-hour service of organ music played automatically by the Perpetual Wurlitzer and broadcast by concealed loud speakers all over the cemetery.

Then, leading out of the vestry, the Bride's Apartment (for one was married at the Tiny Church as well as buried from it)—the Bride's

Apartment that had just been redecorated, said the chauffeur, in the style of Norma Shearer's boudoir in *Marie Antoinette*. And, next to the Bride's Apartment, the exquisite black marble Vestibule of Ashes, leading to the Crematorium, where three super-modern oil-burning mortuary furnaces were always under heat and ready for any emergency.

Accompanied wherever they went by the tremolos of the Perpetual Wurlitzer, they had driven next to look at the Tower of Resurrection—from the outside only; for it housed the executive offices of the West Coast Cemeteries Corporation. Then the Children's Corner with its statues of Peter Pan and the Infant Jesus, its groups of alabaster babies playing with bronze rabbits, its lily pool and an apparatus labelled The Fountain of Rainbow Music, from which there spouted simultaneously water, coloured lights and the inescapable strains of the Perpetual Wurlitzer. Then, in rapid succession, the Garden of Quiet, the Tiny Taj Mahal, the Old World Mortuary. And, reserved by the chauffeur to the last, as the final and crowning proof of his employer's glory, the Pantheon itself.

Was it possible, Jeremy asked himself, that such an object existed? It was certainly not probable. The Beverly Pantheon lacked all veris-imilitude, was something entirely beyond his powers to invent. The fact that the idea of it was now in his mind proved, therefore, that he must really have seen it. He shut his eyes against the landscape and recalled to his memory the details of that incredible reality. The external architecture, modelled on that of Boecklin's Toteninsel. The circular vestibule. The replica of Rodin's Le Baiser, illuminated by concealed pink floodlights. The flights of black marble stairs. The seven-storey columbarium, with its endless galleries, its tiers on tiers of slab-sealed tombs. The bronze and silver urns of the cremated, like athletic trophies. The stained glass windows after Burne-Jones. The texts inscribed on marble scrolls. The Perpetual Wurlitzer crooning on every floor. The sculpture . . .

That was the hardest to believe, Jeremy reflected, behind closed eyelids. Sculpture almost as ubiquitous as the Wurlitzer. Statues wherever you turned your eyes. Hundreds of them, bought wholesale, one would guess, from some monumental masonry concern at Carrara or Pietrasanta. All nudes, all female, all exuberantly nubile. The sort of statues one would expect to see in the reception room of a high-class brothel in Rio de Janeiro. "Oh Death," demanded a marble scroll at the entrance to every gallery, "where is thy sting?" Mutely, but eloquently, the statues gave their reassuring reply. Statues of young ladies in nothing but a very tight belt imbedded, with Bernini-like realism, in the Parian flesh. Statues of young ladies crouching; young ladies using both hands to be modest; young ladies stretching, writhing, callipygously stooping to tie their sandals, reclining. Young ladies with doves, with panthers, with other young ladies, with upturned eyes expressive of the soul's awakening. "I am the Resurrection and the Life," proclaimed the scrolls. "The Lord is my shepherd; therefore shall I want nothing." Nothing, not even Wurlitzer, not even girls in tightly buckled belts. "Death is swallowed up in victory"—the victory no longer of the spirit but of the body—the well-fed body, for ever youthful, immortally athletic, indefatigably sexy. The Moslem paradise had had copulations six centuries long. In this new Christian heaven, progress, no doubt, would have stepped up the period of a millennium and added the joys of everlasting tennis, eternal golf and swimming.

All at once the car began to descend. Jeremy opened his eyes again, and saw that they had reached the further edge of the range of hills, among which the Pantheon was built.

Below lay a great tawny plain, chequered with patches of green and dotted with white houses. On its further side, fifteen or twenty miles away, ranges of pinkish mountains fretted the horizon.

"What's this?" Jeremy asked.

"The San Fernando Valley," said the chauffeur. He pointed into the middle distance. "That's where Groucho Marx has his place," he said. "Yes, *sir*."

At the bottom of the hill the car turned to the left along a wide road that ran, a ribbon of concrete and suburban buildings, through the plain. The chauffeur put on speed; sign succeeded sign with bewildering rapidity. MALTS CABINS DINE AND DANCE AT THE CHATEAU HONOLULU SPIRITUAL HELPING AND COLONIC IRRIGATION BLOCK-LONG HOT DOGS BUY YOUR DREAM HOME NOW. And behind the signs the mathematically planted rows of apricot and walnut trees flicked past—a succession of glimpsed perspectives preceded and followed every time by fan-like approaches and retirements.

Dark-green and gold, enormous orange orchards maneuvered, each one a mile-square regiment glittering in the sunlight. Far off, the mountains traced their uninterpretable graph of boom and slump.

55 Pipe City

As the depression deepened, California had a special problem. For many people who were unemployed, the decision to flee the rigors of the eastern or midwestern winter for the milder climate of the Golden State was an easy one. Thousands of such homeless individuals roamed the West, and this selection tells of their attempts to improvise shelter. The author is Upton Sinclair, who wrote unceasingly in an effort to correct the inequities in California life. He redoubled his efforts during the depression, even entering politics to run for governor in the historic EPIC campaign of 1934.

As a place of residence for human beings, a piece of concrete sewer pipe, while still aboveground, and before it has become part of a sewer, has some virtues and some defects. It is durable, and requires no repairs. It is rainproof—at least until the rain has gathered on the ground. It provides plenty of ventilation. It will not be blown over by a "santa ana," nor wrecked by the earthquakes which are common in California. Finally, it is impossible for an automobile to come crashing through the side of it— something which has been known to happen to frame and stucco houses along California highways.

On the other hand, it is rather difficult to close the two entrances to such a residence. You can draw a board cover or a sheet of tin up against the opening; but you cannot pull it close, otherwise it will fall over; and a gust of wind may take it away at the very time it is most needed. You cannot drive a nail into concrete—not unless you have money to buy a special kind of nail. The early dwellers in Pipe City suffered much discomfort, until some genius bethought himself to fasten a length of rope to each of the board covers or pieces of tin. When these ropes were drawn together and tied, there you were, safe and snug.

In the city of San Sebastian, California, was a concern which manufactured concrete sewer pipe, and this concern had a large quantity of pipe stored on a vacant tract; rows upon rows of unconnected pipe joints, each five feet in diameter and ten feet in length. They were near the waterfront, and the railroad passed, and the tops of the freights, especially the gondolas, were crenelated with men and boys, riding here and riding there, anywhere that was a different place. The riders would see these pipes, shining in the sunlight, gay and festive with yellow underwear and blue shirts laid out to dry, and groups of men sitting about, smoking pipes and chatting. The riders would descend and make inquiries: "Hey, buddy, do the bulls let you alone here?" The answer being satisfactory, they would unsling their bundles and file a claim.

Only when the sun went down, and fog began to creep in from the bay, did they discover the defects of five-foot sewerpipe as a residence for grown men. In the first place, you can't stand erect in it; and when you lie down, you discover that concrete is one of the chilliest substances invented. The nights are always cold in California, and one man could not sleep alone in Pipe City, unless he had more bedding than most wanderers carry. When you got yourself a sleeping-partner to warm you, you made the discovery that the tilt of the floor made it impossible to turn over without butting him in the ribs. When you tried sleeping, one at one end of the pipe and the other at the other end, you had to decide whether you would rather have your partner's feet in your shins, or have them in your face. From disagreements about this resulted many pummeling matches in the dark interiors of this city of forgotten men.

You might solve the problem by begging, borrowing, or stealing a tiny wood stove, and a couple of pieces of rusty pipe. This would establish you among the aristocracy of the settlement. You would set up your stove in the lee end of your home, and make it firm and snug; you would gather driftwood along the waterfront, and with stones pound or smash it into the

right sizes; and then, when the sun went down, and the fogs stole in, you
could crawl inside and spend a night in lonely solitude—alternately baked
when your fire burned and shivering when it didn't.

But in the morning hunger would drive you forth; you would stand in
the breadline for the requisite number of hours, and after you had filled
your belly with thin soup, thin coffee and thick bread, you would come
back and find your stove and stovepipe gone. How were you going to find
them in a city with so many hiding places? The history of international
diplomacy proves that men who steal will also lie, and they will fight to
defend their stealings. Pipe City in the end was forced to establish a
government and elect a "mayor" and a "policeman"; and presently it had
all the phenomena of graft, politics, "Reds," revolutions.

The materialist interpretation of history was vindicated in this
community; for it was the rigidity of sewer-pipe dimensions and the lack of
heat-retaining qualities in concrete which governed the laws of hospitality
in the unusual community. The prowler in the damp and chilly night
would stop at an entrance and say: "Any room in there, buddy?"—and if it
was an aristocratic place, possessing a central heating plant, he would hear
a surly: "All full up." But if it was a place which depended upon human
heat, he would hear the question: "You got any cooties on you?" If he
answered: "No, but I got some smokes," he would hear, "Come in," and a
scuffling of men moving up to make room.

The more there were in a pipe, of course, the warmer they all slept. You
put yourself crosswise, and if you had anything soft you put it under the
base of your spine; your head lay back against the rounding wall behind
you, and your feet were braced against the rounding wall in front. If you
tired of one position, you could slide back, and sit up; or you could slide
farther down, and bend your knees at a sharper angle. You could not
straighten your legs except by crawling over the legs of the others, and
facing the wind and the rain outside.

One of the luxuries of life in Pipe City was a dry board, to keep your feet
away from the concrete. Not all knew this—only those who had become
permanents, and learned how pleasant it is to take off your shoes, and rub
one foot against the other to warm them. Nearly everyone had matches, and
either a pipe or cigarettes; when they struck a match, you saw four pairs, or
sometimes five, of socked feet, or maybe of bare ones. You slept the night
with men whose faces you had never seen, and whom you knew only as
trouser-legs, socks, and odors.

It was difficult to read in such a place, and few men tried it. But on cold
nights they had to crawl in early; and then, huddled together, they talked.
They talked about the scraps of news they had picked up in papers by the
wayside; they talked about baseball scores, and later in the year, football;
they talked about breadlines, missions, and other places to get food; they
talked about women and adventures with them; they talked about the races,
and various kinds of gambling—few of which could be carried on inside a
five-foot sewer pipe; they talked about politics, and how rotten it was; they

talked about economics—why times had got so bad, and the chances of their getting better. More and more they were becoming interested in economics, for the depression was finishing its third year. They had been told that prosperity was just around the corner, but the corner seemed as far away as ever, and they were beginning to ask if it was a roundhouse.

56   Labor Strife

The most spectacular strike in the state during the depression was in San Francisco. It originated on the docks where longshoremen, growing desperate as a result of starvation wages and uncertain work, took advantage of pro-labor New Deal laws and organized. Under the leadership of the talented Harry Bridges they were finally successful. The following has Rory O'Brien cast in the role of Bridges and graphically portrays the historic events in the summer of 1934. Note that the employers sincerely believed that the revolution was at hand.

On July first, the Industrial Association of San Francisco, demanding police protection, announced its intention of opening the port. At 1:27 in the afternoon of the third, the steel doors of Pier 38 on the Embarcadero rose, and five trucks, loaded with perishable merchandise, rolled out, preceded by eight radio patrol cars.

Since daybreak that morning hundreds of pickets and labor sympathizers had swarmed the waterfront; at eleven the police, on foot, on horseback, and in cars, moved in and proceeded to clear the area in front of the pier. As the trucks came into view, the strikers surged forward and the Embarcadero became a vast tangle of fighting men. Bricks flew and clubs swung. The police fired over the heads of the mob with revolvers and riot guns; clouds of tear gas swept upon the oncoming rioters and sent them to the right-about with streaming eyes. Armed with any sort of missiles, with crowbars and railroad spikes, the men returned to the attack. Officers were dragged from their horses and pulled from their cars. Men went down right and left with cracked heads. At short range the police discharged gas shells from the revolvers. As the crowd fell back, the bluecoats threw hand grenades of gas and shot other grenades from gas guns. Dense crowds lined every rooftop and leaned from every window in the neighborhood. The gas seeped into the buildings, restaurants, and factories, driving those inside to the streets. By midafternoon the Embarcadero had been cleared, and a casualty list recorded twenty-five maimed and wounded—thirteen police, twelve strikers.

It was but a preliminary skirmish to the battle which was to be fought two days later. The Fourth being a holiday, no unloading was

From *Flint* by Charles Norris. Copyright 1944, 1971 by the author. Reprinted by permission of Dr. Frank Norris.

attempted. Promptly at eight o'clock on the morning of the fifth, as trucks began to transport more merchandise from Pier 38, a crowd of five thousand strikers surged out to stop them. Eight hundred police officers were on hand and with gas and clubs routed the rioters, and once again the Embarcadero was cleared and once again it was littered with prostrate bodies. The strikers retreated to the slopes of Rincon Hill. Firing their revolvers and swinging their long riot sticks, the police charged up the hill, driving the men up the steep slope. Tear-gas shells ignited the dry grass, and presently the hillside was in flames. The fire department arrived to the scream of sirens and turned high-pressure streams of water on grass and pickets alike. Gas and gunfire at last drove the men into the city, and the police took command of the hill.

From the windows of the president's office in the Wickwire, Rutherford Building, J.O.B., his son Stan, Syd Watterbury, and three other officials of the company stood watching the melee, only part of which was visible, but the roar of battle, the crash of splintering glass, the crackle of gunfire, the angry shouts of men, and the sound of fighting, struggling, and grappling was terrific.

"My God, it's a riot! It's murder and bloodshed!" Stan exclaimed.

"It's revolution," his father said sternly.

At noon there was an interval, but shortly after one o'clock the battle recommenced. A large crowd of strikers had gathered at the Long-shoremen's headquarters on Steuart Street and filled the narrow thoroughfare from wall to wall. The police proceeded to disperse this crowd and charged with tear-gas bombs and clubs. Presently there was the angry bark of pistolfire, and a score of men littered the sidewalks, either lying silently where they fell or crawling painfully away on hands and knees. Two were dead.

At five o'clock the same afternoon the National Guard, fifteen hundred strong, helmeted, bayoneted, equipped with automatic rifles and machines guns, moved in and took charge of the Embarcadero.

The governor of the state issued the following statement:

> Forbearance with the striking longshoremen in San Francisco has passed the point of common sense and good citizenship. The acknowledged leaders of the strike defied the state government and sought to overthrow the authority of the state government in its operation and maintenance of the state harbor facilities at San Francisco.
>
> The situation cannot be endured. I have ordered the National Guard of California to move into the San Francisco strike area, safeguard life, protect state property, and preserve order.

The following day the Joint Marine Strike Committee, of which Rory O'Brien was a member, published and widely distributed among labor circles a bulletin calling for a general strike.

The National Longshoremen's Board appointed by President

Roosevelt announced that, in compliance with its request that all issues be submitted to arbitration, replies had been received from employers and strikers. The longshoremen insisted that the matter of a closed shop and control of the hiring hall be agreed to before arbitration began. They also reiterated their position that the grievances of the seamen be considered before any union on strike would return to work. The employers insisted on the open shop—freedom to hire union or non-union workers at will, and refused to recognize the Strike Committee.

On Sunday, July 8, at a mass meeting of the Teamsters' Union, Local 85, in Dreamland Auditorium, members of that union voted to stop hauling on the following Thursday unless the maritime workers' strike and the longshoremen's strike had at that time been definitely settled. If the teamsters walked out, their action would completely paralyze all movements of freight or merchandise in the community.

Public sentiment in the city was crystallizing rapidly. People in every walk of life were mobilizing at opposition polls of opinion. Lukewarm or undecided attitudes were rare. San Francisco was a city divided into two clear-cut factions—those supporting the strikers and those opposed to them.

On Monday following the day in which the two men had been killed, the Longshoremen's Association staged an impressive and dramatic funeral for them. At half past twelve, services were begun at the International Longshoremen's headquarters on Steuart Street, in front of which the men had fallen, and in which their bodies had lain in state since Saturday. The parade was well organized, and in solid ranks, eight to ten abreast, thousands of strike sympathizers, with bared heads, accompanied the trucks bearing the coffins up Market Street to an undertaking establishment in the Mission two miles distant.

It was a spectacular and stirring sight, as thousands of men and women, to the solemn cadences of Beethoven's dirge, silently followed the dead and the attendant trucks piled high with wreaths and floral tributes. With measured step the vast procession of mourners marched up the main artery of the city. The police, at the request of the longshoremen, were nowhere in sight, and the latter, with blue bands about their arms, directed traffic. Sidewalks were lined with women, children, and soberfaced men of every walk of life. Hours passed and still the column moved onward. A great hush lay over the line of march, broken only by the rhythmic tread of trudging feet. Tramp—tramp—tramp, on the workers plodded, bare-headed, not talking, not even a cigarette. Tramp—tramp—tramp, grave and grim, on they came; there seemed to be no end to the procession. Long after the trucks bearing the coffins and flowers had passed from sight and the strains of the funeral music had been lost in the distance, the phalanxes of the marchers escorting the bodies of their fallen comrades continued. It was a demonstration dramatically conceived, dramatically carried out, and it left Stan Rutherford with a feeling of solemnity and respect, and a feeling of apprehension as well.

He and Syd Watterbury had gone out to lunch together, and as they emerged from the restaurant after their meal the long column of labor sympathizers was solemnly passing in the street. Stan had been aware earlier that morning that there was to be a funeral procession, but he was unprepared for the drama of the spectacle—the endless ranks of sober faces, bared heads, and the slow cadence of marching feet. Tramp—tramp— tramp. No noise except that. The band with its muffled drums and its somber music had long since passed. He recognized that he was looking upon something vastly more significant than a tribute to two longshore- men who had been shot by officers of the law. On the marchers came—hour after hour—ten, twenty, thirty thousand of them. Tramp—tramp—tramp. There was no break in the march; there was no division into corps or companies; there was no halting or hesitation. A solid river of men and women who believed they had a grievance and who were expressing their resentment in this gigantic demonstration.

.   .   .

On Sunday 115 of the 120 unions in the city—each union represented by five delegates—voted for a general strike to begin at eight o'clock the following morning.

Industry promptly came to a standstill. Factories shut down; streetcars ceased to run; taxicabs disappeared from the streets; grocery stores, already stripped of most of their stocks by foresighted housewives, closed their doors and put signs in their windows, "Closed Till the Boys Win" or "Closed for the Duration of the Strike." Highways leading to the city were blocked and picketed. Nothing moved except by "permission of the Strike Committee." Deliveries of gasoline, food, vegetables, milk, coal, wood, and other necessities of life stopped. Movement of all supplies was paralyzed within a distance of one hundred miles north, east, and south of the city. Food on hand was not sufficient to last the inhabitants of the Bay region a week.

Three thousand more troops were ordered to San Francisco and the area of martial law was extended to include the fruit and vegetable districts adjacent to the waterfront. Streets were barricaded and the approaches manned by machine guns mounted on trucks. The mayor appointed a "Citizens' Committee" of five hundred representative men. Oakland's mayor announced he had sworn in three thousand citizen vigilantes. An additional five hundred were mobilized in Berkeley and five hundred more in Alameda. At the Labor Temple some nine hundred union delegates were in almost continual session. At the same time large orders of gas equipment were immediately placed by the police department, and in addition gas and gas grenades were ordered by the Waterfront Employers, various packers' associations and warehouse distributors, a prominent San Francisco daily, a number of commercial houses, and the Occidental Oil Company of California. Every union man in the Bay district was out except the electrical and typographical workers, who voted to continue at their jobs, thereby assuring the community light, power, communication, and newspapers.

The morning the walkout became effective, the Strike Stratgey Committee announced that regular deliveries of all commodities would be made to the families of the strikers, but no provision was made for supplying food to the rest of the city's population. Nineteen restaurants at scattered points in the downtown section were permitted to remain open so that the workers might be fed. All theaters, night clubs, and barrooms were ordered closed, and the sale of intoxicating liquor was prohibited.

"Who's running this city?" J.O.B. demanded, shaking his fist in the faces of the family circle grouped around him. "Our mayor and supervisors, or this damned, self-appointed Strike Committee? They permit nineteen restaurants to do business so that they and their hooligans can be fed! The rest of us can starve. Do you call that taking over the reins of government or not?

"But what's going to happen?" Frances asked anxiously. "My grocer, my butcher tell me: 'Sorry, Mrs. Rutherford, we're cleaned out!' They have some canned goods, but we can't live solely on them—and how long will *they* last? The government ought to take over, don't you think? Why, we haven't any gasoline for our cars! We can't even get downtown! The streetcars have stopped!"

"You're telling me!" her husband growled. "Don't I have to walk to my office every morning and walk all the way back! It's lucky we have the telephone. What're you going to do when they shut off your light and your water and begin to sack your homes and stick up folk on the streets?"

"Oh, oh, oh," wailed Bessie, "Can't we go somewhere? Can't we get out of this terrible city? Surely there's some place that's safe!"

"They're just after my furs and my jewels," Grandmère asserted, sitting bolt upright in her chair and shaking the white curls of her marcelled wig. Her wrinkled hands were crossed in her lap, and every now and then her false teeth clicked audibly. "I'm not going to be run out of my home. I'm going to stay right where I am. Let them come and try to rob me if they dare."

" What will you do if they do?" Lloyd asked amiably.

"I'll have the law on them," Grandmère replied stoutly."

"Well, there isn't any," Lloyd reminded her.

"You men—you men—you men," cried Grandmère, her choler rising, "you've got to *do* something! You can't sit round here like a lot of nincompoops and let that rabble run our town. Where's your manhood? I declare, I'd do something, and do it in a hurry, before I'd let women and children starve."

"To say nothing of the livestock that's cooped up in pens down in Butchertown," Stan tossed in casually. "I only heard today that there are twenty-seven hundred hogs locked up down there that haven't had a single thing to eat for the past five days."

"Oh, don't tell me such things!" cried Grandmère.

"Couldn't we—all of us—go down to Charmion's and Reggie's at Visalia?" Frances queried. "Surely they have plenty to eat down there. Wouldn't that be a good idea? They'd be glad to have us, don't you think?"

"I won't budge an inch," Grandmère asserted.

"But, my dear," Bessie pleaded unhappily, "what are we going to eat? I've got a ham and a few chickens, and that's about all. The cook hasn't a bit of flour or sugar and not even an egg!"

"If you decide to go to Visalia," J.O.B. put in, "how do you propose to get there? Of course you could walk from here to the ferry, take a train, and we'd carry your suitcases for you . . . well, we might even have to do that," he ended soberly.

"I have an idea," he said after a moment when nobody spoke; "I've got an idea of how to break this strike," he continued, "if only I can get co-operation of a sober-minded, clear-thinking element in this town. If I can persuade some of those boys to work with me . . ."

His voice trailed off into silence. The others looked at him expectantly, but J.O.B. only stared at the floor.

Lloyd finally asked: "What you got in mind?"

"Well, if we could run some of these radicals out of town, the communist element and the Reds—this fellow Rory O'Brien, for instance—the conservatives might swing some weight."

"How do you propose to go about it?"

"It would take some strong-arm methods, of course," J.O.B. said thoughtfully. "I can give 'em the information—I can get it from the Industrial Association—but they'll have to furnish the man power; I can promise them all the police protection they want."

He fell silent again, scowling and thinking. Then with sudden determination he turned to Stan.

"Come on," he said, "let's see where we can get with this scheme."

. . .

The general strike was over within the next two days. Several factors contributed to its collapse.

The Strike Strategy Committee permitted the men operating the municipally owned streetcars to return to work, since, being under a civil-service status, they would lose their jobs and all privileges unless they did. The committee also authorized the opening of thirty-two additional restaurants; while Rory O'Brien still railed and harangued the labor delegates, the group which usually supported him was either absent or had grown strangely inarticulate. It was clearly apparent that the ranks of the radicals had thinned, and there was less incendiary talk. Addresses by conservative leaders were no longer greeted by catcalls and boos, and their advice and admonition could be heard. The partial restoration of streetcar service and the opening of more restaurants gave the impression that the grip of the Strike Committee was loosening. This had a disheartening effect on the unions across the Bay who were just beginning to organize; there did not seem to be much use in promoting general strikes elsewhere if the strangle hold in San Francisco was weakening. Primarily it was public opinion, fanned by the press, and hourly growing more vociferous and exasperated, that ended the general walkout. It was the highhanded ruling of the Strike Committee, permitting certain restaurants to open while others remained closed, which more than anything else aroused people's indignation.

At quarter past one in the morning of July 19, after a turbulent all-day session, a resolution to terminate the general strike was put before the delegates of the various unions. By a standing vote of 191 to 174 it was adopted.

The next day labor poured back into industry in a great sweeping tide. Traffic was resumed, autos honked, trucks rumbled through the streets, chimneys smoked, hammers rang, saws whined, steel clanged, whistles blew, restaurants began serving customers, and thirsty men crowded barrooms.

The longshoremen and seamen, however, refused to capitulate, and the teamsters still boycotted the Embarcadero. The Market Street Railway employees too decided to wait until they were assured their lot would be ameliorated.

A week passed, and finally the longshoremen decided to ballot secretly, with the result that by a majority of four to one the men approved going back to work, provided their differences with the employers were settled by arbitration and the demands of the seamen would be taken care of as well. The Market Street Railway strikers also agreed to arbitrate. The next day the governor of the state ordered the evacuation of the troops from the Embarcadero.

The President's Mediation Board lost no time in arranging for a vote by the seamen to decide who should represent them in collective bargaining. Prior to the strike some seamen belonged to the Marine Workers' Industrial Union, a larger group to the International Seamen's Union, and a still larger group to no union at all. The vote when counted advocated a return to work pending arbitration and named the International Seamen's Union as the official bargaining representative.

Thus the waterfront strike came to an end.

57 The Grapes of Wrath

California's greatest writer and only Nobel prizewinner in literature, John Steinbeck, was another who felt strongly the dehumanizing impact of the depression. Observing the harsh treatment of the Okies and the Arkies in the Salinas Valley, he traced their pilgrimage from their former homes to California, the land of promise. He was so effective in portraying the plight of the migrant workers and their families that he shocked many

people, and one county banned *The Grapes of Wrath* from its libraries
and burned the copies available. The obvious message in this passage is
that there is something wrong with a society which will destroy food
while people are starving.

Along the rows, the cultivators move, tearing the spring grass and
turning it under to make a fertile earth, breaking the ground to hold the
water up near the surface, ridging the ground in little pools for the
irrigation, destroying the weed roots that may drink the water away from
the trees.

And all the time the fruit swells and the flowers break out in long
clusters on the vines. And in the growing year the warmth grows and the
leaves turn dark green. The prunes lengthen like little green bird's eggs,
and the limbs sag down against the crutches under the weight. And the
hard little pears take shape, and the beginning of the fuzz comes out on
the peaches. Grape blossoms shed their tiny petals and the hard little
beads become green buttons, and the buttons grow heavy. The men who
work in the fields, the owners of the little orchards, watch and calculate.
The year is heavy with produce. And men are proud, for of their
knowledge they can make the year heavy. They have transformed the
world with their knowledge. The short, lean wheat has been made big
and productive. Little sour apples have grown large and sweet, and that
old grape that grew among the trees and fed the birds its tiny fruit has
mothered a thousand varieties, red and black, green and pale pink,
purple and yellow; and each variety with its own flavor. The men who
work in the experimental farms have made new fruits: nectarines and
forty kinds of plums, walnuts with paper shells. And always they work,
selecting, grafting, changing, driving themselves, driving the earth to
produce.

And first the cherries ripen. Cent and a half a pound. Hell, we can't
pick 'em for that. Black cherries and red cherries, full and sweet, and the
birds eat half of each cherry and the yellowjackets buzz into the holes the
birds made. And on the ground the seeds drop and dry with black shreds
hanging from them.

The purple prunes soften and sweeten. My God, we can't pick them
and dry and sulphur them. We can't pay wages, no matter what wages.
And the purple prunes carpet the ground. And first the skins wrinkle a
little and swarms of flies come to feast, and the valley is filled with the
odor of sweet decay. The meat turns dark and the crop shrivels on the
ground.

And the pears grow yellow and soft. Five dollars a ton. Five dollars for
forty fifty-pound boxes; trees pruned and sprayed, orchards cultivated—
pick the fruit, put it in boxes, load the trucks, deliver the fruit to the
cannery—forty boxes for five dollars. We can't do it. And the yellow fruit

falls heavily to the ground and splashes on the ground. The yellow jackets dig into the soft meat, and there is a smell of ferment and rot.

Then the grapes—we can't make good wine. People can't buy good wine. Rip the grapes from the vines, good grapes, rotten grapes, wasp-stung grapes. Press stems, press dirt and rot.

But there's mildew and formic acid in the vats.

Add sulphur and tannic acid.

The smell from the ferment is not the rich odor of wine, but the smell of decay and chemicals.

Oh, well. It has alcohol in it, anyway. They can get drunk.

The little farmers watched debt creep up on them like the tide. They sprayed the trees and sold no crop, they pruned and grafted and could not pick the crop. And the men of knowledge have worked, have considered, and the fruit is rotting on the ground, and the decaying mash in the wine vats is poisoning the air. And taste the wine—no grape flavor at all, just sulphur and tannic acid and alcohol.

This little orchard will be a part of a great holding next year, for the debt will have choked the owner.

This vineyard will belong to the bank. Only the great owners can survive, for they own the canneries too. And four pears peeled and cut in half, cooked and canned, still cost fifteen cents. And the canned pears do not spoil. They will last for years.

The decay spreads over the State, and the sweet smell is a great sorrow on the land. Men who can graft the trees and make the seed fertile and big can find no way to let the hungry people eat their produce. Men who have created new fruits in the world cannot create a system whereby their fruits may be eaten. And the failure hangs over the State like a great sorrow.

The works of the roots of the vines, of the trees, must be destroyed to keep up the price, and this is the saddest, bitterest thing of all. Carloads of oranges dumped on the ground. The people came for miles to take the fruit, but this could not be. How could they buy oranges at twenty cents a dozen if they could drive out and pick them up? And men with hoses squirt kerosene on the oranges, and they are angry at the crime, angry at the people who have come to take the fruit. A million people hungry, needing the fruit— and kerosene sprayed over the golden mountains.

And the smell of rot fills the country.

Burn coffee for fuel in the ships. Burn corn to keep warm, it makes a hot fire. Dump potatoes in the rivers and place guards along the banks to keep the hungry people from fishing them out. Slaughter the pigs and bury them, and let the putrescence drip down into the earth.

There is a crime here that goes beyond denunciation. There is a sorrow here that weeping cannot symbolize. There is a failure here that topples all our success. The fertile earth, the straight tree rows, the sturdy trunks, and the ripe fruit. And children dying of pellagra must die because a profit cannot be taken from an orange. And coroners must fill in the certificates— died of malnutrition—because the food must rot, must be forced to rot.

The people come with nets to fish for potatoes in the river, and the guards hold them back; they come in rattling cars to get the dumped oranges, but the kerosene is sprayed. And they stand still and watch the potatoes float by, listen to the screaming pigs being killed in a ditch and covered with quicklime, watch the mountains of oranges slop down to a putrefying ooze; and in the eyes of the people there is the failure; and in the eyes of the hungry there is a growing wrath. In the souls of the people the grapes of wrath are filling and growing heavy, growing heavy for the vintage.

58   The Day of the Locust

Nathanael West was a successful screenwriter in the 1930s. In his novel *The Day of the Locust* the main character, Tod Hackett, is a painter who has just arrived to work in Hollywood. In this selection a typical make-believe scene on a movie lot is presented. In addition, West evaluates the unusual types of people one meets in a walk down Hollywood Boulevard. The description of the weird variety of houses encountered in Hollywood is bitter but accurate.

Around quitting time, Tod Hackett heard a great din on the road outside his office. The groan of leather mingled with the jangle of iron and over all beat the tattoo of a thousand hooves. He hurried to the window.

An army of cavalry and foot was passing. It moved like a mob; its lines broken, as though fleeing from some terrible defeat. The dolmans of the hussars, the heavy shakos of the guards, Hanoverian light horse, with their flat leather caps and flowing red plumes, were all jumbled together in bobbing disorder. Behind the cavalry came the infantry, a wild sea of waving sabretaches, sloped muskets, crossed shoulder belts and swinging cartridge boxes. Tod recognized the scarlet infantry of England with their white shoulder pads, the black infantry of the Duke of Brunswick, the French grenadiers with their enormous white gaiters, the Scotch with bare knees under plaid skirts.

While he watched, a little fat man, wearing a cork sun-helmut, polo shirt and knickers, darted around the corner of the building in pursuit of the army.

"Stage Nine—you bastards—Stage Nine!" he screamed through a small megaphone.

The cavalry put spur to their horses and the infantry broke into a dogtrot. The little man in the cork hat ran after them, shaking his fist and cursing.

Tod watched until they had disappeared behind half a Mississippi steamboat, then put away his pencils and drawing board, and left the office. On the sidewalk outside the studio he stood for a moment trying to decide whether to walk home or take a streetcar. He had been in Hollywood less than three months and still found it a very exciting place, but he was lazy and didn't like to walk. He decided to take the streetcar as far as Vine Street and walk the rest of the way.

A talent scout for National Films had brought Tod to the Coast after seeing some of his drawings in an exhibit of undergraduate work at the Yale School of Fine Arts. He had been hired by telegram. If the scout had met Tod, he probably wouldn't have sent him to Hollywood to learn set and costume designing. His large, sprawling body, his slow blue eyes, and sloppy grin made him seem completely without talent, almost doltish in fact.

Yes, despite his appearance, he was really a very complicated young man with a whole set of personalities, one inside the other like a nest of Chinese boxes. And "The Burning of Los Angeles," a picture he was soon to paint, definitely proved he had talent.

He left the car at Vine Street. As he walked along, he examined the evening crowd. A great many of the people wore sports clothes which were not really sports clothes. Their sweaters, knickers, slacks, blue flannel jackets with brass buttons were fancy dress. The fat lady in the yachting cap was going shopping, not boating; the man in the Norfolk jacket and Tyrolean hat was returning, not from a mountain, but an insurance office; and the girl in slacks and sneaks with a bandanna around her head had just left a switchboard, not a tennis court.

Scattered among these masquerades were people of a different type. Their clothing was somber and badly cut, bought from mail-order houses. While the others moved rapidly, darting into stores and cocktail bars, they loitered on the corners or stood with their backs to the shop windows and stared at everyone who passed. When their stare was returned, their eyes filled with hatred. At this time Tod knew very little about them except that they had come to California to die.

He was determined to learn much more. They were the people he felt he must paint. He would never again do a fat red barn, old stone wall or sturdy Nantucket fisherman. From the moment he had seen them, he had known that, despite his race, training and heritage, neither Winslow Homer nor Thomas Ryder could be his masters and he turned to Goya and Daumier.

He had learned this just in time. During his last year in art school, he had begun to think that he might give up painting completely. The pleasures he received from the problems of composition and color had decreased as his facility had increased and he had realized that he was going the way of all his classmates, toward illustration or mere handsomeness. When the Hollywood job had come along, he had grabbed it despite the arguments of his friends who were certain that he was selling out and would never paint again.

He reached the end of Vine Street and began the climb into Pinyon Canyon. Night had started to fall.

The edges of the trees burned with a pale violet light and their centers gradually turned from deep purple to black. The same violet piping, like a Neon tube, outlined the tops of the ugly, hump-backed hills and they were almost beautiful. But not even the soft wash of dusk could help the houses. Only dynamite would be of any use against the Mexican ranch houses, Samoan huts, Mediterranean villas, Egyptian and Japanese temples, Swiss chalets, Tudor cottages, and every possible combination of these styles that lined the slopes of the canyon.

When he noticed that they were all of plaster, lath and paper, he was charitable and blamed their shape on the materials used. Steel, stone and brick curb a builder's fancy a little, forcing him to distribute stresses and weights and to keep his corners plumb, but plaster and paper know no law, not even that of gravity.

On the corner of La Huerta Road was a miniature Rhine castle with tarpaper turrets pierced for archers. Next to it was a little highly colored shack with domes and minarets out of the *Arabian Nights*. Again he was charitable. Both houses were comic, but he didn't laugh. Their desire to startle was so eager and guileless.

It is hard to laugh at the need for beauty and romance, no matter how tasteless, even horrible, the results of that need are. But it is easy to sigh. Few things are sadder than the truly monstrous.

Chapter 11

World War II

World War II

The four years of the war were second only to the gold rush as the most formative influence in the history of the state of California. War industries such as steel, shipbuilding, aircraft, and armaments formed the basis of aircraft and aerospace as well as consumer oriented industries in the postwar years. The tremendous influx of people to work in the war plants, to train at one of the many armed forces installations, or even to pass through the state en route to a destination in the Pacific theater, made many more individuals familiar with the attractions of California life, and a high percentage of them returned permanently after the war.

Even before the war began, California's depression-plagued industries were stirring with orders for the British war machine. This was only a prelude to the rapid expansion which followed Pearl Harbor. The Los Angeles area was the scene of most of the aircraft production while the Bay area concentrated on shipbuilding. In addition to giant corporations like Kaiser Shipyards and Lockheed Aviation, there were thousands of small plants doing subcontract work. All needed workers, which were often recruited from distant points. The human problem of training and fulfilling the needs of these workers taxed the state's resources, but the vast production of war goods was proof of the successful results. In addition, the state was the main staging area for supplies and men to be shipped to the Pacific.

The war years provided work opportunity for many and even large profits for some. Unfortunately, there were also many who suffered in wartime California. Ethnic minorities such as blacks and Mexican-Americans had difficulty breaching the barriers of discrimination and obtaining jobs on an equal basis. They were also prevented from obtaining housing in many instances. But those who suffered most were the Japanese-Americans who were interned for the duration of the war with a consequent loss of earnings, businesses, farms, and homes.

59   Samson Duke

As American involvement in World War II neared, California's economy benefited from it. The concentration of shipbuilding in the Bay area and aircraft in the Southland spawned an economic upturn that quickly erased memories of the depression. Anticipating the change, some men made fortunes by building houses with deflated depression money and selling them at war-inflated prices. The following selection is from a novel dealing with construction and real estate speculation in the Los Angeles area. The excerpt demonstrates how "patriots" with money could avoid the draft. This was common throughout the nation and was not confined to California alone.

By the end of 1940 Samson had close to two thousand units finished or under construction representing a total value of six million dollars in which his equity roughed out at a million. So well had they been financed that his cash investment in all was less than a hundred thousand dollars. There was a lot at stake now, more than he had ever imagined, and when the Selective Service Act was instituted and he had to register for the draft he made a careful study of the situation and proceeded with plans to keep on the home front.

So-called "defense plants" were springing up everywhere, vacant stores and backyard garages were converted into machine shops, guys with two hundred bucks and a steady hand were going into business, the aircraft plants were building assembly lines, the tooling for war had begun. They weren't taking men his age yet—it was a peacetime army—for defense; no boy would be sent overseas the president said and so forth. . . . War or not, overseas or at home, the army meant a uniform and it took you out of circulation. The place to be was out, making things a war used up and selling it for as much as you could get. In the army cooks became clerks and clerks became tank commanders and sometimes even generals and there were gravediggers too. There were many ways to dodge the draft, some brought shame, others honor, presidential citations, and a million bucks. He was only nine years old at the outbreak of World War I, but he remembered casualty lists and war millionaires, the Marne and Chateau Thierry and burgeoning industry. And when the war was over the rich slacker was twice blessed when he gave a man with a stump a job. Samuel Johnson once said that patriotism was the last refuge of a scoundrel but he was talking of a different brand. During a war patriotism was a deadly blunder.

The first thing Samson did was to contact Howard Ebberly. He met the senator in his Los Angeles office, freshened his memory concerning the cash he had funneled into his campaign, and then questioned him. He wanted all the information he could be given about the draft, who they were going to take, and who might get a deferment. He made it very clear that the only reason he came to see him was that he wanted to do his duty and be sure his talents were not dissipated in a position that could be filled by a clod.

"They might take me in the army and have me shoveling horseshit or digging graves. They do that, you know."

"How about a desk job . . . in Washington. Or maybe in L.A.?"

"That's just it. At best I'd be a clerk. And God knows they have enough of those around. Listen, Howard," he said, with all the patriotic fervor he could pitch, "I want to help my country. If I have to do my duty on the home front, then damnit I'll give up the glory."

Ebberly asked him the number and location of his draft board.

"I think Charley Simpson is on that one. He lives in the neighborhood and I know he heads a board. I'll talk to him."

"Remember," Samson said, as he left. "I don't want any favors. Just information."

He got the information the next day.

"Charley's your man all right. They won't be taking men your age for awhile. Maybe never. Unless we get into a war. He also told me they're going to lay off men in essential industries. They'll take married men with children first."

That was all he wanted to know. Now he went to see Tipton. Martin covered his disappointment about the resumption of Samson's relationship with Posey with a good-natured observation that Posey's rejection confirmed his good taste, a young woman worth pursuing would have better sense than to play with a man who rolled over the side of fifty.

With Martin he was candid. "I had to register for the draft. And I don't want to end up a buck private in the army. I want to buy a defense plant."

Tipton laughed.

"What's so funny?"

"Three other clients are looking for the same thing. An actors' agent, a stockbroker, and an attorney. Looks like there won't be enough of them to go around."

"How would you like to be bugled out of a cot at dawn and have some asshole with two or three stripes on his arm screaming at you before breakfast?"

"I wouldn't like it. But war is hell, remember? And Mr. Hitler can't be talked to anymore, he's got to be shot at. If some of you didn't think he was a funny man with a mustache and others that he was a savior this wouldn't have happened. There was a time he could have been stopped with a slingshot. Now it's going to take everything we've got, and England and France, and God knows who else."

"That's just it, Martin. It's going to take everything we've got, including married men without children age thirty-two."

"Tell me, don't you think there are such things as just wars? Don't you realize if Germany takes over Europe we're next?"

"I don't think Hitler's going to take over Europe. And if he does there's an ocean separating us. Anyway, that's not my immediate concern. There'll be plenty of itching suckers in line to sign up. There always have been. I don't like soldiering, don't like orders shouted at me, lousy food, lumpy beds; I like to sleep late, go to bed when I damn please and I like living. Now, what do you suggest?"

It looked like Martin was going to try one more recruiting pitch, then he smiled wryly. "All right, get your defense plant."

"Any ideas?"

"Try an ad. Put it in the *Times* classified. Money to invest in machine shop, defense plant. Something like that. You'll get answers."

He put a box ad in the following day and within two weeks received over a hundred replies. He weeded through the letters, checked half a dozen and ended up talking to the most likely prospect in a plant on Robertson Boulevard. It seemed to have everything he wanted: small, but still big enough to have landed a contract with Douglas for some magnesium parts, adequate equipment, room for expansion, and a hungry owner with big dreams, a head full of tools and dies and hands that could tear down anything and put it together blindfolded. Jack Gilbert was thirty, he told Samson, had a fused hip, was 4F and was tooled up for the duration. They were seated in a glass-enclosed crib that served as his office from which he could watch every worker without rising from his chair.

"The help you get these days. . . . " He shook his head. "You gotta watch them like a hawk."

"What did you make before you got into aeroplane parts?" Samson asked.

"A little bit of everything. Rebuilt transmissions, rear ends, made a few parts for a local washing-machine company. Did a little tool and die work too." He held up his hands and spread his fingers. "They can do anything," he said, looking at them admiringly. "With the right tools I could do surgery on a fly."

They toured the shop, he explained the machines, caressed them like pets, showed Samson the tool room, wiped his hands on some waste, and returned to the office.

"I'm running twelve hours a day now," he said. "Soon it'll be twenty-four. I need more machines and a building for them. The shack next door is for rent. It'll take two big turrets and a half-dozen engine lathes. And there's room for storage."

Samson asked about his rent, the length of his lease, cash position, and accounts receivable. He had two years on his lease and an option for five more and as his receivables grew his cash position became weaker.

"I can hock my accounts but it costs too much. Anyway, that'll only take the pressure off for awhile. I want to buy more machines and take the place next door. I think this is just beginning. We're in for a long war. What do you think, Mr. Duke?"

Samson agreed and they got down to specifics. The book value of the plant was twenty-five thousand dollars on which he owed five. He wanted an investor to put up an equal sum plus an amount to match the accounts receivable, out of which he would clear the debts and create a fifty-fifty partnership.

"Would you be active?" he asked.

Not to be active would not go well with the draft board. He told Gilbert he would have to be on the payroll, act as controller, but that the work would be done in his own office where he expected him to send daily reports. The salary could be small.

"I draw a hundred and fifty a week now plus a little for expenses," Gilbert said. "It may sound like a lot, but I'm always here. Put in sixteen, eighteen hours a day."

He had Martin's office send a man down to check the books and found them sound. The deal was made. The business was to be incorporated, each was to receive fifty per cent of the stock. They were to draw profits moderately and only after a reserve was built up. And Gilbert was to make all decisions.

"It isn't that I want to be the boss," Gilbert explained as they sat in Tipton's office before signing the papers. "It's just that I built this from a bench lathe in my garage. It's like you raised a kid."

They signed the documents, agreed that Martin's office would do the auditing, and then he invited Gilbert to lunch.

"You have no idea how big this thing can get," he told Samson over coffee. "It's just a question of getting help, the machines and the space for them. There's talk that Douglas is going to hire thousands more. Lockheed, too. I can get all the orders I want. But I got to deliver on time and the parts must fall in the tolerance. Now it's easy, but later on it'll be stuff within one-ten thousandths. Engine lathe work, highly precision. Maybe tools and dies. That'll be big money."

He not only bought insurance against the draft, he thought as he left Gilbert, it looked like the business could pay all the premiums and leave a bundle besides.

60 Harvest of Hate

Japanese-Americans had integrated themselves into California life (70,000 were American born), and they were ill-prepared for the violence of the hate campaign waged against them during the war. Even Governor Culbert Olson and state Attorney General Earl Warren, both of whom had distinguished themselves as civil rights advocates, joined the popular attack. These innocent people were forced to leave their homes, farms, and businesses with little advance warning and often at great financial loss. They were sent to relocation camps away from the coast. The federal government ultimately compensated them in some small part for the monetary losses they suffered, but nothing could repay them for the insult to human dignity they endured. The following tells of "the worst single violation of the civil rights of American citizens in our history."

There was a mountainous heap of baggage on the platform beside the train, where men were busily loading the baggage car. More people were arriving all the time struggling with their bags and bundles of bedding, some brought to the station by friends, some who came by streetcar.

There were young and old, rich and poor, weak and strong. The fifteen hundred persons brought together by Army orders were from all stations of life. There were humble peasant farmers in dark suits and white shirts and wives in chain store dresses. There were the well-to-do and sophisticated city dwellers with all the style and savoir faire of the elite. There was a small group of college girls in bright sweaters and sleek slacks, one with her identification tag and her Phi Beta Kappa key mingling with ironic intimacy on her sweater front. There were high school boys, scowling and angry over the stupidity of it all, and young men from the University cut deep by the knife thrusts of suspicion aimed at them. There were babies in baskets, and a bride and groom who had married at the last minute to keep from being sent to different camps.

There were the old. And the crippled. And the blind. There was an old man dying of cancer. And one on crutches barely able to stand. Some crippled with rheumatism and others worn out from age and hard work. Pathetic figures.

There were little tots toddling on their first uncertain steps, already tired and fretful, reflecting in their unhappy faces the strain under which their parents had labored the past few days. Anxious lines around the eyes of tired fathers and mothers as they tried to comfort their children and wondered what was in store for them. Would there be good food, or any food? Milk? Would there be medical care? What would happen to their little ones now the parents were no longer able to look to their welfare?

There were quiet, acquiescent little women. Issei women. What flight of the imagination would be required to regard them as dangerous!

The military dragnet had been no respecter of persons. It had been drawn through the designated area with merciless efficiency, into the sanctuary of the old and infirm as well as the able, and had dragged them forth from the comfort and warmth of their firesides and beds. Here they stood, many with difficulty, desolate and shivering in the chill evening air from the sea, waiting to entrain for internment—and, for some, eventual death. Pullman accommodations had been provided for the sick and aged, and they were being put on board as rapidly as possible.

The swarming people who filled the platform to overflowing were unusually orderly for such a large number under difficult circumstances; and there was something incongruous in the presence of military police stationed at intervals the entire length of the platform. Towering over this throng of subdued little people, they looked as much out of place as stage settings inadvertently left from a previous act. The young people eyed these guards with unbelief and resentment.

From *Harvest of Hate* by Georgia Day Robertson. Reprinted by permission of the California State University-Fullerton Library.

There was a veteran of World War I limping about on an ill-fitting artificial foot; he had left his own in France a quarter of a century before. He was wearing a worn and faded overseas cap at a jaunty angle and was stumping about talking to everyone, trying to bolster morale.

"Heh! Where you going, Charley?" someone yelled.

"Military secret," the vet retorted with a resounding laugh which brought some smiles where scowls had been.

61 Brood of Eagles

Southern California had long been the center of the nation's aircraft industry but it had to expand rapidly to meet wartime demands. Employment in the aircraft industry was 30,000 in 1937 and soared to a peak of 2,100,000. Crash programs were created to train the many inexperienced workers. The following selection mirrors the experience of many young women who worked in war-time aircraft plants. It was exciting to feel that you were gainfully employed, and also making a real contribution to the war effort. But, naturally, there were also less pleasant experiences.

She loved the sights and the sounds and the smells of the shop, and she gloried in the sense of freedom that went with her job. And she loved the night.

Until 4:45 in the afternoon the front offices were still occupied, but by 5 o'clock most of the front office people were gone, and the materiel offices and planning departments and vast engineering drafting rooms were almost deserted; but in the shops, the sounds and the smells were all a part of the night: the clomp of the shears and the high-pitched scream of the shapers, the whirr of drill press, lathe, and milling machine; the snap and thud of punch press, drop hammer, the whine of giant hydro; the insane chatter of rivet guns in fuselage, wing, empennage, final assembly; the sweet smell of the paintshop, and the stench of the anodic tanks; the odors of rubber and plastic and leather and cut micarta; the new-car smells of finished assemblies stacked in stockrooms.

She loved the outside work area where standlights drove back the darkness, and cables wound beneath your feet, and the constant thunder of great engines filled the night. Men, casting odd shadows in the glare of the standlights, climbed in and over airplanes, ministering to them, pampering them, preparing them, as trainers prepare racehorses, for their ultimate effort.

Oh, there were the unpleasant parts, too. That night over near the foundry, the night of the Factory B blackout on orders from the area defense command: one moment there was light and activity; the next moment the entire plant was dark—"Jesus, what's happened?" somebody said.

And then the announcement over the public address that the plant was on a red alert, that everyone was to stay where he was, that supervisory personnel would be wearing luminescent armbands, and that there was no cause for panic . . .

Edna had her notebook; she found that she was clinging to it with both hands. No cause for panic—well, probably not; on the other hand, the darkness was so intense, and people she could not see were all around her, men, no other women here in the foundry drop-hammer area; she herself had just been passing through; she stayed where she was out in the alleyway, and it seemed that time would never pass.

The first shock had worn off. In the work area where the big hammers stood, someone said in a high falsetto, "Take your hand off my ass! Not you! You!"

And another voice said, "Jesus, if they're blacked out in those front offices, think of all the nooky standing around for grabs." And then, "Goddam it, whose feet you think you're standing on?" There was the sound of minor scuffling. "Knock it off, huh? You can't see a damn thing— Hey! Jesus! Hold still, will you: Can't you—?"

Edna had heard the sound countless times before, but never isolated and underlined by the surrounding silence like this: the small click as the drop-hammer release was tripped; the faint whirring sound as the great punch of its own weight and guided by the vertical rails fell toward the anchored die; the thud that shook the floor as the punch and die came together with irresistible impact. This time the final sound was somehow muffled, and wrong. Edna held her breath and the silence was a sudden roaring in her ears.

A man's voice, uncertain, quavering, said, "Jesus Christ! Somebody light a match! Goddam it, will somebody—?"

A match flared. Edna could not keep herself from looking. A man seemed to be kneeling in front of the drop-hammer bed, but his head and shoulders simply weren't there; where they should have been was only the enormous punch buried in the die, and blood oozing darkly. This much she saw before, mercifully, the match went out.

The voice which had called for light said, "For Christ's sweet sake, get the punch up! Get it off him!"

And another voice, calm, scornful, said, "Without power just how in hell are you going to lift a half-ton punch? And if you did, what good would it do? He's formed like a piece of cowl panel, and that's all there is to it."

Someone vomited then; the sound was unmistakable. And the endless waiting went on.

It was forty minutes before the lights came on and there was power to raise the punch—but the moment there was light, Edna hurried on her way without looking back and failed to forget what she had seen. She heard the official version of the accident later: a man named Joe Black, drop-hammer helper, had lost his balance and started to fall and, in reaching out for support, had accidentally tripped the hammer release . . .

And there was the late afternoon when she was walking along the main alleyway that led down into the major assembly departments—and the new safety engineering display pulled her right up short: there in the glass case was a drill motor containing perhaps fourteen inches of a broken extension drill. Wrapped around the extension drill was a quantity of long brown hair to which was still attached a large patch of bloody human skin—the woman had been scalped.

Women with long hair were supposed to wear hairnets in the shop. Edna stared at the display and shuddered. For a few days, anyway, she thought, hairnets would be very popular. She hurried on.

Some of the people she met were oddballs, but she had expected no different: many were lazy, and some were foul-mouthed, and few knew anything about the plant beyond the immediate knowledge required for their own little jobs. Many cheated: the crap game in Stock 10 had been going on for two years and would continue uninterrupted until the end of the war; bribing a section timekeeper was frequent practice when you felt your luck was running and you wanted an hour or two with the dice.

But there were others, too, and it was the presence of these that restored the balance in her mind. That nice little old fellow in Stock 12 who wore gloves all the time. He maintained an inventory that could be counted on, a rarity, and because of it he was the love of all night dispatchers who worked into Department 12—never in his stockroom was there a last-minute hysterical call for parts shown to be in stock that were nonexistent. It was not until Edna had known him for some months that she found out he was also a senior partner in a downtown stock brokerage firm and worked nights at Dancer just because he wanted to help.

There was that girl over in the wing section one night. She was on the upper level of the jig, bucking rivets, wearing a loose hanging shirt over her slacks and, obviously, to the delight of her fellow workers on the floor, no brassiere. She had put down her bucking bar as Edna was passing once and was unbuttoning her shirt; then she held it wide and thrust out her breasts. "All right, you jerks," she said. "Have a good look. Then let's go back to work."

There were day crew people who stayed over occasionally on nights, and some of these, wearing oval badges (salary instead of hourly wage; hence no extra pay at time-and-a-half) worked around the clock, or longer, if necessary: as, for example, when on the Kestrel line the new turrets would not fit, daymen from engineering, planning, experimental, and the shop stayed on the job until the redesign was accomplished, proved out, and into production—something like 30 hours; and the line did not stop, or even slow.

There were dispatchers she knew who on occasion punched themselves out on the clock at close of shift, and then stayed on illicitly, without pay, chasing or herding parts through the shop simply because they did not trust their follow-up men to carry on with sufficient urgency.

There were the blind shopworkers with their marvelous Seeing Eye dogs. Each dog wore on his harness his own identification badge complete with picture, and had his own small palette beneath the bench where his master worked. Despite the confusing sights and sounds and smells, the warning bells, and the occasional horns of passing trackless trains, never once did Edna see one of these dogs make a mistake about which bell meant which message.

They did not stir for the bells announcing the quarter shift ten-minute smoking break when their masters merely stepped out into the white-lined areas; but they recognized immediately the lunch bell, and were up and ready for their harnesses if their masters were going outside the plant for lunch. And there was never any question in the dogs' minds when close of shift came and the five-minute warning bell said that it was time to tidy up the bench and get ready to leave. The dogs did not even mind being patted by strange hands on their way to the time card rack and the outside gates.

"The thing I can never get over," Edna told another dispatcher one night, "is that the dogs seem to be enjoying themselves." Maybe, she thought, it was because they felt they were doing something useful—like herself. In some ways she felt happier, more dedicated than she had ever felt in her life.

62 Skip to My Lou

The shipyards of the Bay area were as indispensable to victory as the aircraft plants, and they too had to take workers of all backgrounds. In this selection a recruiter is visiting an Arkansas community to lure people to California, "the Land of Promise." It is ironic that only a few years before, California leaders had devised schemes to send the unwanted Arkies home. When these people did reach the shipyards they found conditions vastly different from what was promised. There were often no trailer-mobiles for them to live in, restaurants and stores were crowded, and their children were lucky to find seats in the packed schools. Many stayed only a short time, returning home as soon as they had the money.

Men, and boys who took their places in the fields beside the men, began filing into the big auditorium and taking the seats along the aisles. There was a great shuffle of feet as they moved over the hardwood floor and slid into the seats. There they sat in silence, fanning their faces with their hats, and looked up to the stage, where California Bartlett and his man secretary sat between the sheriff and his two deputies in the row of chairs before the

From *Skip To My Lou* by William Martin Camp. Copyright 1945, 1972 by the author. Reprinted by permission of Doubleday.

drop curtain. In the front center of the stage was a speaker's stand, like the pulpit in a church, and over it was draped an American flag. A larger flag hung down over the drop curtain, and to the left of the flag was a big cloth sign, pinned to the curtain. In letters big enough to read all the way to the back of the auditorium, the sign said:

WELCOME TO CALIFORNIA!
UNCLE SAM NEEDS MEN TO BUILD SHIPS.
ALL EXPENSES PAID. GOOD WAGES.
EARN WHILE YOU LEARN.
CASH PAID IF YOU SIGN A YEAR'S CONTRACT.

R. T. ("California") Bartlett
Agent.

Motto: "My Word's As Good As My Bond!"
COME TO CALIFORNIA!
UNCLE SAM NEEDS YOU!

This was the first thing that greeted them as they entered the hall, and from where Uncle Yancey sat at the right of the speaker's stand he could watch their faces as they read the sign while walking to the front to take their seats.

Vigo Hoxie and Judd Cossey came in together—and Uncle Yancey, holding his guitar on his knee and his harmonica on the wire contraption around his neck, watched Vigo as his mouth dropped open when he saw the big flag and the sign, and his lips began to move as he read the sign aloud to Judd. Then, after looking at the faces of California Bartlett and his secretary, a man named Bolger, and Sheriff Lawson and his two deputies, Vigo glanced over at the end of the stage and saw Lou's uncle Yancey and nodded and pointed for Judd to see.

Uncle Yancey was adjusting the wire contraption around his neck and fitting the harmonica into the grip that held it before his mouth when Sheriff Lawson gave him the nod, and Uncle Yancey sounded his "A" and tuned the strings to the key of the mouth organ, and began playing "Skip to My Lou." He would play and pick a stanza, then sing the words to the stanza, then go back to playing his mouth organ and picking the cords and making the runs on the guitar. Two by two the men took up the rhythm and began tapping their feet and slapping their knees, keeping time with the cadence of it. Presently, attracted more by the music, which could be heard echoing through that big hall all the way out to the lawn in front, the men began to fill the hall and stand along the sides by the windows.

Within a few minutes the place was packed with old men and young men from all over that part of the state of Arkansas. Vigo recognized men he hadn't seen in years, men from Harrison, Boone County, and from all that rich country in the valley of Crooked Creek; North Fork, on the White River, and Cotter and Yellville, Salem, Mountain Home, Calico Rock, and Rogers and Huntsville, and all the mountain regions and valleys, hills and hollers of the Ozarks in the northwestern part of Arkansas.

Finished with "Skip to My Lou," Uncle Yancey arose, holding the guitar by the neck, and bowed. The hall echoed with the stomping of feet and men slapping their hands on knees covered by the thin, tightly drawn blue denim of their overalls. Someone called out, "Play 'Barbara Allen'!" And someone else yelled, "Play 'Turkey Shivaree'!" and "Play th' Jawbone Song!"

Still half bowing and not knowing whether to announce that this was the end of the entertainment or whether to continue with his playing, Uncle Yancey looked back over his soulder at California Bartlett, who was smiling, and then at the sheriff, who nodded. Mr. Bolger, sitting with the money sack between his feet on the floor, was clapping wildly and laughing and talking to California Bartlett.

"Play 'Little Birdie, Little Birdie,' " someone down front yelled, and Uncle Yancey looked down and saw that it was Vigo, who was clapping his big hands and laughing. His voice was heard above everyone else's, and because it was Lou's husband, and because there was a moral in it for everyone, including Vigo, Uncle Yancey began with "Little Birdie". . . .

After that they cried for more, and again the sheriff, who by this time was monopolizing California Bartlett with his talk, gave Uncle Yancey the nod, and he proceeded with the song they asked for, and everyone kept time with the tapping of their feet and the slapping on their knee.

> *"My ole Miss is mad at me,*
> *'Cause I wouldn't live in Tennessee,*
> *Wah jawbone to my jangle lang,*
> *An' a wah jawbone to my jangle lang. . . ."*

When the laughter and applause quieted after that, Uncle Yancey got up and walked over to the speaker's stand, where the flag was draped, and raised both hands and, according to instructions from Sheriff Lawson, he asked:

"Now, who's a-goin' t' Californy, th' Land of Promise?"

A few raised their hands, and the others clapped and stomped their feet and yelled, filling the hall with their noise. As an old road agent, who had sold bug juice and patent medicine for ten years with Colonel West, Uncle Yancey could tell that this crowd was in the right humor to buy anything, do anything, or say anything. Right now, he thought, if he had some of old Colonel West's tonic, he could clean up a fortune this evenin', right here. Any man who couldn't sell this crowd of mountaineers on the idea of going to California wasn't much of a salesman, he thought. Why, in the humor they were in, he could talk 'em into high-tailin' it straight out for California, afoot and ahorseback, right now.

The sheriff arose in the midst of the applause and walked up to stand at the speaker's stand.

"This here feller, California Bartlett," the sheriff was saying, "travels around in one of them trailer automobiles, a-packin' his own printin' press fer printin' up them yaller circulars that everyone in this room got, an' two special deputies an' a man secretary to protect th' great amount o' cash he totes aroun' with him t' give away t' fellers like me an' you t' pay their expenses t' California so's t' hep build them ships. An' he's come here today to Berryville, th' gateway to the Ozark country, to get good, big, strong men like you to pitch in an' build ships. Now, without further encroachin' on his time, I give you California Bartlett, the man whose word is as good as his bond—Mister Bartlett, step up hyar!"

Bartlett cleared his throat as he arose and walked toward the stand, his long arms dangling at his sides and his acre of back and shoulders swaying a little from side to side, his head held high and his red hair glistening in the light.

A breeze was blowing across the auditorium from the open windows. There was an immediate uproar as the men and boys caught sight of the big man, who towered a full head and shoulders above the sheriff and who dwarfed the speaker's stand which stood before him. Bartlett stood a good six feet six inches in his white Palm Beach suit, which made him look even bigger. When he opened his big square jaws, his voice boomed out over the heads of the men and boys sitting with their mouths agape, their hats poised in midair from their fanning.

"Gentlemen," he began, waving his right arm in a wide sweeping motion, "I'm indebted to"—and he turned around and made an uplifting motion with his hand—"to Uncle Yancey Jolly for putting across this meeting today. When I was in eastern Oklahoma they told me that if I was looking for a man to make my appearance in the Ozark country a success, Uncle Yancey Jolly of Berryville, Arkansas, was the man!"

Uncle Yancey half rose to acknowledge the clapping and stomping which went up from the men out front. Just as he rose, Mr. Bolger came up and took him by the arm and led him to the front of the stage.

"Gentlemen," Bartlett went on, as he raised his right arm upward to indicate silence, "it's worth a fortune to me to get a meeting like this together. And"—he reached down and put his big hand into the moneybag Bolger had brought up, and drew out a wad of greenbacks—"and, gentlemen, just to show you how much I think of Uncle Yancey an' his guitar playing and harmonica blowing, I want to present him with a little token of my gratitude and esteem." Turning, he said, "Uncle Jolly, I want to present to you, out of my own funds, *the sum of fifty dollars for your work here today!*"

One by one he counted out five ten-dollar bills. There was a big intake of breath all over the hall as everyone watched him count out the money and lay it in Uncle Jolly's shaking hands.

"Take it, Colonel," he said, bestowing a title upon Uncle Yancey.

Then turning to the audience, he said, "Now, gentlemen, that is only a sample of how much we out in California value the talents of you good people of the Middle West."

As Bartlett talked on, Uncle Yancey backed to his seat in the center of the stage, under the great flag, and sat down weakly. That was the finest piece of showmanship he had ever seen, he thought. It had the desired effect, for if there was a man in the auditorium who was not in the proper frame of mind before, he was now.

"I hold before you," California Bartlett was saying, "copies of work contracts which I will ask each and every one of you to sign at the conclusion of my remarks. And upon the signing of one of these contracts, each man will receive the sum of fifty-seven dollars and fifty-five cents for the payment of first-class railroad fare from here to California.

"And on top of that, gentlemen," he added, "I will add, out of the funds of the shipyard people whom I represent, the sum of twelve dollars and forty-five cents, making a grand total of *seventy dollars* to each and every man who signs a contract here today."

It seemed as if not a man breathed, and California Bartlett lowered his voice as he talked fast.

"Mind you, men, this is not a gift. It is an advance—a loan—which will be deducted from your first month's salary in California."

And as though he had read their minds, he answered their question by saying, "Seventy dollars is nothing compared to the wages you will earn. We have just begun to lay the groundwork for the biggest shipbuilding program in the world. The first ship was launched last August. You will be trained and well paid. Many of you will make enough *in one week* to repay the advance in full!"

There was loud applause, and when it had quieted, he went on:

"California *welcomes* you now. California offers a job for every one of you now and in the great future in store for that Golden State in the West..."

His big voice rumbled on as he told of the good rich land fully irrigated, the great green pastures, the forests full of great flocks of game, the streams where fish were abundant and where wild rice grew to feed the flocks of wild ducks and geese which blacked the skies over the hunting grounds in season.

There were no skeptics among the men who sat there now with their hands clasped over the knees, their heads to one side, their eyes big as walnuts, and their mouths open as they listened. He told them of the new homes which would be waiting for them there, modern homes with every luxury, good hospitals and schools, old-age insurance and security for the future. And when he had finished he took his place at the table on the end of the stage and spread out the contracts and laid beside them pencils and pens and ink bottles. Bolger, his secretary, and Sheriff Lawson and his two deputies came over, and while Bolger sat in the chair beside Bartlett the sheriff and his deputies stood guard behind them.

First in line and on the stage was Ab Turrell. California Bartlett looked at him, extended his arm across the table and shook hands with Ab, a tall, skinny mountaineer who had a houseful of young ones, mostly boys.

"Ab Turrell. Abner's th' first name."

Bolger wrote Ab's name at the top of one of the contracts in a blank space among the fine print.

"Religion?"

Turrell said nothing.

"Any skills? That is, are you a mechanic, carpenter, welder?" asked Bolger.

Ab shook his head. "I can fix farm machinery. An' I can fix fences, nail boards, build houses."

California Bartlett looked at him a moment, glanced back at Sheriff Lawson, who nodded.

"Put him down as a carpenter, Bolger," he told the secretary.

Bolger wrote quickly, then reached into the bag.

"I got two growed-up boys," Ab said. "Both over sixteen. How about them?"

California Bartlett looked at the sheriff, who nodded.

"Fine, upstandin' boys," said the sheriff.

"All right. You can sign up for them, too," said California Bartlett. Names Abel and Cole. Cole is seventeen, Abel sixteen."

Bartlett's secretary filled out two more contracts, and Ab Turrell signed them.

"Two hundred and ten dollars to Mister Abner Turrell," the sheriff called out.

Ab swallowed hard, took the money and shoved it into his pocket quick. He was so excited that he nearly fell from the stage as he tried to find the way out of the auditorium.

The next man in line was Shadder Bob.

"Name?" asked Bartlett's secretary.

"Shadder Bob."

"How's that?"

"Shadder Bob."

"Is that your full name?" the man asked him.

Shadder Bob nodded.

"Religion?"

Shadder Bob stood silent, and the secretary repeated: "Religion? Are you Protestant or Catholic?"

Shadder Bob laughed. "I ain't no Catholic, mister," he said. "I got enough trouble jus' bein' colored!"

Shadder Bob signed up for himself and his seven sons, and then, one by one, the others came up in the line, signed the contracts, took their money, and yelled and laughed as they ran out of the auditorium, past the long line of waiting men and boys, who shifted nervously from one foot to another, shoved their hands deep into their pockets, bit off the ends of tobacco twists and plugs, rolled their own cigarettes, licked the paper and twisted the ends and lit them, drawing hard on them and blowing the smoke above their heads. Some stood still, gazing out over the hills where the sun cast moving shadows of the clouds.

63   Bright Web in the Darkness

The shipyards required large numbers of welders and there were numerous intensive training programs to prepare them. But, as badly as they were needed, there was still widespread discrimination against ethnic minorities. In many cases companies tried to hire everyone but were kept from doing so by the unions, which used a variety of tricks to deny membership to blacks as the following illustrates. In addition to being denied equality on the job, members of ethnic minorities also confronted discrimination in schools, housing, and other public places.

For the final session of the welding class, they went down to the shop in the basement as usual, but no one did much work that evening. The instructor, visiting from one bench to another, repeated the latest shipyard jokes, asked where each one expected to hire out, warned them not to fall for any sucker tricks when they went up for their tests. He never liked to see too many old students come back to take his course over again—that was hard on a teacher's reputation; and wishing them all good luck, he dismissed the class half an hour early. However, they used up the rest of the time packing their helmets and coveralls, goggles and gloves, saying good-by several times inside and once more on the steps of the school.

Charlie was waiting there for them.

With Reverend Beezely and the white girl, Sally O'Regan, they crossed the street to the cafeteria for their coffee.

"This will be my last night waiting on counter," Sally O'Regan announced. "For the rest of my life, I hope, believe me, if only I can pass that damn test tomorrow. I'm going right over when I get off work in the morning. Shall we go together?" she asked.

But Joyce said she had to report to her job and request time off from her foreman; and the Reverend explained that he was waiting on the application he had put in at the housing project because he wanted to move his family to San Martin Village before he switched to a job in the shipyard over there. Joyce noticed that he seemed to have no doubt of his ability to pass the welding test; however she was relieved that Sally O'Regan appeared less confident, because this kept company with her own uneasiness. Yet she had not wanted to make any arrangement for going to the test *with* Sally. She knew she would do better alone—and hoped no one else from the welding class would show up at the same time.

Sally O'Regan had just received her first letter from her husband, she told them, in which he wrote that he had been assigned to the armed guard pool, although she did not know exactly what that was. Charlie explained it meant he would be one of the navy gunners aboard the merchant ships. "Why, I'll probably run into him myself one of these days, Mrs. O'Regan," he cried. "What does he look like?"

Medium height with dark curly hair, Sally said; and whispered to Joyce, "I want to pass that test tomorrow so I can write him I'm really a welder. I bet that'll take him down a peg or two."

They parted, laughing, at the streetcar stop.

She and Charlie rode out to the Hendersons' where they sat with their arms around each other on the bottom step of the stairway. He left early, not to keep her up too late the night before her examination, he said. But in her room, when she turned off the light and lay down in bed, her anxiety overcame her at once and she knew it would have been better had she stayed longer with him. Trapped half-way between sleeping and waking, she labored the whole night long welding seams. Or trying to. But the rod refused to melt. The arc was never hot enough, the machine refused to operate properly. The metal peeled off in flakes like hard butter instead of flowing out as it should, and when finally the examiner came to her, the two pieces of steel she had been supposed to weld fell apart of their own weight. By daybreak she had repeated this process four or five thousand times. She was exhausted, and convinced that she was certain to fail the test.

But she passed it. Before noon that morning she was back with her cleanup gang, carrying the welder's certificate in her handbag. The other women were jubilant; and even the sour, straw-headed carpenter congratulated her. After work, Mr. Henderson drove her to the Welders' and Shipbuilders' Union Hall out on Folsom Street in San Francisco.

She joined the line near the front entrance where a sign announced: *Welders' Clearances Issued Here.* A man who had been standing at the doorway came over to her, tapped her on the shoulder and motioned her upstairs. On the second floor, she found another window and another line, but here the people waiting were all colored. The man at the window was white, and Joyce could see that those ahead of her in the line were passing him money, for their dues payments, she supposed. When her turn came, she held out her welder's certificate and opened her billfold.

"We got no call for women welders right now," the man told her. "Got a long waiting list. Put your name down if you want." He passed her a sheet of paper on a clipboard. "We'll send you a card if something comes up. Don't know when that'll be. If you go around to the laborers' union, they probably put you to work right away."

Joyce shook her head and went down the stairs, back to the car where Mr. Henderson was waiting.

"That don't sound right to me," Mr. Henderson said.

When Charlie came for her at six, he threw up his hands and shouted, "My God Almighty, what a dirty run-around!" Charlie took her out to the liquor store on the corner where there was a phone booth, and they found Sally O'Regan's telephone from information, and called, waking her. The union had given her a welder's clearance right away, she told them, and she was supposed to start work that night at midnight.

"We better get ahold of the Rev," Charlie said.

Reverend Beezely was asleep too when they came, but his wife waked him and he padded out of the bedroom in a pair of straw sandals and a dressing gown that struck him above the knees, while the sleeves ran out halfway between his elbows and his wrists. He sat rubbing his eyes with his knuckles as Charlie told him what had happened, and Joyce kept saying to his wife Janet, "Oh, we shouldn't have waked him up!"

"I expected this might happen," the Reverend Beezely said. "Yes. Don't worry about waking me, it's almost my supper time in any case." And turning to Charlie: "You asked the other evening why I was leaving my soft berth, as you like to put it, Charles, to go into the shipyard."

Charlie nodded and placed his hands with the fingers together in a gesture of repentance.

"Perhaps we'd all like some coffee?" the Reverend suggested. "This is happening every day, in every shipyard all over the West Coast," he told them. "Our people work as laborers, janitors, they work in the cleanup gangs; and nobody minds that. But as soon as we learn the higher skills, as soon as we seek admission to the skilled trade unions, then our difficulty begins. If you and I had been white, Miss Allen, the shipyard would have trained us on the job and paid us for learning. But we are not white, so we have to enroll in a class on our own time. Then the union tells us they have no need for welders. Yes. The shipyards place notices in the newspapers saying come one come all to the shipyards. Learn as you earn. They hire every man and woman to whom the union will issue a clearance. We know that. Everybody knows it. *Learn as you earn*," he repeated. "Perhaps we will. Yes. I hope we will learn."

His wife brought a tray of coffee cups and Reverend Beezely passed around the canned milk and sugar, then poured milk in his own cup, filling it to the brim. As he continued talking, he held the cup half raised to his mouth in the long fingers of his hand, while Joyce wondered how he could keep from spilling it.

" . . . the National Negro Improvement League here, of which I am a member," he was saying, "has undertaken to draw together a committee, of shipyard workers, ministers, several lawyers perhaps, to seek ways of protecting our people. We intend to petition President Roosevelt's Fair Employment Practices Board to hold a hearing directly on shipyards. But all this is a slow process. It won't get you your job as welder, Miss Allen. Not today or tomorrow."

64 Zoot Suit Riots

Japanese-Americans and blacks were not alone in feeling the sting of wartime discrimination. In 1943 an incident involving a group of Mexican-American youths dressed in long jackets and tapered trousers, which were contemptuously called "zoot-suits," dramatized the situation. Some of these juveniles, angry because servicemen were dating their girls, beat up some sailors. In retaliation, mobs of hoodlums (including many servicemen) roamed the streets of Los Angeles attacking persons of Mexican descent indiscriminately. It has even been alleged that the police assisted this brutality. The following tells of the terror which a Mexican-American teenager experienced in this riot.

Angel knew that he was kidding himself. He knew it from the minute he got to school. He knew it from the way everyone acted. He knew it from the over-protective attitude Kenny and Virginia took toward him. He knew it from the way they tried to talk him out of going down to the theater. He knew it from the way Mr. Heller tried to nail him after class. But it was not until he had started the long walk to town and saw the black, streamer headlines of the late afternoon papers that he realized how foolhardly he was being.

ZOOTERS THREATEN L.A. POLICE
We're Meeting 500 Strong Tonight and We're Going to
Kill Every Cop We See

It was not too late to turn back and go home. He went into Pablo's Hamburger Stand. The place was deserted. The groups of Mexican boys and girls that frequented the joint had disappeared. Angel sat down on the high stool near the counter. Presently a large Mexican woman bustled out. Angel ordered a hamburger and a coke for his dinner. The woman served him wordlessly. There was nothing to talk about. Angel finished eating, paid for his meal, and started out. As he reached the door the woman called to him.

"*Muchacho,* you better stay home tonight."

Angel nodded his head briefly, and left.

What was the matter with him? Why was he determined to go to the theater tonight? The drive that was impelling him was self-destructive, stupidly self-destructive. He did not care to analyze it. Whatever the compulsion was, it was not alloyed by curiosity. He had no desire to see what was going on. He knew what was going on. Even without having seen what he had already seen as a prelude, on the stage of the Super Star Burlesque Theater, his imagination was vivid enough to picture the happenings of the past week end without any outside help. Nor was he drawn by an irresistible desire to be back in the theater; quite the contrary, he had come to detest the Super Star Burlesque Theater. He had made up his mind to quit after last Thursday night. If anything, he was going to town in order to tell Mr. Geeslar that he would have to find another boy for the balcony, and to pick up his check. At least, his last reason had seemed a good one when he woke up this morning. Right now it did not seem so urgent.

Angel picked his way through the thickening masses of fevered humans who were gathering at the focal point, Main Street, like white cells around an infection. Mr. Geeslar stared at Angel, appalled, as the boy entered the theater.

"Who the hell told you to come down here tonight?" he demanded.

"You said to come back Monday. Anyway, I need my check." He wasn't going to tell Mr. Geeslar he was quitting until he got the check. He knew Mr. Geeslar.

"The hell I did!" Mr. Geeslar took the cigar stub he was chewing on out of his mouth and spat. Then he grumbled: "Well, get the hell upstairs. I'll bring your check up to you. Goddam fool!" As Angel started up the stairs, Mr. Geeslar called out: "Soon as everybody's seated and the house is dark, you scram outa here, see!" Angel nodded and continued his ascent to the balcony.

He stood near the balcony exit doors, watching the stragglers come in and find their way to their seats in the murky light. He was most anxious now to leave before the show started, but Mr. Geeslar had not come up with his check yet. In ten minutes the show would start. The house was two-thirds empty. Evidently the burlesque show could not compete in attractions with the arena outside. There was a quiet knock on the exit door behind him. Startled, Angel turned his head and cocked it to one side. The knock came again. He did not know what to do. His heart began to beat rapidly. The picture of the soldiers and sailors dragging the *pachuco* onto the stage flamed into his mind. He pulled himself together. The quiet persuasiveness of the knock was not that of any enemy. He turned around and opened the door a few inches. It was Fern. She was dressed in her street clothes. She didn't have to go on until the last part of the show.

"Angel!" she whispered in a frightened voice. "Come out here."

Angel looked at her. Her face was mottled with color under the heavy make-up; her hair disheveled; her breathing heavy, as if she had been running and the exertion was too much for her.

"Fern!" he queried anxiously, stepping outside and leaving the door slightly ajar behind him.

"Close it! Close it!" she panted.

"I won't be able to get back in," said Angel. "What's the matter?" In spite of his effort at composure, some of the woman's alarm was beginning to find an answering nervousness in himself.

"Close it. You don't have to get back in. Beat it, kid. I run all the way up here. I'm a wreck." She leaned against the railing, trying to catch her breath. "It ain't the exercise," she murmured, as if Angel might possibly report this lack of vitality on her part to the boss, "it's the scare they give me. I was late tonight—getting through that damn mob—and then I seen them sailors with their sticks and ropes coming into the house. Mr. Geeslar was yelling at them that the house was empty, that everybody was staying out on the streets to see the show. But I didn't wait for nothing. I kinda had a feeling you'd be up here tonight. Kid, I never run upstairs like this in my life. Listen." They both stood tensely still. From the interior of the house, back of the exit door, a rising crescendo of human sounds filled the air.

"Beat it, kid. Run. Don't bother about me. Go on. Beat it."

But Angel insisted on helping her down the steep flight of iron steps. "God, I don't know how you're going to get outa this! Honest to God, I don't!" she kept whispering shakily.

Just as they reached the bottom of the stairs, two sailors and a civilian looked down the narrow alleyway. The figures of the boy and the woman stood fully illumined in the light over the stage door, which was directly under the fire escape.

"Bejeesus," yelled one of the sailors, "they're even taking our whores away from us."

With a loud guffaw of appreciation, the three men tore down the alley. Fern gave one brief scream and ran to the stage door, beat wildly on it, and within a second had disappeared inside. Angel looked around. There was no place to run. It was a deadend alley. He took a desperate plunge in the direction of the oncoming men, seeking to dive between them. Someone grabbed his leg. Curses and obscenities filled his ears. Flailing out wildly with his fists, he fell. His head struck the pavement. He knew they were tearing off his clothes. Through the dark painful stupor that seemed to be spreading down from his head through every part of his body, he heard one say, "He's out!" And the others reply, "Aw, he's just playin' possum!"

When they went away, Angel lay still for a long time. He was not unconscious; only badly stunned. He could hear the clamor very plainly— the roar of the mob, the sirens of the police, the carnival laughter of the crowd. He could even hear the faint sound of the orchestra from the interior of the theater, playing, "Roll out the barrel—we'll have a barrel of fun." The show was in full swing.

Chapter 12

The New Age of Technology

The New Age of Technology

The era since World War II has seen California experience its most rapid growth. The economy sputtered briefly immediately after the war and then soared to new heights when the Korean War began in 1950. Rapid migration into the state has always been an important factor behind economic booms, and population increased in the 1940s by fifty-three per cent, and in the 1950s by forty-eight per cent. In 1962 the state surpassed New York as the nation's most populous and by 1970 there were 19,953,000 persons in California, making the increase rate for the decade twenty-seven per cent. This slower rate of growth began with a downturn in the number of newcomers in the years after 1964. In that same year a state agency had projected a 1970 population of 21,690,000 and that of 1975 as 25,000,000, predictions that were to prove wildly exaggerated.

In the first twenty years after the war, many people justly felt that in California the great American dream was to be realized. The economy was bolstered by all of the forces which had helped California in the past: nation-wide prosperity which provided a market for the state's burgeoning agricultural produce, investment capital for building and industry, growing numbers of retirees and tourists who brought money with them, and a sophisticated aerospace industry. Finally, the boom developed a momentum of its own as the constant inrush of people created ever-growing needs for new housing, new services, and a wide variety of consumer products.

The economy began to slow down in the mid-1960s, either as a result of the slackening pace of growth in the indigenous population, or the lessening of the number of migrants into the state. The leveling off of population growth was due, in part, to emphasis upon zero population growth which caused a sharp decline in the birthrate. Air pollution, congestion in the cities, and racial unrest all helped to discourage possible migration. By the mid-1970s revised projections suggested that the decade would record the lowest population growth in the state's history. This end of the population expansion itself dried up potential jobs. Defense spending declined rapidly after 1967 also, and a national downturn in the economy contributed to California's problems.

In the years since the war, California politics have also assumed importance and have attracted national attention because of their unusual character. The large number of recent arrivals, combined with the mobility of Californians, has helped blur party loyalties and create a vast independent vote. Weak party structures in turn force candidates to run on their own. Hence, state politics have been dominated by powerful personalities. Earl Warren, the only triple winner as governor, had a long and distinguished career also as Chief Justice of the United States Supreme

Court. Richard Nixon's career as congressman, senator, Vice-President, and President prompted many national political observers to analyze the nature of California politics. Interestingly enough, novels of political fiction abound for this period, while other aspects of the state have been neglected.

65   Peacetime Industry

As the end of the war neared in 1945 many feared that war-inflated manufacturing would collapse and there would be a return to depression conditions. Unemployment did remain high between 1945 and 1950, and there was a slight exodus from the state—which was more than offset by new arrivals later. Not until the outbreak of the Korean War in 1950 did California's manufacturing boom again. The following selection tells of the changes faced by one aircraft firm and how it made the transition from a war economy to that of peace.

The first sign of wilt at Amcraft was unspectacular and expected. A young riveter got married and became a housewife. A die-maker went back to his farm and bought a new tractor with his wartime savings. One of Lonnie's assistants tore up his draft-board registration card and disappeared to paint gaudy swirls for a world suddenly able to appreciate the finer things. A radar technician cashed his E-Bonds and became proprietor of a radio and television repair shop. A stockroom clerk noted for her unsmiling attention to work suddenly became gay, threw up her job and stayed home sewing new curtains for the living room: the boys were coming home and hers among them. In the design room a New Englander who had found California too new and uninhibited moved east to the more congenial clime of Fall River, Massachusetts. Paul Esterbrook got a job in North American Aviation's new aerophysics laboratory as soon as restrictions on changing jobs were rescinded. Several Bachelors of Science pondered the future, estimated the number of Bachelors of Science who had been first lieutenants in the army and returned to college to become Doctors of Philosophy. One odd, disgruntled character quit to take a job selling life insurance.

All in all, about two thousand workers voluntarily left Amcraft to return to familiar lives and old hopes renewed, to new ventures and deferred dreams. They were not badly missed. Rather, the shrinkage was welcomed as an orderly, easy way to convert to less hectic peacetime operations. These were the amateurs that were leaving, and their departure would leave an efficient, hard core of professionals to deal with the great days ahead.

And for months following the end of the war the days ahead did promise to be great days, prosperous days bright with newness and change. There were the problems of sonic flight to be mastered, jet planes to be built, the embryonic guided missiles to be perfected. Peace, with its inevitable lessening of military demands, was in itself auspicious, for men like Humbler thought they saw at last a way clear of abject dependence upon governmental contracts. Every airline needed bigger, faster transports. Hundreds of thousands of aviators and air-crewmen were becoming civilians, forming a new, air-minded market for the helicopters and flivver planes which could turn Southern California into a new Detroit. Large corporations had learned that it was economical to let their executives use company-owned transports for trips between far-flung factories. Moreover, a nation hungered for all manner of durable goods after years of war—and there were the ruined cities of Europe to prove the aircraft industry's ability to mass-produce, and there was war-made money in company treasuries to bridge the troublesome transition to the manufacture of civilian goods. Factories were bigger than ever before, their machine tools were new and of the latest design, the staffs of engineers and machinists the best ever assembled in the industry. Equally important was the experience of the past, a guide to what not to do. This time, vowed aircraft industrialists, they would diversify their products, manufacture civilian goods as well as airplanes, and so become immune to the whims of erratic appropriations from Congress and election-year economics. This time, things would be different.

With the sun shining and the hay ready to be made, the aircrafters took to the fields. Lockheed worked the flaws out of the Shooting Star, built a transport, tinkered with plastics. Boeing designed jet planes and an egg beater. Ryan Aeronautical's choice of a sure-fire seller was a streamlined casket called the Grecian Urn. Mammoth Douglas undertook a private plane for civilians, a cargo plane for the Air Force, a dive bomber for the Navy, a jet plane for the National Advisory Committee on Aeronautics and a rocket for the Army; it also built unsinkable aluminum rowboats. Northrup tried nightfighters, flying wings, artificial limbs for amputees and motor scooters. North American built private planes, fighters, missiles and an atomic reactor. Hughes Aircraft, that odd sport of the industry, designed giant helicopters and fighters, almost flew a wooden flying boat with six engines and built an electronic altimeter while its president crashed airplanes and discovered chesty beauties for the movies and one of its officials entertained congressional investigators with tales of girlie-girlie parties honoring wartime procurement agents. Amalgamated Aircraft received an Air Force contract for a design study on a rocket engine, commenced research on a small electronic computer, and produced a sleek automobile trailer equipped with a picture window and a retractable television antenna.

It took about a year for the inevitable to appear on papers in comptrollers' offices, on balance sheets and stockholder reports.

The industrialists who had produced thousands of planes in the last year of the war were badly, almost ludicrously fooled by the deceptive lures of peacetime. As civilians, the million men who had served in the Air Force were eager to buy houses, cars, baby cribs and television sets but were perfectly content to do without a private airplane. The boom in airline travel did not occur. Corporations supplied their needs for transports from the abundant supply of surplus military aircraft. Fishermen seemed content to row wooden boats, and tradition seemed to favor awkwardly shaped egg beaters and clumsy, ornate caskets. The market for motor scooters and artificial legs was soon saturated. The war-work wanderers who had lived in trailer camps suddenly craved two immovable bedrooms and a bath. And the old stand-bys, the armed services, were too embroiled in feuds, too confused by the strategic implications in atomic weapons, too badly hamstrung by economies rooted in approaching elections rather than national safety to do more than spoon-feed aircraft suppliers and sustain a flicker of life.

Soon, Consolidated, Ryan, Northrup saw profits wither. North American lost eight millions on its private plane alone. Hughes ceased manufacturing airplanes altogether. Lockheed, Douglas laid off thousands of skilled workers. Like the rest, Amcraft delayed as long as possible, hoping for a miracle, existing on tax carry-backs and financial fat. Then, reluctantly, Humbler accepted the verdict of his board of directors and let Whitelaw act. The result was quick, heartbreaking, almost unbelievable.

As an integrated manufacturing machine, Amcraft ceased to exist. A work force of five thousand became a feeble cadre of eight hundred and fifty. The two night shifts disappeared; entire buildings became silent shells, parking lots turned into vacant acres, the tracks of railroad sidings corroded with rust. Warehouses were empty and locked. Vacated drafting boards were removed from the design room at night, stealthily, like bodies too obscene to be viewed by the survivors who returned at dawn. No one was free of the dread that tomorrow or next week, or next month, his turn would come.

It was at this time that the great, raddled camouflage net was removed from overhead. Some found the new brightness and sense of spaciousness a good omen. Others found their portent for the future in the dummy cow that had so long grazed above the rooftops. Scabrous and weatherworn, missing a leg, it lay amid weeds near the main gate, a sight for each entrance, each exit.

66   Sargossa City

In the 1920s California first began to build small houses specifically for retirees. The advent of social security and the proliferation of private and public retirement programs plus national prosperity meant that people were retiring early and could afford some luxury in the sun during the twilight years of their lives. The landscape was soon dotted with "Sun City," "Leisure World," or comparably named self-contained communities where young people were prohibited from living. The sales hoopla and extravaganza used to promote those developments in the 1960s was strikingly similar to that employed by the realtors of the1880s or the 1920s—as the following relates.

A highway the color of elephant hide took them through Indio, and Nina saw the old California decrepitude of swept front yards, and the bones of farm machinery rusting in the sun. Beyond lay the folds of the true desert, where waves of heat and fantastic patterns of cactus came together in a beauty both fragile and intense in this old forge of the sun.

The chartered busses were farther back along the highway when Nina first saw the Sargossa Sea: an unrolled sheet of blue construction paper, shimmering some miles ahead in a basin of rock.

As they drove faster past road signs pointing to Sargossa City, the arrows of wood became larger until the signs were tall as a fender, and then larger than the car. At the turnoff, the last sign was two stories high and pointed toward the lake: Playground of the West. Retirement Acres.

In the shadow of the two-story roadside arrow of wood, Mayo stopped the Ghia. With his help Nina made out the stakes of Aero Acres, where taxi strips for the family airplane branched off to each lot. On a rising shelf of land to the right she made out one golf green, its purple flag blinking in the desert sunshine. Below, at the end of a sickle-shaped road, an A-frame sales office was a daub of redwood and sparkling pane-glass beside the water. As Nina watched, the lake went calm. The water changed to blue tin, flattened by the great hammer of the sun.

"So there you see it," Mayo told her, and put his arms around her. "There you are, complete. Ready to roll—a Community Center and a really good restaurant. Also ten thousand Senior Citizens on the way in chartered busses from all over Southern California. I mean, it's all there, and we have got to make it to the sales meeting. . . ."

"Five years." As Mayo spoke Nina understood he did not really want to leave this shadow of a two-story road sign, for in this optimistic light Mayo saw Sargossa City as already completed and glittering.

"Less than five years," and Nina understood for the first time that beneath an Ohio innocence Mayo Sergeant had been born with the talent of firm humorless belief. "Then God knows how much one lot will be worth. Why, look at Cutlass Island!"

Because he believed, because his talent seemed to show her what she herself ought to become, Nina put her head on his shoulder. Besides, she remembered her uncles and her father from Bakersfield always said, "Five years, even less" about every acre of California ranch land they ever optioned or sold. And those men were native sons, to the man.

Then Mayo drove them so fast down the sickle-shaped road that they seemed to be in an airplane diving on the sales headquarters beside the lake. Where Sutter and Crockett and Via LBJ came together at the Towne Center, they parked.

Quickly Mayo led her to the front of the A-frame, the shadow of its beams massive above water. A narrow, tilting pier extended into the lake. Sargossa was below sea level and water near the shore was only a few inches deep.

"Marina here in ninety days," Mayo said, "then this building becomes a country club. For boaters."

Behind the windows, Nina saw the other people: a man in a Stetson hat; a pair of knickers walking through a slant of lights; bell-bottomed slacks; women's legs, all in a row, going toward one end of the room.

When her eyes adjusted to the draped darkness, and when she felt the elegance of the lounge and the sudden cooled moist air that was like velvet when she breathed, Nina saw the other realtors. They sat at bridge tables, or stood in clusters around the Coke machine; they relaxed on ice-blue sofas or in groups of four around the artificial palms.

"Time everyone. Almost time."

The sales manager called them to order, his silver spoon rapping a coffee urn. For twenty seconds there was silence, the kind that precedes a wedding.

"In exactly ten minutes, colleagues, our first bus unloads. Just beyond those windows!"

From the back of the room a realtor applauded.

Nina understood that the sales manager was Dr. Harvey Scholes, once a college president, but now at Sargossa; he had come here from Penjy Farnham's last development at El Paso Highlands. Doctor Scholes held up his hand for silence. His prematurely white hair was the color of the spoon he held aloft like a small silver lightning rod.

"Colleagues, I want every prospect out there greeted. I mean, extend the hand of fellowship. I do not want to bring these good people to our Sargossa City and *sim-ply let them ro-am.*"

In the front row one salesman brought out a notebook so that Doctor Scholes would see him write it down.

"Don't for one moment forget it: you are realtors—one and all! You have a responsibility to these good people. We must give them the complete Sargossa story. I mean the facts: Aero Acres has two planned runways of three thousand five hundred feet. We have two planned marinas, each launching one hundred and thirty boats an hour.

"Don't forget their golf course. Tell your golfers the whole story in *one* phrase."

Dr. Scholes held up both hands, to catch the ball. Eight men from the side of the room said it with one voice:

"A view of the sea from every tee."

The salesmen were warming up.

"But, men—yes, and you ladies—" he bowed half from the waist but did not stop talking. "Out there today, remember: Eighty-seven percent of married *unrest* comes from money trouble.

"I could not sleep at night if I thought the good people coming here today—instinctively, to find a home—I could not *sleep a wink* if they ever felt—now or in the future—burdened with nigg-ling lit-tle payments. We want, we demand one hundred *percent* satisfaction with every lit-tle bit of paper we write today."

In the middle row one man wearing knickers said, "HEAR, HEAR."

"Bring your clients this far! There's no waiting."

Dr. Scholes gestured toward the executive wing of the A-frame where his "closers" worked.

"I'll get four today."

Another voice said, "I'll do ten today."

Voices spoke, all through the darkened room, giving themselves confidence, "I'll sell five," "Six," and finally a mellow voice above her own head that Nina recognized as Mayo Sergeant's said, "I'll do twenty-two. Or bust."

Harvey Scholes said, "Ah, Mayo Sergeant," and began a round of applause that was picked up around the room.

At Sargossa, Mayo was already more than a salesman. He was a personality, and he knew it.

Outside Nina heard an air horn; the first bus stopped on the ramp. Harvey Scholes looked toward the ceiling. In a mellow air-horn voice he said, "Get out there. And sell!"

The salesmen cheered and broke ranks. They swept Nina out the door and into the sunshine.

Before the first bus door opened, Nina heard the oil-drum thump of the development band. In costumes of the Caribbean, the musicians came around a corner and circled the ramp, and when the last three busses pulled into the line the musicians formed in a half-circle and began furiously to sing:

SARGOSSA CITY
Where de sun she do shine
SAR-GOSSA CEE-TY
Where de climate she sublime
SARGOSSA CITY
Where she make fun all de time .

SAR-GOSSA CEE-TY
She will cost you one dime,
Aaaaaa-dime!
Aaaaaa-DIME!

All the bus doors opened and Nina saw older couples and newlyweds, fathers and sons, secretaries with a day off; ladies with dogs, gentlemen with canes, all in a line, come down the steps. And finally the bus drivers took wheelchairs from the groin of one bus for two arthritic passengers, here only for their health.

. . . Ohhh, she will cost you one dime . . .

From behind a small outcrop of land, two fast white motorboats, side by side, came across the water of the Sargossa Sea. A girl in a white bathing suit was balanced between the shoulders of two men. She waved as they roared past that gaping shore. The boats, in unison, swerved. White spume from propellors and water skis rose in the desert air. The crowd on the ramp was stunned by the noise and the girl in white riding between the water skiers. As they watched, the boats went back behind the outcrop of land.

Nina turned, but Mayo had already met his first client.

The lady was not young—but not old, either. She wore a broad white hat and sensible shoes. Mayo had his hand raised, protectively, and it seemed to Nina that Mayo Sergeant had known this woman all of his life.

I'll do twenty-two . . . .

Nina suddenly realized she was alone on the ramp, between a row of parked busses and the lake. From above she felt the hammer of the sun on her face and her temples. She turned sideways, but the sunlight leaped up from the water and battered her eyes; she turned from the lake, but a whirlwind of dust came down from Aero Acres, and across Via Harding, and turned off Via LBJ, and cut through her blouse like a scythe. And not yet noon.

Nina went back to the wall of the A-Frame headquarters. Above her, beyond the golf green where two rows of runway stakes came together in a point of white at the water's edge, she saw him: dust spurted from the rear wheels of the Ghia; then she saw him posed by the golf tee, swinging an imaginary driver; she saw him with a dozen older women, each woman holding one white hand to the brim of a white hat. Then Mayo Sergeant was at the water's edge, and now walking with an older couple beyond the row of palms, the fronds brown in this brown wind. She heard Mayo's voice, and the air horn of his famous Ghia; she saw him at ease, eating just outside a "closer's" booth. Then a bugle blew across the landscape. Noon.

The double doors slid open. The Senior Citizens went eagerly past the trestle-board tables and took box lunches of fried shrimp or fried chicken. They smiled at each other, neighbors already, their dentures white as their shirt collars. Doctor Scholes greeted them all at the coffee urn—and he also watched the members of his Calypso band who were doubling as bus boys. . . .

SARGOSSA CEETY.

Where de climate she sublime

Then community singing. Nina watched Mayo on the trestleboard table, making a dozen different hats out of white lunch boxes, putting on a different hat each time he led them into one of the old songs. Finally Mayo made a duck hat out of two boxes, and led all the other salesmen in a realtor's version of the "Stanford Farm." . . .

Ohhh, here-a-lot, there-a-lot, Everywherrrrre, a lot-lot . . .

Even after the rooms were empty again and the white lunch boxes were scattered across the carpets and the ice-blue sofas and even out on the ramp like chunks of snowmen fallen from the desert sky, and even when Nina was alone again, she understood that when Mayo Sergeant stood on the trestle board and sang, he was not cheap, or even deceptive. Mayo really was boyish and enthusiastic, very much like a younger son, away from home for a long time, but glad to be back once more. The Senior Citizens wanted to sing with him.

By late afternoon, Nina thought of the waters of Cutlass Bay. The green of the sea was a green dream—and nothing was sold yet. At five o'clock the air horns called everyone back to the busses. The newlyweds, and the two people in wheelchairs, and two horse players in striped suits, who had gotten on the wrong bus in the first place, came back to claim their seats for the ride back along the valley, and to coastal cities beyond. As the caravan of busses pulled out, the sun overheard bunched its shoulders in the sky, and posed for a final drop into the blue haze west of the mountains.

67 Huelga

One group that did not participate fairly in the post-war prosperity was the workers in the fields. California's agriculture, the state's leading industry, has had a historic tradition of enjoying the benefits of cheap labor, most of it foreign-born. Because of crop specialization, there is an intense demand for labor at specific times. The perishability of many crops makes it imperative that the labor to harvest be available when needed—or the farmer faces disaster. And the owners of the state's agribusinesses especially fear a strike at such a critical time. They were particularly pleased with the *bracero* program as it gave them the control of their field hands which they desired. In 1965 Cesar Chavez led a strike (huelga) against the grape growers of Delano which was not successfully concluded until 1970. This is a fictional insight into one phase of the strike.

Roberto watched, and the *huelga* was on. The sun was up. The sheriff's cars were parked between the strikers and the workmen. The workmen were getting out of the bus and being ushered into the fields. The strikers were in line along the public dirt road and yelling in chant. There were four sheriffs, and their two cars were parked on the farmer's property. One sheriff, the one with stripes, was leaning on his car. Arms folded. He watched silently. With his back to the farmer's property as he faced the *huelguistas*, the strikers, and the *huelguistas* were calling. Yelling, pleading, and begging for the workers not to go to the fields. To quit and join them. Now. Quickly. To come to them. Their brothers. Their fellow field workers. Their brother *campesinos*. And not be afraid.

The foreman, thirty-some yards behind the sheriffs, was telling the workmen to get out of the bus and go into the fields. That everything was okay. Not to pay attention to those troublemakers. Roberto and his two friends obeyed and followed the other workmen out of the bus, by the big tractor machinery, and into the fields. They began to work.

The *huelguistas* screamed!

The sheriff, the one with stripes, put on his sunglasses as the sunlight brightened, and there he stood. By his car. Uniform and gun. Arms folded. And the others copied his style, and they all watched silently. The sun climbed higher, and the heat of the day began, and the *huelga* continued.

Now Roberto and his group of field hands, *campesinos*, were working in mid-field, and the *huelguistas* were far away. Way over there on the public dirt road, and their calls were not too loud or bothersome. Roberto now worked fast and picked many tomatoes. He wiped the sweat from his brow. He looked across the field and saw the line of *huelguistas*. They were dressed much like himself, and they were waving flags and calling. He watched.

"Boy! Get back to work!" It was one of the foremen. A *pocho* Mexican foreman. There were now many foremen on this job, and they were all moving about and telling the workmen that everything was okay. Not to worry. They were doing the right thing. That those, on the road, were just lazy, no-good troublemakers. "I said, get back to work! Pronto!"

"Hey," said another foreman to this first foreman. "Don't yell at our men. Take it easy." Then this second foreman smiled at Roberto. "He didn't mean to yell at you, kid. Go back to work." He smiled again. Roberto thought his smile-of-concern seemed very unnatural, but he said nothing and went back to work. Picking fast. Carrying fast. Dumping fast. And once again picking. Soon they were by the edge of the field again, and there were the *huelguistas* on the public road. Very close. They were waving red flags with a black bird in the center and calling and pleading, and it was all so very loud that Roberto could not do his work. He stopped and looked at the *huelguistas*. Many other workmen had stopped also. Even Aguilar and Luis were not working so good now. The *huelguistas* stopped yelling and began talking. They explained that this particular ranch was on strike. On *huelga*. For them to go and work elsewhere. That this ranch had a particularly bad reputation for treating *campesinos*, field workers, very unjustly. That they paid bad wages and lied about the number of boxes one picked. That they robbed one. To please come with them. That united they could overcome . . . for the hearts of men were . . .

Suddenly a car came racing at the strikers. Roberto, in the field, watched. The car was new and golden, and it was coming up the road, raising dust, and going straight at the line of *huelguistas*. The *huelguistas* watched. Mouths open. And the car came. One striker ordered everyone to keep his place. The *huelguistas* held. The car kept coming fast. Not showing any intent of turning, and now the long golden El Dorado was only a few feet away from the group of strikers, and one *huelguista*, a young Mexican boy of fourteen, screamed and dodged away, and then all the strikers scattered. The car came to a skidding stop. Dust clouding all around, and a big man leaped out of the car. Bellowing! He was tall, raw-boned, and dark and very un-Mexican. His arms were hairy, his head was balding, and his face was shaved but shadowed with beard. He continued. Cigar in mouth.

"What the hell's going on here!"

The sheriff with stripes came over to him. Slowly. Respectfully. And began explaining.

A *huelguista*, young and tall and very much the all-American, came over. "I'm an attorney!" he shouted. "And I want this man arrested!" He was yelling at the sheriff. He was very excited.

The sheriff and the big man with the cigar looked at the young man, and, together, they said nothing. The clean-shaven boy ran his finger through his longish blond hair, looked at the four sheriffs, and trying to keep cool, said more quietly, "I'm an attorney, and I want this man arrested."

"Who's he?" asked the big man, and pointed his cigar at the young attorney.

"I don't know," said the striped officer. "One of the Chavez attorneys, I guess. But, getting back to my point, we're here to keep the peace, and please, Mr. Anderson, I don't want you doing things—"

"Boy!" said Mr. Anderson. The attorney had come closer to them. "What's your name?"

"Michaels. Jim Michaels."

"Well, Jim Michaels . . . get back over there." He pointed with his long cigar. "This is private property."

Jim Michaels backed up three paces to the public road. He yelled, "Sheriff! I want that man arrested on attempted hit and run!"

"Hit and run?" laughed Anderson. "Hell, who's running?"

Jim Michaels shuffled his feet in the dirt. He was twenty-five and so uptight that he could hardly think. Last year he had graduated second in his law class from Stanford Law School and he knew the law, and this damn sheriff wasn't doing his job. "Arrest him for the . . . Sheriff, hell, you saw him. Do your duty!"

"Look, boy . . ." said the sheriff, and drew out the word "boy." "I'm doing my duty. I'm keeping the peace. And I suggest you go talk to Mr. Chavez and find out what your duty is. Understand?"

The young attorney kicked the dirt. He was boiling. He went back to his group of thirty or forty *huelguistas* and they began talking on the bullhorn to the workers in the field. Roberto and the others all stopped their labor and listened. Even Aguilar and Luis. The car and the scattering of the strikers had caught their attention. They now listened. Giving their undivided attention. The sheriffs all drove off. The big man, Mr. Anderson, turned on his car radio real loud. Blasting rock music. The man on the bullhorn had to speak louder. The foremen began coming up to the workers and telling them individually that everything was okay. That legally these lazy troublemakers were in the wrong. That the sheriff had gone to get a warrant for their arrest.

Two pickups came up, in front and in back, of the long golden El Dorado and put on their radios also. More blasting modern music. The workmen began going back to work.

The bullhorn screamed.

It was a Mexican girl on top of the old panel truck, and she was a sight to see. She wore black pants and black boots and had one hand on her hip, another on the bullhorn, and she was screaming, cursing, and laughing. Roberto smiled. There she was, tall and slender, and she was *a toda madre*, a real live mother, and many men stopped their work. This woman, this girl, was not asking them nicely to stop their work and come and join them. No! She was yelling at them, saying they were cowards, not men, if they allowed a *patrón* to rob them of their dignity. Then, having their attention, she moved her hips and called to the heavens for them to be men, true Chicanos, Mexican-Americans, and not crumble to this *gringo* boss! That they too had their rights! That sure, right now, they were young and all the fields were in harvest and they were making good money. But let the work die down a little, and they'd be fired! Or get a little old, reach the age of forty or just thirty-five, and they wouldn't be given jobs!

"And you know what I say is true!" she continued as the radios blasted rock music in front of her, trying to drown her out. "My own father, not yet forty, cannot work because of a back injury he got on a ranch. And does he get compensations, no! He doesn't! Because farm workers had no disability compensation until a few years ago, while all other workers have been getting it for years! And years!

"And unemployment. Do we get that? No! While all other workers have been getting unemployment insurance for years! Please, be men!

And see the future and think of your children. Your children! And improve their world! Their chance for education and a better world! Join us! For, UNITED WE CAN OVERCOME. . ." A roaring echo began coming from the distance. Roberto stopped watching the girl on top of the old panel and looked. Two gigantic tractors were coming. They were pulling plows, huge steel discs, and raising a great cloud of dust. The girl stopped, she saw, and her face twisted with fear, but then she held . . . swallowed and continued talking as fast as she could. "Think of your children! Do this for them! Join us! And united we shall overcome!" The two tractors, driven by two Mexicans, came on. Anderson and his foremen got in their vehicles, radios blasting loud, and drove off to a comfortable distance. "Oh! Deep in my heart, I do believe! We are not alone! We'll walk hand in hand and someday we shall . . ."

The first tractor, huge and all iron, passed by in front of her and threw up a fantastic wall of dust with its huge steel disc. The girl began coughing and choking. A *huelguista*, a young Chicano with an Ivy League shirt and longish hair, leaped up on the panel with her and tried to help her down. She pushed him aside. She screamed. "JOIN US! NOW! DON'T YOU SEE WHAT THEY DO!" She was choking and crying, and now Roberto, for the first time, wished to quit and go to her. To them. Over there. He threw down his tomatoes. He began to go. A foreman yelled. The girl saw. She scree-eeee-ched with delight. The first tractor had gone by, and she could see. "Come! That's right! Please! Give me your name! Give me your name!"

Roberto began to speak. Aguilar grabbed him.

"Don't!" said Aguilar.

Roberto looked at Aguilar.

"Leave him alone!" yelled the girl. "If he wants to quit, it's not your concern!"

Aguilar was saying, "Don't be a fool! We're illegal. You'll be deported."

Roberto's eyes blinked and he held . . . remembering all his months of labor to get here.

"Leave him alone!" Then, in a very feminine voice, "Please, good-looking. Tell me your name."

"Roberto," he said, shaking his arm loose from Aguilar. And eye-to-eye he stared at Aguilar, but then went back to work as the second tractor came in front of her.

"Roberto?" she called out. "Did you say Roberto?" The second wall of dust raised up in front of her. She coughed, she choked, she called, "Roberto? Roberto! Roberto! Oh, that is my father's name, and he is brave and strong and would not let them . . ."

She was drowned out. The two tractors were now going back and forth in front of her and the *huelguistas* and all was a wall of dust and the roar of the tractors and the blasting radios from the owner's El Dorado and his foremen's pickups was all too much. But still the *huelguistas* held their ground on the public dirt road in the cloud of dust and kept chanting their protest as the tractors raced before them dangerously close. Finally a few strikers backed up across the road and got inside their cars and rolled up their windows. The girl was choking and coughing, but she held her post on the old panel and continued using the bullhorn. The two tractors picked up their pace. Going by, cutting near the edge of their property line with their great sharp discs, turning about and coming back. Then the panel truck was bumped. It rocked. The girl fell. *Huelguistas* rushed to her aid. Someone screamed.

Screamed a sound of pain. Not protest. And Anderson rushed forward. His face truly looked concerned. He stopped the tractors. The dust was terrible. No one could see anything. Anderson stood there. Tall. Boss-solid. And waited for the dust to settle.

Roberto, in the field behind Anderson, was not 'working. No one was working. All eyes held in wait.

Finally one could see. The girl was down, and there were a group of *huelguistas* around her, and someone was crying in terrible pain. Anderson walked up and saw . . . the person in pain was a young boy. The one that had panicked when Anderson had raced up in his El Dorado. His leg was all bloody. It looked like his foot was cut off. The girl who had been up on the panel was bent over him. She saw Anderson. Savagely she turned and leaped at him.

"You murderer! You pig!"

It took the attorney, Michaels, and two others to get her off the big man. Still she screamed at him. She had clawed his face and he was bleeding, but she wanted more. Michaels told two *huelguistas* to hold her. He went back to Anderson.

"Mister," he said very evenly. "We're going to sue you. Believe me, we're going to sue you, and you're going to pay with every damn cent you've got!" Anderson said nothing and touched up his face with a handkerchief. "Look at that boy! Not even fourteen, and your tractor cut off his foot!"

"The boy was trespassing," said one of Anderson's foremen. "I was over there, and I saw the whole thing. One of them"—he pointed to the *huelguistas*—"got in the panel and backed up into the tractor and knocked the girl off."

"Liar!" yelled the young Chicano with the Ivy League shirt. "I was going forward, and your tractor ran into me!"

"Bullshit!" said the foreman. "You backed up and knocked the girl off, and then this kid, trying to be a hero because he was a chickenshit a little while ago, rushes out to help her and goes into the disc!"

"Liar! The tractor came at us!"

"No sirreeeee!" The foreman shook his head with much vigor. "That tractor was within our property line. You all were trespassing, and that's a fact!"

"You're a goddamn liar!"

"Listen, punk!"

"All right," said Anderson, "enough! We can each tell our story when the sheriff comes." He turned to Michaels. "Michaels, I'm radioing into my office for the sheriff. Do you want me to get an ambulance out here?"

Michaels looked at the young boy. "No. We'll take him. It will be faster." He turned to his fellow *huelguistas*. *"Amigos, por favor,* help this boy to my car. And you, Teresita," he said to the young girl with black pants and boots, "get in with him." And he shook his head, kicked the dirt, mumbled to himself, and got in his car, a small foreign-made station wagon, and drove off. Down the road he stopped. He yelled for somebody else to drive. He had to stay. He had to make sure the sheriff got the right story. The Chicano with the Ivy League shirt ran up, got in the little wagon, and drove off.

Michaels came back to the scene of the incident. "Everyone step back," he said. "Don't destroy this evidence. Please, get back. Don't mess up these tractor prints." Anderson was with his tractor drivers. They were starting up the tractors. "Anderson! Don't you dare! Those tractors stay where they are!"

He rushed at Anderson. Yelling and ordering. Roberto and all the men in the field watched. The foremen weren't telling them to get to work any more. The foremen were all watching also. Michaels was raging. Anderson, twice as wide as Michaels, smiled. Cigar in mouth. Michaels yelled at the tractor drivers and told them that these vehicles were evidence, and if they moved them, they would be breaking the law. One driver stopped his tractor, turned off the motor, and got down.

"Keep your tractor," he said to Anderson. "I quit!"

The *huelguistas* yelled, "Bravo! Bravo! Tell it to him again!"

The tractor driver smiled hugely and yelled, "I QUIT!" And he walked over to the strikers. The strikers cheered him and rushed forward to meet him, embrace him, and give him many great compliments.

The other tractor driver, a Mexican also, was hesitant. He sat on his tractor. He looked from boss to young man to boss. Anderson took the initiative and walked up. He mounted the abandoned tractor. He started it up and drove off. The other driver followed him. Halfway down the field, he, Anderson, stopped, called one of his foremen, and told him to take the tractor into the yard. The foreman obeyed quickly, and the other driver followed. Anderson lit up a new cigar, smoked, watched the two tractors go down the way, and then turned, coming back down the field. Tall. Alone. Boss. Solid. And all the foremen saw him, became his once more, and began telling the workmen to get back to work. Quickly. Quickly. Aguilar went back to work. Roberto didn't. He gave true witness.

Luis patted Roberto on the shoulder and said, "Tonight, we'll talk. Not right now. Come. Let's get back to work."

Roberto nodded . . . and he went back to work, but he couldn't figure it. Hell, where was Aguilar's bravery? Where was Luis's smartness?

What were they doing letting an old balding boss and a bunch of fat-ass foremen treat their people like this?

He jerked at the tomatoes. Hard! He was mad. A foreman yelled at him. He whirled. Ready to fight. The foreman, a big fat *pocho* Mexican, stepped back. Surprised. Robert held . . . eye-to-eye. Unto death. Ready to go *a la prueba*. Then felt someone pulling him around. It was Aguilar. Aguilar was telling him to get back to work. Aguilar was apologizing to the foreman. Aguilar shoved Roberto to the tomatoes. Roberto, after a minute, began picking. And across the field on the public road the strikers were with their flags once more, and they were chanting: *"Huelga! Huelga! Huelga!"* And the sun climbed higher and the day grew hotter.

68   The Patriots

One facet of California politics in the 1960s was the rise to prominence of right-wing political extremism. Secret organizations of self-styled patriots were formed, several of them based on the premise that Communists had infiltrated important positions in the community, state, and nation. A factor in the rise of such organizations generally was fear of the changing society. On the local level school boards were a favorite target, and in one California community several teachers and principals were harassed for suspected anti-American leanings. This selection relates how one "patriotic" group operated.

Secrecy lent The Patriots' meetings an air of excited melodrama. Here was an elite membership of the right people, each of whom possessed a deep reserve of local power, and the secrecy made them feel more important and more powerful. They loved it. They went to complicated lengths to maintain just the right amount of mystery to baffle observers. Each member was a personal FBI unit with a code name—Retired General, Taxpayer, Patriotic Citizen, Member of DAR, Loving Father, and Alert. Such names were employed in anonymous phone calls and letters to the papers and to teachers, ministers, social workers, school presidents, and school-board members.

Miss Lucy Andrini was Cameron Pitt's most devoted and admiring follower. She employed the pseudonym Joan of Arc. As a student at the Dominican convent, she had played the role in the annual Easter play. That was before she became an heiress. She had inherited almost enough to pay for twenty-two years, eleven months, and twelve days of caring for her whining old mother; of accepting imperious commands, rebukes and abuses; of feeding her mother's two spoiled poodles; and of

From *The Lost and Found* by Ann Chidester. Copyright © 1963 by Ann Chidester. Reprinted by permission of McIntosh and Otis, Inc.

preparing mountains of soft, bland diet which the old lady spat over her clothes, the furniture, and the floor.

During these years of simulated meekness and servitude, Miss Lucy had also taken orders from her brothers, their wives, and a clan of nieces and nephews. Toward the end, the blue shade of approaching death showed around her mother's thin nostrils, and Miss Lucy whispered in her ear, "Mother? You make *me* richer than the others. I don't have a husband or a child, so I got to have *some*thing. I want your money and your land, you hear? You promised me that if I stayed home to care for you. So put it on paper right now, Mother, or I'll walk out of his house and never come back. *Then* Artie or Frank'll move in with their wives. Oh, that'd be the day! You better get the priest up here to witness it, so there'll be no doubt." Dutifully, in a final daydream, happy to be done with the world's ways and her daughter's virility, the old lady had signed over all but minor bequests to Lucy.

Now, Miss Lucy—alias Joan of Arc—went around in worn tweeds, winter and summer, her feet eased in scuffed tennis shoes. Her huge knitting bag was always nearby. Local wits said that, along with her stomach pills, she carried a loaded gun. She had her own little clique in The Patriots. These ladies were terrified of her lest, in a moody moment, she might strip them to the bone with her fearful tongue. She had a bad odor, too, though no one dared tell her. These days, with time on her hands, she could sit by the bay window for hours, watching and noting the passage of each pedestrian. In this way, she put bits of puzzles together to foretell scandals.

Her little group consisted of four wealthy widows. There was Luke Egan's mousy little wife, widowed at forty and still acting like a silly young bride; Leon Andrini's pretty Flora, lacking in intellect but gifted in making money, who feared Khrushchev might attack her and poked under her bed and into closets with a broom handle every night; Jane Ellen Bartless, a Florida woman who inherited oil leases from a husband well aware of her extravagances and clever enough to leave her money in trust, so that by the end of each month she had to go whining to Miss Lucy to borrow at seven and a half per cent; and Cleo Harper, a Christian Scientist, an aged sorority girl and an active clubwoman who spent her days writing letters to congressmen.

These four arrived early and separately with an elaborate show of stealth, leaving their big cars parked in side streets a few blocks from Charlie Best's drugstore. Miss Lucy, as usual, was already waiting for them. Together, they composed a vociferous claque for Cameron Pitt. He thought of them as ladies of position who shared his fear of the creeping Red invasion. Also, when he mentally added up their finances, he realized they could walk with the Queen of England without needing to borrow from her. All of them trembled when they thought of a brutal Communist invasion—rough, barbaric men forcing their way into their clean orderly houses, telling them what to do. God knows, no American man had succeeded in doing so!

Charlie Best's drugstore was a very new cement building awash with thin green lights for this meeting. Inside, the air was cool as in a cave with blue flickers of mirrors, chrome, and glass. The diffused light lay coolly over the massive counters in which costume jewelry, perfume bottles, and glossy soaps glinted like cats' eyes. Charlie himself, unctious and assured, received each member at the door. These were his best customers, and he clicked open the locked door, waited for the evening's password—Remember Gettysburg—and bowed from the waist like a headwaiter as they passed.

The women crowded into a booth like high school girls. Their faces were bright with anticipation. Nothing was so exciting as these meetings! They smelled of bath powder and laundry starch. Charlie, who knew what he was doing every minute, prepared each one a Coke with fresh lime and flirted with them out of his soft little eyes.

The ladies bent toward Miss Lucy. "What about Mrs. Ryan? You phone her?"

Miss Lucy put on a solemn, grave face. She studied her slim hands, for she loved her hands now that she could care for them properly—white, slender, heavily jeweled, and perfectly manicured twice a week, they must reveal her true personality, her womanly self. She looked with dark passion at the back of Charlie Best's handsome head where his hair curled sweetly over his fresh shirt collar.

"I followed instructions."

"Oh, we know that!" they quickly assured her.

"To the letter. I told her our decision. Will you believe it? She never spoke one word when I finished talking? I could hear her breathing at the other end of the line. She was waiting for me to give myself away, but I plain told her and hung up, like I was instructed. Also, I told those ranch hands of mine, believe me! Eight of them signed up for the union, and I got their names—never you fear. They thought I wouldn't know, but you can buy anything. I told them! I didn't feel we, any of us, had disloyalty coming to us. During the Depression, if we had a dollar our people got fifty cents of it, and that's the way it's always been here, but these Okies can give us real trouble. Nowadays, they've got too much swagger—too much education for their brains and station in life, I say. They don't know their places any more. Next year I'm hiring braceros and no one else. It comes to that—everyone's been telling me, but, no, I wanted to employ our own if I could—as long as I could." She sighed and shook her head.

They sighed with her—poor, lonely women left to run the complex kingdom of ranches, oil leases, manure and chemical businesses, banks and wineries and cotton ranches. Poor, weak little widows.

As they were whispering together, swinging their tired feet—Miss Lucy wore plaid tennis shoes to important events—the others began to arrive. There were red-faced Colonel Beasley Gifford who still hoped to command, though he was over fifty; Judge Howland, enjoying the company of typical Americans, anything to take away from his mother's

Mexican ancestry; groups of Joe Andrini's huge cousins with flashing diamonds and neon silk ties and bland smiles; two general practitioners, a veterinarian, a skin specialist, and three dentists, all of whom knew where the money was; Claude Winship, chief accountant for the land company and eager to be a state senator; Archer Hayden whose cattle brand was famous; the Egans, five handsome men in spotless Stetsons, none of whom spoke at these meetings, though they listened and watched and went away whispering excitedly among themselves, and about twenty rich ranchers, most of whose parents had spoken with accents of one kind or amother, whose roots were not yet deep in what they hoped was a classless society.

Often The Patriots met in one of Egan's barns or in Hayden's dairy office, as immaculate as any surgery, or in Miss Lucy's ranch house, deserted now that she no longer housed a foreman and his family. They pretended among themselves that people did not know or watch these meetings—and hoped they did.

"Tell us, Miss Lucy, what that smart reporter said when you phoned him?" Mrs. Bartless asked.

"Well! You'll never guess that Mrs. Deladier's going to make him editor. Yessir, God's truth, she is. I heard it from the horse's mouth, just about. Of course, he may or may not have known that when I called him. He kept asking my name, and I kept telling him, 'I'm a patriotic American citizen, telling you for your own good.' And I told him the Bible opposes socialism and the UN—I told him he'd better think about Cain some more. And I said if he was smart he'd write things we patriotic Americans wanted written. Or else." Her face showed her bewilderment.

"Oh my," they all sighed. Miss Lucy was wonderful, wasn't she? As good as any man too!

"Yes, but he said this odd thing. He said wasn't subsidy welfare in a way? I mean, taking subsidies for crops we didn't grow? Really, that young man is dangerous, I fear, and I doubt Mrs. Deladier realizes that, because if she knew she'd get rid of him, and I mean so to inform her."

"Oh, would you?" they asked. "You'd tell her?" Amy Deladier was more frightening than Miss Lucy because she was not a Patriot, though she surely ought to be, and she said such surprising things, like a young girl fresh out of college and full of high temper.

69   The Politics of Fear

In 1934 the defeat of the EPIC movement demonstrated what unlimited supplies of money and a good public relations firm could do in California politics. Since the war the computer and scientific sampling of voter opinion have contributed to a concentration of control in the political realm by efficiently analyzing information about the electorate and supplying it to politicians. Much of this control is based upon fear: fear of Communists, fear of student radicals, fear of blacks, fear of labor, or just fear of the unknown. The following selection deals with the way in which this control is exercised.

"You don't deserve to know, Terence," Mike said. "You don't really deserve to know how Cromwell will win, but I'll tell you. See, we know a few things about the undecided voters. And they're the ones that will decide the election . . . like always. We know that they're the people who are worried about something. So they hold off, don't make up their mind, keep trying to decide."

"So what, Mike?" Notestein said. "That's old stuff. But how are you going to find the undecided votes? And what do you do when you find them?"

"First, you find big groups of people that are worried," Mike said. "You don't worry about isolated individuals; big clots of worried people."

"Like the old-age people in the primary," Georgia said. "Tell them abut that, Mike."

Mike looked at her and smiled.

"O.K.," Mike said. "You brought it up, so we'll tell Terence about it. Remember, Terence, in the primary we didn't run much of a campaign. We did that deliberately. We didn't want a lot of excitement. We just wanted a slow, average primary. Because that brings out an almost equal number of Democrats and Republicans. Normally they would tend to favor Daigh because he's better known and if we hadn't done anything he probably would have won both nominations. But we did something. We talked to Mr. Appleton, one of the old-age leaders who, for some reason, seems dedicated to Cromwell. And very quietly, with no fanfare, we sent each person in the state over sixty years of age a letter."

"Tell them what the letter said, Mike," Georgia said. She looked at Hank as she spoke.

"Scared people don't vote for something, they vote against something or somebody," Mike said. "They vote their fears. So the letter, which was signed by Mr. Appleton, didn't even mention Cromwell. It just reviewed Daigh's voting record. In the last paragraph it just raised a doubt . . . a little tiny subtle fear that Diagh might not be for old-age pensions. That's all. And that's the only thing we did during the primary capaign. The only thing."

"How do you know the letter did any good?" Hank asked. "People might have voted against Daigh for a thousand reasons."

"Good question," Notestein said. "How do you know the letters worked, Mike?" He looked over the edge of his glass at Mike.

From *The Ninth Wave* by Eugene Burdick. Copyright © 1956 by Eugene Burdick. Reprinted by permission of Houghton Mifflin Co.

"Because we had a polling service take a sampling of all people over sixty in the state and see how they voted," Mike said. He grinned. "They voted eight to one for Cromwell. And the letter didn't even mention him. It just raised a doubt about Daigh. That's all it did. Raised a doubt that he might not give them a bigger pension or might reduce the pension they're already getting.

Unaccountably, for no reason that he understood, Hank felt a tiny gush of terror somewhere in his mind. Mike had just described a simple political trick and suddenly, inexplicably, the leakage of terror started in Hank's mind. For a wild second he tried to reason the matter out. But it did not make sense. Then he looked at Notestein. Notestein was holding the martini glass against his lip and faintly, almost audibly, his teeth were chattering against the glass.

Hank looked down at the white scraped turkey bones on his plate. He turned them over with a fork. Notestein had felt it, too. The terror flowed evenly across Hank's mind; was almost beyond control.

Then it came to Hank. Mike had just proved that he could do it; he had supplied the final piece of evidence. He had proved the point.

"That's not enough," Hank said, without thinking, blindly. "You need more than just the old-age vote. You have to pick up five hundred thousand votes to win in the general."

"That's right," Mike said, and his voice was hard and flat. "And up in an office on the top floor of the Golden State Building, we've got a research staff picking out every group, every locality, every organization that's got something to worry about this year."

"For example?" Notestein said. His eyes were bright and he had taken the glass away from his teeth.

"For example, Buellton," Mike said, "The little town of Buellton. A few restaurants, half dozen motels, a few gift shops. Five hundred people of voting age. They all make their living off the traffic that goes past on Highway 101. It runs right through the town. But the state engineers have a plan to by-pass Buellton. Make a new freeway that runs a mile south of the town. Every person in Buellton thinks it will ruin the town if the highway is moved. So you suggest to them that Daigh wouldn't object if the highway was moved. You don't have to say what Cromwell would do. You just let them know that Daigh favors moving the highway. That's enough. They won't care what Cromwell stands for. They'll vote against Daigh. And the only person they can vote for is Cromwell."

"How are you going to let them know?" Hank asked.

He was hoping that Mike would not have the answer. But he knew that Mike would. His fingers were trembling and he put them under the table.

"Lots of ways" Mike said. "Maybe you send a liquor salesman into Buellton. You have him mention in a few liquor stores and bars that Daigh is tied up with the asphalt interests and they want the new highway to swing around the town."

"What if Daigh doesn't have an interest in the asphalt business?" Hank asked.

"You think I'm going to say that the liquor salesman should say it, anyway," Mike said. "Well, you're wrong. Because what he says has to be plausible. The people in Buellton might check around. So if Daigh doesn't have an interest in the asphalt industry you look around until you find something he has done or said that indicates he would favor the new highway. Like a vote he cast for a highway appropriations bill four years ago that authorized a highway that by-passed a few towns. There's always something. And you have the liquor salesman say that. That's all you do."

Chapter 13

Clash of Cultures

Clash of Cultures

Californians like to boast that opportunity in the Golden State is open to all who are willing to work. The fact that the state is dotted with enclaves of enclaves of Italians, Armenians, Spanish, Basques, Portuguese, and many others of foreign extraction who have "made it" is pointed out as proof of the relative equality which exists. Unfortunately, however, western America has been mainly a white man's country, and discrimination against those of darker skin has been common. Such people have been tolerated, if at all, only so long as they accepted their role as servants for white masters.

The Anglos who came during the gold rush treated the native-born Hispanos with contempt in their own homeland, and, as one scholar puts it, "The Decline of the Californios" took place rapidly after statehood was attained. Fictional literature perhaps over-compensates by elaborating on the historical myth of the Spanish Arcadia when everyone was happy before the Anglo corrupted this blissful state. While singing the praises of this bygone era, writers ignored one real descendant of that past, the Mexican-American. Even great authors sometimes depicted the happy well-adjusted *paisanos* while ignoring their lack of social, political, and economic equality. Only in recent years has available writing effectively probed the problems of this largest of the state's ethnic groups.

Blacks were among the first Spanish settlers and grew slowly in numbers until World War II. In 1940 there were only 124,306 blacks in California; in 1951 there were 462,172, but this figure had grown to 1,400,143 by 1970. Overt discrimination was probably less common against blacks in California than in other parts of the nation, but they were still kept "in their place" by covert means. Discrimination also grew as blacks grew in number. There were few novels written about the state's blacks until World War II. The numerous books dating from that period probably came from the pens of black writers who came to California to take war jobs. Since the recent civil rights agitation, and especially since the Watts riots, fictional literature about blacks has multiplied.

Orientals have been the recipients of more maltreatment by the dominant white man than any other ethnic minority. For more than three quarters of a century the Chinese were abused at every opportunity. Excellent workers, they were preferred by employers, but hated by Anglo workers who felt that they were unfair competition. Laws deprived them of the protection of the courts while white hoodlums cut off their pigtails, pillaged their restaurants, splashed mud on laundry they were delivering, or chased them with fierce dogs. Harsh treatment and exclusion laws kept their numbers small so that by 1938 there were only 28,812 in the state. White writers have made Chinese customs the subjects of countless novels and short stories. Chinatown is a popular scene for expression of the clash of Occidental and Oriental manners. Some works treat the Chinese with sympathy and understanding, but there are but few works by their own countrymen.

There is an extensive literature concerning the Japanese by Anglo authors. Much of it depicts them as a threat to the Anglos of California, repeating popular beliefs that there was a gigantic conspiracy financed by the Japanese government to buy up the best land in the state. Writings by Japanese-Americans stress common cultural conflicts and, naturally, treat the wartime relocation extensively.

American Indians, the "first" Californians, were harshly treated by the Anglos from statehood on; and their plight has not improved in the twentieth century. In recent years they have left their reservations for the cities where they have had a most difficult time adjusting. Unfortunately, their conditions have not bettered economically in their new surroundings. Indians are often depicted in Western literature, but only a few writers have treated their contemporary situation with sympathy and understanding.

70   The Chinese

The Chinese, with their strange dress and habits, were discriminated against from the time they first arrived in California in large numbers in 1852. The prejudice was steeped in economic fear, for it was believed the Chinese presence depressed the prevailing wage. For that reason attacks upon them increased as hard times increased. The problems of these immigrants were expressed by one in these words: "To be starved in China or stoned in America was the alternative that confronted my countrymen." Note the viewpoint of the Chinese towards the workings of American institutions.

To be starved in China or stoned in America was the alternative that confronted my countrymen, so they came to a strange and inhospitable land and faced the angry foreign devils, smiling much and complaining little as they took bread and stones together. Having no official to speak for them, either to beg tolerance or to demand justice, they formed themselves into societies, according to the district whence they came, for their mutual benefit and protection; and when the presidents of these societies met together to consider matters of moment affecting all Chinese alike they were known as the Six Companies. But even they

From *The Night Tide* by Grant Carpenter. Published in 1920.

could not obtain justice, and in consequence there was much discontent among my people.

When the Six Companies ordered a great public meeting to discuss the matter, Quan Quock Ming, who had been mentioned frequently as a man of great learning and wisdom, though his face was scarcely known, was invited to attend; and everyone was astonished when he strode in quite late and, without pausing even to look to the right or the left or to make the usual salutations, took the seat of honor at the left of the president, Lee Tsi Bong, but his appearance was so impressive that none of the other presidents dared to ask him to take a lower seat, though they scowled with displeasure.

Through the whole meeting he sat on the edge of his chair with his knees wide apart and a hand on each, his shoulders straight, his head erect and his eyes fixed upon the scrolls from the classics that hung on the wall opposite; and Lee Tsi Bong seemed to shrink and Quan Quock Ming to expand with each moment that passed, until all spoke toward him, though he noticed them no more than a joss would a rag-picker or a woman.

"Honorable sirs," spoke Lee Tsi Bong, "this is a strange country of strange people and strange ways; a country where men respect even a bigfooted woman but have no reverence for their elders; where women are permitted to associate with men in public places and even to transact business; where no one worships his ancestors, and few have ancestors to worship; where all touch the filthy hands of one another on meeting instead of each shaking his own; where men take off their hats instead of their shoes on entering the home of a friend; where all have pale sickly faces and staring eyes, and the men have big beards and bald heads; where young men have the effrontery to wear beards before they have lived forty years; where every one boasts loudly of much law and great justice for all, though there is none for us. Now what can we do about all this?"

"The *fan quai* have many magistrates," said Chew Foo, the interpreter, "and lawyers are as numerous and as busy as cockroaches in a kitchen. Each has many rooms filled with books, and every book is filled with laws upon every subject that men may dispute over—even laws concerning the driving of horses, the catching of shrimps, the picking of chickens, the beating of wives and all such trifling matters. Yet, when we have disputes and buy a big lawyer at a high price, we often lose, though we have plenty of money to pay the magistrate."

"Now I would like to know what sense there is in buying a lawyer to lose a case, when one can just as well lose without paying a copper cash!" shouted Jeong Chuey, the merchant, and everyone said:

"*Hi low!* That is true!" and all nodded their heads many times.

"Even when a magistrate is paid by us to decide a cause in our favor," continued Chew Foo, "another magistrate says he was wrong and orders him to decide against us, but we never get our money back.

There is a magistrate for widows and orphans, a magistrate for promissory notes and other debts, a magistrate for gambling and a magistrate for murder, and there are still other magistrates over all these to say that the lesser magistrates are ignoramuses. There are magistrates for the city, for the district, for the province and for the whole country. Our disputes are taken from one to another, and before each a lawyer reads from his books saying the law is thus and so; and then the opposing lawyer reads from other books saying it is not thus and so, but this and that. The magistrate listens, finally saying what the law is, and then the lawyer who is dissatisfied takes the matter before another magistrate, who says that the first made a mistake. If anyone ever finds out what the law is, there are other officials who change it at once, so that no one ever knows it, though it is the law that everyone must know it. So if you pause to look into the windows of a *fan quai* and a foreign devil kicks you, you say to yourself: 'That must be a new law' and you pass on. It is not so in our country, for there the law is certain, the decision prompt and the punishment swift."

71   The Japanese

The Japanese, who began arriving in the state in increasing numbers after the passage of Chinese exclusion measures in the 1880s, were at first welcomed. Like the Chinese they were diligent workers, but they had none of what the Anglos saw as the "bad habits" of their fellow Orientals. Furthermore, they usually came as a family unit; thus, there were more field hands available. This selection is remarkable as it was written in 1907 when anti-Japanese antagonism was most extensive, but its conclusions remained true for a long time. These migrants were welcome as long as they were content to remain as servants but weren't wanted when they sought to acquire land and compete with their former white masters.

This gentleman was the first to indicate that they had not driven out to Lumalitas to discuss the weather and the scenery.

"Best come to business," he said, abruptly. "Judge, will you do the talking?"

But Judge Leslie, who was a modest man, waved his hand deprecatingly. "The idea is yours, sir, and yours is the right to state the case."

The host hastily poured whiskey-and-soda lest he should look haughtily expectant.

"It's just this, Mr. Gwynne," began Boutts, in his sauve even tones. "We have seen your ads. We know that you contemplate selling off a

From *Ancestors* by Gertrude Atherton. Published in 1907.

good part of your ranch—Well, there was a buzz round town when those ads were read, and I was not long passing the word that there would be a mass-meeting that night in Armory Hall. That's where we thresh things out, and in this case there was no time to lose. We had a pretty full meeting. Judge Leslie took the chair, and I opened with some of the most pointed remarks I ever made. I was followed with more unanimity than usually falls to my lot. The upshot was that resolutions were passed before nine o'clock, and a committee of four was appointed to wait upon you to-day—and endeavor to win you to our point of view," he continued, suddenly lame, for by this time Gwynne, forgetting Isabel and his good resolutions, was staring at the common little man with all the arrogance of his nature in arms, and the color rising in his cheeks. Mr. Boutts's hands gripped his knees as if for anchorage, and he proceeded, firmly: "No offence, sir, I assure you. This is a free country. The man who tells another man what he'd orter do should be called down good and hard. Nothing could be further from our intention. The meeting was called only in the cause of what you might call both self-defense and patriotic local sentiment, although it's a sentiment that's local to about two-thirds of California—only we do more acting and less talking than most. It's now some weeks since we adopted resolutions in a still bigger mass-meeting and got the best part of the county to subscribe to them; on the ground that an ounce of prevention and so forth. So we just hoped that as you have come to live among us you could be brought to see things from our point of view."

He scraped his hair forward and dropped his voice confidentially, at the same time darting a sharp glance through the open window beside him. "It's this Japanese business. The Chinese, back in the Seventies, was not a patch on it, because the Chinee never aspired to be anything but house servants, fruit pickers, vegetable raisers and vendors on a small scale, and the like. The agitation against them which led to the exclusion bill was wholly Irish; that is to say it was entirely a working-class political agitation, because the Chinee was doing better work for less money than the white man. The better class liked the Chinee and have always regretted the loss of them; and to-day those who are left, particularly cooks and workers on those big reclaimed islands of the San Joaquin River, where they raise the best asparagus in the world—yes, in the world, sir—get higher wages than any white man or woman in the State.

"But these Japs are a different proposition. They're slack servants, unless they happen to be a better sort than the majority, and that unreliable you never know where you are with them. And being servants is about the last ambition they've come for to this great and glorious country. They're buyin' farms all up and down the rivers, the most fertile land in the State, to saying nothing of some of the interior valleys. You see, there were big grants like Lumalitas at first over a good part of California. Then the ranches of thousands of acres were cut up and sold into farms of three or four hundred acres that paid like the mischief so long as the old man stuck to business himself. This he generally did; but times have changed, and now all the young men want to go to town; and most of the big farms have been cut up into little ones and sold off to immigrants and the like. Well, that's the Japs' lay. They like things on a small scale and know how to wring a dollar out of every five-cent piece. No one's denying they're smart. They slid in and got a good grip before we thought them worth looking at. Now we're saddled with about thirty thousand of them, and more coming on every steamer from Honolulu and Japan. Some years ago when they began to find themselves as a nation, and rebel at the foreigners that were ruling things through the open ports, they let it be pretty well known that it was going to be Japan for the Japanese. Well, now the sooner they know that it's California for the Californians the better it will be for all hands. We don't go round lookin' for trouble, but if it comes our way we don't mind it one little bit. We'll tolerate the Japs just in so far as we find them useful, and useful they are as servants; for if they don't hold a candle to the old Chinee, they're a long sight better than our lazy high-toned hired girls, who are good for just exactly nothing; and we need a certain amount of them for hire in other fields; but as citizens, not much. We've put a stop to that right here, in this country at least; and so, Mr. Gwynne, that's the milk in the cocoanut, and we hope that you'll see things our way, and not sell any of your land to the Japs."

"You see," interposed Judge Leslie, that Gwynne might not feel himself rushed to a decision. "These little men, while possessing so many admirable traits that I am quite willing to take off my hat to them, are not desirable citizens in a white man's country. Not only is their whole view of life and religion, every antecedent and tradition, exactly opposed to the Occidental, so that we never could assimilate them, never even contemplate their taking a part in our legislation nor marrying our daughters, but—and for the majority of the people this is the crux of the whole matter—commercially, and industrially, they are a menace. With their excessive frugality they can undersell the most thrifty white man, both as farmers and merchants; and the contempt they excite, particularly in this state of extravagant traditions, is as detrimental in its effects as their business methods; the more a man exercises his faculty for contempt the more must his general standards sink toward pessimism, and pessimism is neither more nor less than a confession of failure in the struggle with life. I never was much of a fighter, so I believe in eliminating the foe whenever it is possible. At all events we have made up our minds to eliminate the Jap, what with one motive and another, and I think we will. It may come to war in time—when the United States are ready—but we Californians have a way of taking matters into our own hands, and as war is a remote possibility, and we have little prospects of legislation—what with the treaty and the unpreparedness of the country for war—we just do what we can to freeze the Japs out. If we must have small farmers and our own young men have other ambitions, there are plenty of good European immigrants, and it is our business to encourage them. We assimilate anything white so quickly it is a wonder an immigrant remembers the native way of pronouncing his own name. But the Oriental we can't assimilate, for all our ostrich-like digestion, and what we can't assimilate we won't have. It is also true that we don't like the Jap. He antagonizes us with his ill-concealed impertinence under a thin veneer of servility; and superior as he is, still he has a colored skin. Now, right or wrong, Christian or merely natural, we despise and dislike colored blood, every decent man of us in this United States of America. Your sentimentalists can come over and wonder and write about us, reproach us and do their honest ingenuous best to convert us, it never will make *one damned bit of difference*. We are as we are and that is the end of it. The antagonism, of course, only leaps to life when the colored man wants equal rights and recognition, something he will never get in the United States of America, as long as the stripes and the stars wave over it; and the sooner the sentimentalists quit holding out false hopes the better. As to the Chinese, it is quite true that there was no objection to them outside of politics. And the reason was, they kept their place. The antipathy to the Japanese extends throughout all classes. Every thinking man in the State is concerned with the question. California will be overrun with them before we know where we are; and we are hoping that other counties will give an ear to the wisdom and farsightedness Mr. Boutts has displayed, in proposing that no more land shall be sold or rented—to the Japanese. They can work for us if we have need of them, for a while, but they cannot settle."

Gwynne had been thinking rapidly as Judge Leslie drawled out his homily. In his new apprehension of latent weaknesses in his character he was indisposed to yield to pressure, but he was equally desirous not to let the turmoil into which his inner life had been thrown lead him to any ridiculous extremes; not only interfering with his prospects, but converting himself into chaos. He was extremely anxious to make no mistakes at the outset of his new career, beset with difficulties enough. Their words had every appearance of being a just presentment of a just cause. He didn't care a hang about the "Jap." For the matter of that, he reflected with some bitterness, he didn't care a hang about California. At this point in his reflections he became aware that Colton was turning his head with a sort of slow significance. He looked up and watched a pale eyelash drop over a deep gleam of intelligence. Mr. Leslie finished speaking, and Gwynne replied with an elaborate politeness, which might be his vehicle for spontaneous sympathy or utter indifference,

"Thank you all very much for your confidence in me, and also for preventing me from making what no doubt would have been a serious mistake. I have no desire whatever for the Japanese as a neighbor. I was one of the few to recognize the menace of Japan to Occidental civilization when all the world was sympathizing with it during its war with Russia, and they will get no encouragement from me. So the matter is settled as far as I am concerned."

72   The Lonely Crusade

Historically, blacks were spared the harsh discrimination suffered by
Orientals in California. The reason for this was that their numbers were
small. But as blacks came to the promised land in search of economic
opportunity they, too, felt the oppression of the dominant white. This
selection tells of "the lonely crusade" of one black man who was born in
California and sought to improve his position in life. Although the black
probably had a greater chance to succeed in the Golden State than
elsewhere in the nation, he was still denied equality because of the color
of his skin.

Lee and Ruth had been married for eight years that spring of 1943. For Lee
their marriage had been the beginning of his life. Before had been nothing
but a bewildering sense of deficiency and a vague fear of momentarily being
overtaken by disaster.

At the time of his birth in 1912, Negroes were only servants in
California. His parents, Tom and Anna, worked as domestic servants on
a Pasadena estate, and he was born in the pleasant little servants' cottage
out in back. In later years when he wondered why he was the only child,
his mother told him that he had caused a problem by his birth, and her
"missus" had asked her not to have another.

The schools in Pasadena were not segregated. But the Negro
students were known to be the children of the servants and were treated
as such.

When he first entered school, Lee was the only Negro in his class.
Even then before it was given other meaning, his black skin was a
handicap. It made him hard to hide. Whatever he did, he was always
caught.

But it was not until his first year of geography when he was nine
that he came to understand the stigma of his skin. All the class learned
that black people were heathen savages, many of whom were cannibals
besides. The teacher explained, however, that those in America had been
Christianized. But even with that, it was a hurting thing to learn.

Soon afterwards in his history class he learned that Negroes had
been slaves. For a time he wondered if his parents were still slaves, but
he was too ashamed to ask them.

In 1926 he was fourteen. He was in the eighth grade. Outside of the
curriculum he had not participated in any school activities. He had
never had a buddy. The white students had not been deliberately
unkind; they had ignored him.

He had learned nothing to make him proud of being a Negro and
everything to make him ashamed of it. The most complimentary thing
he had learned concerning Negroes was that they had been freed from
slavery. He had never heard the mention of a Negro above the level of a
servant. When asked concerning his nationality, he did not know

From *The Lonely Crusade* by Chester Himes. Published in 1947.

whether to say he was an American or a Negro.

He came to believe that something was lacking in Negroes that made them less than other people. In gym, during showers, he carefully observed the white boys. The only difference he discovered was the color of their skin, and this seemed no superior attribute. In his first year biology class, he asked about the qualities of skin a number of questions that caused the teacher embarrassment. The teacher kept him after class one day to find out what was troubling him.

"Is white skin better than black skin?" Lee asked bluntly.

"There is little difference in the skin itself," the teacher carefully replied. "But the color of skin—along with other things, of course—denotes the division of the races."

Lee was not answered, but at least he knew that white skin of itself was no advantage.

Perhaps the difference was in girls, he thought. He had heard sly talk among the white boys that the vaginas of Chinese women extended crosswise. This decided him to hide in the girls' gym and watch them undress. "They don't look any different," he observed. They weren't even prettier.

Then he was caught, expelled. His parents were discharged, requested to leave the city. It happened with such sudden devastation, devoid of warning or appeal, that he was terror-stricken. He could not understand what he had done that called for so great a penalty. The year before, a white boy, halfback on the football team, had been caught in the very act with a girl. Though he had been expelled, nothing had happened to his parents, his home had not been destroyed, his family had not been banished from the city overnight. What Lee Gordon could not understand was why his spying on the white girls in the gym was considered so much worse.

"Were you after one of those little girls?" his mother asked.

"I just wanted to see them," he replied fearfully.

"For why?"

"Just to see if they were different."

For a long moment she simply looked at him. Then she said in a voice of positiveness: "You're just as good as any white person. Don't you let nobody tell you no different."

"Now all you got to do is prove it," his father said, whether sincerely or satirically Lee Gordon never learned.

But his mind would not dismiss it so easily as this. He came to feel that the guilt or innocence of anything he might do would be subject wholly to the whim of white people. It stained his whole existence with a sense of sudden disaster hanging just above his head, and never afterwards could he feel at ease in the company of white people.

His parents moved to Los Angeles where his father got a job as janitor in a department store while his mother did daywork in Beverly Hills. Lee entered Jefferson High School where the enrollment was almost equally divided between Negroes and whites. Slowly he overcame his constant trepidation, but the harassing sense of deficiency still remained because just the fact of different color didn't answer it. Nor could he forget what had happened in Pasadena.

He came to wonder if there was something about white girls which grown-up white people were afraid of a Negro finding out—some secret in their make-up that once discovered would bring them shame. It made him curious about white girls, but filled him with caution too. Sometimes he watched them covertly but never made advances; he did not want to bring disaster down again. At the time of his graduation he had never said more than a dozen words to any white girl in his class.

Late one night the following summer as his father left the store where he worked, he was mistaken for a burglar by policemen and shot to death. The Negro churches organized a protest demanding that the officer be punished. But the city administration contended that it had been a natural mistake, and nothing was done about it.

Lee had never loved his father nor greatly respected him and was not deeply grieved by his death, but he felt an actual degradation by the callousness of those responsible. The fact that they called it a "natural mistake," as if all Negroes resembled criminals, only confirmed what he had learned in Pasadena. But to know that any Negro might be killed at any time a white person judged him to be a criminal filled him with a special sort of terror.

After that he was afraid to be caught after dark in white neighborhoods. Each time he left the Negro ghetto he felt a sense of imminent danger, as if any moment he might be mistaken for a thief and beaten, imprisoned, or killed. It made just walking down the street, just crossing Main Street into the poor white neighborhood beyond to buy a loaf of bread, a hazard.

A collection of twelve hundred dollars was taken up among the department-store employees and the members of the police force. The policeman who had fired the fatal shot gave one hundred dollars and got his picture in the paper. The owners of the department store gave two hundred dollars more.

And this too seemed more degrading than charitable. If this was what his father's life was worth to all these people, a Negro's life was nothing. He had once read where a pedigreed dog was worth more actual money and held in higher esteem. For the first time bitterness came into his life. He lost all ambition. Why try to be somebody in a world where he resembled a criminal and was valued at less than a pedigreed dog? But afterwards it served as a spur to his ambition. He would prove that he was worth more than that. He might never become important, but at least he would make white people give him more consideration than they had given his father. He made a vow he would pass beneath the earth no common shade.

With the fifteen hundred dollars donated for his father's death, he entered the University of California at Los Angeles. In many respects he found college but a repetition of the grammar school in Pasadena on a higher level. But he went prepared for the lack of Negro recognition in American education, and he expected no honor for himself. At home his mother was finding it difficult to make ends meet. To help pay his way Lee washed dishes and waited table in the white fraternity houses.

On the whole, his college life was not unpleasant. He kept away from where he was not wanted, and had a few companions among the students both Negro and white. The Negro students had activities among themselves, and a Negro fraternity was represented. But Lee did not have the time or money it required to take part. He lived just beyond the edge of social life, concentrating on his studies.

After his first year he majored in sociology. His greatest interest was in the how and why of people—what it was in some that gave them a sense of superiority, and what was lacking in others that contributed to this feeling of inadequacy. And though he learned much about the sources and the causes, he never learned about the logic of it.

The most unpleasant thing that happened to him occurred at a lecture on minorities in his sociology class. The young professor compared the problems of the Negro minority with the problems of the homosexual minority, contending that of the two the latter suffered the greater discrimination. Lee drew the implication that black skin was also being considered as an abnormality. This he rejected bitterly, denouncing the parallel drawn as stupid and malicious; and was asked to withdraw from the class.

He graduated in the spring of 1934. The only employment that he could find for Negro college graduates was in domestic service. This he refused to do.

The neighbors condemned him for sitting home and letting his aging mother support him by working in the white folks' kitchens. It was then he first got on his muscle; he resented their pious judgments. He could not begin life as a domestic servant; nor did his mother want him to.

The day before that Christmas his mother died. Some said from overwork. Others said from heartbreak over seeing her son go bad.

After that the only thing that kept him going was a posed belligerence, a high-shouldered air of bravado, disdain, even arrogance. For many times he went hungry. And always he went alone. . . .

He met Ruth in March 1935. He had stopped to get cigarettes in a drugstore on Central Avenue. A former classmate from the university looked up from his soda.

"Hey, Lee, whataya know, boy?"

Lee turned. "Hello, Hank, what's new?"

"The white folks on the top and the niggers on the bottom. But that ain't new."

"Make 'em kill you," Lee said with a laugh.

"They doing that without my help," Hank replied dryly, then added: "Say, I want you to meet this gal. Ruth Roberts, Lee Gordon."

She turned from beside Hank on the soda fountain stool and smiled. Both she and Lee knew at that moment that they were made for each other, as it is given to some people to know.

"Ruth and her mother are here on a visit; she's a St. Louis gal," Hank went on. "Pretty, isn't she?"

But they were not listening. She looked at Lee through eyes like two lighted candles in a darkened church, and in them he was seeing the end of loneliness and the faintest stir of meaning in a meaningless world. They were together then in wonder, and in time following they were together in each other's hearts.

One night in April as they stood in the hard, cold rain where Skid Row crosses Main Street aching with desire for each other, he reached for her hand and said spontaneously:

"We could get married."

She was the first girl whom he had loved, and the only one. But he had not intended to ask her to marry him. She was a college graduate with at least the promise of a better future than himself.

But her reply: "Yes Yes!" had been waiting for the question.

Her mother disapproved. It was not that she disliked Lee. Only that she could see no future for a Negro of Lee's temperament. After all, most Negro college graduates had served an apprenticeship with mop and pail before they got ahead, she pointed out. Once during a dinner party at a dentist's convention in Atlantic City, which she and her late husband had attended, some prankster had shouted: "Front, boy!" and all but one of the successful dentists stood quickly to attention, she related laughingly.

Nevertheless, the following day she went with her daughter to the Justice of the Peace where Ruth and Lee were married. And the following day she went home.

At first their marriage was like a tale by Queen Scheherazade set to music in a blues tempo, the bass keys sounding out a series of shabby rooms that somehow anchored their sordid struggle for existence—room rent when it was due and enough food for each meal coming up. Not once during that time did they buy any salt, or sugar either, until each landlady in turn learned to keep hers put away. And the treble keys sounded laughter in the night.

Marriage made him break his promise to himself. He worked at many jobs that he had refused before—bus boy in a hotel dining-room, porter in a downtown drugstore, laborer in a cannery during the spinach season. And as often, he did not work at all.

For two months Ruth was seriously ill. He sat beside her bed and nursed her back to health. He never paid the doctor who treated her.

But they braved the hunger and the illness, and the next spring he got a job at the country club serving drinks in the taproom. It was the best job he had ever had, a job where all he had to do to earn fifteen dollars or more each night was just to be a nigger. But he was afraid of the members when they became drunk. They said things to him even a nigger should not be expected to take. What finally gnawed him down to a jittery wreck, however, was the fear that one might ask the price to see his wife, as one had asked another of the waiters. He simply quit.

He had thought that with Ruth he would never be afraid again. But it merely changed the pattern of his fear. Now it was the fear of being unable to support and protect his wife in a world where white men could do both. A fear that caused him to look inside of strange restaurants to see if Negroes were being served before entering with his wife.

Slowly, this changed the pattern of their relationship. For he could not contain his fear or resolve it. His only release for it was into her through sex and censure and rage.

Twice they were refused service in downtown restaurants. Each time he stood there in that blinding, fuming, helpless fury, moved by the impulse to beat the proprietor to a bloody pulp, restrained by the knowledge of the penalty. As enraged at having Ruth witness his cowardice as at being refused.

Each time having to decide before jerking her out into the street the value of his pride and how much he was prepared to spend for it.

Each time accepting Ruth's tense entreaty: "Let's go, Lee. Don't get into any trouble; it's not worth it."

Each time lying awake all night, hating her for offering him the easy and sensible way out. Tortured by the paradox of managing to live on by accepting things that afterwards made him want to die.

73   The Plum Plum Pickers

Most ethnic minority immigrants have been integrated into American life by the time of the third generation. Mexican-Americans have not generally followed this pattern largely because the continual influx of migrants from south of the border, legal and illegal, has helped keep the Hispano culture alive. In many large cities, they have their own world which is distinct from that of the Anglo, complete with businesses, newspapers, television and radio stations. A person can live out his life in the barrios of San Antonio or Los Angeles and seldom hear English spoken. This makes assimilation especially hard for the young people who don't really belong to the Mexican world of their parents, are educated for entry into the Anglo society, but face rejection by many in that society. This is Margarita's dilemma in the following.

Throwing back her covers, Margarita tiptoed barefooted to the window and ducked under the drawn window shade. She liked looking out at dawn. Her favorite game, whenever she awoke early enough, was looking out through the window when dawn was coming on. She was half dreamy, half awake, in a world alone, all her own, all by herself, the only real privacy she could ever find. She loved life, she loved the world and everything in it. She was thrilled with the bigness of her capacity for love, and most of all she loved watching the way the sun came up faithfully every morning, lighting everything up so beautifully. The sky began to barely burn light gray on the horizon, exposing the profiles of the nearby Diablo Mountains as a long, low range of hills, darker than the houses and orchard trees on both sides of the Drawbridge High School buildings. Some of the lights were still lit on the school grounds, burning with a light purple glow on tall thin posts.

She heard the motors of the powerful, heavy trucks along the nearby Bayshore Freeway, taking produce up the Peninsula to San Francisco, or up the other side, the Nimitz Freeway to Oakland. She liked the peacefulness of the countryside under its cool misty cover and, as the sun got ready to lift itself above the mountain humps, its rays lit the undersides of some long, low slivers of clouds, setting them aglow with a wedge of silvery orange fire against the gradually lightening, brightening gray sky. She liked it just the way it was. It was so peaceful and calm. She wished she could stop it, the whole process, that it would stay exactly that way forever. She hated the thought, she hated the prospect of having to face another day filled with hatreds, fights, and unknown ordeals. She knew life could be so beautiful, but its beauty eluded her. What did she have to do to suck the joy out?

High school, everybody said, was supposed to be so much fun. It wouldn't be bad if only the kids would leave her alone. The Anglo boys teased her unmercifully. "Hey, Margarita—give me one of your sexy looks." That was their way of complimenting her. Well, she hated it. The blonde girls were jealous, mean or nasty, and always superior and often suspicious of her. But why? Why? She didn't like having the world split between Mexican and Anglo, but that was how it was, and she tried to make the best of it. She wasn't always successful. The teachers were all right. But so innocent. What it was, they really didn't care. They didn't like getting involved. They didn't want to probe too deeply. Besides by instinct they couldn't help siding with their own kind, with their own Anglo kids, against the Chicanos. Or else they'd do something worse—they'd be patronizing toward her, dripping with false sympathy, and that was much, much worse. She could stand on her own feet. She didn't need any special favors. All she wanted, wanted, all she asked for and seldom got was plain, simple, decent, ordinary kindness. Most of the kids fortunately were indifferent toward her and left her alone. Some of them, however, the tormentors, liked occasionally going out of their way to be real mean.

Drawbridge High wasn't a big school. It was brand new, though, with long low pretty pinkstoned buildings. Only two years were in, and Margarita was keeping pace with its growth and progress. She wished oh many times she wished she could quit school altogether. Not for any reason she could put her finger on. She was just plain unhappy. What good was school doing her? She didn't find school stimulating. She liked to study things she liked, but what was the use? And all the kids were always yapping away about which college they were going to go to. No thank you. What, and go through all this stupid nonsense all over again? What good were books if people insisted on being so mean? And what good was studying if no one gave you any credit for knowing anything? She knew she could learn anything she put her mind to. She knew she could get all the good grades she wanted to, just by concentrating. But why do it? When all they did was laugh and tease and poke fun at you and your looks? Lucky she wasn't ugly like some of the jealous gueras, but she sometimes felt it was better to be a repulsive, ugly blonde guera than pretty, Mexican, and dark skinned. That was the way it was. And that was the way it was always going to be. What good did it do to be ambitious? And a girl? And a Mexican girl? She knew those things bugged Danny too, but Danny at least had his sports and the track team and the swimming team, and he could laugh and play big man and fight back and so they respected him. But she didn't want to fight back. She was always being goaded and annoyed and insulted in mean little ways. Always having to smile back. Always having to go out of her way. Always avoiding conflicts. She didn't like it. That was why she wanted to quit. She wished she could. . . .

She admitted to herself that she secretly liked the way boys looked at her. She knew she thrilled at their longing. But she didn't like the way they teased her unmercifully. They always did it in front of other girls. For their benefit, it seemed. She couldn't stand being teased, toyed or played with. She knew it was their way of flirting with her but still she didn't like it. She was really too grown up for them. They seemed so like children, immature and spoiled. She was already dreaming of having a proud blue-eyed prince for a husband, a lover who would give her everything she wanted from life, who would fight for her and relieve her emptinesses.

There were some Anglo boys she liked but she would never dream of letting them know. The Mexican boys, the Chicanos, treated her diffidently, either with distant disregard, as though waiting, or, some she didn't like, with mean looks of longing in their narrow black eyes. Some of them scared her, but not in a mean way. She would always take care of herself with that kind. But the Anglos, the gueros, who liked to jostle and joke. . . . She wished she could stop smiling at them when they did it and show her anger but she smiled each time they hurt her and she did it only not to give her hurt away and also and especially for the gueras. The gueras considered her their rival maybe because the boys teased her and paid her so much attention. She could tell. She could tell from the way they studied her from the dormers of their lightly made-up eyes, and from the way they smirked behind their upraised arms. As though making believe they were only coughing. But also really making sure she saw. . . .

Slowly, shyly, timidly, the sun's edge peeked above the distant range, a tiny pinpoint of fire at first. She looked at it in fascination. A brand new sun. Another brand new kind of life. A brand new hope. It glowed fiercely. It shimmered. It hung suspended. It nestled for a split instant between a cradle of small peaks like an incandescent orange topaz. It grew bright, hotter, and more dazzling each fragment of a second. She imagined it to be a giant sizzling jewel, perhaps an engagement ring that her princely lover came all the way across the heavens to give her to wipe out all the misery she was suffering. Then the yolk burst. The orange ball tugged itself free of the mountain peaks and blazed so fiercely it burned everything in sight—the trees, the morning mountain, the school, her eyelids. Too bright. Too hot for her to look at directly any more.

She turned her eyes away, seared, sizzled.

It was going to be another hot day again.

Where did she come from? Why was she here? Lupe often talked about Mexico and Guadalajara, but Mexico was nowhere for her. It was as foreign to her as Belgium. Did that mean she had no home? In Mexico she had seen that, except for the very rich, just about everybody was very poor. Two extremes. At least here in her country, in the U.S., everyone that wanted to could work and not be ashamed of being poor, or partly poor, or poor in the sense of not starving but perhaps not having everything you saw in sight in all the shop windows or TV ads or big discount houses. Or even of being just a poor slob of a worker, for everybody worked at something. Still, there were times she couldn't help feeling she didn't belong, even though she had been born right here in Santa Clara, an American born, a citizen by birth. What good was it? What was the good of being born a perfectly good, honest, private, legal citizen of the United States of America if everyone was going to snarl Mexican to your face like it was some hateful word? Where did she belong then? Back in her mother's home town? In her father's? In Salpinango? In Guadalajara? Would they send her back there? But what if she wasn't from there, from any of those places either? What then? She didn't belong there, in old Mexico, either. She was California born, California . . . which once was Mexico. California—which once belonged to her people, for hundreds and thousands of years. And now she didn't belong. In Mexico, on her two brief visits, the native Mexicans there always considered her as an American. She also sensed they also thought her family was very rich because she had pretty clothes. True, she had brought her prettiest dresses; but she'd made most of them herself, and had earned the money for the yardage either babysitting or picking prunes. How could she explain that they weren't rich? That although her father earned more money in a month than most of their relatives earned in a year still didn't make him rich because the cost of living was so high in the U.S.? But how do you explain to poor people, who are poorer than you, that you aren't rich? The answer is . . . .

The answer is, you don't explain. You can't.

The sun vaulted higher. Margarita continued standing there, letting its hot head press down hard on her cool forehead. Its heat felt odd, against the cool pane of that early morning hour. Summer—and summer picking. The household was beginning to stir now. Her mother was moving about in the kitchen, moving pots softly, putting water on to boil, and her sisters in the bathroom were running water. They were all getting ready for another outing, another day's prune picking in family summertime.

Prune picking was essentially and practically a family job. It was more fun and more practical that way. The prune growers preferred families to single pickers. The Delgado family lived right in the middle of the biggest prune county in the world, and there was nothing, absolutely nothing to gathering prunes. Papa Pepe went off to his regular job in the cannery when he wasn't running crews for Roberto Morales. Daniel, big man, would have nothing to do with prune picking. Mama protected him. Serafina liked spoiling him. Daniel liked strutting about showing off his flamante clothery and driving his dad's car around town when Pepe didn't need it or used his pickup instead. Danny chauffered them to that day's picking, then went off on his rounds, looking for big things to do with his big time with other big do-nothings. When asked what do you do that for by his older sister Rosa, he'd reply laughing, Sure—what for?

The orchard owners were good employers. The prune gatherers got as much work as they wanted, and in return they always showed up and executed their agreed contract as promised. It was a good agreement, and mutually beneficial. The prune pickers didn't have to travel around the country, like so many hapless migrant workers, so many now that they were coming in thick like flies to help with all of the heavy crops now ripening, the apricots, the pears, and later the walnuts. The pickers got their wages, and the growers kept their land. Everybody was happy. Even the bankers. Serafina was especially happy to see Mr. Turner so pleased; it was a sure sign that his bank vaults were probably spilling over, and nothing made her happier, for that meant more work for her and hers. She didn't care how much richer the rich got. She didn't like all that radical talk among her compañeros about how the rich ought to be stripped of every dollar and every hectare of land. That was terrible. The rich had earned what they got. They worked hard. They suffered. They sometimes lost, she had heard. They risked their capital. And without them, where would she, and all other poor families be? No, it was good to have good, fat, rich, and—yes—even greedy capitalists in their midst, for that way they all had work and they all could work to their hearts' content, from sunup to sundown if they wanted to, to be able to keep alive. They should be grateful, not critical, her compadres. How ungrateful they were!! But she pardoned even them, for they did not know what they did in condemning the poor, abused capitalists.

Serafina found she could always work her brood as a family unit just as much or as little as they pleased. All they had to do was put in time pretty steadily to make it worth the while. It was necessary to get up early to get out to the orchards. At summer all the kids thought of was playing, for nothing, so outdoor work was good for them. Pepe shrugged his shoulders, letting mama control this aspect of the family's recreation. Pepe took care of the heavy bills, the house payments, the car, the utilities, the food. The money mama wanted and that the kids helped earn helped her buy extra clothing and small luxuries for themselves. It wasn't any longer needed just to keep themselves alive, as had been true in the past, and as was still true of many migrating families she knew.

Daniel drove them over to the new section. Mr. Schroeder was there with Manuel, looking down the rows of trees, in his brand new green pickup. Laid out in many rows, plenty of shade in the long slanting rays of the sun, the kids leaped out of the car like so many dolphins, happy, yelling, hooting, and rolling over each other.

Then the long, monotonous day's work began.

74 Rabbit Boss

Of all ethnic groups in California, American Indians occupy the lowest rung of the economic and political ladder, have the shortest life-expectancy, fewest years of education, and the lowest income. At one time confined to reservations and rancherias, these "first Californians" have drifted into the cities in search of a better life. This selection is from a recent novel about the tragic experiences of four generations of a Washo family of the California-Nevada Sierra region.

"Four, I ate four,"the girl dropped the bones in her uncle's plate.

"Joe likes to hear what us Indians are doin for ourselves."

"No he doesn't."

"Count 'em, that's four."

"Don't you, Joe."

"That's only three and a half."

"What, three and a half what?" Felix questioned his brother-in-law, the smile on his face stretching out in all directions.

"Three and a half chicken bones."

"So what has that got to do with what we was talkin about?"

"Everything, one's a neck. She said she ate four and everybody knows there ain't hardly no meat on a neck. It only counts for half."

"That was a fat chicken," the girl insisted.

"What's this got to do with what I was talkin about," Felix repeated, his smile stretched so far it was about to snap.

"Everything, Indians only count for half, half man, they ain't white."

"I don't think that's fair, Joe. Every time we talk you find some way to bring the conversation around to the fact that I'm only half Paiute."

"I wasn't talkin about you, Felix, I was talkin about chicken necks and Indians."

"Well, I'm an Indian."

"Then you're only half. Best you can ever be is half."

"That's just why we have meetin's. That's just the reason."

"You won't find the other half there."

"How do you know, you never been to none. Why don't you come and find out."

"Don't have to, I already know."

"How do you know?"

"Because every Sunday I come over here you start in talkin about those meetin's for the Indian to better himself and you ask me to go."

"So how do you know they don't do any good?"

"Cause you're still only half."

Felix pressed his cigarette butt in the slime of gravy on his plate, it made a small hiss and he spoke, "What do you think you are, whole, one hundred percent?"

"Didn't say that."

"You can't, that's why. You don't have the nerve. You don't do anything for yourself. Your hire on for a day or two whenever some rancher in the valley needs fencin or buckin hay or an extra hand with the cattle."

"I am the Rabbit Boss."

"But you're not a Washo Rabbit Boss, you're a strawhat, a *hired* whiteman Rabbit Boss."

"Ain't no difference as I see it, Rabbit Boss is Rabbit Boss no matter what time he's living in, any end you look through it's all the same."

"The same," Felix leaned across his plate, his smile stretched so tight it was twitching. "How can you sit at my table, in my house, and tell me it means the same where I know it don't. How can you abuse your own people who were real Rabbit Bosses, respected men that were needed for all to survive. How can you compare yourself to them that did something, something noble. You! You're nothing but a strawhat, a hired Indian with a rifle, hired by a whiteman to keep the rabbits from chomping up all his range grass or his stupid cattle from fallin into their holes and breakin a leg that holds up all those pounds of money meat. You're a hired game warden, you ain't even that, you're just an exterminator. That's it, an exterminator, like one of them guys you get when the termites is eatin your house and you get him quick so's he can exterminate before the house comes fallin down round your ears."

"Ain't no termites in this valley, too cold."

"That's not what I meant."

"Well that's what you said."

"Example, Joe," Felix let out a sigh and sat back in his chair, lighting another cigarette. "Just an example. Can't you understand what an example is?"

"No, it ain't got nothin to do with me."

"Why do you do what you do Joe?"

"It's the only thing for an Indian to do."

"It isn't, that's just the point," Felix was leaning over his plate again. "There ain't too many Indians left in this valley anymore, and those that are all have some kind of job."

"So do I."

"But it's not a respectful job."

"Is to me."

"But it isn't to *them*."

"It's not *their* job, it's mine."

"Your job is outdated, Joe. They have no need for you. You're just cheaper than poison."

"It would kill the cattle, they tried it once."

"The whole idea of what you're doin is out of time. You're the last livin Rabbit Boss there is, I haven't heard of any others in the complete State of California, and there's certainly none over the hill in Nevada. When you die it's over. No one will care, let alone notice."

"What's that got to do with me?"

"It's got everything to do with you, you're an Indian."

"But you're talkin about a dead Indian, makes no difference to a dead Indian if it's over when he dies."

"You're not dead yet."

"So what are you going on about Felix?"

"Joe, I'm talkin about you, your past and your future. Before *they* came a little over a hundred years ago there were over three thousand of your people, now you're lucky if you can scare up three hundred Washo. The Washo, the Paiute, all the Indians got to get together and join with the whiteman before we don't have anything to join with. They made a mess of this country of ours and this is the Indian's last chance to straighten them out. If we get organized and join them as an organization of people then we can point to a nobler way of life through example. Examples of art and nature and brotherhood and . . ."

"Felix," Birdsong interrupted. "Why is it every Sunday you go on about how Indians are the last hope. You tell me the same thing week after week, year after year, you never even bother to change the words around a little, and you go over to Truckee and tell it to those people at the meetin's and then they tell it back to you again and back and forth it goes, you all tellin each other how if *they* don't recognize you as an organization *they* will come to ruin just like that place in history called Rome, because you're the last hope, and all the while *they* keep going on like they always been, without you, and all the time no closer to that Rome place than when *they* was tearin the mountains down for gold and silver or rippin the trees from everywhere to put up houses. *They* didn't need you then and *they* don't need you now, and if *they* do reach that place like Rome there won't be no redman alive to see it."

"Joe, you're an ignorant man and a twice as ignorant Indian."

"Goodbye," Birdsong stood up quickly, the chair falling to the floor behind him.

75   The New Centurions

Blacks in California benefited from the civil rights agitation which began in the 1950s. But efforts to attain equality with whites by nonviolent means were set back as a result of the Watts Riots in Los Angeles in August 1965. The riots were responses to problems such as housing discrimination, unemployment, inadequate public transportation, and long-standing resentment over police brutality. The week-long holocaust left thirty-four dead (mostly blacks), 1,032 injured, 3,500 arrested, and $40 million in property damages. This selection is from a novel by a Los Angeles policeman on duty during the riot. Unfortunately, the attitudes expressed by the police in this novel represent a not unusual approach.

Before driving three blocks south on Broadway, which was lined on both sides by roving crowds, a two-pound chunk of concrete crashed through the rear window of the car and thudded against the back of the front seat cushion. A cheer went up from forty or more people who were spilling from the corner of Eighty-first and Broadway as the Communications operator screamed: "Officer needs help, Manchester and Broadway! Officer needs assistance, One O Three and Grape! Officer needs assistance Avalon and Imperial!" And then it became difficult to become greatly concerned by the urgent calls that burst over the radio every few seconds, because when you sped toward one call another came out in the opposite direction. It seemed to Serge they were chasing in a mad S-shape configuration through Watts and back toward Manchester never accomplishing anything but making their car a target for rioters who pelted it three times with rocks and once with a bottle. It was incredible, and when Serge looked at the unbelieving stare of Jenkins he realized what he must look like. Nothing was said during the first forty-five minutes of chaotic driving through the littered streets which were filled with surging chanting crowds and careening fire engines. Thousands of felonies were being committed with impunity and the three of them stared and only once or twice did Peters slow the car down as a group of looters were busy at work smashing windows. Jenkins aimed the shotgun out the window, and as soon as the groups of Negroes broke from the path of the riot gun, Peters would accelerate and drive to another location.

"What the hell are we doing?" asked Serge finally, at the end of the first hour in which few words were spoken. Each man seemed to be mastering his fear and incredulity at the bedlam in the streets and at the few, very few police cars they actually saw in the area.

"We're staying out of trouble until the National Guard gets here, that's what," said Peters. "This is nothing yet. Wait until tonight. You ain't seen nothing yet."

"Maybe we should do something," said Jenkins. "We're just driving around."

"Well, let's stop at a Hundred and Third," said Peters angrily. "I'll let you two out and you can try and stop five hundred niggers from carrying away the stores. You want to go down there? How about up on Central Avenue? Want to get out of the car up there? You saw it. How about on Broadway? We can clear the intersection at Manchester. There's not much looting there. They're only chunking rocks at every black and white that drives by. I'll let you boys clear the intersection there with your shotgun. But just watch out they don't stick that gun up your ass and fire all five rounds."

"Want to take a rest and let me drive?" asked Serge quietly.

"Sure, you can drive if you want to. Just wait till it gets dark. You'll get action soon enough."

When Serge took the wheel he checked his watch and saw it was ten minutes until 6:00 P.M. The sun was still high enough to intensify the heat that hung over the city from the fires which seemed to be surrounding them on the south and west but which Peters had avoided. Roving bands of Negroes, men, women and children, screamed and jeered and looted as they drove past. It was utterly useless, Serge thought, to attempt to answer calls on the radio which were being repeated by babbling female Communications operators, some of whom were choked with sobs and impossible to understand.

It was apparent that most of the activity was in Watts proper, and Serge headed for One Hundred and Third Street feeling an overwhelming desire to create some order. He had never felt he was a leader but if he could only gather a few pliable men like Jenkins who seemed willing to obey, and Peters who would submit to more apparent courage, Serge felt he *could* do something. Someone had to do something. They passed another careening police car every five minutes or so, manned by three helmeted officers who all seemed as disorganized and bewildered as themselves. If they were not pulled together soon, it could not be stopped at all, Serge thought. He sped south on Central Avenue and east to Watts substation where he found what he craved more than he had ever craved for a woman—a semblance of order.

"Let's join that group," said Serge, pointing to a squad of ten men who were milling around the entrance of the hotel two doors from the station. Serge saw there was a sergeant talking to them and his stomach uncoiled a little. Now he could abandon the wild scheme he was formulating which called for a grouping of men which he was somehow going to accomplish through sheer bravado because goddammit, someone had to do something. But they had a sergeant, and he could follow. He was glad.

"Need some help?" asked Jenkins as they joined the group.

"The sergeant turned and Serge saw a two-inch gash on his left cheekbone caked with dust and coagulation but there was no fear in his eyes. His sleeves were rolled up to the elbow, showing massive forearms and on closer examination Serge saw fury in the green eyes of the sergeant. He looked like he could do something.

"See what's left of those stores on the south side?" said the Sergeant, whose voice was raspy, Serge thought, from screaming orders in the face of this black hurricane which must be repelled.

"See those fucking stores that aren't burning?" the sergeant repeated. Well they're full of looters. I just drove past and lost every window in my fucking car before I reached Compton Avenue. I think there's about sixty looters or more in those three fucking stores on the south and I think there's at least a hundred in the back because they drove a truck right through the fucking rear walls and they're carrying the places away."

"What the hell can we do about it?" asked Peters, as Serge watched the building on the north side three blocks east burning to the ground while the firemen waited near the station apparently unable to go in because of sniper fire.

"I'm not ordering nobody to do nothing," said the sergeant, and Serge saw he was much older than he first appeared, but he was not afraid and he was a sergeant. "If you want to come with me, let's go in those stores and clean them out. Nobody's challenged these mother-fuckers here today. I tell you nobody's stood up to them. They been having it their own way."

"It might be ten to one in there," said Peters, and Serge felt his stomach writhing again, and deliberately starting to coil.

"Well I'm goin in," said the sergeant. "You guys can suit yourselves."

They all followed dumbly, even Peters, and the sergeant started out at a walk, but soon they found themselves trotting and they would have run blindly if the sergeant had, but he was smart enough to keep the pace at a reasonably ordered trot to conserve energy. They advanced on the stores and a dozen looters struggled with the removal of heavy appliances through the shattered front windows and didn't even notice them coming.

Chapter 14

A New Society?

A New Society?

To many, California is the window to the future, or as the poet Richard Armour has put it:

> So leap with joy, be blithe and gay,
> Or weep, my friends, with sorrow.
> What California is today,
> The rest will be tomorrow.

In 1966 the British Broadcasting System saw California as a probable land of tomorrow. They filmed a television program projecting what the future world would be like, and based it on the Golden State. To large numbers of Americans who flocked westward after World War II, California symbolized another chance at fulfillment of the American dream. Here they hoped to enjoy the good life where drudgery, toil, and the ravages of nature would be minimized. One engineer, fleeing Long Island, when asked why he came to California, replied, "It's not the better job that I'm interested in alone. It's the way of life." In other words, the state is still for many the land of promise which draws the hopeful seeking that better way of life. Life in California still vibrates with opportunity. Despite smog, congestion, and the brutalization of the landscape, it is still one of the most beautiful areas of the world. Thousands of people who are free to make a choice still prefer California as the most desirable place in the world to live. Many who return to the rigors of an eastern or midwestern winter soon retrace their steps and come back to California. It remains a place of refuge for healthseekers from the rest of the nation.

With all of its advantages, California gave indications that man's hopes for this paradise might be shattered in the last quarter of the twentieth century. The new society which had emerged had its manifestations of vulgarity, hedonism, materialism, and superficiality. Many essays and scholarly articles have sought to analyze these deficiences. And with the economic slow down of the mid-1970s, and the shortage of energy, these efforts increased. Fiction writers have often grasped the tenor of this new California society far more effectively than scholars, examining its good points as well as its bad ones.

Alison Lurie, in *The Nowhere City*, was a bitter critic of much she saw in and around Los Angeles, yet she caught the promise of this new society also. Her novel's main character is amused by Los Angeles' bewildering array of architectural styles but sees a positive contribution from this effort: "Let them build and tear down and build again; let them experiment. Anyone who can only see that some of the experiments are 'vulgar' should look into the derivations of that word. . .

" 'You're really going all the way out to Los Angeles?' some of his friends had exclaimed, men who spoke daily in familiar terms of ancient Mesopotamia or Transalpine Gaul. Paul had his answer to this. Historians looked backwards too exclusively, he said. Los Angeles obviously expressed everything towards which our civilization was now tending. As one went to Europe to see the living past, so one must visit southern California to observe the future."

76 I Loved You, California

In the fall of 1962 the Golden State passed New York as the nation's most populous state. This prompted many questions about the nature of the number one state. Leading magazines, newspapers, and even books attempted to answer why people found California so attractive. The state's own humorist, Richard Armour, offers some observations in the following poem. Beneath the poem's veneer of fun, some important points are raised about the emerging new society. Note, especially, Armour's belief that California was what the rest of the nation would become.

California, here they come:
Doctor, lawyer, merchant, bum.
They come by car and train and plane,
Straight from Kansas, Georgia, Maine,
Massachusetts, Minnesota,
Iowa and North Dakota.
Rich folk, poor folk, young folk, codgers,
Moving westward like the Dodgers.

Here they come, and here they are,
Living, dying in a car,
Ever moving, dawn to dark,
Looking for a place to park.

Drive-in movies, drive-in cleaners,
Drive-in spas for burgers, wieners,
Drive-in banks and colosseums,
Drive-in (one-way) mausoleums.

Under and over
    In Chevy or Cad,
Some, caught in a clover
    Leaf, slowly go mad;

From Look, September 25, 1962. Reprinted by permission of Richard Armour.

While some, with scant leeway,
    Slow-reaction-time men,
Miss a sign on the freeway,
    Aren't heard of again.

Here, superlatives abound;
"Best" and "most" are all around:
Finest roads and oldest trees,
Biggest universities,
Hottest day and highest lake,
Lowest point and hardest quake,
Most of most, no ifs or buts,
First in peaches, pears—and nuts.

        Divorce?
        Of course.

Build a house upon a hill,
Or a cliff, so that you will
Get a view of row on row
Of other houses down below.
Out with trees, and don't lament;
Fill the valleys with cement.
Thus is nature redesigned
By the modern one-tract mind.

Bulldozers aren't dozing
    By night or by day;
They're opening, closing
    And gnawing away,
Making molehills of mountains
    (The golf course now rules),
Turning lakes into fountains
    And swimming pools.

Hail the warming sun above,
Golden Bear and poppy love;
Hail the jackpots, crackpots, crooners,
Fog and smog and displaced Sooners.
Life begins at sixty-five,
When the pension checks arrive;
Then, with smiling, carefree faces,
Off to Bingo or the races.

So leap with joy, be blithe and gay,
    Or weep, my friends, with sorrow.
What California is today,
    The rest will be tomorrow.

What California then will be
   Is something I'd as soon not see.
                    Richard Armour

77 A Time on Earth

America has been described as a nation of immigrants, and California is surely a state of immigrants. Recent surveys indicate that three-fourths of its citizenry was born elsewhere. Californians are also especially mobile; they move an average of once every four years while the national average is once every seven years. These factors contribute to feelings of rootlessness common to many of the state's citizens. The transplanted Californian often misses his friends and relatives, and even the seasonal changes "back home." However, when he does return to his former place of residence he usually finds that things have changed so much that he no longer belongs there. Friends and relatives have passed on or have no place in their lives for the one who left them so long ago. Many Californians, disgusted with smog, traffic, or the deterioration in life style, have returned to the small towns from whence they came only to return sheepishly to California in a year or so. Vilhelm Moberg, who wrote several novels about Swedish migration to America, probes the problem of the immigrant who feels as though he doesn't belong in his adopted land but who also feels that he no longer belongs to the land of his birth. This is the plight of many Californians.

The place where I live is on the shore of the Pacific. The greatest of the world's oceans surges just outside, and Room 20, the Pacific Hotel, Surf Street, Pine Beach, is my home on earth.

My room has two windows. Through the one facing the street, I see automobiles and trucks moving in an endless stream; through the other I watch the arching rollers of the ocean. The roar of traffic and the rushing of surf—the noises from the street to the east and the water to the west—blend in my ears. The cars on Surf Street sound like the whirring of a giant spinning wheel, increasing, while the thunder of the sea rises and falls with the movement of the waves, like breathing from the depths of the world's lung. The engines roar, crash and rattle; the waves of the deep smash themselves against the rocks of the shore with the sound of great guns, so that the water shoots upward and washes the tops of the cypresses. In daytime the voice of the town prevails, at night that of the sea. By day the noise of engines holds sway over my ears; at night the ocean rules alone.

The sound of the street is as young as the street itself, the sound of the sea as old as the elements. The motor voice will fall silent and the spinning wheel stop, while the ocean continues to hurl its breakers to the beach. Then the sea will be the sovereign ruler by day and by night.

I live between the man-made and a primal element, being myself an incidental phenomenon on the earth. Between the ephemeral and the eternal I have my home.

In this incidental existence I am one of the inhabitants of the little town of Pine Beach in Southern California, one immigrant among the mass of immigrants from Europe. Here the weather is pleasantly mild, the sun pleasantly hot, the wind pleasantly cool, the sea water pleasantly warm. Orange trees grow, and fine fruits ripen. This is the last settler-state, the last frontier. An average of 1,700 people arrive here on each of the 365 days of the year. The daily throng of newcomers is large enough to form a community of its own; a new town could be founded here every day. Young people come to our coast in search of the ancient, original sources of joy—sun and sea—and here they start a new life.

Here, for the young, life feels young. For me, Albert Carlson, an old immigrant, it is otherwise. I am of an age when the power of renewal is lost. The days have now come when I no longer experience anything that seems to me worth experiencing.

At one stage in my life I had a series of places to live in. I lived in houses, equipped and furnished with all the mechanical gadgets that man has invented for his greater convenience and comfort. I had spacious houses to live in, but I never felt at home in any of them. I did not stay long in any of them. I had several dwellings, but no home.

Here in my hotel room with the number 20 on the door I shall stay as long as I can. I wrote recently to my elder son, who was christened Albert after me: "I intend to stay here in Pine Beach and live in a hotel for the rest of my life, if I can afford it. I shall sit here at my window, looking out over the Pacific and thinking about some of the things I've done and known."

From now on I want to be stationary. The later years of my life have been largely spent in traveling. The object of a journey is to arrive at a certain geographical point; yet for my journeys there was no goal anywhere on the globe. Judged by results they were futile: they had no results. I sought something that I was forced to seek, but the goal was within the traveler himself and not to be found elsewhere: I was looking for protection against my awareness. That is what kept me on the move, pursued me and forced me to fresh departures. Journeys for me were like narcotics against pain; they relieved the symptoms but never touched the cause.

How many times in my life have I moved from place to place! But for me physical removal solves nothing.

· · ·

I have just returned from a journey to the place where I was born. Only a week ago I was at the other side of the world. A week ago I was sitting in another hotel room. This hotel was in an industrial community in Småland, Sweden, and the room was much like my present one in the Pacific Hotel, Pine Beach: it was entirely modern, and fitted out on the American pattern. Motor traffic rolled along the street outside, though more sparsely, and the makes of the vehicles were in most cases the same as on Surf Street. Next to the hotel, as here, was a filling station where brands of oil were advertised in English. In the center of the town was a bar where ice cream, Coca-Cola and hamburgers were served, and where there was also a jukebox which emitted a ceaseless stream of songs and dance music: hits from America. Above the counter hung a sign: DRIVE-IN BAR. Posters announced that the "Sweden Artists" were appearing in a Jack Dalley Show in the Folk Park, and that the Andersons' enormously popular twist band, "New Sound Twist Pop," provided the dance music.

America had overtaken me and was moving into my old home district. Each time I have been back to my country I have noticed the changes: each time, Sweden has become less Swedish.

Now, by the roads of the air, I had made another journey home, but not to stay. Not for a moment did I imagine that a final return to Sweden was possible for the old emigrant who bore my name. The Swedish-Americans of my age who go back to find the home of their childhood are the victims of self-deception. There can be no return to that country for anyone. I can go back in the superficial sense, to the soil, the houses, trees, waters, fields. I can go back to things, but never to the domain of childhood. There can be no retracing of one's steps to the world of growing up, for this world has turned into dreams and memories forever. Here I stand rebuffed outside a door that is barred.

After more than forty years in the United States I have become a foreigner in the land where I was born and bred. Father and Mother are dead, my brothers and sisters are dead. Some of my relatives survive, and some contemporaries I knew in my childhood, but among them I am almost entirely forgotten. I am just a name to be mentioned with the added comment: "He went to America."

. . .

Now I felt just like that ghost in the legend, who could not find his bride or his home. I was an unknown person in an unknown place which was inhabited by unknown people. I had been absent for a shorter period than the man in the legend, for only forty years had elapsed since I lived in that parish; but it might just as well have been three hundred years. It would have made no difference, for I could not have felt more of a stranger. I had emerged from the past and was haunting my home. . . .

Never again shall I see the place where I was born.

After six weeks as a ghost in my old mother country, I came back to the land where I shall die.

78 The Glad and Sorry Season

Loneliness is a way of life in California, especially for the newcomer. Churches stress their social advantages, newspapers advertise social clubs, and computerized dating and apartments for singles are common. A curious aspect of this loneliness, of not having someone to talk to, is the prevalence of radio talk shows. They are available at all hours of the day and night, and provide an outlet for the individual who has only the four walls to converse with. Much of what these people have to say may not be worth saying, but such shows are very popular. This selection tells how a recent arrival from New York City views this kind of radio outlet for suppressed emotions, and how she deals with her own loneliness.

September

Dear E. R.:

I started working today. It's a long and tedious job. I'm responsible for arranging telephone interviews on a two-way radio program that's on the air from 2 P.M. until 6 P.M. There are about ten arranged calls between the host and various movie stars, politicians, rioters, creeps, and crazies. When the host is not talking to someone notable, he's answering the phone and trying to make conversation with the inhabitants of this city who have nothing better to do than call radio programs and holler out their guts and broadcast their stupidities. I have to monitor all the calls as they come in and make the decision about which will make interesting air fare. It's just horrendous.

John Stagg is really a nice guy. I know pretty faces of that sort throw you, but ask Oliver. He liked him and I'm sure he would have even if John hadn't brought him a frog. Anyway, John's the typical Good Liberal, if such a thing is possible; he tries to be gracious and talk to the nuts decently, but you can't imagine the vitriol and spleen that gets vented. There's some kind of mechanical cutoff so that the robots who listen to the program in their cars or kitchens don't hear the filth. But we hear it. Every other call I pick up I hear someone calling me a kike, fag, commie, fink and/or pervert. And I can't hang up on them. I have to be polite and see if I can calm them down to some semblance of sanity and then turn them over to John to talk to on the air. One of them saved up till he got on the air and then threatened to bomb John's house and have his wife's face scarred. All this because Stagg is in favor of gun legislation. Can you imagine! I don't know if this kind of two-way radio thing is happening in New York, but it's the Big Thing here. By the time I get home my head is crammed with noise and insanity, but it always has been, come to think of it, and at least now I'm getting paid for it.

The real-people interviews are kind of fun. It makes me giggle when I have to call the White House and arrange for the Secretary of State or whatever to be available for the phone. And then I have to kind of chat along and set up x number of questions that will be covered on the phone call during air time.

Occasionally we do an in-studio interview. A sort of interesting guy came in yesterday. He's the publisher-editor of one of those fringe magazines like the East Village Other, but on slick paper. Quite attractive. He used to work on the New York Times, with by-lines and everything, and gave it all up to drop out into the world of the misplaced comma, the complainer, the protester, and the dirty classified ad. Not to mention dirty fingernails. But he asked me out to dinner. There is a suspicious light mark on his wedding-ring finger. Just like Italy, I suspect, where the ring gets hidden in the pocket at the beginning of the rendezvous. But I am going crazy. I'm also having this weird "acting out" problem, as they say in the shrinkery business, and I've just been madly running around and screwing everything that moves. Anyone who comes through the door gets a boff, and it's weird because most of them are old friends of Catherine's who don't know she's in Synanon, and people who work at the radio station (which I think is a bad idea), and assorted freaks and strangers. It's an eerie business. I don't want any of them, I don't like any of them and I just can't keep it from happening.

I haven't been able to write to Max in a while, and obviously it hasn't thrown him into wild despair because he hasn't written to me either. So at least the magazine man has made a dinner offer and maybe I can taper off behind Mexican food. You know that indiscriminate balling has never been my scene, but I have never had such horrors about being by myself before. I can't read, I can't sit, I can't watch the magic box, and I don't want to make idle chatter. What I do make is a rotten lay. It must be like banging Pinocchio and no compliments and return engagements are forthcoming. Thank God. This too shall pass. Hopefully before I get the clap, which is an illness my horoscope says I am prone to. Hee-hee. It's not as bad as it sounds. I don't think.

And don't kiss Oliver for me, I'm probably contagious. And love me in spite of myself.

                                                                    Sarah

                                                            September

Dear Max:
    Things are going along smashingly for a change. My job is fantastic. I get to have all the fun. Yesterday was a black militant named Frank Rage (his real name and his constant state) and an inventor named Sweetsby, who develops weapons for the police to use in riot situations. He and Rage loved each other a lot. We got four phone calls saying they were going to blow up the station. Two from blacks and two from whites! John Stagg, who is about as left-wing as your brother Salvatore, the priest, didn't know where to look first or what to say. It

ended up quite terrifying, with Sweetsby telling Rage that he could rant
all he wanted to but when push came to shove "we have the might, we
have the guns, we have the money, and you will have nothing but more
of the same."

At that point I wanted to go out and buy Rage a gun myself, if he
promised to get Sweetsby with it first. Poor John. His intentions are
good, and his effectiveness little in the world. But one would think that
he was the reincarnation of Marx, Lenin, Stalin, and maybe Trotsky too.
Letters have been coming in threatening his life, and mine occasionally.
I prefer the ones that offer Christ as a solution. I wish I knew if it was to
be laughed at or not. Everyone hates us. The blacks who come in for
interviews put us down for not having any blacks on the staff. I'm the
staff. Am I supposed to quit? The rednecks tell us we're nigger lovers,
the Jews holler we're Arabs, and the Arabs yell that we're Jews. That's
close but not really important. And the cuckoos. What vile and deranged
people live here. They're everywhere I guess, but insanity in the tropical
sun, coming out of the mouth of a blond, blue-eyed, cute person is very
frightening. Fortunately I don't have to see them, but they sound bad
and frightening on the phone, and when I'm marketing or in the
laundromat I always wonder whether the person next to me isn't
someone who called the program one day and threatened to kill me, or
called me a kike. So, I'm a rag when I get home.

The fringe benefits of these jobs are always rather nice. You get put
on the screening lists of all the movie companies, so that you can
sensibly discuss the latest epic with the inarticulate producer or director,
so you get to see a lot of good movies, free, and a lot of bad ones, which I
really like best. And loads of free records and invitations to cocktail
parties and all that sort of thing. Being the Lady Producer of the fastest-
talking show in the West I bound around constantly and dine out
frequently on one-liners laid on the air waves by various Birchers and
"in" people.

Doesn't that make you happy? Do you love the idea of me being
Miss Gadabout?

Darling, I'm writing this in the studio . . . and it's time to start
answering the phones. Come to think of it, why don't we set up a call
with you? You can expound on the inner meaning of advertising.
Wouldn't that be fun, and I could get to talk to you. Let me check and
see if they want one of those and then I'll call you like a lady and ask.

ciao
Sassy

October

Dear Edith:
I really was thinking about hopping a plane and coming to New
York for a couple of days but things have taken a turn for the better (or

worse, I don't know which). I had jokingly suggested that we arrange a long-distance telephone call for the show in which John Stagg would interview Max and get the low-down on the advertising world. Stagg thought it would work, didn't question my judgment about who would be the best spokesman for the Ad Biggies, and told me to go ahead and fix it up. I called Max and he said he thought it would be funny to do but that he would prefer to handle it from here, where he expects to be shortly. You can expect not to hear from me until after he's gone.

And don't call because I won't answer the phone. I promise a play-by-play description. He seemed anxious to see me. God knows I'm anxious to see him. So, we'll see.

The job is a bitch. I'm in a state of babbling collapse. The other day we had an in-studio go-round with the world's foremost consumer of acid; he appeared with a cohort, a snappy-mouthed writer. It was a loony tune. The Healer, as he calls himself, ranted and raved about how HE had the answers to the world's problems, how HE could revolutionize civilization and return the human being to a proper human condition— one of lovingness and enlightenment—and incidentally how HE had passed a bad check off on the airline to fly from his home to our studio, and how HE and how HE. The writer, who had been very silent during most of the interview because he was loaded and hallucinating, finally came through with one line that justified his entire presence as far as I'm concerned. When the Leader finished his twenty-minute monologue about how marvelous HE is, the writer shrieked, "And ladies and gentlemen you have been privileged to hear the Leader in his present state of Purification. Can you imagine what an earful he would have given you before the dissolution of his ego?" It all made me very happy. I'm allowed carte blanche in the booking of the show and am busily giving every nut and marginal in the vicinity free air time. It makes me laugh a lot.

79   The Dharma Bums

California has been the first home to a number of youth movements, two of the best-known being the "beat" generation of the 1950s and the "hippy" culture of the 1960s which made a household word of Haight-Ashbury, a San Francisco neighborhood. In the following selection, Jack Kerouac tells what it was like to be a part of the beginnings of what became known as the "beat" movement. At the heart of the movement were its poets, and readings like the one described were common. Kerouac also suggests the important part which some Oriental philosophies, especially Zen Buddhism, played in "beat" poetry and life style.

From *The Dharma Bums* by Jack Kerouac. Copyright © 1958 by Jack Kerouac. Reprinted by permission of The Viking Press, Inc.

Anyway I followed the whole gang of howling poets to the reading at Gallery Six that night, which was, among other important things, the night of the birth of the San Francisco Poetry Renaissance. Everyone was there. It was a mad night. And I was the one who got things jumping by going around collecting dimes and quarters from the rather stiff audience standing around in the gallery and coming back with three huge gallon jugs of California Burgundy and getting them all piffed so that by eleven o'clock when Alvah Goldbook was reading his, wailing his poem "Wail" drunk with arms outspread everybody was yelling "Go! Go! Go!" (like a jam session) and old Rheinhold Cacoethes the father of the Frisco poetry scene was wiping his tears in gladness. Japhy himself read his fine poems about Coyote the God of the North American Plateau Indians (I think), at least the God of the Northwest Indians, Kwakiutl and what-all. "Fuck you! sang Coyote, and ran away!" read Japhy to the distinguished audience, making them all howl with joy, it was so pure, fuck being a dirty word that comes out clean. And he had his tender lyrical lines, like the ones about bears eating berries, showing his love of animals, and great mystery lines about oxen on the Mongolian road showing his knowledge of Oriental literature even on to Hsuan Tsung the great Chinese monk who walked from China to Tibet, Lanchow to Kashgar and Mongolia carrying a stick of incense in his hand. Then Japhy showed his sudden barroom humor with lines about Coyote bringing goodies. And his anarchistic ideas about how American don't know how to live, with lines about commuters being trapped in living rooms that come from poor trees felled by chainsaws (showing here, also, his background as a logger up north). His voice was deep and resonant and somehow brave, like the voice of oldtime American heroes and orators. Something earnest and strong and humanly hopeful I liked about him, while the other poets were either too dainty in their aestheticism, or too hysterically cynical to hope for anything, or too abstract and indoorsy, or too political, or like Coughlin too incomprehensible to understand (big Coughlin saying things about "unclarified processes" though where Coughlin did say that revelation was a personal thing I noticed the strong Buddhist and idealistic feeling of Japhy, which he'd shared with goodhearted Coughlin in their buddy days at college, as I had shared mine with Alvah in the Eastern scene and with others less apocalyptical and straight but in no sense more sympathetic and tearful).

Meanwhile scores of people stood around in the darkened gallery straining to hear every word of the amazing poetry reading as I wandered from group to group, facing them and facing away from the stage, urging them to glug a slug from the jug, or wandered back and sat on the right side of the stage giving out little wows and yesses of approval and even whole sentences of comment with nobody's invitation but in the general gaiety nobody's disapproval either. It was a great night. Delicate Francis DePavia read, from delicate onionskin yellow pages, or pink, which he kept flipping carefully with long white fingers, the poems of his dead chum Altman who'd eaten too much peyote in Chihuahua (or died of polio, one) but read none of his own poems—a charming elegy in itself to the memory of the dead young poet, enough to draw tears from the Cervantes of Chapter Seven, and read them in a delicate Englishly voice that had me crying with inside laughter though I later got to know Francis and liked him.

Among the people standing in the audience was Rosie Buchanan, a girl with a short haircut, red-haired, bony, handsome, a real gone chick and friend of everybody of any consequence on the Beach, who'd been a painter's model and a writer herself and was bubbling over with excitement at that time because she was in love with my old buddy Cody. "Great, hey Rosie?" I yelled, and she took a big slug from my jug and shined eyes at me. Cody just stood behind her with both arms around her waist. Between poets, Rheinhold Cocoethes, in his bow tie and shabby old coat, would get up and make a funny speech in his snide funny voice and introduce the next reader; but as I say come eleven-thirty when all the poems were read and everybody was milling around wondering what had happened and what would come next in American poetry, he was wiping his eyes with his handkerchief. And we all got together with him, the poets, and drove in several cars to Chinatown for a big fabulous dinner off the Chinese menu, with chopsticks, yelling conversation in the middle of the night in one of those freeswinging great Chinese restaurants of San Francisco. This happened to be Japhy's favorite Chinese restaurant, Nam Yuen, and he showed me how to order and how to eat with chopsticks and told anecdotes about the Zen Lunatics of the Orient and had me going so glad (and we had a bottle of wine on the table) that finally I went over to an old cook in the doorway of the kitchen and asked him "Why did Bodhidharma come from the West?" (Bodhidharma was the Indian who brought Buddhism eastward to China.)

"I don't care," said the old cook, with lidded eyes, and I told Japhy and he said, "Perfect answer, absolutely perfect. Now you know what I mean by Zen."

"I had a lot more to learn, too."

80   Angle of Repose

The "hippy" culture was various in its manifestations and not easily defined. However, many so-called "hippy" groups were alike in their attempts to establish Utopian communities. Communes sprang up all over California. Each had its own unique origins and goals, but all were concerned with building a society which would be counter to the dominant culture, rejecting the values of "The Establishment."

In the following selections from a novel by Wallace Stegner, the narrator talks about what he sees as the major flaw in the commune movement—lack of a sense of history. Extending California's present-oriented viewpoint, many young people knew little of the past and refused to acknowledge value in learning it.

Nevertheless, neither Ada nor I should expect a girl of twenty to sit in this quiet place very long, working seven days a week for the Hermit of Zodiac Cottage. For reasons best known to herself she chose to cut away from the Berkeley scene and rusticate herself here. But here she is a stranger to everybody she used to know, including her old schoolmates. They have nothing to offer her, she has nothing to give them except an occasion for a lot of lurid gossip. Probably she *was* the brightest student in Nevada City High, as Ada resentfully says. Somewhere, sometime, somebody taught her to question everything—though it might have been a good thing if he'd also taught her to question the act of questioning. Carried far enough, as far as Shelley's crowd carries it, that can dissolve the ground you stand on. I suppose wisdom could be defined as knowing what you have to accept, and I suppose by that definition she's a long way from wise.

Anyway, this afternoon when I was sitting on the porch after lunch she came in and without a word, with only a prying, challenging sort of look, puckering up her mouth to a rosebud, handed me a sheet of paper. It was mimeographed on both sides, with stick figures and drawings of flowers scattered down its margins—a sheet that might have announced the Memorial Day picnic-and-cleanup of some neighborhood improvement association. I've got it here. It says

MANIFESTO

WE HOLD THESE TRUTHS TO BE SELF EVIDENT TO EVERYBODY EXCEPT GENERALS, INDUSTRIALISTS, POLITICIANS, PROFESSORS, AND OTHER DINOSAURS:

1) That the excretions of the mass media and the obscenities of school education are forms of mind-pollution.
We believe in meditation, discussion, communion, nature.

2) That possessions, the "my and mine" of this corrupt society, stand between us and a true, clean, liberated vision of the world and ourselves.
We believe in communality, sharing, giving, using without using up. He is wealthiest who owns nothing and needs nothing.

3) That the acquisitive society acquires and uses women as it acquires and uses other natural resources, turning them into slaves, second-class citizens, and biological factories.
We believe in the full equality of men and women. Proprietorship has no place in love or in any good thing of the earth.

4) That the acquisitive society begins to pollute and enslave the minds of children in infancy, turning them into dreadful replicas of their parents and thus perpetuating obscenities.

We believe that children are natural creatures close to the earth, and that they should grow up as part of the wild life.

5) That this society with its wars, waste, poisons, ugliness, and hatred of the natural and innocent must be abandoned or destroyed. To cop out is the first act in the cleansing of the spirit.

We believe in free and voluntary communities of the joyous and generous, male and female, either as garden communities in rural places or as garden enclaves in urban centers, the two working together and circulating freely back and forth—a two-way flow of experience, people, money, gentleness, love, and homegrown vegetables.

NOW THEREFORE

We have leased twenty acres of land from the Massachusetts Mining Corporation in North San Juan, California, four miles north of Nevada City on Route 49. We invite there all who believe in people and the earth, to live, study, meditate, flourish, and shed the hangups of corrupted America. We invite men, women, and children to come and begin creating the new sane healthy world within the shell of the old.

What to bring: What you have.
What do do: What you want.
What to pay: What you can.

FREEDOM   MEDITATION   LOVE   SHARING   YOGA

Address: Box 716, Nevada City, California

When I finished the front side and looked up, Shelly was watching me, moodily running a rubber band through her front teeth like dental floss. She said nothing, so I turned the sheet over. On the back were three quotations:

Let the paper remain on the desk
Unwritten, and the book on the shelf unopen'd!
Let the tools remain in the workshop!
Let the money remain unearn'd!
Let the school stand!

My call is the call of battle, I nourish active rebellion.
He going with me must go well arm'd,
He going with me goes often with spare diet, poverty,
angry enemies, desertions.

WHITMAN

The practice of meditation, for which one needs only the ground beneath one's feet, wipes out mountains of junk being pumped into the mind by the mass media and supermarket universities. The belief in a serene and generous fulfillment of natural desires destroys ideologies which blind, maim, and repress—and points the way to a kind of community which would amaze 'moralists' and eliminate armies of men who are fighters because they cannot be lovers.

The traditional cultures are in any case doomed, and rather than cling to their good aspects hopelessly it should be remembered that whatever is or ever was in any other culture can be reconstructed from the unconscious, through meditation. In fact, it is my own view that the coming revolution will close the circle and link us in many ways with the most creative aspects of our archaic past. If we are lucky we may eventually arrive at a totally integrated world culture with matrilineal descent, free-form marriage, natural-credit Communist economy, less industry, far less population, and lots more national parks.

GARY SNYDER

Let these be encouraged: Gnostics, hip Marxists, Teilhard de Charlin Catholics, Taoists, Biologists, Witches, Yogins, Bhikkus, Quakers, Sufis, Tibetans, Zens, Shamans, Bushmen, American Indians, Polynesians, Anarchists, Alchemists . . . . . . Ultimately cities will exist only as joyous tribal gatherings and fairs.

BERKELEY ECOLOGY CENTER

I passed the sheet back.

"Keep it," Shelly said. "I've got more. What do you think?"

"I like the part about the home-grown vegetables."

"Come on!"

"What do you want me to say? OM?"

"Whether it makes *sense* or not."

"It's got plenty of historical precedents."

"What do you mean?"

"Plato," I said. "In his fashion. Sir Thomas More, in his way, Coleridge, Melville, Samuel Butler, D. H. Lawrence, in their ways. Brook Farm and all the other Fourierist phalansteries. New Harmony, whether under the Rappites or the Owenites. The Icarians. Amana. Homestead. The Mennonites. The Amish. The Hutterites. The Shakers. The United Order of Zion. The Oneida Colony. Especially the Oneida Colony."

"You don't think there's anything in it."

"I didn't say that. I said it had a lot of historical precedents."

"But it makes you smile."

"That was a grimace," I said. "A historical rictus. One aspect of the precedents is that the natural tribal societies are so commonly superstition-ridden, ritual-bound, and war-like, and the utopian ones always fail. Where'd you get this?

"It was handed to me."

"By whom? Your husband?"

"So to speak." She scowled at me, pulling her lower lip.

"Are you being asked to bring what you have to this joyous tribal gathering?"

Letting go of her lip, she smiled with a look of superiority and penetration, as if she understood my captious skepticism and made allowances for it. "I didn't say." But then the smile faded into a discontented pucker, and she burst out, "If something's wrong with it, tell me what. I've been trying to make up my mind if anything is. It's idealistic, it's for love and gentleness, it's close to nature, it hurts nobody, it's voluntary. I can't see anything wrong with any of that."

"Neither can I. The only trouble is, this commune will be inhabited by and surrounded by members of the human race."

"That sounds pretty cynical."

"Well, I wouldn't want to corrupt you with my cynicism," I said, and shut up.

But she kept after me; she was serious.

"All right," I said, "I'll tell you why I'm dubious. These will be young people in this garden commune, I assume. That means they'll be stoned half the time—one of the things you can grow in gardens is *Cannabis*. That won't go down well with the neighbors. Neither will freeform marriage or the natural-credit Communist economy. They'll be visited by the cops every week. They'll be lucky if the American Legion doesn't burn them out, or sic the dog catcher on their wild life children."

"None of that has anything to do with *them*. It only has to do with people outside."

"Sure," I said, "but those people aren't going to go away. If they won't leave the colony alone I'll give it six months. If it isn't molested it might last a year or two. By that time half the people will have drifted away in search of bigger kicks, and the rest will be quarreling about some communal woman, or who got the worst corner of the garden patch, or who ate up all the sweet corn. Satisfying natural desires is fine, but natural desires have a way of being both competitive and consequential. And women may be equal to men, but they aren't equal in attractiveness any more than men are. Affections have a way of fixing on individuals, which breeds jealousy, which breeds possessiveness, which breeds bad feeling. Q.E.D."

"You're judging by past history."

"All history is past history."

"All right. *Touché*. But it doesn't have to repeat itself."

"Doesn't it?"

She sat regarding me in a troubled way, puckering up her mouth and making fishlike, *pup-pup-pupping* noises with it. "I don't see why you're *opposed*," she said. "It's one thing to think it's sure to fail, but you sound as if you thought it was *wrong*. I suppose you think it's lunatic fringe, but why? You can't think the society we've got is so hot. I know you don't. Haven't you sort of copped out yourself? What's this but a rural commune, only you own it and hire the Hawkes family to run it for you?"

"Do you resent that?" I said.

"What? No. No, of course not. I was just asking something. Take marriage, say. Is that such a success story? Why not try a new way? Or look at your grandfather. Is this manifesto so different from the come-on he wrote for the Idaho Mining and Irrigation Company, except that he was doing it for profit? He was trying something that was pretty sure to fail, wasn't he? Maybe it wasn't even sound, maybe that sagebrush desert might better have been left in sagebrush, isn't that what you think? All that big dream of his was dubious ecology, and sort of greedy when you look at it, just another piece of American continent-busting. But you admire your grandfather more than anybody, even though the civilization he was trying to build was this cruddy one we've got. Here's a bunch of people willing to put their lives on the line to try to make a better one. Why put them down?"

"Look, Shelly," I said, "I didn't start this discussion. It doesn't make that much difference to me what they do. You asked me what I thought."

"I'd really like to know."

"Is that it?" I said. "I thought you were trying to convert me. That'd be hopeless. I wouldn't live in a colony like that, myself, for a thousand dollars an hour. I wouldn't want it next door. I'm not too happy it's within ten miles."

"*Why?*"

"Why? Because their soft-headedness irritates me. Because their beautiful thinking ignores both history and human nature. Because they'd spoil my thing with their thing. Because I don't think any of them is wise enough to play God and create a human society. Look. I like privacy, I don't like crowds, I don't like noise, I don't like anarchy, I don't even like discussion all that much. I prefer study, which is very different from meditation—not better, different. I don't like children who are part of the wild life. So are polecats and rats and other sorts of hostile and untrained vermin. I want to make a distinction between civilization and the wild life. I want a society that will protect the wild life without confusing itself with it."

"Now you're talking," Shelly said. "Tell me."

"All right. I have no faith in free-form marriage. It isn't marriage, it's promiscuity, and there's no call for civilization to encourage promiscuity. I cite you the VD statistics for California as one small piece of evidence. I'm very skeptical about the natural-credit Communist economy: how does it fare when it meets a really high-powered and ruthless economy such as ours? You can't retire to weakness—you've got to learn to control strength. As for gentleness and love, I think they're harder to come by than this sheet suggests. I think they can become as coercive a conformity as anything Mr. Hershey or Mr. Hoover ever thought up. Furthermore, I'm put off by the aggressively unfeminine and the aggressively female woman that would be found in a commune like this. I'm put off by long hair, I'm put off by irresponsibility, I never liked Whitman, I can't help remembering that good old wild Thoreau wound up a tame surveyor of Concord house lots."

It was quite a harangue. About the middle of it she began to grin, I think to cover up embarrassment and anger. "Well," she said when I ran down, "I stirred up the lions. What's that supposed to mean, that about Thoreau?"

As long as I had gone that far, I thought I might as well go the rest of the way. "How would I know what it means?" I said. "I don't know what anything means. What it suggests to me is that the civilization he was contemptuous of—that civilization of men who lived lives of quiet desperation—was stronger than he was, and maybe righter. It outvoted him. It swallowed him, in fact, and used the nourishment he provided to alter a few cells in its corporate body. It grew richer by him, but it was bigger than he was. Civilizations grow by agreements and accommodations and accretions, not by repudiations. The rebels and the revolutionaries are only eddies, they keep the stream from getting stagnant but they get swept down and absorbed, they're a side issue. Quiet desperation is another name for the human condition. If revolutionaries would learn that they can't remodel society by day after tomorrow—haven't the wisdom to and shouldn't be permitted to—I'd have more respect for them. Revolutionaries and sociologists. God, those sociologists! They're always trying to reclaim a tropical jungle with a sprinkling can full of weed killer. Civilizations grow and change and decline—they aren't remade."

81 Oil Spill

On January 28, 1969, a blowout occurred at an oil well being drilled in the Santa Barbara Channel. Most of the nearby beaches were covered by the oil, and many people were driven from their homes by the foul odor of the gooey mess. Loss of fish and wild fowl was extensive. This tragedy has been described as "the ecological shot heard around the world." Spurred in part by the Santa Barbara incident, Congress passed the National Environmental Policy Act, a basic step in the fight to halt man's devastation of his environment, and people of all political backgrounds joined forces in Get Oil Out (GOO) to protect the area from a repetition of the disaster. Ross MacDonald, a Santa Barbara resident and prolific author of mysteries with a California setting, uses the oil spill as background for a novel and explains the impact of the spill upon people.

I flew home from Mazatlán on a Wednesday afternoon. As we approached Los Angeles, the Mexicana plane dropped low over the sea and I caught my first glimpse of the oil spill.

It lay on the blue water off Pacific Point in a freeform slick that seemed miles wide and many miles long. An offshore oil platform stood up out of its windward end like the metal handle of a dagger that had stabbed the world and made it spill black blood.

The flight steward came along the aisle, making sure that we were ready to land. I asked him what had happened to the ocean. His hands and shoulders made a south-of-the-border gesture which alluded to the carelessness of Anglos.

"She blew out Monday." He learned across me and looked down past the wing. "She's worse today than she was yesterday. Fasten your seat belt, Señor. We'll be landing in five minutes."

I bought a paper at International Airport. The oil spill was front-page news. A vice-president of the oil company that owned the offshore platform, a man named Jack Lennox, predicted that the spill would be controlled within twenty-four hours. Jack Lennox was a good-looking man, if you could judge by his picture, but there was no way to know whether he was telling the truth.

Pacific Point was one of my favorite places on the coast. As I made my way out to the airport parking lot, the oil spill threatening the city's beaches floated like a depression just over the horizon of my mind.

Instead of driving home to West Los Angeles, I turned south along the coast to Pacific Point. The sun was low when I got there. From the hill above the harbor, I could see the enormous slick spreading like premature night across the sea.

At its nearest it was perhaps a thousand yards out, well beyond the dark brown kelp beds which formed a natural barrier offshore. Workboats were moving back and forth, spraying the edges of the spill with chemicals. They were the only boats I could see on the water. A white plastic boom was strung across the harbor entrance, and gulls that looked like white plastic whirled above it.

I made my way down to the public beach and along it to the sandy point which partly enclosed the harbor. A few people, mostly women and girls, were standing at the edge of the water, facing out to sea. They looked as if they were waiting for the end of the world, or as if the end had come and they would never move again.

The surf was rising sluggishly. A black bird with a sharp beak was struggling in it. The bird had orange-red eyes, which seemed to be burning with anger, but it was so fouled with oil that at first I didn't recognize it as a western grebe.

A woman in a white shirt and slacks waded in thigh-deep and picked it up, holding its head so that it wouldn't peck her. I could see as she came back toward me that she was a handsome young woman with dark eyes as angry as the bird's. Her narrow feet left beautifully shaped prints in the wet sand.

I asked her what she was going to do with the grebe.

"Take it home and clean it."

"It probably won't survive, I'm afraid."

"No, but maybe I will."

She walked away, holding the black struggling thing against her white shirt. I walked along behind in her elegant footprints. She became aware of this, and turned to face me.

"What do you want?"

"I should apologize. I didn't mean to be discouraging."

"Forget it," she said. "It's true not many live once they've been oiled. But I saved some in the Santa Barbara spill."

"You must be quite a bird expert."

"I'm getting to be one in self-defense. My family is in the oil business."

She gestured with her head toward the offshore platform. Then she turned and left me abruptly. I stood and watched her hurrying southward along the beach, holding the damaged grebe as if it were her child.

I followed her as far as the wharf which formed the southern boundary of the harbor. One of the workboats had opened the boom and let the other boats in. They were coming alongside the wharf and tying up.

The wind had changed, and I began to smell the floating oil. It smelled like something that had died but would never go away.

There was a restaurant on the wharf, displaying on its roof a neon sign which spelled out "Blanche's Seafood." I was hungry, and went that way. On the far side of the sprawling restaurant building, the wharf was covered with chemical drums, machinery, stacks of oil-well casings. Men were debarking from the workboats at a landing stage.

I went up to an aging roustabout with a sun-cracked face under a red hard hat. I asked him what the situation was.

"We ain't supposed to talk about it. The company does the talking."

"Lennox?"

"I guess that's their name."

A burly straw boss intervened. He had black oil on his clothes, and his high-heeled Western boots were soaked with it.

"You from a media?"

"No. I'm just a citizen."

He looked me over suspiciously. "Local?"

"L.A."

"You're not supposed to be out here."

He nudged me with his belly. The men around him became suddenly still. They looked rough and tired and disappointed, ready to take their revenge on anything that moved.

I went back toward the restaurant. A man who looked like a fisherman was waiting just around the corner of the building. Under his ribbed wool cap, his face was young-eyed and hairy.

"Don't mess with them," he said.

"I wasn't planning to."

"Half of them came from Texas, inland Texas. They think water is a nuisance because they can't sell it for two or three dollars a barrel. All they care about is the oil they're losing. They don't give a damn about the things that live in the sea or the people that live in the town."

"Is the oil still running?"

"Sure it is. They thought they had it closed down Monday, the day she blew. Before that she was roaring wild, with drilling mud and hydrocarbon mist shooting a hundred feet in the air. They dropped the string in the hole and closed the blind rams over her, and they thought she was shut down. The main hole was. But then she started to boil up through the water, gas and oil emulsion all around the platform."

"You sound like an eyewitness."

The young man blinked and nodded. "That I was. I took a reporter out there in my boat—man from the local paper named Wilbur Cox. They were evacuating the platform when we got there, the fire hazard was so bad."

"Any lives lost?"

"No, sir. That's the one good thing about it." He squinted at me through his hair. "Would you be a reporter?"

"No. I'm just interested. What caused the blowout, do you know?

He pointed with his thumb at the sky, then down at the sea. "There's quite a few different stories floating around. Inadequate casing is one of them. But there's something the matter with the structures down there. They're all broken up. It's like trying to make a clean hole in a piece of cake and hold water in it. They should never have tried to drill out there."

The oil men from the workboats went by, straggling like the remnants of a defeated army. The fisherman gave them an ironic salute, his teeth gleaming in his beard. They returned pitying looks, as if he was a madman who didn't understand what was important.

I went into the restaurant. There were voices in the bar, at the same time boisterous and lugubrious, but the dining room was almost deserted. It was done in a kind of landbound nautical style, with portholes instead of windows. Two men were waiting to pay at the cashier's desk. . . .

I ordered bourbon on the rocks. Then I made the mistake of ordering fish. It seemed to taste of oil. I left my dinner half eaten and went outside.

82 The Corrosion of the New Society?

In recent years more and more observers of the California scene have been deeply concerned at the direction it has been taking and have been increasingly pessimistic about the Golden State realizing its potential as the terrestrial paradise. Books with such titles as *Eden in Jeopardy, The*

Destruction of California, and *How To Kill a Golden State*, along with essays such as "Brutalizing the California Scene," attest to the widespread concern. This selection recounts many of the arguments which are raised to alert the state's populace to the danger.

Following the meal, Caddy introduced the customary featured speaker. Los Angeles Lovely dealt in what was known as "challenging" guests and paid good fees. It encouraged controversy and, to the distaste of some supporters, occasionally went far into left field. In their time, with appropriate thrills of disgust, the garden club members, clubwomen, social climbers, civically righteous and retired bankers had heard out disgruntled architects, worried biologists, manic city planners, anxious politicians, embittered men from the Atlantic Seaboard, traffic experts, hopeless demographers, a Scandinavian industrialist trying to dispose of a monorail system that had been rejected in South America, and any number of academic types brooding upon the more noxious effusions of a mechanistic civilization. Today's star turn was a professor A. B. Wyitt, late of the liberal arts department of Laguna Seca Junior College, and an alleged authority in socio-economic dynamics and urban redevelopment.

"This is going to be a tedious early afternoon," Junior whispered.

But Garnet thought Professor Wyitt looked interesting, if not promising. He assumed the lectern without notes, a tall, slim, good-looking, smiling man, boyish in appearance, whose age was hard to guess. He had light brown hair and light blue eyes, and wore the standard academic outfit of sports jacket, button-down shirt and skimpy dark slacks. Although he seemed a pleasant sort, not like many of the agitated types for which LAL provided a forum, he wasted no time on the usual preliminary jokes or raillery. His first words, delivered without a "Madam President" or other salutations, were arresting: "You people, presumably the influentials and opinion-makers in this disorderly collection of unlovely communities called Los Angeles, the victims of an unbridled growth, ought to be ashamed of yourselves. You've made a mess of it. You have raped and debased a pretty country and a promising city, and I doubt if there is any way for you to escape the consequences except by packing your air-conditioned automobiles with a few necessaries and fleeing at once, two steps ahead of an overwhelming deluge of men, women, children, pollution of air, soil, water and the mind, cars, trucks, police regulations, basic housing, third-rate schools, taxes, public indebtedness, scoundrelly super-patriots and universal vulgarity. The Queen of the Angels is indeed the first true megalopolis, stretching some two hundred miles along a superb, climatically serene coast from the Mexican border to a befuddled, fumbling anachronism known as Santa Barbara. If Los Angeles is the flesh and spirit of what is to come elsewhere, then men are well advised to push out into space. I call your attention to the irony of the fact that much of the thinking and tinkering necessary for interstellar voyages is being done in your own area. Is it possible the urge to depart has more appeal here than in cities less favored by sunshine, gasoline fumes and the quick buck artists?"

"Oh, boy," Garnet said, and was touched and amused. "Listen to him. He sounds authentically bugged."

A. B. Wyitt went on to deal with certain numbering facts. Los Angeles, situated in the most populous state in the Union, was second in size nationally and had nearly four million citizens. The people of the county (of the same name) in which it sprawled in an abandoned orgy of rapid accretion numbered almost seven million. No one spoke anymore of the city as such, for who could distinguish between a central section decaying and forsaken and the innumerable collections of tract houses attached to shopping districts in Alhambra, Artesia, Azusa, Bell, Cudahy, Covina, West Covina, Dairy Valley, Duarte, El Monte, Glendora, Hawaiian Gardens, Hermosa Beach, Hidden Hills, Huntington Park, Industry, Inglewood, Lakewood, La Mirada, Long Beach, Monrovia, Norwalk, a hundred mobile-homes estates, and fifty other puffy little enclaves, all merged one into the other and utterly undistinguishable? To the four points of the compass the bulldozers rumbled and gouged, removing orange groves and row crops and gashing the hills for building pads, and the paving contractors spread their acres of blacktop. Westward the tall buildings rose on bits of property far too valuable for anything but immense concrete rabbit warrens, poking up out of the smog. In Civic Center, amidst the blue-brown haze, the city fathers labored to produce great piles of stone and steel in a diversity of heavy, pudgy styles, crowned by a prevailing mediocrity. And parking lots served for the sweep of the eye—they were the important item, with white-painted lines for the cars to stand in.

"Only the police building is handsome," Wyitt said. "Is that intentional, the mark of a cellular society? Is planting trees the extent of your obligation to your successors? You haven't done much besides that, except talk."

New York alone exceeded the Queen as a financial giant. The third largest complex of the nation's manufacturing was here. Perhaps the future safety of the United States lay with Los Angeles, for the central coils of the defense industry—brain trust, allied universities, experiment, development and manufacture—were here entrenched. Miles of residences went up overnight, as nowhere else, and with them the highest rate of real estate foreclosure in the country. Employment, aerospace, agriculture, minerals, motion pictures, television, international trade, fishing, non-durable goods production, tourism, sports attendance, motorcar sales, homosexual activities: the Queen was queen of all. Her magnet was stronger than ever: the outsiders came in by the hundreds every day. Megalopolis would have fourteen million inhabitants by 1980, or considerably better than half the total population of California, and probably thirty million in the second decade of the twenty-first century

The sum total was staggering and incomprehensible. Possibly only a computer could see the picture as a whole. That would be appropriate in the hyper-city devoted to electronics and automation.

"However," Wyitt said, "give a moment of merciful consideration to your typical Angeleno, your householder and taxpayer. He's a suburbanite in this apotheosis of suburbia. He just came here, and so he is not responsible for the trap you've got him in. He is young—Los Angeles is a young town, new all over again and progressively younger in each fresh wave of immigration, and old solely in mistakes—and he has a wife and is breeding too many children. You'll have to supply schools for those kids, as nearly as you can at the rate of one a month, and add new colleges at tremendous expense from public funds to educate youth beyond its fundamental intelligence in order to equip it for the demands of a profoundly changing technology. Your man has been plunked down in a ramshackle social structure, without traditions or continuity; he lacks relatives and old friends and a definite niche in a pecking order to occupy, and his church, if any, can't satisfy him. The astronauts and the rockets have been out where God was always supposed to be and haven't seen Him. He must have abdicated, or anyhow abandoned Los Angeles. The Angeleno is afloat without rudder or sail on a heaving sea of emotional insecurity. He has no roots, no standards, no permanent goals; he's unattached and mobile—a third of the families move once every year. Materially he is well taken care of. He has a pasteboard, cut-out assembly-line house built to last nearly through a twenty-year mortgage; a dieted, nervous wife, clad in pants somewhat resembling his own, interested in the P.T.A. and banning the bomb; his children are healthy, though jumpy from the violence they watch on television and the fierce competition in the schools. Doctors can assure him of a frightful old age of creeping decrepitude if he abstains from cigarettes and saturated fats. His assets include such items as an electric razor and toothbrush, a washer-dryer, a tape recorder, martinis, tranquilizers, and news magazines to simplify his opinions. Unemployment insurance, unlimited credit, pension funds and the promise of government medical care seem to take care of the future. He is living in the most modern city in the world, surrounded by all the dubious attributes of the new civilization. Carbon monoxide is the breath of life to him."

Wyitt thought the Queen did have a god of sorts, a Moloch, to whom incredible sacrifices had been offered. It was the motorcar. Everything bowed to its demands. The city was ripped apart, whole neighborhoods obliterated, natural beauties buried under tons of concrete, to afford swift, deadly, unending passage for the cars. To give them standing room required thousands of hot, bare, repellant surfaced acres. They clogged the streets, fouled the atmosphere, dimmed the sight, killed and maimed. Dedication to them was complete; every man was a priest. No right-thinking citizen would consider using a public transportation facility unless he was short of funds or deprived of his driver's license. In each heart the ultimate bliss was equated with three hundred horsepower, elephantine size, low lines unsuitable for human ingress and egress, bright paint and gleaming metalwork, and time payments. People were born in them, grew up in them, had intercourse and conceived in them, and of course died in them. But one day soon Moloch would command the last measure of devotion—stoppage, suffocation and ruin.

"He's a nut," Junior said softly. Garnet didn't hear her; she had her whole attention fixed on the speaker.

"You say you don't have extensive slums," A. B. Wyitt told them. "What nonsense! How many of you have really driven around your immense city, how many ever bother to leave your comfortable neighborhoods? You have slums everywhere. Only the climate has prevented them from becoming quite as dirty and distressing as those to the east. Your kind of disintegration is unique; you have new slums, areas which have fallen into disrepair within the space of a decade, through inadequate building codes, lack of planning and venal politicians. Look at Hollywood, Santa Monica, Venice, Hermosa Beach, Lincoln Heights, Boyle Heights, the great reaches south of Olympic Boulevard to the ocean, the dreary compounds in the San Gabriel Valley, the stark and treeless monotony of Orange County tracts which have aged a little, the stinking, explosive jungle that is Watts. You are consistently discriminating against and hedging the opportunities of that substantial part of your population composed of Negroes and Mexicans. So far you have been saved from their organized resentment by mere size and diffusion—nobody can mount a protest or a revolution in so vast and disorganized a place. The confusion and compartmentation and absence of cohesion fogs men's brains. But that won't necessarily last forever."

The professor's voice, which was gradually rising in volume, began to take on organlike notes. He had the quality of the evangelist in him, and his listeners, who were stiffening in a growing hostility and mild shock, nevertheless pricked up their ears at a change toward reasonableness and a call for enlightened action; they were accustomed to such appeals, some of them actually pitiful. Wyitt, harsh but never losing his good-humored air, obviously wanted to help them, however much they had provoked his contempt. He had suggestions. They could perhaps repair their errors and those of their unmentionable predecessors. The hodge-podge of disparate architectural atrocities could be stopped or refined. Urban redevelopment might yet save the atrophied, crumbling plexus of the Queen. A decent social order would cure the sickness of the Mexican and Negro minorities. Planning and severe new laws could blunt the rapacity and destructive instincts of the tract promoters. Ugliness was not an immutable law of nature. Asphalt could give way to the spaciousness of the Lord's own green and pleasant earth. Moloch and his foul breath was not irresistible. The lovely contours of the land did not have to vanish beneath the earthmovers and dump trucks. No Sermon from the Mount compelled the faithful to remove vegetation, allow narrow streets, perch crackerboxes on hills, erect tall glass cubes festooned with aluminum, build miserable miles of identical tiny houses on equally tiny lots, block off every view with billboards and the astral glow of tubular glass signs, smother the central organism of a living city by splattering dismal replicas of it in miniature for a hundred miles. They were not bound by oath to prevent man from standing upright and having natural space for breathing and recruiting his soul. Nor had God enjoined against parks and healing profusion of nature. Sour water, littered sands and thick air weren't inevitable. The Queen was capable of reformation. She had risen repeatedly on her ephemeral ruins. It was still possible to make her the prototype of an incalculable new world.

"You are the influentials here," Wyitt said, "the people who should accomplish this. You could substitute grace and abundance and simplicity for disorder and an appalling, tasteless modernity. It's in your hands. But you have to take a stand against greed and ignorance and eyes that cannot see and minds that cannot understand the good of the multitude is the good of the individual. In terms of historical time, you have about five minutes. This is your last chance, and I advise you to apply yourselves right now to distinguishing between healthy growth and the unchecked spread of a civic carcinoma called megalopolis . . . Thank you for listening courteously to somebody who has nothing but contempt for most of the manifestations of your chosen abode."

The applause he received was scarcely shattering. Madam President did not bother to thank him, and declared the meeting at an end. Chairs scraped, voices made a babel, and LAL adherents headed for the exit.